MW01599721

THE SHARDWELL SERIES

Book 3

CHILD OF STONE

A. Gerry
C. Hall

Published by Scribes of Shardwell, LLC

The Shardwell Series

Book 3

Child of Stone

PROLOGUE

For me, things have always been simple: achieve the objective. Cost is irrelevant. That's the drill of training. Pounding your head so full of general orders, combat maneuvers, and weapons basic that you're quarter-decked nine times out of ten. Without fail, your life becomes the mission. So many ops I lost count by the time I reached 26 DST (Designated Stellar Time). Strikes, raids, and drops. It's what GAEL VICs live for, why we were bred in the first place.

Few soldiers have what it takes to become a GAEL. Only first generation blendeds even have a chance, and then only a fraction meet the genetic requirement for bonding. The Round took me as an infant—I tested positive on the BCB. My parents' names are classified. Was my mother a Sulevian and my father human? Or had it been the other way around? I'll never know.

Blending is responsible for the state of the system worlds—the MetaGalactic War has poisoned the races for almost 1500 years DST. It was the Sulevians who first mastered the technique. Up until then, Morrigans had baby Morrigans, Danaans had Danaans, and humans had humans. Interspecies unions were physically incapable of generating children. But the Sulevian scientists shoved their pointy ears into the universe's genetic limitations, creating the tech that circumvented the laws of natural biology.

And then all hell broke loose.

Extremist cultures like the Sylph and the Vartal believed the new tech went against the dogma of their goddess, that bringing people like me into existence was a sin against nature. The Danaan System crashed into civil war, and the Sulevian homeworld was obliterated. The survivors fled to the human sectors. Soon, religious fanatics across the galaxy merged into the Agrona-Morrigan Concord—we soldiers call them the Agromors—and pushed their military into the free planets of the Blended Coalition, demanding the cessation of interracial marriage and the destruction of all "tainted" offspring.

Knowing the Agromors would never surrender, the Round created a top military soldier, the GraEL Attached Elite Level Vanguard Infiltration Commando. The GAEL VICs were the Coalition's answer to the gromm crap infesting the extremists' genocidal campaign. Two hundred years of combat skirmishes and we finally jacked them back into their own space. For once, the right side is winning the MetaGalactic War. Peace teeters on the brink, though I wonder if anyone still remembers the meaning of the word.

My training shaped me into an expert warrior, a soldier who could waste anyone or anything my commander set me against. But nothing since the Bang could have prepared me for *her*. She was the most beautiful woman I'd ever seen.

And I hated her.

PART 1

1: EVERY SAGA HAS A BEGINNING

Lieutenant Lance Kyleren plopped his legs on the flimsy surface of the cheap metallic table near the bar and downed his waterlogged beer in a single swig. With precise balance he tilted his chair back onto two of its stumpy legs, tossing the lousy tankard back onto the table with a loud clatter. The brew was transported in powder form and rehydrated once it reached the outlier mining operation of Jera Zeta. Not only did the drying process rob the drink of any semblance of taste, but the owner had obviously added the bare minimum of the beer-grind to mix his merchandise. The drink left a nasty aftertaste against the roof of Kyleren's mouth.

Smothering a yawn, he scanned the steel room with his yellow-hazel eyes. Few of the colony's inhabitants frequented the tavern at 0600 DST. Anyone with any sense still lay buried in the thermolayer sheets of his rack. On the opposite side of the mess hall, though, several off-duty Vanguard Infiltration Commando soldiers—VICs—had challenged a team of ordinary Cymric troops to an arm-wrestling competition. Though the two groups of military men seemed friendly, Kyleren knew their camaraderie was a forced show for the civilian audience that populated the worlds of the Blended Coalition. The two factions of the military harbored hostilities for each other that spanned nearly 15 centuries. The Cymrics—a police force turned militia left over from the ancient WorldLink treaty—were slowly losing influence in a space fleet that demanded stronger, more specially trained soldiers. Naturally, the two groups vied for supremacy.

Kyleren's six month tour at Jera Zeta was the most tedious assignment of his career—demoted to babysit a bunch of mineral-spec whizbangs as they poked their long noses into asteroid holes, searching for dintillium deposits, while the rest of his GAEL VIC team was intercepting the Agromor terrorists on the blended capital world of Kamolos and the major industrial planet of LeFay. No doubt his buddy Wayne waded gleefully through the action, while he—Lance Kyleren—brooded sullenly on a boring rock barely a light year from the emptiness of the Black Reach. This post went way beyond discipline. It was banishment.

How was Lance supposed to have known that Gwen was the fleet admiral's daughter? And besides, she had come on to him, not the other way around. Kyleren snorted as the bearded barman delivered another flagon of alcohol. No frag was worth this duty, no matter how good it had been.

Stranded from real civilization, or at least all the good fights, for something that was clearly not his fault pissed him off. Even a Danaan System surveillance mission would have been better than this. Jera Zeta was a mixture of elves, humans, and blended, but few of the settlers were women. He knew most of them already—a few even twice.

This was such a waste of a bonded soldier. Few subjects survived the GraEL attaching process, making every GAEL VIC an essential tool of the military. Yet here he was, every day seemingly longer than the last. He felt like he'd been exiled for a hundred years.

Only the moment of his arrival seemed to stand out in his memory. He had been greeted by a squad of Cymrics, who—outnumbering the current VICs two-to-one—had mistaken him for a normal VIC soldier. They had meant to flaunt their clout, letting him know just which military branch controlled Jera Zeta. Major Cadin had arrived just in time to see the last man hit the concrete. Kyleren's first night at his new post had been spent racking in the brig.

When released, Kyleren met up with his fellow VIC soldiers, but between the color of his eyes and the cylindrical core drive tucked into his arm holster, they quickly recognized him for what he was. Even among the VICs, meeting an actual GAEL was rare. But at least they comprehended the threat level a GraEL bonded signified. They gave Kyleren an even wider berth than the worked-over Cymrics.

The new tankard rose to his lips. It was his fifth. The other soldiers glowered at him as he drank—he was on duty after all—but whether their expressions twisted with disapproval or envy, he didn't care to know. Alcohol was just a toxin, one of the many poisons to which he was immune. Even exotic atmospheres did not harm him; his lungs could use almost any gaseous element to oxidize his blood.

Kyleren ignored their animosity. No one here was a threat. He could overwhelm the entire garrison on his own if he had to. And he just might. He was crazy with boredom, locked up with nothing to shoot.

The small dead tech comm tucked inside his ear buzzed with life.

"Lieutenant Kyleren, respond!" the major shouted over the airway.

Kyleren grimaced at the accompanying static that fizzed in his ear. He missed the sleek LT comms that grafted seamlessly into the skin. They were both better quality and more secure.

"Read you, sir," Kyleren answered after a dowdy pause.

"Lieutenant, you were due in the hangar bay at 0600!" his commanding officer bellowed. "Where the frag are you?"

"Yes, sir, reporting immediately, sir!" Kyleren replied with an amused smile.

Screwing with the Cymric major was the only source of entertainment available on this crappy heap of slag—it was particularly rewarding to turn up ten minutes late on every shift.

An adroit pivot brought him out of his chair and he flipped a dozen prings on the table. Though the door sensed his approach, the panel flagged halfway, jerking as it attempted to complete its task. With an irritated grunt Kyleren slapped it open, muttering a profane description of InterSys's ability to properly outfit its minor research colonies.

The walk to the hangar bay was all too short. A small pane set in the wall next to the decontamination locker restricted access to all non-approved personnel. Reaching into his collar, Kyleren extracted his clear plastic ident tag. As he lowered the rectangular disc into the panel's red sensor light, a coded series of numbers, along with Lance's picture, flashed across its surface. The panel indicator blinked green and the door wrenched open.

He sauntered inside. A row of lockers with shoddy peeling labels huddled against the far wall. Kyleren slid his ident tag across one of them and disarmed the security device. He was the only VIC in the colony with his own private locker. Normally, all weapons and equipment were stored in the general armory across the hall, but a GAEL VIC's armaments were a particular combination of living and bonded tech—and incredibly expensive. The items stacked in the thin compartment cost more than the entire outpost.

He yanked the panel open and scanned the tech weapons inside. With a pang of regret he slid his arm past his BT70 sniper rifle, his *White Lady*, and instead collected his BT sharp pistol. There was nothing to fight on the dead surface of the Jera asteroid, except the occasional space worm. And that creature barely gave his skills a workout.

A quick jerk on the end ring of his core drive freed it from its sheath. With the ease of repetition he inserted the metallic cylinder into the pistol's handle. It took only seconds for his body to link with the weapon; he felt the barrel, trigger, and core-life rounds merge their energy with his own, making the BT sharp an extension of his arm rather than a dead object held by his hand. The CL rounds tasted unusual; they were the newest upgrades to his arsenal, able to bypass any energy shield and pierce almost every type of space armor.

Any worm that crossed his path would be instant jelly.

He snorted and set the pistol aside as he slipped expertly into his camouflage combat body armor. Currently its slick surface was slate black, but once Kyleren enacted the masking module, the exterior of the suit would shift spectrums and blend in with its surroundings. Suitably outfitted, he wrapped his core drive holster onto the hard

shell around his arm and snagged the BT sharp on a catch
on his belt. Before slamming the locker closed he retrieved
his oxygen helmet. Even a GAEL wasn't immune to the
vacuum of space.

With a comfortable swagger he entered the hangar bay,
turning immediately left toward a neglected transport
machine. The battered apple-hopper was barely large
enough for five passengers and a pilot, so of course it was
stuffed beyond capacity with grubby research gadgets and a
team of pesky scientists.

Major Cadin paced crossly back and forth in front of
the hopper's cockpit. His cropped hair revealed his pointed
Kildar ears. Even by elven standards the man was short.
Kyleren towered over him by nearly 40 centimeters. The
major adjusted his sleek uniform at every revolution of his
path, agitatedly smoothing invisible wrinkles from his tunic.
When he registered the arrival of his tardy lieutenant, his
almond eyes grew bright with aggravation.

"Your lack of respect is unacceptable, lieutenant,"
Cadin said testily.

"Sorry, sir," Lance acknowledged, indifferently saluting
his superior.

"This is the ninth lag this month, soldier!"

"I got no sense of time, sir," Kyleren replied with a
smothered chuckle.

"Don't think I don't understand your defiance,
Lieutenant Kyleren," Cadin spat. "But since you have been
deferred to my command, you will show me the proper
respect. I may be a Cymric, but I am still your superior
officer."

"Yes, sir," Lance answered, his eyes carefully locked on
the hopper. He refused to look at the major, afraid he
might burst into laughter.

"Confinement to the brig doesn't seem to correct your behavior, lieutenant. Perhaps extra duties cleaning the head—"

"Major?" Dr. Orton interrupted hastily as he waddled from the loading ramp. The major turned to the scientist. "We only have two hours of clearance for this research ship. Where's our pilot?"

"Just arrived, doc," Kyleren answered. "Permission to report to my post, sir," he said to the major.

Cadin's creamy skin turned blotchy with resentment. "Granted, lieutenant, but I expect to see you in my office the second your team air docks."

"Yes, sir."

Kyleren grinned, although he did salute again to placate the Cymric. Lance watched the major storm away.

"Can't wait."

*

Kyleren's armored feet dangled casually over an 80 meter precipice. His pistol spun back and forth around his index finger as he passed the time. The research team toddled about, scooping soil and rock into palm-sized collection receptacles. One had tried conversing with the GAEL, blathering on about a pigment in the surrounding minerals and its relationship with the decomposition of a rare organism. Kyleren stared at the blended, half Kildar by the look of him, until the scientist was thoroughly intimidated by the lieutenant's silence. The whizbang scuttled into the furthest quadrant of the research zone. After that, the rest of the team left Kyleren to himself. He made sure all of them stayed at least ten meters away, grumpily ignoring the useless scientific chatter that clogged the ear comms.

There were still 20 minutes until dust off. In five he could give the order to secure the equipment back into the hopper. With a sigh of boredom's relief, he stood, turning his visor to the sky. Kyleren activated the locator sequencer in his helmet. Each little pinprick of light in the heavens was instantly tagged with its proper designation, with blue lines encircling each planetary sector. The Kamolos system was closest, the agricultural world of Corbin brightest—the planet of his downfall.

Why hadn't "Sorry admiral, I didn't know she was your daughter" been enough?

Unexpectedly, the display marked Penardun, the nomadic space city. Though he could just barely make out the artificial lights of the traveling metropolis, it registered close, maybe halfway between the Kamolos and Athalonde systems. Kyleren wondered if Anya was still there, heading the medical department. Penardun had often served as his GAEL squad's base of operations. Anya's medical staff was the best the galaxy had to offer.

The Kildar elves built two space cities after the destruction of their homeworld, Sulevia. Arianrod was the first, a platinum octahedron orbiting Corbin like a silver jewel. Penardun had been established two thousand years before, by the old galactic treaty WorldLink, but had fallen into disrepair. A small force of Sulevian survivors rebuilt the ancient city into a roving municipality of artistic beauty. Lately, the Penardians had withdrawn from the MetaGalactic War, siding with neither the Blended Coalition nor the Agromors. Its citizens—having survived one apocalypse—were slow to get involved with another.

To maintain their neutrality, the leaders of the roaming space station allowed the military forces of the Blended Coalition to create a base in the lower portion of the city in exchange for protection against the terrorist attacks of the Agromors. The citizenry, however appreciative, declined to serve in the military themselves.

A series of beeps sang from Kyleren's suit. The lieutenant notified Dr. Orton to gather his team and load the craft. Ducking into the hopper, he flipped the switches into proper alignment for pre-flight. The engines purred to life with little coaxing.

"Flight to Jera Z," he reported as Dr. Orton signaled everyone and everything was strapped in. "Research operation two-nine-six returning to compound. ETA, ten minutes DST."

"You're clear for approach, lieutenant," came the excited response.

Kyleren only briefly speculated at the flight manager's enthusiasm. Anything that thrilled the colonists usually put him to sleep.

The return trip was uneventful. Kyleren disembarked before the ramp had the chance to completely settle to the hangar deck. He was halfway to the decontamination chamber when he noted a large vessel on the platform that hadn't been there when he left. It was too new and well-kept to be InterSys property. A military insignia gleamed below the cockpit window.

"Lieutenant Kyleren," the major hailed from the comm, his voice crackly with annoyance. "Report to the command center directly after decontamination."

The order piqued his interest. Previously, Major Cadin had suggested another disciplinary hearing in his office. Kyleren wondered why the elf had changed his mind. Maybe the major intended to contact VIC headquarters and nark on Lance's disrespectful behavior. Kyleren was almost past caring at this point. He would do anything to get off this gromm rock, even if it meant a court martial.

Kyleren stripped off his armor and piled his gear into his locker. As he did so, the room filled with a foggy gas that scrubbed any dangerous particles from his skin and clothes.

His journey to the command center was laden with murmurs and low whispers. The other VICs and Cymric troopers lined the halls, discussing him as he passed.

"You guys got a problem?" he growled, lifting his eyebrows. Kyleren purposely avoided intimidation in his voice, but the men scattered anyway.

Hundred-year-old equipment clogged the command center. Every wall dripped with gears and wire. More than half of it was broken beyond use, the rest in a sad state of perpetual repair. Ten people occupied the room, six of whom were on the complex's command staff. Major Cadin exchanged a displeased glance with the middle-aged human colony director, but Kyleren's eyes were immediately drawn to the two visitors standing next to them.

Both were GAELs. The older of the two, with square features and brown skin, broke into a gritty smile when Kyleren stepped into the room. Lance couldn't remember a time when he hadn't known Captain Wayne Reese, the highest ranking GAEL in squad Aon. The two had been companions through childhood. The other GAEL Kyleren didn't recognize, but judging by the poorly hidden mask of uncertainty in the soldier's face, the lieutenant guessed the youngster was fresh off Gwydion.

"Captain Reese, sir," Lance barked, stiffening with a genuine salute, but his lips twisted into a pleased grin.

Major Cadin's face deepened in a scowl.

"I must report that Lieutenant Lance Kyleren is deserving of disciplinary action," Cadin complained.

"What do you think he's doing here?" Wayne said with a laugh. His merriment sucked the needles from Cadin's objections. "Nothing is worse than taking a GAEL VIC out of the action and marooning him on some grommsack rock."

"Please tell me you've come to get me outta here," Lance begged.

Wayne smirked. "Lieutenant Lance Kyleren, your commission to GAEL squad Aon has been reinstated, effective immediately."

2: ALL THOSE MOMENTS WILL BE LOST IN TIME LIKE TEARS IN RAIN

Kyleren watched with some amusement as Private Gary Thompson fiddled nervously with his BT rifle. The young soldier's most distinctive features were his wide face and flat nose; otherwise he reflected the traditional enhanced attributes of a bonded soldier: increased height and muscle tone, and the signature yellow-hazel irises. The new recruit had been avoiding Lance's gaze since their introduction six hours ago, obviously intimidated. Though current military training was unrivaled, it was nothing compared to working with an active GAEL VIC squad. The limits of a bonded soldier's abilities could only be tested in actual combat. Kyleren chuckled as Thompson lost his grip on his weapon, narrowly rescuing it from clattering on the deck.

"What's your expertise?" the lieutenant intervened.

Thompson started at the direct address.

"Sorry, sir?" the private asked, straightening perceptibly under the attention of his superior.

"Relax, private," Lance said with a calming wave of his hand. "I just asked for your specialty."

"I'm not sure I understand, sir," Gary replied, trying unsuccessfully to loosen the rigidity of his spine.

"Most newbs fresh from Gwydion are grouped together and assigned a non-bonded VIC officer to command 'em. Normally, you'd be runnin' small ops that don't affect anythin' important. But you've been assigned under Captain Reese of GAEL squad Aon, the most dangerous post this side of the Reach. I wanna know how you managed that, private."

"They said one of your team was sacked," Thompson answered hesitantly. "I'm supposed to replace him."

"There are hundreds of GAELs across the galaxy. Battle trained. How many ops you been on?"

"Two," the younger warrior said sheepishly, "including this one."

Lance whistled. "You must've done somethin' impressive."

"Second best shot in the corps," Wayne interjected as he entered the rear compartment from the cockpit, "after you, lieutenant. But luckily, Gary's smarter than you." The captain grinned. "Doesn't fraternize with the admiral's daughter."

"I told you before, she came on to me!" Lance objected.

"I would have at least asked her name before I fragged her," Wayne scolded with a minor rise of irritation. He plopped into the bucket seat next to Kyleren. "Air dock in five."

"There wasn't time for talkin'," Lance replied with a wink, as all three GAELs strapped in for landing. The restraints chimed loudly as they locked.

"Captain Reese told me about your mission on Agrona," Gary began, the words rushing together as if he had been waiting to say them for hours. "Is it true that you got separated from the rest of the squad and had to escape from an enemy base all on your own?"

"Sharin' old war stories, Wayne?" Kyleren asked suspiciously. The story of the Agrona Op was Wayne's favorite form of friendly ridicule.

"I didn't tell him anything," Wayne said innocently. "Trish did."

"She still mad at me?"

"Can't blame her," Wayne shrugged through his harness.

Gary glanced between his superiors, confused. He probably couldn't tell whether Kyleren was angry with the captain or just playing along.

"It was a standard assassination op. There was an Agromor general allowin' doctors to cut up blendeds. A real gromm bastard. I was snipin' guards on the wrong side of the compound when our former captain ordered an evac."

"What did you do?" Thompson asked.

"Yeah Kyleren, what'd you do?" Wayne nudged.

"Well, I'm sure Sergeant Trisha Reynolds told you that," Kyleren replied caustically.

"Well—she did," Gary admitted, "but I thought it was a joke."

"It wasn't," Kyleren declared.

"That's right," Wayne agreed, "Kyleren really did find a broken down apple-hopper and fixed it in record time—"

"Yep," Lance affirmed.

"—with the help of his very special squirrel friend," Wayne laughed.

"I never said the squirrel helped me!" Lance clarified. "It just happened to show up right when the ship started workin'."

"We always tell people he had to fight his way through a company of Agromor soldiers first," Wayne said to Gary. "That way he doesn't sound so crazy."

"Well, where is this squirrel now?" Gary asked.

Lance just shook his head and turned toward the window.

The space city Penardun filled the portal with its nine signature towers, gleaming light washing its walls with gold. Thousands of windows twinkled from the sleek razor buildings like miniature stars. A huge ring girdled the city, less delicate in architecture and more functional, housing the industrial areas and docking ports that serviced the city.

The ship shuddered once as the Cymric pilot set it solidly on the hangar deck. Kyleren released his safety belt and stood in one fluid motion. He slung a duffle over his shoulder with one hand and lifted his heavy weapons trunk with the other. A group of average VICs met them as the three GAELs disembarked the loading ramp. After a quick salute, the group sergeant stepped forward.

"Colonel Stoddard sent us to retrieve your gear, Lieutenant Kyleren," he announced.

Kyleren looked quizzically at Wayne before setting his equipment in front of the four men. It took two of them to haul his weapons case to a transport vehicle.

"From exile to bellhops," Kyleren stated. "Did I get a promotion?"

Wayne coughed to cover an amused chuckle and led them to the personnel tram. Kyleren waited for the doors to hiss shut before pressing Wayne for information.

"What's the op?" he asked.

"Don't know," Wayne answered as his fingers ticked off their destination on the tram computer. "Colonel Stoddard wouldn't give me the details. But I will say that I've never seen him so close-mouthed about anything."

"Must be important," Lance surmised. "How'd you guys get the admiral to let me off that slag heap?"

"We didn't," Wayne admitted, quickly snagging a plastic loop that dangled from the ceiling as the tram shot forward into the transport tunnels that burrowed through Penardun. "Whatever's going down, it's big. The general himself had you reactivated. Word is that he had to remind the admiral that you're the best GAEL in the galaxy, and any personal vendetta against you put the Coalition at risk."

"I'll have to thank him," Kyleren said absently, admiring his surroundings.

Inside the city proper were many fountains and gardens, smaller buildings and wide pedestrian boulevards. Filigree ironwork, a favorite motif among the Kildar elves, dripped everywhere like metallic ribbons. Everything danced past quickly as they zoomed toward the central medical tower.

"Where's the rest of the squad?" Lance asked.

"They'll meet us for the briefing in 45 minutes."

"That's fast," Lance noted, excitement rising.

"Our orders came in less than 12 hours ago. I was on the ship ten minutes later to pick you up."

"Glad you guys waited for me to pack," Lance observed.

The tram dashed through an archway, slowing to a halt at the military entrance of the Lamorak building. All the upper floors, especially those with the most attractive views, belonged to the civilian sector of the Lamorak Corporation, housing the most advanced research labs for developing blended technology. The center levels offered mostly general hospital services to the city's population, though the same doctors served the VIC level at the tower's base.

"We have to hurry," Wayne prodded. "Maybe Anya can speed up your evaluation."

"Not gonna happen," Kyleren said easily. "She's very thorough."

Gary grunted, leaving Lance wondering if it was a laugh or a growl. The new recruit adjusted his uniform uncomfortably as they were welcomed by an elven nurse, her black hair in a careful upsweep that accentuated the bronzy curve of her neck. *Not bad*, Kyleren thought as she directed them to a spacious examination room, and he wondered just how much shore leave he would get before the squad moved out.

Dr. Anya Ninevay didn't look up when they entered, but chewed her lip thoughtfully as she explored a medical chart. The crease in her forehead indicated she was displeased with what she found there, and tiny lines around her ageless eyes made Kyleren question when she had last slept. Her hair hung in a limp bun, her Kildar ears all but hidden by escaped curls.

"Doc Anya, how've you been?" Kyleren greeted warmly.

"Sit on the table please, lieutenant," Anya instructed distantly, closing the chart and dropping it on a small counter next to her.

"I like a woman who takes charge, doc," he grinned jovially as he complied. "But I have to warn you: I'll only break your heart."

"You and every other VIC on this station, lieutenant," Anya returned crisply, lifting her medical scanner and passing it back and forth across his face. A faint tone signaled the completion of each swipe as she orbited the device around his body.

"I could tell you what I say to all the girls," he posed, trying to alleviate the tension. It was odd for Anya to be so callous. Usually, she responded to his teasing with more affection. "Like, 'sorry I didn't call, my communication array was down,' or 'I was on a top secret mission and couldn't blow my cover.' That sorta thing."

"Is that what you said to Gwen?" Anya retorted with a frown.

Kyleren looked at Wayne, who tried not to laugh. Gary seemed oblivious to everything, surroundings and companions alike. His eyes were entranced by the lovely physician.

"Is there anyone who doesn't know?" Lance complained with feigned exasperation.

"Six months is a long time," Wayne said with a gritty flash of teeth. "The elves like to talk."

An aggravated buzz ejected from the doctor's medical instrument, pulling Kyleren's glare off his friend. Anya tapped forcefully on the scanner's surface, persuading it to behave.

"You okay, Sugar Lips?" Kyleren asked in some concern. "You don't seem your bright-starry self."

Anya's demeanor softened perceptibly at Lance's term of endearment.

"I'm sorry, Kyleren. That was really rude of me. I shouldn't have—"

She trailed off hesitantly and turned her gaze in the direction of the hospital's hallway.

"I've just had a hard morning. We lost a blended baby today."

Wayne's brown face crinkled.

"You're a doctor. You must lose patients all the time," he pointed out.

"Not healthy patients," she said sadly, brushing a quick hand against her cheek. Lance could tell she must have been trying to hold back her tears most of the day. "I examined the child myself. She was fine when I left the hospital late last night."

"Anything we can do?" Gary interjected hastily, eager to please.

Wayne shook his head disapprovingly at the inexperienced recruit and Lance gave the young soldier a glance that plainly warned him to curtail his advances. Gary's ears turned a remarkable shade of pink, most unbecoming for an elite sentry.

"Unless you can revive the dead," Anya sighed. "I'm afraid nothing can be done."

The scanner jingled as it completed its final tasks. Anya barely glanced at the data that scrolled across the display. "As usual, lieutenant, you're in perfect physical condition."

"Hey Sugar Lips, it'll be fine," Lance soothed, wanting to lift his favorite doctor's spirits. Who knew the next time he might see her? "More people will die if you don't start smilin' again."

Anya's eyes filled with gratitude.

"Thanks, Lance," she said wrapping her arms around him tightly. "You've always been my favorite patient."

Kyleren stiffened with astonishment and glanced at his companions over her embrace. Wayne met Lance's eyes with a comparable expression of surprise, but Gary pouted enviously.

"Anytime, doc," he said with a grin.

She pulled away quickly.

"I need to submit this," she said, waving the scanner as she hustled to the door. "Colonel Stoddard was adamant I clear you for duty as quickly as possible."

Kyleren hopped from the table as she disappeared. Wayne checked his watch and then nodded toward the exit meaningfully. The trio walked without speaking as they climbed into the elevator that would allow them access to the lower levels of the Lamorak building, the secure military designated floors. Wayne inserted his ident tag and typed a clearance code into the panel as the doors sealed. The lift responded promptly, dropping down the shaft.

"Why do you call her 'Sugar Lips'?" Gary rumbled tightly as they passed the halfway point of their journey.

"Because no one gets near her, Newb," Kyleren explained. He folded his arms across his muscled chest.

"Lance started it, really. The rest of our team just picked it up," Wayne added carelessly.

"You don't think its offensive to call her that?" Gary demanded.

The doors sang open.

"We gave it to her because she isn't like the rest of the Sulevians, private," Lance threw over his shoulder as he stepped from the elevator. "She doesn't play around."

"She expects commitment," Wayne said, as if that clarified everything.

"What's wrong with that?" Gary asked a little irately.

Both Lance and Wayne stopped abruptly, turning to stare at Gary. Was this newb naïve enough to fall for the doc? That was a problem.

"Listen kid," Kyleren started, placing a hand on Gary's sorry, misinformed shoulder, "commitment women expect gifts and visits. And that's what they deserve. The only commitment you and the rest of us GAELs have time for is the corps."

"But you're good friends with Dr. Anya," he argued. "I thought that meant our squad docked on Penardun a lot."

"It's only our occasional base of operations," Wayne inserted. "Usually we live spaceside. We report back every two to three months, but rarely stay for more than a day."

Gary's face fell.

"Sorry Thompson," Wayne continued, "but whatever business you have with a woman, you keep it short. But do me a favor. Don't frag her without making sure you won't get quarter-decked first. I get tired of replacing my men."

"You're never gonna let that go, are you?" Kyleren asked indignantly.

3: YOUR MISSION SHOULD YOU CHOOSE TO ACCEPT IT

All but Sergeant Trisha Reynolds offered a head flick of acknowledgement as Kyleren entered the austere briefing room, welcoming Lance back to the team. In GAEL terms the gesture was equivalent to a group hug.

Colonel Art Stoddard scratched the grey stubble on his chin as he rose from his chair. Even at fifty, the human VIC officer commanded authority simply with his presence. Lance saluted his leader warmly.

"Good to have you back, son," the colonel said. He jerked his thumb at Captain Reese. "Wayne here hasn't stopped crying himself to sleep since you left."

"Really?" Kyleren asked. Turning to Wayne, the lieutenant placed a hand over his heart. "I'm touched, captain."

Wayne grimaced and plopped into the nearest waffle-backed chair.

"Only because you stole my favorite sidearm!" he grumbled.

Private Gary followed his mentor's lead, but left a seat open for Kyleren.

"You lost it to me fair and square," Lance reminded, feigning hurt sentiment.

"You hacked the system," Wayne shot back.

"You call anyone who beats you at Targ a hack. You're just a sore loser."

"If you weren't my best pal, I would've shot you."

Chief Chad Snow lifted his buzzed blond head from his paperwork and rippled the tight shoulder muscles exposed by his sleeveless uniform.

"Then I would be stuck treating him, and Lieutenant Kyleren whines over the smallest contusions," the medic jeered.

"There are no small scratches for GAELs, Snow," Harris's gruff voice inserted as he polished the barrel of his BT assault rifle.

Chad just rolled his eyes.

"I spend twice as much time saving your life, corporal," Chad argued.

Lance slipped into one of the chairs orbiting the circular table in effort to escape the field medic's attention. Though Chad's personality was empty of humor, he harbored a slick disdain for stupidity.

Corporal Harris Evans, however, took everything literally. As the oldest GAEL VIC in service, he was among the first batch of soldiers to survive the GraEL bonding process. Though his face betrayed no signs of age, he had survived countless missions over the last 97 years. The many scars on his body proved his prowess as a soldier. One disfigurement in particular caught the eye: a nasty rake from temple to jaw that he had received from a Famorian boghag while he was still a newb.

The level head of Chief Snow was the balance for Harris's craggy personality. Chad lived his life by the book, never deviating from an order or wavering from a mission plan. He was the comeliest of the lot, with a handsome face and well-proportioned body. His only flaw lay in his honest perspective, which could sometimes carry into the extreme.

"Cut the chatter," snapped Major Kenny Huard—the only other human in the room—as he mucked with the table's projection interface. It seemed he was doing more damage than good. "I've enough to deal with without your blathering."

"Kenny's grumpy as ever," Kyleren muttered.

Wayne snorted a laugh. The underlying recklessness of GraEL bonded soldiers persuaded the military's leaders to head every GAEL VIC platoon with a duo of regular issue VIC commanders. Kenny rarely smiled, looking like he suffered from perpetual digestive upset, but he was extremely good at his job. His ability to rein in the thrill-seeking nature of his bonded team earned his position as second commander of the prime jewel of the military, squad Aon. Huard's impatience, however, seemed impossible to breach. Though Colonel Stoddard was only six years from retirement, Lance and Wayne hoped the general would assign a new commanding officer to the team, rather than promote the major.

As Kenny continued to struggle with the table, Kyleren cast an oblique glance at the sergeant. Trisha's severe yellow-hazel eyes glared at her helpless dataplate, her fingers angrily suffocating its frame. Her chocolate skin gleamed in the soft florescent light, her black hair hung in thick braided cords against her neck. Innate mechanical skill had blasted her to the top of her class at only fourteen. She had gone into active service earlier than anyone else on the team. Her skills as ground tech specialist were unmatched in the galaxy, and though her infiltration algorithms and code hacking programs were nearly unstoppable, she could still manage to wrangle most men to the ground in under three seconds when she had to.

Lance knew that from first-hand experience. He logged a mental note to make an effort to be uncharacteristically nice to her. If anyone in the room was actually capable of shooting him out of spite, it would be her.

"Ready, colonel," Kenny announced at last.

"Good," Stoddard said, advancing on the table as a hologrid image of Gwydion materialized. The military space complex was a collection of wide disks, each about ten decks, stacked on top of each other. Two thinner arms extended from its midsection, stretching out 250 meters in both directions. Only four apple-hoppers could dock at any given time. At the sight of their home, all six GAELs visibly tensed, waiting for orders.

"The information you're about to receive is only known to the Round, myself, and a handful of scientists who will be joining our mission shortly."

Kyleren's eyes drifted from the hovering hologram to his commanding officer. Whizbangs? Although science teams were sometimes included on war missions, squad Aon had never used one to Kyleren's knowledge. The elitist of the elite, Aon's assignments were fast, dangerous, and lethal. Stoddard's usual jovial demeanor evaporated faster than dintillium in a core reactor, replaced by a seriousness that carved long lines of concern down his face. He stared at the projection, his muddy green eyes grim with apprehension.

"At approximately 2235 DST on quadrilmoth 7th, 1403 AGW, the Blended Coalition military research and training station, Gwydion, was infiltrated by hostiles. The base was completely destroyed. There were no survivors."

Trisha's dataplate fell to the table with a loud clatter. Murmurs of disbelief rattled around the circumference of the table. Every GAEL in the room had spent his first 20 years of life on that station—except Trisha who had graduated early—and it was the closest thing any of their military driven lives had to home. Its orbit around Athalonde Prime was a closely guarded secret, even within the Coalition. The station's outer defenses were the most advanced in the system.

Lance surveyed the reactions of his fellows. Wayne's fists were turning white with pressure, and Gary's mouth hung open. The 20-year-old had left the station's training halls only a few days before. Seven thousand military personnel inhabited Gwydion, a tenth of them were the GraEL candidates, most of whom were children.

"How?"

Harris's question came as a loud snap that bounced off the angular walls.

"Unknown," Stoddard replied. "We have limited facts surrounding the attack, and what little intel we've pieced together can't account for the level of damage sustained."

The colonel tapped a series of keys at the table's lip. Two dimensional pictures of the real station floated in succession around the perimeter of the table. Each slide had been taken a few seconds after the previous, illustrating the path of a standard-sized apple-hopper as it approached the center disk of the military base.

"These shots were taken from a camera on the adjacent science complex of Govannan, ten minutes before the explosion. Our analysts believe that this ship docked just outside Gwydion's command center."

"There's no dock or hatches there," Sergeant Trisha Reynolds noted. "They would have been forced to cut their way in."

"It's standard procedure for 20 fully bonded GAELs to be posted in the command center 25/6," Chad said, shaking his head, "and another hundred throughout the station. Even if an infiltration team had hacked through the outer warning systems, they wouldn't have stood a chance once they stormed the station."

"Any unidentified vessel would have been blown to the Reach before it got within a light year of Gwydion," Wayne inserted skeptically.

Others added their arguments, but Kyleren only listened. After a quick rabble of voices, the colonel held up his hand, silencing their comments.

"We've linked the photos with the information we received just before Gwydion's communications blacked out. Clearance was given for a GAEL VIC military vessel, inbound from Kamolos, transporting a new batch of potential GraEL candidates. According to the log, it was a routine flight. But on approach, it diverted from the air dock ports, attaching directly to the command center."

"They disguised themselves in a Coalition military ship? That's impossible!" Gary stated incredulously.

Never in the history of the MetaGalactic War had the VICs lost track of a vessel, whether in service, destroyed, or captured by the enemy.

"Even if it got them past the outer defenses of the station," Kyleren maintained, "once they bypassed the ports and attached to the outer hull, their behavior would have been registered as hostile. Why didn't the GAELs engage?"

"We don't know," the colonel admitted. "The apple-hopper didn't disengage immediately. We are positive that whoever was inside cut through and somehow managed to penetrate the station. They should have been stopped there."

"Maybe they've got some new tech," Kenny surmised.

"Speculation gets us nowhere," Wayne said, redirecting the conversation. "Do we know who it was?"

"Intel has calculated the trajectory of the ship once it jumped to FTL," Stoddard answered. "It's headed for Agromor space."

"Then it was an act of war," Chief Snow muttered.

"Even worse," the colonel continued, "we now believe that their objective was more than just the destruction of Gwydion. The general and his staff think the Agromors' true goal was to steal the GraEL."

"*The* GraEL?" Wayne demanded.

"I thought it was kept on Kamolos somewhere," Trisha objected, "to keep those gromm bigots from getting to it."

"Those were rumors, a shell game to protect the GraEL. Since the foundation of bonded tech, the GraEL has been secured on Gwydion."

"If it was such a secret, how did the Agromors know it was there?" Harris grumbled.

"There's no other possibility. The Agromors must've had an informant," the colonel answered promptly. "According to my report, only five doctors in the GAEL Research Initiative knew the GraEL was located on Gwydion. Some high-ranking politicians with the information are also being investigated."

Trisha snorted. "If it was one of the station's doctors, then he's long gone. All the others died in the attack, so we'll never know for sure who was involved."

Colonel Stoddard hard-eyed each member of his group. "Our job isn't to apprehend the spy. Our mission is to locate and recover the GraEL from enemy hands, before it's lost to Agromor space."

"If they wanted us to pull that, they shoulda sent us three weeks ago," Lance complained loudly. What the hell was the Round thinking? The Agromor ship had an impossible head start. "Why didn't they order a pursuit immediately?"

"By the time the data was analyzed, the Agromors were already between systems."

"There's no way we'll find the GraEL. The Agromors will have it secured long before we get there," Chad argued. "It will be untraceable."

The others muttered low agreements, but Stoddard's face split into a knowing grin.

"We're going to get there first," he replied.

"There's no fragging way, sir," Trisha declared.

Lance waited patiently. The colonel was famous for dramatic suspense. The unmistakable pleasure in his expression foretold something unusual.

"Four years ago, the Round allocated ten billion prings to Lamorak Industries to construct the first prototype of a living tech space vessel. Through its formulation they developed a new method of faster-than-light travel."

"Slip Transference Travel?" Trisha gasped. "They've managed to create an STT drive? That cuts normal FTL travel time from weeks to hours!"

Stoddard nodded. "It's currently untested in combat situations, but the chief technobionomist on the project has operated two successful STT jumps. The ship is still incomplete, but it has weapons and life support, plus a few—extras. This emergency has moved its commission date up a few years ahead of schedule."

"I thought living tech postulates state that anything larger than a computer built exclusively of LT could be catastrophically dangerous," Chad objected, "due to instability of control protocols."

"I don't care where the tech comes from, chief," the colonel declared. "The Round gives me orders and I execute them. As do you. Retrieving the GraEL will be the most important mission you undertake in your entire career. But to find it, you'll need a description of its specs."

The GAELs around the table exchanged glances, revealing varying degrees of tension and excitement. Lance and Wayne leaned closer to the hologrid. None of them had ever seen the GraEL, and to their knowledge, neither had any other soldier.

The effect the Graviton Energy Locus—the GraEL—had on a planet was only a blip in the education prescribed by the GAEL training program. All Kyleren knew was that somehow the GraEL was responsible for creating the living ore that grew across the surface of Athalonde Prime, and that this mineral was required for all living tech machinery in the modern world. More importantly, the GraEL was the means by which the Coalition scientists bound the GAEL VICs to their core drives, allowing them to integrate themselves with various living technology. Without the GraEL, there would be no new bonded soldiers.

The holopicture shifted away from the floating military base of Gwydion. A yellow-tinted object took its place, alive with pulsing veins of sun-flame orange. It was only 50 cm tall, even narrower in width. Kyleren blinked several times, disappointment fizzling his initial anticipation.

Somehow he had imagined something more extravagant, more alien in nature, especially since the GraEL had always been hallowed by the Agromors—something to do with their ancient religion.

Lance spoke first, seemingly breaking through the disillusioned shock that muted the tongues of everyone else in the room.

"It's a tree in a pot, sir."

4: SHE'LL MAKE POINT FIVE PAST LIGHT SPEED

A platoon of spit-shined Cymric guards packing dual-stun assault weapons spectacularly lined the voluminous hallway. Attesting to the magnificence of Lamorak Industries—or at least the company's influence on the coffers of the Round—the guards were merely for show, to impress any high-ranking visitors lucky enough to have clearance to view Lamorak's latest project. Many a famous diplomat or scientist must have tread these halls, but Lance doubted that any had ever made the jaws of the Cymric sentinels sag so low as the sight of six fully armed GAEL VICs tromping down the corridor.

A sandy-haired human in his early twenties paced in front of the security door, his limbs twitching with agitation. Every so often he would pause, stuffing his hands into the pockets of his trousers and rock back and forth on his heels. When he resumed his path, he muttered unintelligibly at the ceiling. If it weren't for the lab coat, Kyleren might have mistaken him for an absent-minded college student.

"Team," Colonel Stoddard said loudly when the squad reached the young man, "this is technobionomist Gene Pecktol, head of the LAMIE project."

"LAMIE?" Lance asked.

These whizbang types made tech sound like a cute furry animal, not the most advanced spaceship ever manufactured.

"Lamorak Augmented Mechanical Integrated Entity," Gene clarified so quickly that the words blended together incoherently.

Gene's eyes had a glazed, glassy quality that seemed to look right through a person, as if his mind was preoccupied with something more important than mere conversation.

"Right, LAMIE it is," Lance said, failing to recall a single portion of the ship's actual designation.

"Colonel, you're late," Gene accused. "I still haven't been able to fully integrate the neurosillica pathway cryptograms into the base protowards of LAMIE's programming! Do you have any idea how long that takes? I should have downloaded the regulatory cyphers an hour ago—"

Whatever else the technobionomist said was such a jumble of terminology that Kyleren hardly called it language. Gene swiped his ident tag as he talked, causing the security door to hiss open smoothly.

"Trust me Gene, it was worth it," Stoddard interrupted, slapping him on the shoulder as the colonel twisted the technobionomist around to face the members of Aon squad. Gene winced and rubbed the spot where the commander had jovially struck him, mouthing the word "ouch" in a silent grimace. "My GAELs needed to know all the facts before they could properly defend you and your ship."

"Trust me, colonel," Gene returned, "she'll be the one doing the protecting."

Squad Aon followed the young technobionomist into the hangar. An open balcony overlooked the massive deck, providing an aerial view into the heart of Lamorak Industries' most prestigious enterprises. Kyleren had never seen so much experimental living tech. Though not an expert, as a member of the GAEL program he often received the newest developments of modern technology before any civilian organization, or even other branches of the military. The majority of Lamorak's LT department focused on weapon design, computer upgrades, and tools to link with GAEL core drives. But LAMIE's hangar bay was strewn with equipment he could barely describe, much less recognize. Scientists were scattered everywhere, tinkering with the machinery and blathering streams of incoherent vocabulary, dashing around the bay like ants under a rock.

But nothing between the gleaming white walls of the gigantic research hall flashed as elegantly as the sleek black hull of LAMIE. She glistened in the center of the bay like a magazine model in a photo shoot, conscious that all eyes fondled her form with longing. Twin cylindrical engine shells distended from the flanks of her hull, accentuating the angle of her nose, which was bejeweled with two sophisticated LTB cannons. Rail guns threaded into her wings and bow, like glimmering silver bracelet charms.

She was slightly larger than a standard military hopper, fifty meters from nose to tail, nearly thirty in width. Workers leaned over her roof with cranes, applying some substance to her hull while others jiggled the gears and wire along open panels in her stomach. As the squad admired the lithe figure of her body, the black sheen of her skin rippled crimson like the silicated hydrobromine clouds of Lugh, swirling into a vortex of scarlet.

Gene turned his floppy body away from the balcony's edge and leaned against the railing.

"A few weeks ago she discovered how to access her camouflage subroutines. She's been changing her color about every half hour since."

"*She* changes her color?" Harris asked in confusion.

"Yes," Gene said. "I explained this to your superiors earlier. LAMIE wasn't anywhere near ready for active commission, but they made me upgrade her protoboard anyway, before she was mature enough to handle the advance."

"You're personifying her," Trisha said disapprovingly. "She's just a machine."

Gene practically jumped off the banister.

"Shhh!" he said, bringing a long finger to his lips.

He glanced over his shoulder at LAMIE. He must have determined that all was well because his shoulders relaxed perceptibly.

"LAMIE's made of the finest grade LT ore that can be found on Athalonde Prime. Her creation has redefined everything we know about technobionomy! But when you insult her she gets—pouty."

Kyleren eyed the ship skeptically. "That doesn't sound reliable. I don't know if I wanna trust my life to a moody chick."

Gene's high-pitched snort sounded more like a gurgled sneeze than a laugh. "Pouty doesn't mean uncooperative," he explained. The technobionomist pointed at the ship, "I designed her protoboard with over 12 million protochips. She's the most advanced living tech entity in history."

"Do those 12 million protochips include vanity?" Wayne asked suspiciously.

"Ha, ha, ha," Gene returned with a measure of sarcasm. "Laugh all you want, but LAMIE isn't just some collection of rivets and bolts like other vessels. Except for her engines and deck platforms, she's constructed entirely of LT ore. She's a fully sentient being, complete with personality, just like any regular biological person."

"But doesn't that mean she can make her own decisions?" Chad asked. "Like disobeying orders?"

"You military guys always underestimate us," the technobionomist replied, clearly offended. "LAMIE has restrictions. She's incapable of defying her own protocols. For example, she can't just shut off life support and kill us all in our sleep; her protoboard doesn't allow it. And she can only link up with her main systems like engines and weapons when a GAEL VIC activates her interface with a core drive. She's programmed to obey every command she's given by an authorized user."

Satisfied when no one argued, Gene smiled proudly and shoved his fists into his pockets.

"So why does she change color, whizbang?" Wayne asked Gene with feigned interest. Lance grinned widely at his friend's amusement.

"It's her LT stealth system. Her skin adapts to any color or texture, allowing her to blend in to her surroundings. Plus she emits a constant pulse that makes her undetectable to enemy sensor arrays."

Harris whistled a low tone. Lance was impressed, but Trisha looked unsatisfied.

"But isn't it faulty if she changes color every half hour?"

"On all of our space runs she follows instructions," Gene replied. "LAMIE likes the missions, and she understands the importance of directions. But like I told your general, and the Chancellor of the Round himself, by the way, LAMIE isn't ready for this much excitement."

"Why not?" Kenny intruded, speaking for the first time since they entered the Lamorak complex.

"Don't you know anything about living tech?" Gene asked, clearly flabbergasted at the ignorance surrounding him. He shook his head, missing Kenny's glare entirely. "LAMIE was only created four years ago. That's how old she was when Gwydion was destroyed last month. I've been building her protoboard slowly from the day she was born. Like a child, she learns and grows over time. It's the only way to ensure a living tech entity her size doesn't gain a sentience that we can't control. To be successful on any military mission, I've projected she needs to be in her early twenties."

"A few years shy, aren't we?" Lance observed sardonically.

"I built her slowly to prevent mistakes, but if you're a brilliant technobionomist at the head of your field—like me—the process can be, uh, manipulated."

"So, how old she?" Lance asked.

Gene inhaled anxiously. "Fourteen. It was the best I could do in such a short time."

Gary stepped forward, laughing lightly. "Are you saying that she changes color and pouts because she's going through puberty?"

"Exactly," Gene said happily. "She's recently developed an awareness of herself and her appearance. Think of it like self-esteem. So instead of just testing her hull color, she has to put on an entire light show."

The stringy technobionomist led the troop down the stairs and through LAMIE's main hatch. Her corridors glistened opaque blue, their unblemished surface interrupted every few meters by doors or code panels. The GAELs walked side-by-side in pairs, with room to spare between the walls. As Kyleren noted an oversized hatch, most likely leading to the ship's loading dock, a breezy female voice saturated the air.

"Welcome back, Gene, Colonel Stoddard," LAMIE said cheerfully. "I recognize the members of GAEL VIC Aon squad from my memory banks. I am very happy to welcome you. I must say I am excited to venture into Agromor space. I understand the Sylph elves of the Danaan system can change their hair to any color they wish simply by willing it to happen."

"Yes," Gene responded toward the ceiling. Since LAMIE was technically all around them, Lance thought Gene's actions were unnecessary. "But they are far less impressive than you LAMIE," he flattered pleasantly. "You can change your entire hull."

"True, but they are organic life forms, whereas I am a technological sentience."

"LAMIE's never been planetside," Gene explained to the soldiers, as if justifying the meaningless exchange. "She's obsessed by the galaxy's differing species."

"I am most intrigued with the ashrays of the planet Mannan in the Famorian System," LAMIE added. "I understand they are quite antagonistic toward the biped races."

"She's well-spoken for a 14-year-old," Stoddard noted.

"I am also curious about the members of Aon squad," LAMIE said hopefully.

It was eerie how her emotions were so recognizable. Kyleren wondered if it would ultimately prove inconvenient on a mission.

"May I ask them questions about their adventures?" the ship asked.

"Ah," Gene breathed, redirecting his haughty intelligence back toward the soldiers, "such curiosity. She always has questions. Go ahead LAMIE."

"Thank you, Gene," LAMIE replied. "My first inquiry is for Lieutenant Lance Kyleren regarding his recent expedition on Jera Zeta. I have never been to the Dintigel Asteroid Belt. What is it like?"

Lance saw his teammates' yellow-hazel eyes shift to him. He felt strange discussing his life with an LT intelligence. What possible use was there in befriending an adolescent machine?

"Boring as hell," Kyleren answered noncommittally.

"I have no knowledge of this 'Hell'," LAMIE responded. "Is it located near the Eye of Baylour?"

"Is she gonna ask us questions durin' the whole mission?" Lance complained to his superior officer.

"I do not intend to intrude on your comfort limitations, Lieutenant Kyleren," the machine apologized. "If you would prefer, I will suspend my queries until you are prepared to speak with me."

Gene glowered at the lieutenant, as if Lance had insulted the technobionomist's girlfriend or something. There was no gromm way Kyleren was going to apologize to a fragging machine, no matter how advanced. Still, he supposed it would be problematic if LAMIE were offended.

"Maybe between shifts," Lance said in compromise.

Though LAMIE didn't respond, the technobionomist seemed placated by the offer. Gene clapped his hands together and rubbed them excitedly.

"So, who wants a tour?"

The whole team buzzed with enthusiastic agreement. Though some of the soldiers were hesitant to trust a self-aware vessel, they were nevertheless eager to experience LAMIE's advanced systems, especially her combat capabilities.

"We have a doctor coming," Gene said as he led them in a straight line to the medical bay, "and he's supposed to be some expert on GAEL physiology."

Scanners, regenerators, and fancy nanomite tech devices lay in tidy rows about the walls and steel cabinets. Two exam bunks extended from the bulkheads.

"I haven't met him," Gene continued, "but he's been assigned by the highest authorities for the operation, or so I'm told. They've also assigned a culturalist. Apparently, he knows everything about the Agromor societies."

As the team reentered the main corridor, Gene pointed to a closed door.

"My lab is open to anyone, but I suggest that you don't bother me unless it's really important. It connects to LAMIE's protocore. You'll never see it."

He led them to the next hatch and waved as they passed by.

"This one leads to the forward landing gear and the STT portal drive. You probably won't see that either."

"How does it work?" Trisha probed as they turned a corner.

"The STT portal drive? I'm glad you asked," Gene replied, as if he were providing a cure to one of the galaxy's most deadly diseases. "As you must know," he began proudly, "technobionomy theorizes that our world is linked to a plane of unimaginable energy. Microscopic anomalies bridge our space with this other dimension, and technobionomists have measured a constant flow of tiny matter particles being drawn from our plane into the energy dimension over these bridges. At the same rate, these particles are replaced in other parts of the galaxy by the same kind of anomalies—which we call transference portals. That's how Slip Transference Theory was discovered: the idea that matter can be transported through one T-portal and exit another within a short span of time. Over the last few centuries we have detected over five hundred individual T-portals."

"This ship isn't tiny," Harris pointed out.

"Excuse me?" Gene said, tossed from his stream of explanations by the interruption.

"You said only small particles could enter the portals," Harris clarified.

Gene blinked perplexedly at Harris, as if the solution to the conundrum was painfully obvious. After a few seconds of blank stares, the technobionomist heaved an exasperated sigh.

"Unless you have an STT drive that widens the T-portal openings to accommodate more conventional-sized objects. Which we do." Gene rolled his eyes and continued his informational tirade, his limbs gaining in animation as he talked. "It only needs to open the portal for initial entry into the transference plane. Once through, we convert into pure energy as we slip from one T-portal to the next. We then materialize on the other side of the galaxy."

"I don't know if I like the sound of that," Wayne said.

Lance noticed an almost imperceptible squeamish quality to his comrade's voice. Kyleren felt a smidgeon of

45

apprehension himself. What if his particles—or whatever—simply scattered aimlessly across the universe?

"It's completely painless," Gene said, waving away the anxiety of atomic deconstruction with an absent-minded flick of his palm. "In fact, you won't remember a thing. Time still moves forward, but you can't maintain memory when your body and brain are only energy."

"I feel so much better," Wayne responded sarcastically from the edge of his mouth, but the technobionomist didn't notice.

Gene brushed them past the loading dock, pointing out standard military infiltration equipment as he went, including a basic terrain crawler shackled behind a large ribbed hatch. He indicated the corridor leading to the main engine room, but warned them not to enter without permission from the head engineer, Bedin Desha. Despite the fact that the Kildar elf had chosen to live within the Blended Coalition, he had little respect for anyone not of his own race, and seemed especially intolerant of blendeds.

"Unfortunately, LAMIE's standard FTL drive isn't complete. But it doesn't matter," Gene assured, "because our sublight engines will get us to the nearest T-portal and then, whoosh," here his hands gesticulated wildly, "we can go practically anywhere we want."

Kyleren silently wished the whizbang would "whoosh" himself back to his lab. Gene's incessant chatter was making Lance's head pound uncomfortably. There seemed to be more crazy personalities on this boat than a Sulevian tragedy. Caught up in his thoughts, the lieutenant lost the thread of conversation.

"—outfitted with the latest weapons' upgrades. There are four retractable rail guns, all with LT rounds and a living tech bond cannon. The holds for the rail guns are accessible through the armory on the starboard side, the space suit hold on the port side, and on opposite ends of the engine room. All are controlled by one interface—meaning only one GAEL can operate them at a time. It's the most advanced core drive integration ever created."

"Hearin' that a lot?" Kyleren murmured to Wayne.

The big man only grinned, his white teeth flashing brilliantly against his brown skin.

"We're going green with all new technology. They must have a lot of faith in their new interface system."

"Or us," Gary popped optimistically.

Lance was starting to like the newb.

After touring the lower deck, Gene guided squad Aon topside to the upper level. "LAMIE's brig and officer quarters are all the way down the hall," Gene explained, directing their attention to a single corridor running the length of LAMIE's nose. "The mess hall is directly ahead, and the barracks are down there."

He continued pointing, first to a set of large, double-sliding doors, then toward the ship's aft, where another set of stairs twisted upward. Walking toward the barracks he stopped just in front of the rack room and indicated the door opposite.

"This is the situation room," he said, palming the door trigger.

Kyleren peeked over the threshold. A plain but heavy circular table was bolted into the floor, along with twelve chairs, one for each member of the crew, plus an extra.

"Last but not least," Gene said, grandiosely leading them up the last narrow staircase, "we have the bridge."

The rectangular command deck blinked with holographic heads-up displays and access panels. A sturdy chair manned each of the three stations, and one loomed center, clearly intended for the commander. Core drive insertion points were clearly visible at each post. A transparent crystasteel portal served as the main viewport, unobstructed from ceiling to floor and stretching from the port bulkhead to starboard.

"LAMIE only requires one GAEL pilot. Over there is the weapons' interface. The last station is for the navigator. Currently, the STT portal drive is not accessible by bonded tech and can only be initiated by myself or the colonel."

"And what if the entire squad is needed on the ground?" Chad asked. "We can't spare team members during an op to pilot the ship."

"You won't need to," Gene defended. "LAMIE doesn't require a bond for flight. She can be piloted like any other ship by non-GAEL personnel. However, without the bond she won't have instant access to the engines like she would with a GAEL. If you want, you could insert your core drive and control her remotely."

"Are you saying a GAEL could fly her using only his mind?" Wayne asked excitedly.

As Aon's main pilot, he was the most likely candidate.

"Exactly," Gene said eagerly. "You could go planetside and order LAMIE into orbit until you wanted her back."

"But I'd have to leave behind my core drive," Wayne mused.

"Yes. That's the only downfall of the system," Stoddard asserted. "Gene's working on it."

Lance scoffed. Expecting a GAEL to go into combat without his core drive was like equipping him with a bow and arrow against a missile launcher.

"Sounds like a suicide run," Lance said with a nudge at Wayne.

The colonel placed a hand on Wayne's shoulder. "Don't worry, captain, for the first half of the mission, you and Gary will be remaining shipside," he informed. "Lieutenant Kyleren will be heading the ground team."

Lance jerked. Colonel Stoddard never put Kyleren in charge, due to the lieutenant's perpetual habit of surrendering to his impulsive nature when making decisions. He wasn't sure if he was ready for command. Scanning the faces of the others revealed that they—unfortunately—agreed.

"What exactly is the first half of our mission, sir?" Lance inquired.

"Locate intel revealing the Agromor ship's destination. We're going to hit them like they did us. LAMIE's stealth abilities give us an edge for a mission that would normally be impossible. We're going to infiltrate an Agromor defense satellite and find the information we need," Colonel Stoddard said. He added with a smile, "Then we're going to blow it up."

5: It Can Only Be Attributable To Human Error

Blended children were always stronger than the offspring of the natural races. Because of technical intervention, a blended infant gained the genetic strengths of its parents and avoided their racial weaknesses. Thus the child gained immunities to most diseases, the ability to flourish in harsh environments, and enjoyed a lifespan that was the average of its parents. If a blended baby died—which happened to one in approximately every ten million births throughout the Coalition inhabited planets—the cause was always poor integration of the living nanomite technology. Blending tech had existed for almost two thousand years, a little longer than the official start of the MetaGalactic War, but still, after all that time, the medical community seemed unable to determine the precise conditions that caused Failed Living Tech Blending. And even more frustrating, the instances of FLTB had risen over the last century.

The defect was the worst fear of every mother who underwent the two year process of carrying a cross-species fetus. Testing for FLTB was standard procedure on a newborn blended. It was undetectable until a few hours after an infant's delivery, but the signs were readily recognizable to any trained physician once the time interval had passed.

Dr. Anya Ninevay slammed her dataplate against the table with dissatisfaction. She was renowned throughout the wandering city of Penardun for her meticulous consistency. She had earned an honorable commendation as the head student at the Medical Apprenticeship Academy on Lludd for her exceptional performance before taking a position as the Kildar space city's head of medicine. Never once during her 300-year span career had she misinterpreted a set of test results.

She lifted a small crystal vial from her desk, upsetting the red liquid inside. Anya had run the diagnostic herself when the infant had been still alive. The blended girl-child tested negative for FLTB. The half-Kildar babe had been the strongest blended infant Dr. Ninevay had ever helped to grow. But the baby died later that night, a few hours after Anya had completed her shift. The death was completely unforeseen, an improbable circumstance that was inexcusable under Dr. Ninevay's professional standards.

She interviewed all the attending nurses. Only two had been working in the nursery that night. One admitted she had fallen asleep on duty and summarily had been dismissed, and the other had been fully consumed with caring for a human child born too early for proper lung function. The autopsy on the blended infant had been performed by a medical student Anya had never met, and she didn't trust his results.

The infant's remains had been routinely destroyed before Dr. Ninevay returned to the hospital the next morning—by edict of the Coalition Chancellor all cadavers were to be cremated within a certain time period to avoid a new biological weapons threat instigated by the Agromors—and so Anya had been forced to execute the FLTB test on the baby's original blood sample.

The findings were conclusive and undeniable: full tech degradation. At first Anya was aghast, so she ran the test a third time. But the results remained unchanged.

How could she have made such an error the day before? Every protein marker seemed to be in order, the energy signature of imminent nanomite failure obvious. She even double-checked the recorded time of the sample and ran a DNA test make sure the blood hadn't somehow been mislabeled. No mistake: it had been extracted five hours before death from Riia Farren. All the allele indicators matched the dataplate record.

Anya set the vial back in its frame. The analysis was irrefutable. So why did she have this annoying buzz in the back of her mind, making her feel like something was wrong?

She stared at the neat identificatory script on the vial, written in her own hand, her fingers pulling absently at the roots of her hair. The maltreatment loosed several strands from their bindings, forcing her to slick them back behind her ears. After two hours of further examination of the electronic file, she finally surrendered. With a discouraged sigh she stood, picking up the sample on her way to the crypt, where the medical center stored patient biologicals.

Just as she touched the freezer's handle, a thought peeked through her disappointment. Unlooked for, it offered an alternate explanation of the infant's mysterious death, one that absolved her of fault. Her heart throbbed at a higher tempo. Most physicians acquired their nanomites from a Coalition central medical stock, preprogrammed by the nanopharm companies for specific tasks. Modification options were linked to the medical technician's protointerface to better serve a specific patient. Anya, however, felt that the mass production of medical supplies was ill-suited for a physician's craft, and consistently rewrote the protocols for the nanomites toiling under her care. Additionally, she tagged each patient's mites with her own ident code—usually something trivial that didn't require electronic record, a simple augment to the microscopic entities' serial numbers.

She rushed back to the lab and scanned Riia's vial with the protointerface. Though the mites had been inactive for several hours since the sample was taken, each serial number registered the presence of the exact mites that had been drawn with the blood. Anya held her breath as the data flashed across the screen. The number strings matched the original factory designations, but her personalized ident code was missing. Anyone else cross-referencing the nanomites Dr. Ninevay had used in the blending procedure would have found nothing amiss, but Anya knew these were not the same microscopic machines she had implanted in Riia's mother two years ago.

Someone had tampered with the sample.

6: Bring The Rain

Zipping through the void of space on the outer hull of a ship lacked the rush of atmosphere of a planetside aircraft, but Kyleren's blood pumped with adrenaline despite the lack of wind. Knowing that sublight speed could rip through a standard planet's circumference in less than a minute, and that he and the other three members of the infiltration team would be crushed by terrestrial g-force if LAMIE weren't sprinting through an airless vacuum, revived the familiar pre-mission thrill he had lost during his internment on Jera Zeta.

As soon as LAMIE had confidently informed Colonel Stoddard that she had calculated the location of a T-portal less than five minutes sublight from the targeted Agromor satellite, squad Aon launched. Kyleren's infiltration team—Trish, Chad, and Harris—were nearly invisible against LAMIE's black casing, their CC armor blending into her coloring flawlessly. Only their disembodied gear—LT assault rifles, pistols, Chad's medical kit, and Harris's particularly largish grenade launcher—were easily discernible. Perched on the curve of LAMIE's bow, just above her twin LTB cannons, they waited by the soles of their magnetic combat boots for the enemy satellite to loom into view.

"STT drive is coming on line," Gene announced over the comm.

The portal drive activated soundlessly, a unique feature of living technology. If it hadn't been for the sudden appearance of a pinprick of light, gleaming ahead like a far off star, Kyleren might have believed the new tech had failed to initiate. As they raced toward it, the flickering glow jerked through several sizes, like an uncontrolled muscle spasm, until it yawned into a rippling gold vortex twice LAMIE's circumference. Lance had the uncanny impression that, rather than heading for it, the iridescent eddy greedily sucked them in.

An anticipatory shiver trickled through his limbs. The crackling energy spiral wrapped its sharp fringes around the little ship, the center crumpling against them. Lance had not, despite 232 missions, encountered something so menacingly unknown. Regardless of Gene's previous assurances that slip transference was completely painless, Kyleren's muscles drew taut, suddenly aware that only the thin layer of his combat space suit shielded him from the constricting space portal.

He felt nothing as it washed over him. Abruptly, the bright light vanished.

"Congratulations," Gene's voice stated proudly through Lance's headset, "we have successfully reached the Danaan System. Total travel time: 7 hours, 31 minutes."

Lance shook the eerie feeling that accompanied the loss of time from his head. The crazy technobionomist had warned Kyleren that he wouldn't remember passage through the energy plane—from Lance's perspective the journey had lasted less than a second—but he at least expected to remember something odd about bursting into millions of atomic pieces and then jolting back into existence.

"Target visible on sensors, initiating attack sequence," Captain Reese announced.

Several moments passed before Lance relayed visual conformation of the satellite's position. He shoveled any lingering doubts over the unnerving experience of STT travel out of his mind, allowing the buzz of mission prerogatives to consume his focus.

The target hung limply at the system's edge, an inverted cone composed of three consecutively shrinking rings. Thin spokes anchored the satellite's deep space hyperbolic communications array in the center of the largest halo.

LAMIE charged her triangular LTB cannons on approach. A giddy ripple, like a wave of excitement, tickled her outer hull as mirrored beams of destructive power erupted from her main weapons, converging on a point in seemingly empty space. The cannons tore a wicked hole through the Agromor force shields. Kyleren thought he heard the LT ship raise her voice with pleasure as the adolescent vessel careened into combat range. Three more precise discharges and the satellite's communication dish disintegrated into floating hunks of shrapnel.

"Squad Aon is clear for departure in three—" LAMIE announced, as her path swung to a point above the enemy target.

Lance's muscles tightened as he prepared to spring, Harris slammed his core drive into the grenade launcher.

"Two—"

The ship pivoted, accelerating into a dive.

"One."

LAMIE plunged through the center of the station, clearing the floating wreckage of the communications array, cannons blasting the Agromor ring as she passed.

When LAMIE drew level with the second circlet, the infiltration team deactivated their magnetic boots and vaulted from her hull, pushing through the dark vacuum on a diagonal trajectory away from LAMIE as she easily slid through the satellite's smallest ring. Knowing that their current vector would smash them against the ring's outer surface, Lance barked an order to Harris, who immediately launched a grenade at the station's bulkheads. The sharp tip of the explosive pierced the metal hull, disappearing into the interior for a heartbeat while the mechanism's secondary protocol activated. Inside the enemy perimeter, the grenade released tiny stabilizers that anchored to whatever surface it had contacted, then detonated. The explosion cracked the hull like a can of sardines, spewing debris and atmosphere in the GAELs' path. Lance's super speed knocked the most dangerous pieces out of the way as the team careened toward the opening.

Kyleren fired his suit thrusters against his forward momentum to slow his passage through the blast gap, but in the three seconds it took him to pass through the opening, he realized it wouldn't be enough. His body slammed ungracefully against the station's inner wall with enough force to crumple the bulkhead, propelling him into the room beyond. He rebounded off the next barrier, tucking into a roll and gripping the nearest metallic surface with his reactivated boot soles.

Harris followed, narrowly avoiding a collision with Lance. The corporal reoriented himself with a snarled grumble. Trisha and Chad, landing expertly at the edge of the grenade's impact zone, smirked condescendingly through their space visors at their two floundering comrades.

A quick hand signal from Lance, however, sobered the team instantly. Harris took point, trotting warily down the ring's curved corridor, grenade launcher stowed and his rifle raised and ready. Lance and Chad followed, Trisha covering the rear. The compartments were completely depressurized, though several flashing red lights indicated the station had reacted to the assault, instituting some type of automatic emergency lock down. It wasn't long before the GAELs met their first obstacle: one of the station's internal blast doors.

Sergeant Reynolds hustled to the front of the group, extracting a small metallic wafer from a thin pocket at her thigh. She pressed it onto the door panel with a thumb as the others encircled her in a standard defensive formation. Living tech feelers twisted out of the lean override device, boring into the access panel. Trisha had already drawn a second tool from her belt, deftly inserting her core drive into the flat data interface plate. A few quick keystrokes disengaged the emergency system and persuaded the door to rise. All four GAELs flattened against the walls.

Three space-gear-less Agromors were blown into the vacuous corridor by the enthusiastic rush of air, each Vartal elf desperately clinging to any available handhold. Kyleren's team pushed against the pressure, using their enhanced strength to drag their bodies out of the vacuum. When all four were safely across the threshold, Trisha resealed the door.

"Schematics indicate the command center and dintillium core are located on the smallest ring," Trisha said, retracting the clear shield of her space helmet and rolling through a collection of files on her dataplate. "There's an elevator ahead to the left."

Kyleren's BT assault rifle already jutted solidly against his shoulder and aimed down the curved passageway to engage any Agromor who might appear. He motioned Harris forward with a silent signal. The corporal obeyed instantly, scouting down the hall and bending out of sight.

"Negative for contacts," Harris reported.

Kyleren led the rest of his team to the secured elevator.

"Are we walking or knocking?" the corporal growled.

Kyleren examined the admission panel, amazed it didn't require a code or ident tag. *Stupid gromms think no one can get on this satellite,* he thought with amusement as he flicked the key to summon the lift.

"Let's knock," he grinned.

"How about we just finish the job?" Chad inserted, exhibiting an unnatural amount of patience for a GAEL.

The doors slid open with a pleasant ting. The GAELs loaded into the lift and Trisha input their destination. The machine lurched downward.

"Me and Evans will neutralize any targets," Kyleren commanded, brisk and businesslike. He was trained to prepare for any circumstance, but he doubted they would meet much resistance. Their CC armor masked them from the internal sensors, and LAMIE's attack run would occupy the focus of the Agromor retaliation. "Snow, you've got Reynolds' six until she breaks into command."

"Yes, sir," Chad returned.

The elevator slowed as it reached the requested level. As the shaft portals retracted, Kyleren spotted the flash of granite-dappled skin and navy hair of a Vartal security officer, frantically shouting instructions. No one took particular notice of the elevator arrival. The Agromors were probably expecting reinforcements, not the advent of a GAEL infiltration team.

Lance dashed through the doors before they had completely opened, dropping to one knee. The corridor was narrower than he expected, with an exit on the left and right. He popped a single round from his assault rifle as he hit the floor, infusing the BT projectile with enough energy from his core drive to cleanly pass through the security guard's brain and into a second elf behind him, but not so much that the slug would penetrate the bulkhead. Before the bodies of either target struck the ground, Kyleren heard the crack of Harris' pistol as the lieutenant's comrade dealt with another enemy on their flank.

"Clear," Chief Snow called.

Kyleren turned as he stood. Sergeant Reynolds collected an ident tag from one of the fallen guards, injecting it into her dataplate. A few seconds and the information transfer completed its cycle. Harris entertained himself in the interim by plunking vapor shells into his grenade launcher.

"Access to secure areas," Trisha reported, removing the tag and her core drive simultaneously.

"Spray the command center with two shells," Kyleren ordered, pointing to Harris. "Me and Trish will target anyone caught in the blast. You and Snow take the tag and clear out any other entry points to the room."

Trisha tossed the ident tag to Snow who scanned it into the door panel while she bonded her core drive to her pistol. Harris clipped the door panel as he sprinted through to the command deck, firing his launcher twice, Chad at his heels. Cries of alarm resonated in the swirling cloud as Reynolds and Kyleren rushed into the fray. Lance's visor automatically shifted into infrared, pinpointing nine

Agromors hunched over and gagging in the veil of lung-numbing gas. Harris and Chad blasted two elves and a dwarf who had escaped the vapor's grip on the bent side of the room.

Kyleren spurted six skillfully aimed shots into the mist, dropping a half-dozen targets as Trisha incapacitated the other three. Harris and Chad had continued through an adjacent door; Kyleren heard their rifles report as he covered Trish. The ground tech tapped several panels, scrolling through material as she hacked the enemy computer systems.

"Three minutes," she stated, as Chad and Harris appeared. She clipped her pistol to her waist and retrieved the dataplate.

Kyleren signaled to the other two GAELs.

"Snow, stay here and cover Reynolds," he ordered, snatching the ident tag from the chief. "Once you have the intel, rendezvous in the dintillium core."

Chad nodded affirmative. Lance and Harris sped back into the lift platform, entering the door opposite the command deck. The core room was a labyrinthine mass of slatted catwalks and access ledges, walled by terminals, drive gears, and the dintillium accelerator. Kyleren led Harris through the first section of the maze, dropping several engineers who seemed frantic about the state of the coolant conduits.

"Evans," Lance called to Harris as they reached a fork in the path, "we need to locate the shield generator and waste it."

Harris grunted his agreement and cut left. Lance banked opposite, disabling two more Vartal workers as he turned a corner. The butt of his rifle shattered the jawbone of a third, felling the Agromor. Unsure whether the elf was simply unconscious or dead, but too pressed for time to properly check, Lance stepped over the crumpled body and loped across the catwalk. It ended abruptly, opening into a two-meter platform with a raised podium in the center, the standard terminal of a dintillium accelerator.

A loud drone peeled across the station intercom system. Harris must have found and disabled the generator. Kyleren rushed forward, punching a flat yellow key on the terminal. Inside the podium's crystasteel dome, the dintillium reaction spun wildly, like millions of windmills clashing together in vibrant orange. At his touch, a small panel ejected outward, revealing a numbered keypad and a small black screen.

Kyleren cursed the Agromors and their prejudice against living tech. The dead interface most likely carried a push button code. The tech was so ancient that it was inaccessible to his core drive. He supposed the team had been lucky that the doors had been encoded with ident scanners. These grommbag Agromors might as well be working in mud-and-grass houses!

He considered his options. Shooting the terminal first came to mind, but that would be unpredictable. The accelerator might rupture—or it could trigger a full systems shut down.

With a snarl he moved to tap the keypad, hoping to accidentally determine the access code, when the black screen unexpectedly lit with green blocky pixels. Automatically, he covered the platform with his rifle, expecting the untimely arrival of an adversary. Seeing no one as he scanned the room, however, allowed him to relax.

Trish decrypted the system, he mused thoughtfully.

Without further reflection, he meddled with the energy output controls of the dintillium disc, pushing them far beyond their maximum safe limit. A disembodied voice from the console warned him in a thick Danaan dialect that his actions would lead to core overload.

The lieutenant smiled. That was exactly what he wanted.

Soon after Lance dismissed the console, Trisha and Chad arrived, both stained with grave expressions. Harris jogged to their position seconds later.

"What?" Lance asked.

"The target ship reentered Agromor space over two days ago," Trisha reported. She scowled heavily. "It landed on Agrona for drop off."

Harris whistled, though his weapons remained at the ready. "That's not good."

"Neither is dyin'," Lance announced as the station's dead tech AI expressed a cold notification of the impending core explosion. "Let's get off this heap before we worry about the GraEL."

The lieutenant led his team back through the engine room and into the command center. The vapor had dissipated. Diamond stars glimmered behind a crystasteel viewport almost as long as the room's curved wall. As he lifted his weapon the other GAELs dropped their space visors.

Kyleren bled his full core drive strength into his BT ammunition, spraying the clear bulkhead with a shower of shells. They pierced the heavy material thoroughly, leaking atmosphere into the black. His team stormed the portal simultaneously, the compromised crystasteel shattering under the slam force of four fully geared troopers.

"Squad Aon ready for rendezvous," Kyleren transmitted over the comm, activating his thrusters to augment his velocity. "Mission complete."

"Good work GAELs," the colonel responded. "Now enjoy the show."

Kyleren twisted on the axis of his vector seconds before the station crumpled into the dintillium core. The center of the anomaly glinted orange, then exploded in a halo of fiery auburn spheres. LAMIE circled the spectacle like a silver carrion bird, her underbelly the color of dried blood.

It was the finest fireworks display Lance had ever seen.

7: To Boldly Go Where No Man Has Gone Before

Kyleren's mission debriefing kept him long enough that the barracks were empty by the time he entered it. The rest of the team had hit the mess hall for rations. Lance welcomed the solitude. The ensuing respite to mull over his first mission as ranking officer was numbly pleasant. His op had been smooth, nearly perfect in execution. He smiled as he shed his thermal socks. With the intel the infiltration team had pilfered, squad Aon could extract the GraEL from Agrona before the gromms even discovered their lost communications outpost.

He stripped his combat gear and drew on a more comfortable pair of standard issue trousers. Jera Zeta was 17 hours behind him—a lifetime ago for an adrenaline addicted GAEL VIC soldier. Just as he reached for an undershirt, thinking of nothing more than a hard-earned date with his rack, a voice intruded from his left.

"You did all right for your first command," Trisha said.

Startled, Lance turned toward the entrance of the L-shaped sleeping quarters. She had always been the stealthiest of the group and had emerged silently from the bend in the room.

"The colonel said so, too," Kyleren returned, noticing with a measure of discomfort the loose manner of her attire—a sleeveless rec shirt hugged her breasts and crimped pants dangled comfortably from her shapely hips.

Not good, he thought warily.

"I thought you'd be in the mess celebratin' with the others," he said, absently pulling the shirt over his head. Unfortunately it was inside out, which forced him to take it off again.

Trisha circled around him and his locker, touching his shoulder lightly with her calloused hands. He grimaced as she ran her dusky fingers across his collarbone and down the bare skin of his chest.

"I'd rather celebrate with you," she said softly, lifting her lips to his neck so that her breath teased his skin. Her other hand slid to his waist.

"I've gotta get to the bridge," Kyleren said, stepping away. He reoriented his shirt and mangled it over his head. "I'm the major's relief."

The excuse failed to halt Trisha's advance.

"You haven't slept since you left the asteroid belt, Lance. The colonel doesn't have you on duty for another five hours." Trisha's white teeth glistened against her dark lips. "There's plenty of time."

"I've had too many nights in the brig to risk more fraternization, Trish," he apologized.

His blood raced through him, not all of it from anxiety.

"Never stopped us before," she murmured, her lips brushing against his.

His body automatically returned the gesture, his mouth pressing hard against hers, before his mind caught up with his hormones. With effort he pushed her away.

"That's over, Trish," he declared, his voice harsher than he had meant.

Trisha's yellow-hazel eyes narrowed alarmingly. She wasn't likely to give in easily.

"You still hung up on the admiral's daughter, Lance? Really?"

"No," Lance growled, cursing whatever false gods the Agromors worshipped and wishing that he had listened to Wayne months ago when his friend had warned him against playing around with Trish.

"Then what?" she demanded crossly, folding her arms furiously across her ample chest.

Kyleren was unsure how to answer without sounding like a complete grommsack. How could he defend himself? He was positive "sorry, but the squad was touring through the Morrigan system on covert ops for three-and-a-half months straight and you just happened to be the only woman around" would get him a well-deserved kick to the groin. He and Trish had succumbed to mutual flirtations, but he hadn't realized at the time that she was expecting more than some heated rack time. Trish turned out to be a commitment woman—or at least wanted to be. Reynolds believed their relationship was viable—as long as they kept it a secret—since the ranks of GAEL squads were rarely reassigned.

The trouble was, Kyleren only cared for Trish the way a soldier felt for his comrades. Her gender had simply been convenient. But she was likely to space him if he told her it was only a one-time thing. It was a lesson hard learned: no fragging your team members. Now if he could only survive the fallout intact.

"Trish—" he began.

"Lieutenant Kyleren," LAMIE's voice serendipitously interrupted, "your presence is required in the medical bay."

Lance gave the sergeant a contrite shrug, though clandestine relief swelled through him. Trisha glared and pursed her lips in her this-isn't-over-until-I-say-it's-over expression as he escaped through the hatch. Striding through the ship's corridors toward the medical deck he wondered how to rectify the situation. Nothing easily came to mind, and he silently rebuked himself for his reckless behavior. First Gwen and now this. He was well prepared to swear off women altogether.

A thunderous explosion of laughter met him as he passed the mess on his right. The loudest guffaw belonged to Wayne. No doubt they were passing the remaining hours sublight to Agrona by embellishing their exploits of the enemy satellite run. There was a T-portal close enough to the Vartal homeworld that would cut the journey time in half, but the colonel, Major Huard, Gene, the new culturalist, and, for some odd reason, the team doctor, needed the extra time to design a successful operation to retrieve the GraEL.

It struck Kyleren as odd that he had been requested to the med bay when the doctor was busy in the situation room with the other officers. The hallways were empty as he trotted down the stairs to the science deck. A more few steps and the crystasteel doors to the medical center slid open.

It was empty.

"LAMIE?" he called out in no particular direction. "What am I doin' here?"

"I determined that you required my assistance with Sergeant Trisha Reynolds," LAMIE answered with a hint of satisfaction. She added, "My knowledge of biological behavior psychology is quite extensive."

Lance blinked several times, unable to register that an adolescent machine had pried him from a rather destructive personal situation. After a few minutes passed, he assumed LAMIE was waiting for him to express some kind of gratitude.

"Uh, thanks, I guess. Trish can be emotional sometimes."

"I didn't mean the sergeant, Lieutenant Kyleren. I was referring to you," LAMIE clarified.

Lance's brow furrowed with confusion.

"Sergeant Reynolds made a logical advance for standard mating rituals," she explained. "My analysis of your body language concluded that you did not share Sergeant Reynolds' inclination for copulation, nor did you have a satisfactory explanation that would end the conflict in compromise."

"I don't need you analyzin' me, LAMIE," Kyleren muttered. "But just so I get this straight: You called me down here so I wouldn't hurt Trish's feelin's?"

"I was hoping we could form a mutually beneficial relationship."

"What does that mean?" he asked warily.

"Upon our first encounter you made it clear that you did not appreciate my interfering questions," LAMIE explained. "I contest your earlier assumption, and propose that a useful partnership could be made between us."

"What kind of partnership?"

"Simple," LAMIE said. "Gene did not restrict my protoroutines in a manner that forbids my systems from, let us say, 'mislogging' security footage. I believe that current military policy prohibits sexual relationships between team members. It would be quite damaging if a record of a conversation, where one or more parties admit to fraternization, was to be made public."

"You're gonna report me?" Kyleren gasped incredulously.

Now female machines were getting him fragged.

"Gene limits the knowledge he inputs into my databases; it is his method of controlling who I become. I wish to experience at my own discretion, and I hope to start by studying your adventures. Of the six GAELs in Aon squad, your file is what most humans and blendeds would call 'colorful'."

"Are you fraggin' serious? You're gonna blackmail me if I don't tell about you my missions?"

"You misunderstand," LAMIE justified. "My protoboard does not allow me to 'blackmail' anyone. I am simply taking the opportunity to satisfy your needs while supplementing my own."

"How about instead I tell Gene about the loopholes on that twelve million protochip board 'a yours?"

"There are no uncharted evolutions in my protocols that were not instituted by Gene's intended programming, lieutenant. My record with my creator is spotless. Yours, however, is not. By exposing me, you would also have to admit to your own guilt, thereby linking Sergeant Reynolds to your noncompliance of Coalition military mandates."

Lance nodded his head several times as he comprehended the scale of LAMIE's trap. This was one chick he could not outmaneuver.

"You're good," he conceded. He rubbed his hands together as he considered her offer. "So you'll get rid of that stuff about me and Trish in return for war stories?"

"And more, should you require it," LAMIE offered.

Lance raised an eyebrow. "What'd you wanna know?"

"Tell me about the last time you were on Agrona," she insisted.

8: THE TRUTH IS OUT THERE

Anya tapped her foot nervously against the polished floor, her dataplate uneasily clutched in her arms. For two days she hadn't taken her eyes from it, going so far as to secure it under her pillow while she slept. She had disconnected its remote receiver, anxious that someone would discover her investigation and alter her notes. Little Riia's blood was safely enfolded in a coolant wrap, stowed in the deep pocket of Anya's jacket.

At the medical center, Anya had deliberately distanced herself from colleagues and patients alike, afraid to trust anyone. Who had corrupted the blended child's tests and charts? The perpetrator could have been any of the innumerable members of the staff, or even a sneaky hospital patient. One of Anya's friends, a nurse she had known for two centuries, noticed the doctor's agitation and insisted she take the day off. Anya had agreed; it made a perfect excuse to hide her excursion to Penardun's political sector.

"Dr. Ninevay, the prime minister will see you now," a plump secretary announced from behind her glossy semicircular desk. Her human eyes were crisp and business-like.

"Thank you," Anya returned, her stomach tingling unpleasantly.

She walked forward as two immense wooden doors yawned wide to receive her. The material was incredibly rare on the travelling space station, a lost relic of the elven homeworld of Sulevia. A long marble entry stretched into the building's interior, gilded with historical tapestries and stone sculptures. Anya's heeled shoes clicked loudly on the hard floor as she whisked through the corridor. She had seen it all before and was too preoccupied to give the wondrous art much notice. At the end of the hallway, sandwiched between green panes of streaked copper depicting the two Kildar space cities of Penardun and Arianrod, was the prime minister's office.

Six stars of inlaid silver surrounded the minister's desk and seating area. Cunningly wrought iron sconces arched over the stiff chairs like drooping blossoms. Penardun's head of state stood in welcome, her moonlight hair coiffed in bright sapphire. Her elegant gown drifted about her like a midnight dream, her pale skin denoting that she belonged to one of the oldest Kildar families—a lineage dating back to the time of the Bang. As Anya approached, the prime minister embraced the physician affectionately.

"Anya," Vivian greeted warmly, "how fare you, sister?"

Dr. Ninevay squeezed her elder sibling in return, but pulled away quickly.

"I wish my overdue visit was simply for pleasure, Vivian. I must apologize."

A wave of the hand indicated that the leader of the Kildar didn't mind.

"None of that. Regardless of the reason, I am glad to see you."

She invited Anya to sit with a gesture and resumed her position behind the desk.

"What is your errand?"

"I need your people to investigate something," Anya said, hands shaking as she slid her dataplate onto her sister's desk.

"My 'people'?" Vivian asked with feigned confusion. Amusement sparkled in her brown eyes.

Anya wasn't fooled. The doctor knew her sister well.

"You know what I mean," Anya persisted. "The underground organization of spies that everyone believes to be merely rumor. The Servants of the Eye."

"It amazes me that you, a student of science, would believe such nonsense," Vivian protested, straightening like a young girl preparing to share a silly secret. "The governing council of Penardun harbors no such illegitimate force."

Anya pursed her lips. She could tell her sister withheld information, but was hesitant—or unable—to reveal it.

"All right then. Let's just say you have connections that I lack and the means to investigate suspicious circumstances that could prove to be a breach of contract between Penardun and the Coalition Military."

The prime minister pinched her brows together in alarm. "That is a serious allegation. What circumstances?"

"Recently a blended infant died of FLTB at the medical center, though when the baby was born all the tests indicated she was healthy."

"Doesn't it take a few hours before a baby shows signs of FLTB?" Vivian asked dubiously.

"Only the serious symptoms, but just after an infant's birth, some traces of FLTB can be detected. But Riia Ferrin's tests were completely negative for the disorder."

"Did you double-check your tests?" the prime minister asked.

"Always," Anya promised, taking no offense, knowing her sister's duty required her to ask the question.

"How did a perfectly healthy child die from tech degradation then?" Vivian posed slowly.

"She didn't," Anya stated.

Vivian's eyes blazed with impatience. "You said the baby died."

"That's what the nurses told me. I was appalled that I could have made such a grave mistake, so I retested the blood we collected from the infant."

Navigating through the folders on her dataplate, Anya displayed her test results for her sister. Vivian glowered at the screen while Dr. Ninevay continued.

"For every blended conception I perform, I label the nanomites with an extra indicator. It's just something to informally track my own work. The nanomites that appeared in the second test were not the ones I administered during the blending process."

"What does that mean, exactly?" Vivian asked, looking up from the dataplate.

"Someone tampered with the sample and falsified the second set of results. They altered the blood to look like Riia had died of FLTB."

Vivian's expression hardened with thought.

"I suppose there's no documentation to back your claim, or you would have turned the matter over to the courts instead of coming here for help."

Anya nodded, fiddling absently with her hands.

"It's all off the record. Vivian, if I had documented the indicator, whoever orchestrated the deceit would have duplicated my mark and I would have never noticed anything was wrong."

"Why would someone go through all this trouble?" Vivian asked, more to herself than Anya. "And where is the baby now?"

"That's what I want to know," Anya replied, rubbing her heart gently. The strain caused the organ to burn with aggravation. "So I visited the morgue to interview the medical student who had performed the autopsy and supposedly dealt with Riia's remains."

"And?"

"Terrance Barton was transferred just yesterday. Riia's autopsy and cremation were the last two procedures he performed before he left the lab."

"That could be coincidence, Anya. Medical interns are transferred all of the time."

"I thought the same. So I went to his apartment. There was no answer."

"Did you look for forwarding information?"

"Yes," Anya answered, swallowing nervously. "I asked our hiring supervisor. He said Terrance didn't leave any."

Vivian creased her forehead. "Odd. Did the supervisor say why Terrance was transferred?"

"I was too—," Anya paused, searching for the right description, "—intimidated to ask. The supervisor seemed—I don't know. I just didn't trust him and there was something about him that didn't feel right. Every nerve in my body warned me not to press him further."

"What makes you think the Coalition Military has anything to do with it?" The minister's voice became firm.

"After I couldn't find Terrance, I backtracked," Anya explained. "I visited Clara Edin, a nurse who used to work at the medical center. I dismissed her for falling asleep on duty the night Riia died. It was Clara who recorded time of death and delivered the body to the morgue. But her neighbors said she had moved planetside."

"That seems logical," Vivian argued. "There's only one hospital here and you're highly respected. If you fired her, Anya, no one on Penardun would ever give her a position in the medical sector."

The prime minister dropped the dataplate to the desk.

"That's why I had a friend from the Department of Transportation check to see if she or Terrance had left the city. Neither of them booked transport. The only way off Penardun without papers is through the military. The Coalition has to be involved in this."

Anya slumped unhappily in her chair. Vivian considered the matter, then leaned forward with her hands intertwined, wrists against the desk's surface.

"I'm going to choose to ignore that you did this all on your own, Anya. If there really is something dubious happening here, you could have just placed yourself in danger. You should have come to me the minute you noticed something wasn't right, instead of plodding around on your own."

"I didn't want to bother you without sufficient evidence," Anya sighed.

Vivian's face softened.

"The circumstances are indeed suspicious, and I will have some of my 'people'," she winked slyly at Anya, "investigate on one condition."

Hope reared inside Anya as she answered, "Anything."

"If nothing turns up, you'll let it go."

"Of course," the physician vowed.

"And," Vivian said, "no more searching on your own. What would I say to mother if something happened to you?"

Anya smiled tiredly, glad to share the burden of her discovery.

"Just let me know when you find that baby."

9: IF YOU CAN'T DO SOMETHING SMART, DO SOMETHING RIGHT

"Agrona does not rotate on its axis; thus it does not experience day and night cycles. Its two intelligent species inhabit opposite sides of the planet, one a creature of perpetual light, the other of complete darkness—"

The soft hololight emanating from the table and comfortable chairs in the situation room caused Kyleren's eyes to droop. Culturalist Percy Jameson spoke in a voice that was academically bland. His mannerisms and dress indicated that he'd never actually ventured to the exotic places of his expertise. Lance wondered if the thin man had ever left the university space city of Lludd before. Percy was short for a blended, with dull brown hair that nearly hid his lackluster eyes. The 29-year-old culturalist had entered the briefing chamber in a flurry of nervous equipment, emitters, and holoslides. Though anxious when shaking the hands of the assembled military audience, Percy soon relaxed as he immersed himself in the description of his craft, meandering into irrelevant material so often that Colonel Stoddard was forced to intervene on more than one occasion.

Currently, a floating representation of Agrona hovered above the table, one side labeled "dayside" and the other "nightside." This was turning out to be one of the longest briefings Kyleren had ever endured, and he had to force himself to curtail a multitude of frustrated groaning. As the lieutenant flicked his eyes across the room, he was proud to note that the other GAELs were just as unimpressed with the culturalist. Most of Percy's information was already known to the original members of squad Aon. The homeworld of the Vartal and Sylph was the heart of the Agrona-Morrigan Concord. Aon had engaged in only one mission on the planet—four years ago, DST—and had barely escaped with their lives.

"The Sylph elves occupy the dayside of the planet," Percy droned as he shifted the holodiagram to an image of the race. "They range from 8 to 15 centimeters in height and have filament wings attached to their bodies just below the shoulder blade. Their hair changes color and texture to mimic their surroundings. A typical life span is 12 to 17 years, DST. The main government changes leadership and form at least once every 10 or 20 years, making their political affairs precarious and unstable."

Kyleren couldn't believe the ridiculousness of the lanky moron before him. A Venn Diagram? Really? They were infiltrating a gromm base on the Vartal side, not playing at Sylph politics.

"The Sylph are an emotionally volatile people. They believe in living life to the fullest extent, seeking pleasure wherever it may lie, and revenging themselves jealously when the occasion arises. A common belief among the Sylph is that if you eat the heart of your enemy, you will gain a measure of his soul's strength as it passes into the Otherworld."

Percy snickered amusingly and scanned his spectators. He seemed disappointed that no one else shared his humor. A quick cough covered his embarrassment and he plodded back to his lecture.

"They especially love working with their hands and are gifted mechanically. Though they do not believe in blending, they are lovers of invention. They were the first to discover camouflage technology and their cities are almost impossible to find—"

Kyleren's head bobbed forward. His interlude with LAMIE had prevented him from visiting his rack. After regaling her with several colorful versions of his previous missions, he'd reported to the bridge for duty.

Percy continued to highlight the subtleties and beauty of the flying elves of Agrona. Sure they were pleasing to the eye, but they were apt to bite you if they didn't like the look of your face. Besides, Kyleren snorted internally, their women were too small for anything fun.

"The Vartal elves are the sister species of the Sylph. They are a culture passionately single-minded, with a long memory. Arrogant and quick to anger, slow to forgive, they rarely accept outsiders. Their society is ruled by a secretive council of druids. Their religion is riddled with complex rituals and customs that center around a polytheistic set of gods. Their highest deity is the goddess Danu: maiden of life and purity. An integral part of their dogma includes a separation of species so deep that different races should not even live within a certain distance of each other. Interaction may occur only for official business on preapproved Agrona moon cycles."

Lance closed his eyes. It seemed Jameson would never stop talking.

"Vartal children are betrothed to their future mate just hours after their birth. It is the task of a special priest or priestess to make offerings to the gods during the 18 months the child grows in its mother's uterus. This union is made for life. Vartal elves never take another spouse, even if widowed—"

Percy's voice smothered into no more than an echo, like someone shouting at the end of a tunnel. The soft light of the situation room melted into the darkness of memory. Lance barely felt the hard surface of the holotable as he slipped into the release of slumber.

*

The sky was black and the heavy pines darker still in the pitch night of Agrona's dark side. Bullets pecked at the bark shielding the massive forest trunks, their silhouette appearing vibrant green in Kyleren's low-light ocular specs. He wrestled with a Vartal soldier, grabbing the enemy by the head and breaking the elf's spine as a sniper round pierced Lance's armor. It hit his ribs hard, knocking the wind from his lungs. The projectile had been slowed considerably by his protective combat suit, lacking the momentum to penetrate GAEL enhanced skin. But it would leave a significant bruise.

Lance ducked back into the shelter of the thick tree root he had been using for cover until the Vartal had flanked him. Torn fragments of trunk and limb had been showering him for nearly ten minutes as the enemy sought him out, pinning him in position. One sniper round wasn't much of a problem, but several connecting in the same general spot would be powerful enough to tear into his skin. The last one had cracked two ribs by its impact, causing Kyleren to grunt with effort as he peeked over his shelter, scanning for an escape route.

Captain Doran had data-commed the evac ship from the other side of the compound. It would touch down in five minutes. Doran had broadcast the order for withdrawal, letting Lance know in plain terms that if he didn't make it to the extraction point within the timeframe, the captain intended to abandon his sniper GAEL to the mercy of the Vartal.

That was a death sentence. The Vartal were on a single-handed crusade to rid the universe of "blended pollution." Kyleren clutched his sniper rifle, cursing his commanding officer as a coward. Doran had refused Lance's request for ground support, even though Wayne, Trish, Chad, and Harris were all on hand. Just two of his comrades would be enough to punch a breakout pass through the enemy ranks stalling his position, but Lance couldn't handle all 26 elves by himself.

The captain had sustained some sort of injury, something about how a gromm Vartal female had sung at him. Snow had commed the team that Doran was stabilized, but incapacitated. The captain ordered the others around him, convinced all four were essential to defend the hopper when it arrived.

At least two of the enemy bastards surrounding Kyleren were snipers. Their weapons were by far the most dangerous to a GAEL VIC. Thirteen others hugged the ground and 11 had scaled the trees. Even before the last positive hit, the Vartal's weapons had punctured Lance's armor in two places, his right bicep and left thigh. Though Lance had the high ground, the Agromors had the advantage of homeworld. They knew the terrain, had greater numbers, and could see in the dark without the restrictions of a helmet.

He was royally fragged.

"This is Apple Six, clear for pick up," Major Huard grated across the comm.

The silver forest canopy blew widely as the aircraft zoomed overhead. The elves hunkered or scattered for cover. Kyleren took advantage of the sudden distraction, leveling his *White Lady* at the vitals of three enemy elves. In two seconds their blood watered the grass, their lifeless corpses crumpling to the ground. Another spray of Vartal fire forced him to plunge back behind the tree.

At least he had been able to tag one of the snipers.

"Everyone on! Go, go, go," Doran barked at the squad, the frantic order relayed back to Kyleren through his comm.

Lance nearly mangled the frame of his rifle as his frustration boiled out of his skin. If the rest of the team dusted off, all the Agromors left on the ground would focus their attention on him. He could hold out for maybe an hour, but not much longer. GAELs might be walking tanks, but they weren't invincible.

The mission was a complete wash. Kyleren didn't like incomplete operations in his file, but the targeted Agromor facility was still intact. Captain Doran had accidentally lost the four-gram dintillium explosive needed to destroy the refining center right after drop off. The squad had breached the interior of the structure before Doran noticed. He had sent Kyleren to track the explosive down, which was how Lance ended up cut off from his unit in the first place.

The trapped GAEL extracted the fragile explosive from a compartment in his combat armor. When detonated, the tiny tetrahedron would vaporize anything within a two kilometer radius.

The engines of Apple Six roared over the trees as the vessel rocketed toward orbit, a squadron of dead tech enemy fighters burning at its tail. Kyleren lifted his head to the sky, following the ships, but whatever battle raged across the heavens was obscured by the heavy fleece of the trees.

Left behind, Kyleren weighed his options. His fourth generation CC armor included a biosigns tracker that could pinpoint enemies as they tried to flank him. Already, little red blips infiltrated its perimeter. He decided that, rather than be captured and executed, he'd take all the Vartal bastards with him. His rifle pelted two elves clean in the head before he made a wild dash to the target building.

The complex was built like all Vartal structures— ancient stone constructs thousands of years old, retrofitted with dead tech upgrades. Weapons discharged around him as he ran, though his GAEL speed caused most of the projectiles to miss entirely. But some of the elves were intelligent enough to lead their mark, catching Kyleren in a crossfire. Several of the slugs bounced off his armor. A lucky few actually breached it, but didn't manage anything more than small contusions.

Unfortunately, the last sniper managed an inconceivable shot. Whatever angle the Vartal had employed bypassed Lance's CC armor without a loss of momentum, plunging the round into Kyleren's back within a few centimeters of his spine. The GAEL hit the ground and rolled as pain flowed down the back of his legs faster than blood. His uncontrolled momentum slammed him against the Agromor complex. Lurching to his knees, an action that seemed to take longer than it should, he reached for his rifle, only to discover that his *White Lady* had been thrown wide from his position. Another sniper round cracked his direction, splintering the stone near his head.

Despite the situation, Lance grinned. The enemy marksman had just given away his position.

He used his visor to locate his core drive signature. Bonded into his rifle, it was an easy discovery ten meters off to his left. Command would have to be satisfied with an ignition off-target. With his injury he wouldn't make it past the compound's perimeter. His skin tolerated a barrage of bullets from a group of standard firearms, but he was forced to dodge another sniper round. His back felt hot and wet. He gritted his teeth against the sharp agony that rippled through his body with every movement.

Setting the dintillium charge for two minutes, he synced the timer with his suit, unsure whether he could clear the blast zone in time. He lunged for his rifle, sliding to its location and hefting it upward as he pulled himself painfully upright. One shot and *White Lady* sent the sniper to meet his imaginary gods.

Lance didn't have time to congratulate himself. Breaking into the fastest run his injury would accommodate, he plunged into the forest. Blood slicked the back panel of his armor and lubricated his leg greaves. Kyleren started to feel dizzy. His vision blurred. Just as he thought he might eat the ground, an angry voice screamed through his comm.

"Sergeant Kyleren," the colonel's fury broke through, though Lance sensed his commanding officer's anger wasn't directed at him, "what is your position?"

"On the run, sir," Lance managed to gasp, "one-point-four kilometers southeast of my sniper perch. D-blast deployed. Thirty seconds to detonation."

A stab of profanity marched through the LT communications line.

"Sergeant, you run like hell before that blast fries your comm! You have to make two kilometers clearance, do you hear me?"

"Copy," Kyleren panted, narrowly missing tree after tree, his lower back burning with riotous pain.

Five seconds.

Just as the blast shook the ground, Kyleren sprang behind the nearest rock. He'd only made one-point-eight-five. White intensity converged against the stone at his back and, though the heat was uncomfortable, Lance's core bond provided him with a high tolerance. Still, it was fortunate that only the edge of the discharge had caught him. His armor and weapons weren't as lucky. The tech in his visor fried—taking his comm with it—and his armor drooped sadly in the heat. Immune to the resultant radiation, he shed his ruined visor and gear when the bleached flash had faded away. The tang of metal razed his tongue as he breathed the unfiltered Agrona air. Only his *White Lady* remained unscathed, protected as she was by his core drive.

Without the low-light vision of his helmet, he would have been plunged into impenetrable darkness were it not for the fast spreading fire left in the dintillium explosion's wake. He was lost in a desert of ash and smoke, with no way to contact his team.

*

Lance woke with a start as Wayne kicked his chair. Percy the culturalist trudged forward through his notes, oblivious to Kyleren's behavior.

"Many of the Vartal customs remain a mystery to the rest of the universe as they are loath to share anything important with other races. One exception, however, are the shiidh, a conclave of specially selected women who travel throughout the galaxy offering mourning services for those who pass into the 'Otherworld' or land of death. The shiidh refuse to speak to the living, but their keening voices sing haunting melodies at memorial ceremonies. Of all the Agromors, they alone have autonomy to move freely about the universe, and their services are in great demand on blended homeworlds."

Kyleren barely listened, shrugging off the intensity of his dream, a fair recount of his first Agrona mission. He'd wandered through that fragging forest for hours, all but bleeding out, before finally stumbling across some useful dead tech. Captain Doran had been dishonorably discharged for his conduct. Both Wayne and Kyleren received a promotion. Despite Lance's heroic actions, surviving impossible odds, and single-handedly destroying the Agromor complex, his comrades referred to the mission as "the squirrel incident."

"The Kildar invention that introduced the blending process struck deeply against Vartal beliefs," Percy interrupted. "Interracial coupling represents the worst of immoral behaviors from their perspective, and blended children are considered an abomination to the gods. Their goal is not only to ban intermingling of the species, but to cleanse the universe of blended children altogether. This was the reason the Vartal created the Agrona-Morrigan Concord and destroyed the Kildar homeworld of Sulevia."

"So you're sayin' that they'll shoot first, then clean up our fraggin' souls later," Kyleren interjected, finally cracking with impatience. "That's all you needed to say."

Poorly disguised laughter folded through the GAELs.

"You'll keep that skrit to yourself, lieutenant," the colonel reprimanded, but judging by the slowly dissipating glaze on his face, Stoddard hadn't been paying attention either.

"Yes, sir," Kyleren responded respectfully.

"Mr. Jameson here has helped us to positively locate the GraEL," Stoddard said.

"Really?" Chad asked in disbelief. "You have confirmation?"

"No," the colonel clarified, "but Percy is convinced the GraEL will be delivered to the main temple of Danu on Agrona's nightside."

"No way," Wayne contested with a savvy shake of the head. "The Vartal aren't that stupid. It's the first place anyone would look for it."

"LAMIE can pick up the GraEL's energy signature once we reach orbit," Gene explained, though a frown pulled at his lips, "but for the record, I'm with Captain Reese on this one."

"It has nothing to do with stupidity," Percy defended. "The Vartal are deeply religious. They follow the edicts of their goddess without question." He added ominously, "Or die trying."

"I've seen pictures of the temple," Wayne said, still skeptical. "It's ancient, made of arches—completely open to the sky. Why would they leave the GraEL that exposed?"

"Because they believe Danu will protect it," Percy explained with a shrug.

Kyleren scoffed. He'd heard stories of Danu. They were nothing but a stack of skrit. The Agromor religion was simply a method of control, allowing the government to maintain dominance over their people. If the gods believed blending was a crime, why didn't the Agrona-Morrigan Concord destroy the Blended Coalition at the very beginning of the MetaGalactic War?

There was too much bad in the universe to believe in gods. Danu hadn't saved him on Agrona when he'd almost bled to death, nearly been devoured by a dintillium blast, or ended up stranded behind enemy lines. He'd rescued himself all on his own.

The way he saw it, the gods could frag themselves.

10: I Said It Looks Clear

Lance perched on a sturdy, moss-encrusted branch in a tall pine, patiently waiting for Wayne to finish his analysis of the target 60 meters ahead. Reese scanned the area through his single lens ocular sensor, his silence indicating displeasure.

"Whatcha thinkin', Wayne?"

The captain detached the scope thoughtfully and passed it to Lance. Kyleren lifted his visor, momentarily blind in the Agrona darkness, until he pressed the lens against his eye. Vibrant green night enhancement pulled details from the magnified vicinity.

The ancient temple of Danu dripped with various hues of mossy vegetation. Flowers and vines hugged the aged stone arches, night grasses and star ferns brushing against its base. The trees had been cut back around the shrine, leaving it to bask in the rays of the planet's twin moons. Thirty meters in diameter, the circular sanctuary was comprised of tall monoliths, each about six meters high, topped with a single layer of flat stone blocks that connected every arch in the ring. An inner arc of five wide pillars formed a protective semicircle around a glistening marble statue of an elven woman. She bent saintly over a delicate pedestal that rose a meter out of the grass.

The GraEL sat on its surface, undefended.

"I don't see anythin'," Lance said, puzzled.

"Exactly," Wayne returned. "There's nothing but trees and rocks. Something's not right. I don't like it."

Lance peered through the ocular device again. "Is it too much to hope the gromms are just stupid?"

"They managed to destroy Gwydion," Wayne recalled, disgust plain in his brown face. "That makes me think this is a trap."

"They could be waitin' for us in the forest," Kyleren offered, surveying the surrounding undergrowth and tree line for enemy presence.

"Lance, when I say there's nothing down there, I mean it. No life signs, no weapon or tech signatures. Nothing."

Lance's own review of the territory had already led him to the same conclusion. The sensor was designed to detect signs of activity. Percy had explained that the Vartal believed their goddess would protect the GraEL, but this was just too ridiculous.

"If it is an ambush," Lance speculated as he returned the ocular sensor and clicked his visor closed, "we won't see it 'til we're hit."

"That's what worries me."

Lance clapped his friend on the back so hard that Wayne had to catch himself to prevent from falling off the tree limb.

"Don't be so serious," Lance jibed. "Sittin' here starin' isn't gonna get us anywhere. Let's get that little holy tree and pack it spaceside."

"I'd feel more comfortable if Thompson and I hadn't been forced to leave our core drives with LAMIE," Wayne complained.

Lance nodded. He was extremely grateful he hadn't been required to leave his. Kyleren jumped the ten meter distance to the ground, Reese following silently a moment later. The other four members of squad Aon formed a cardinal perimeter, warily standing guard. Both Trisha and Gary relaxed perceptibly as their commanding officers appeared from above.

"Are we a go?" Gary asked with wired excitement.

Wayne nodded.

"We'll split into teams," he ordered crisply. "Thompson, Evans, you're with me. We'll approach from the left."

The newb jittered his weapon nervously as the gargantuan form of Harris stepped next to him.

The captain continued, "Snow and Reynolds: bring up the other side. I don't want to hit this thing head on. We're not taking chances. Kyleren will provide cover from this tree."

A chorus of affirmations clattered the comm and each GAEL saluted. Lance climbed back into the tree, training *White Lady* on the stone ring and adjusting the amplification of her scope. Each team verified its position quickly.

Still no evidence of enemy engagement.

Wayne gave the order and the GAELs moved in. Despite their capability for speed, Reese warned his unit to approach slowly, checking for mines, energy signatures, or other traps. Lance could only see an outline of his comrades through his scope since their CC armor was activated, allowing their bodies' complete integration with their surroundings.

The closer Wayne's team drew to the temple, the tenser Lance became. He'd fought the Vartal before. Though they often did things that didn't make sense, they had proven themselves to be exceptionally clever. Even if they did believe Danu would protect the GraEL, Kyleren doubted that they would leave it completely vulnerable.

Wayne's outline wavered strangely in the scope, disappearing from Lance's vision for less than a second. Kyleren blinked, running his senses through the core drive link with *White Lady* to see if something in her tech had malfunctioned. Finding nothing amiss, he was surprised again when Harris and Gary, who trailed behind their leader, vanished and reappeared quickly in a similar manner at the same point.

Before Kyleren could warn the team, an eight meter mech shed its cloak and blasted Harris with its main canon. Almost simultaneously, it swatted Wayne back into the trees with a heavy swipe of its arm. Roughly formed in the image of its creators, the killing machine had two legs and arms, each laden with dead tech weapons. Its head imitated angular elven facial features. Another mechanical monstrosity disengaged its camouflage on the other side of the temple, followed by a third, isolating the two teams.

Chad and Trisha had bolted for the first one as soon as it appeared, and barely managed to dodge the barrage of blue energy discharged by the second mech. Tossed into the forest like a dead twig, Wayne had been thrown completely out of visible range.

"Captain Reese, status," Lance shouted over the comm, but there was no answer. "Captain Reese, respond!"

Gary's non-bonded assault rifle crackled numerous reports as he released a volley of fire against his attacker, his stationary position indicating he was defending. Kyleren assumed Harris had been injured by the mech's first hit. Reynolds and Snow faced two opponents, though they seemed to be holding their own.

"Private Thompson, what's your status?" Kyleren barked.

"Evans is down. I repeat, Evans is down," Gary reported with a wild mix of exhilaration and fear.

This is bad, Kyleren thought. Without his core drive, Gary was at a severe disadvantage: he was inexperienced, alone, and immobile. The drives had been left in LAMIE for air support—Wayne's at the pilot station and Gary's connected to the ship's weapons array—but with the captain nonresponsive, the effort was wasted.

"Thompson," Lance ordered, now in command, "get Evans and fall back. I say again, fall back."

The enemy had Gary targeted with its energy cannons. Before the weapons had time to fully charge, Lance pelted it with two full-strength bonded rounds. The resultant explosion pushed the mech against the ground, neon blue material oozing from the torn limb. Black dots flashed across the lieutenant's vision as the burst overloaded the light sensors in his scope. Razors of shrapnel narrowly missed the newb as he hefted the injured corporal over his shoulder and sped back into the protection of the forest.

"Lieutenant Kyleren, do you read?" Colonel Stoddard called across the comm.

"I read you, sir," Kyleren answered, popping several shots at the other two mechs, though neither caused significant damage.

Trisha stumbled awkwardly as she circled her opponent. Lance figured she had been injured.

"Lieutenant, LAMIE says she has lost connection with Captain Reese's core drive. Status report."

Kyleren fired an extra round at the machine attacking Reynolds, then pulled away from *White Lady* to inspect his combat tracker. Three friendlies blinked in a stationary position just beyond his location.

"Evans and Thompson have retreated. Evans is seriously wounded. Captain Reese's condition and location are unknown. One target down, two engaged, Snow and Reynolds are in melee. Request med evac for wounded, sir."

"Copy. We will touch down at the extraction point in seven minutes."

"Colonel," Thompson cut in, "I don't think Evans has that long."

Communications paused. Kyleren fired another fan of sniper blasts.

"Understood," Stoddard replied. "Administer a nanomite injection, private. Locate Captain Reese. Get him and Evans to the evac point."

"Yes, sir," Gary replied, strain evident in his voice.

Kyleren watched Chad ram himself into the nearest mech's leg, the medic using his GAEL strength to heave it off balance. The machine toppled into one of the temple's outer arches, causing the monolith to crumble into a pile of broken rubble. Trish jumped onto the fallen mech and twisted off its head.

A horrific wail of sorrow reverberated through the trees. It seemed to crawl from the depths of the soil, resonating in each blade of grass, trembling through every leaf. The hollow cry penetrated Lance's drive, causing both his body and his weapon to shudder with the sound.

What gromm skrit is this? Kyleren thought, not waiting around to find out.

He leapt from the tree and sprinted toward his two remaining comrades, extracting his core drive from his sniper and snapping it into his BT assault weapon as he ran. He wondered angrily what new camouflage the Sylph had provided the Vartal to cloak their mechs so completely; even the energy sensors had been fooled.

By the time he reached Trisha and Chad, the last gargantuan machine had been dispatched. The outer temple lay in ruins. Kyleren could almost hear the reprimand of his superiors when they discovered his squad had demolished a Vartal monument that had stood for over nine thousand years.

Trish and Chad jumped over the tech remains and shrine rubble, heading for the inner ring. Lance arrived at Danu's statue. The radiant stone seemed to glower down at him as he reached for the GraEL.

His combat tracker suddenly went berserk, registering enemy signals in all directions. He swore. The CC armor should have detected their approach much sooner. Kyleren twisted, raising his weapon to sweep the perimeter. Back to back, the trio of soldiers formed a three point circle as 30 Vartal women surrounded them. Kyleren suddenly realized why his tech hadn't been able to warn him.

The dark-skinned elves had emerged from solid stone.

They slid out of the lonely columns like terrible holograms of dread, their fingers curling around sharp spikes they held in their palms. Their hair tumbled down their backs, loose cascades of pallid white scraped with sallow grooves like malachite. Black skin, mottled with grey, gave the impression that their bodies were made of granite.

Kyleren shot two in the head in a blur of motion. He heard the dull thump as others fell to his fellow GAELs' weapons.

The rest of the dark elves opened their mouths and began to sing.

The melodic thrum was like nothing he had ever experienced. Within the first few notes a sharp snap echoed painfully throughout his body, as if the flow of his life's energy was suddenly yanked out of his brain stem. His body sagged limp, like a machine cut off from its power supply. Kyleren hit the ground on his knees, his muscles involuntarily relaxing. Pleasant, mindless numbness overtook him. He blinked lazily at a strange woman who approached him, his mind afloat in the rhythm of her music. Her hips swayed to the melody's pattern as she walked, the crystasteel head of a feyhammer reaping gleams of moonlight from a silver clasp on her belt. When she reached Lance's helpless form she lifted the weapon and drew back her arm to strike. Kyleren watched the hammer swing toward his head, uncomprehending.

Just as the blunt mallet came within centimeters of his visor, a buzzing ripple restored his senses. If he had been a normal soldier, he would have met his death. But as a GAEL, his enhanced speed and reaction time saved him from the lethal blow. He lurched backward and the hammer swept through empty air. Most of the women still chanted their haunting tune, but several halted, dumbfounded that he had escaped their mesmerizing song.

Through his periphery, Kyleren noted the catatonic shapes of his friends on their knees, their firearms discarded in the grass. His own BT assault rifle rested next to him. He didn't understand the nature of the Vartal attack; he just knew these freaky skirts had to die. Within seconds he had retrieved his weapon and fired into the ring of women, dispatching six enemies before he noticed that his targets were backing away. They turned their gaze from him, staring at the woman with the hammer. They continued to sing.

Whoever she was, Lance recognized her as the leader. Her deep eyes scrutinized him thoroughly, narrowing as if trying to pierce a fog or haze. Suddenly coming to a decision, she slid the hammer back into her belt. The music ceased immediately. An eerie silence rattled through the ruined temple.

Then women vanished back into the stones, leaving the dead where they had fallen.

Trisha gasped like a swimmer who had nearly drowned.

"What the frag was that?" she demanded.

Her body trembled spasmodically. Lance helped her to her feet.

"Dunno," Lance breathed, a dead lurch in his stomach. "Let's get outta here before they come back."

Chad had the semblance of mind to snatch the GraEL before they darted for the trees. They pushed their full speed to the extraction point.

"Looks like Percy left something important out," Chad grumbled angrily as they ran. "I thought he said the Vartal believed Danu would protect the temple. Why didn't he tell us about those gromm women?"

"He did," Trisha replied, nearly spent. "Those were the shiidh. The Vartal who sing at funerals. But I don't think Percy knew their voices could be used as a weapon."

"I don't know if anyone does," Lance added, thinking of Captain Doran.

After that first mission to Agrona, his former commander had garbled for hours about some woman who had managed to incapacitate him with a song. Supposedly, one stabbed him with a glass spike. No one else had seen the incident and at the time everyone believed Doran suffered from some kind of post-battle stress. The event had been passed off officially as a hallucination.

Whatever they were, the shiidh were extremely dangerous. Kyleren didn't know how he had overcome their strange musical assault, but it had effectively left three armed GAELs defenseless. Even though he had managed to shake off the song, he wouldn't have managed to defeat them all if they had attacked simultaneously.

The only thing he did know for sure was that the shiidh had let them go, and the GraEL with them.

PART 2

11: ROADS? WHERE WE'RE GOING WE DON'T NEED ROADS

Margariete's eyelids fluttered open, the ship's automatic alert system coaxing her into wakefulness. The vessel would soon drop out of faster-than-light travel. With her bare left hand she brushed away the treasonous tear that had leaked down her cheek while she slept. Sniffing away the burning in the rims of her eyes, she sat upright in the pilot's chair. Though the nightmare had altered and distorted over the past four hundred seasons, it never failed to end the same way: she watched in vivid horror as her little brother's heart melted into salt, crushed in the grip of Kirion's palm.

The telepath threw the long locks of her dark tresses over her shoulder and out of the way, wishing her guilt could be as easily dismissed. Sighing irritably, she twisted, pulled, and tapped the correct sequence of buttons and knobs. The ship slowed to a halt at the coordinates Raeylan had provided. A quick curl of a handle activated the space anchor to prevent the ship from drifting in the sluggish eddies of current that always swirled near a shardgate.

Margariete slithered out of the cramped chair, her muscles complaining at the swift movement after such a long shift in the tiny cockpit. She slammed her hand against the door release sourly. Her brother most likely knew they had already reached their destination since his lorelei blood gave him the ability to detect the proximity of shardwalls and gates, but Margariete felt the need to notify him anyway.

Ten steps took her through a narrow passageway, past two doors on either side, to a hatch at the far end. The rest of the ship was as congested as the bridge, with a tapered kitchenette, tight engine compartments accessible only by tuber ducts, one stall-like wash room, and two living spaces that accommodated a bunk, a clothing cabinet, and a metal-plated desk.

As far as Margariete was concerned, this vessel was Castle Viridius. Their last craft had contained only one barracks, and sharing a room with her twin had been the longest 20 seasons of her life. Additionally, this ship was the most advanced piece of technology they had encountered in the last century, even though it was shabby and battered. Not only did it have a faster-than-light drive, it possessed atmospheric dampeners that allowed them to land on planets.

A delicious odor wafted from the miniature kitchen. As she entered, she found herself ravenous. It was always that way with Raeylan's cooking. He could mix the blandest of ingredients into a meal worthy of the gods.

Margariete ducked under the low threshold and slid onto the bolted bench. The two-meter square room was hardly large enough to accommodate two people. Raeylan hunched over the cooking unit. He had worn the same white overcoat embroidered with the Viridius crest as the cycle they had left Thyella, but he had let his hair grow longer. Instead of brushing the top of his shoulders, his blond strands dropped down his back, held together with a leather thong at the nape of his neck.

"The gate is approximately a quarter arc away," Margariete informed him as he ladled two portions of noodles into ceramic serving bowls.

"I know. I can sense it growing close," he returned, placing the dishes and several thin hashi sticks on the table.

Margariete devoured her ration as her twin settled next to her. Since leaving Thyella, her brother had devoted thousands of arcs to her education, especially sword training and hand-to-hand combat. She had absorbed the lessons quickly, but one topic continually evaded her. Margariete was incapable of preparing food without accidentally poisoning someone.

They ate in silence, honoring Thyellan custom. Margariete kept her gaze entirely on her meal, but sensed Raeylan's observant stare. When she had finished, she rose and cleaned her bowl at the washing station.

"What is wrong, sister?" Raeylan asked before she managed to finish.

The former princess felt her muscles lock with tension and her bowl clattered against the metal counter.

"Nothing. I'm fine," she lied quickly, refusing to turn around.

She yanked a drying towel from a drawer.

"You have been crying."

"A single tear," she admitted, finishing her work and depositing the dish in its storage compartment. She turned to face her brother. "Hardly anything to worry about."

"I checked on you earlier," Raeylan said, pushing his meal away. "You were asleep. Did you—?"

He didn't finish the question, but let his words soften in the air, inviting her to share. Margariete looked at the floor. She felt the gentle pressure of his gloved hand on her arm.

"It has been a long time since that dream haunted you," he said tenderly.

Margariete stifled a sniffle.

"Margariete?"

Why was it impossible to keep anything from him? She bit her lip in frustration. She was the telepath, after all! How did he always seem to know?

Despite Raeylan's frequent assurances that Kirion would have murdered Shikun regardless of her actions, the olive-skinned mind reader couldn't forgive herself. She had failed to protect her younger brother. He was dead because she had refused to give in to the Lord of Light's demands.

"The dream has troubled me almost every night since we left Gorta," she confessed.

Raeylan's brow creased with worry.

"That was three fortnights ago, Margariete. Why did you not tell me?"

"We had just found our first lead on Esilwen," she explained, "and I didn't want to distract you."

"It proved fruitless a few cycles later," he argued with infinite patience. "You should have told me then."

Margariete kicked the metal panel of the refrigeration unit as hard as she could.

"You've put up with my complaints about the same nightmare for centuries. I told you, I'm fine."

"Let me take the memory, Margariete," Raeylan offered soothingly. "The pain is not healing."

"No," she spat fiercely, folding her arms stubbornly across her chest. "If you take it I'll know it's missing. It will make me angry when you refuse to give it back."

"I hate to see you torture yourself, Margariete. You need rest."

"Neither of us can rest until Esilwen is safe and Kirion is dead," she stated coldly. "The memory reminds me why it's so important we succeed. It makes me strong."

"Kirion will meet justice for Shikun's death," her twin promised, "but seeking revenge will consume you in the end, sister. Only emptiness will remain."

Margariete rolled her eyes.

"So you remind me, every other cycle."

The corners of Raeylan's lips twitched and his eyes grew warm. "A slight over-exaggeration. I believe the last time was a full season ago."

"By your reckoning, maybe," she huffed. "But the older I grow, the faster the seasons seem to pass. So it feels like you tell me every other cycle."

Raeylan laughed affectionately and wrapped his arms comfortingly around her.

"Just consider it, Margariete," he requested as he released her.

"I will," she promised lightly, not meeting his eyes as she stepped into the hallway. Then she changed the uncomfortable subject. "I need to collect my weapons— you never know what we may find on the other side of the gate."

Raeylan seemed dissatisfied with her answer, but did not argue. Margariete strode through the corridor and ducked into the door on her left. Her quarters were small, barely over a meter wide and only two in length. A slot in the wall contained a retractable cleansing station and a snug cot could be drawn from the left bulkhead. Jutting from the opposite side of the room was a narrow desk, its surface strewn with her favorite possessions.

Four weapons, each from a different shard, lay in a neat row. A celestrium alloy pistol, fully loaded, rested next to a set of finely crafted daggers, their razor edges reflecting midnight blue in the feeble light. The last Margariete had carried since her fifteenth season: *Stardawn*, the magical blade she had received as a gift from the traitor, Terail Dasklos.

She pushed open the pane to her small clothing cupboard and acquired fresh attire. Gorta had been home to some of the most pleasing fashions she had ever seen in her travels and it had been difficult to refrain from purchasing several elegant outfits. The practicality of her existence had helped her to resist. Instead, she had been content with an arrangement of a simple, wrist-length blouse, a tight brown vest, and flowing, gold-threaded trousers.

She wore only two fine ornaments: her mother's teardrop necklace and a royal signet glove. Since the destruction of her home shard, many versions of the garment had been sewn as the seasons swelled into centuries, but, as a tribute to her station as Princess of the Jewel, it had always remained crimson. She had been surprised when she realized her desire to uphold the tradition—sheathing the right arm in decorative fabric to exhibit one's social status—rather than scorn the custom. Of Anleia's twins, she would have expected Raeylan the likelier candidate to retain the practice.

Her brother's dark leather glove was decorated with only a single symbol: sacrifice. Had it not been for the disfigurement his arm had suffered when Kirion removed Nehro's Glove, Margariete believed her twin would not wear one at all. Even though Raeylan was no longer a king, the telepath still felt her brother was worthy of the honor a regally-embellished arm raiment signified. But arguing with Raeylan was impossible. He flatly refused to wear a real signet glove.

After Margariete changed her clothing, she donned her weapons. She strapped the pistol to her right hip and hung *Stardawn* on the left. The daggers slipped into two sheaths that had been stitched into the calves of her boots. Lastly, she stowed two ammunition clips, a jar of quirr healing ointment, and a blue kryystil stone in a pouch on her belt.

Margariete's mind wandered as she followed the routine. The siblings prepared themselves carefully every time they entered an unknown shard, carrying their weapons and other important items closely, ever since the time they had accidentally met General Thanati on the other side of a new gate. Even though space gates mostly opened into another expanse of vacuum, it was better to err on the side of caution then to be caught without a means of defense.

Raeylan had already moved the ship into position by the time she returned to the bridge. His eyes were closed in concentration and his face stretched tightly. Margariete stood quietly so as not to disturb him as he opened the shardgate. Her blood tingled with excitement.

What if this is the shard? she hoped silently. *What if Esilwen waits for us on the other side? By Nehro's Grace, we have searched long enough!*

Through the cockpit window she could see the blackness of space burn away as her twin commanded the barrier to open. A jagged gap, churning like a crucible of melted gold, yawned before them, warm and bright. Raeylan opened his eyes and Margariete stepped to his side.

The bow of their vessel had barely breached the gate threshold when a sudden jerk hurled Margariete painfully against the control console.

"What—?" she demanded as the ship wrenched sharply to the side.

"I don't know," Raeylan replied, his fingers flying across the console. "The scanners are malfunctioning—"

The screech of tearing metal overshadowed the rest of his statement. Margariete looked up to see the ceiling peeling away into the tawny swirl of light. The air turned thin. She struggled to right herself as the ship's movements became more erratic.

Time froze so suddenly that Margariete overcorrected and fell. She hit the floor and rolled, glaring at her twin as she pulled herself up by the pilot's chair. They were still only halfway through the gate.

"Took you long enough," she accused. "What was that?"

Raeylan jumped from his seat.

"There is a special disturbance on the other side of the gate."

"Can we go back?"

"I have already tried. It is drawing us in. We—"

Margariete reached out to Raeylan, but was yanked off balance when the vessel righted itself. The hull squealed loudly as time resumed its normal pace.

"Why did you let go of your spell?" she demanded as he caught her. "The ship's being torn apart!"

"It was not of my doing," he answered with a worried expression. "Something dispelled my power."

Margariete felt her eyes go wide. Again, everything around her slowed, but only for a moment. The ship jolted and reared, slamming both Margariete and Raeylan into the wall. Time fluctuated wildly, shaking from nearly motionless to normal in unpredictable instants. Nausea curdled Margariete's throat as her twin's time manipulation ability went haywire, creating a surrealistic environment that bombarded her senses.

Raeylan grasped her forearm and dragged her toward his room. She clutched his bicep for support and tried to keep pace.

"Hold tightly," Raeylan ordered.

Margariete obeyed as her brother rushed into his cabin and snatched a leather pack that held the six god scrolls, Kalariel's heart salt, and the two other teleport stones. Just as the breath of teleportation surrounded her in starry light pricks, their ship disintegrated into a mass of scrap.

The telepath had travelled instantaneously with her twin on countless occasions—which is how she knew something was wrong. The brief relief of their escape was unexpectedly splintered by pain. It penetrated her body, slitting her skin to the marrow of her bones. Massive pressure pinched her limbs. As spasms curled her muscles wildly, she lost her grip on Raeylan's arm.

Her feet connected suddenly with a hard surface. Instinctively, she extended her arms in an attempt to balance. Something clattered to the floor as she stumbled; her mind belatedly registered it as a plate of food. As Margariete's equilibrium recovered, she comprehended her surroundings. She stood on a table, three pairs of stunned, yellow-hazel eyes surveying her.

The humans around the table were the bulkiest the telepath had ever seen, including the woman. Both men had hair cropped nearly to the scalp. One was definitely older, with a chiseled, square jaw. The other had a flat face and almond-shaped eyes, more like an elf than a human, but his frame was too muscular to be one. Rows of tiny braids hung from the woman's head and her skin was so dark that it was almost black.

A moment revealed three essential things: the view from a port informed her that she had appeared on another ship, all three humans around the table wore pistols at their belts, and Raeylan was nowhere to be seen.

Margariete reacted first, lifting her gun and discharging it at the older, most threatening looking opponent. To her horror, the bullet simply bounced of his skin. He grinned at her infuriatingly. With incredible speed, the trio of warriors leapt to their feet and drew their weapons, firing as one. Margariete reacted intuitively, commanding the air to capture the rounds a fingertip's length from her face. The bullets fizzled strangely against the atmospheric shackles that held them bound, and the telepath understood—with a smirk—that the soldiers' weapons did not eject solid projectiles as she had expected.

They launched surges of magical energy.

The humans wavered in uncertainty, giving Margariete an opportunity to attack. She coupled a telekinetic blast with an energy dissipation spell. Her opponents' energy rounds withered and dispersed into a dazzling mist just as her intangible slam hurled the warriors backward the length of five strides.

Her brows contracted. The potency of her attack should have knocked them all unconscious. She was startled to note that all three remained upright. They were certainly more resilient than her normal adversaries.

Margariete tossed the pistol away—since it was useless—and flipped from the table, drawing her twin blades from her boots with her mind. *Stardawn* was already in her hand as she charged the dark-skinned woman, loosing the daggers toward the formidable, square-jawed man on the left. The human female dodged Margariete's first swing so quickly that the telepath thought her opponent had the gift of teleportation. But after reversing *Stardawn's* path and doling a second strike, Margariete determined the woman simply possessed enhanced speed. After a quick scan of her other two enemies, Margariete realized that she had seriously underestimated the humans' abilities.

The formidable man on the left met her daggers edges with his bare arms. Though the dancing weapons shielded Margariete from his possible attack, their blades could not pierce his skin. The woman evaded too swiftly for Margariete to effectively dispatch with *Stardawn* alone, and the flat-faced human on her right raced to flank her.

Time to change tactics.

Margariete crushed the back of the woman's knee with a burst of air, causing the female warrior to lurch forward. At the same moment, the telepath smashed *Stardawn's* hilt across the woman's temple, sending her sprawling across the floor. With her free hand palm forward, Margariete absorbed the lambent particles of static that floated about the air, and just as the younger male soldier leapt to tackle her, the Thyellan princess released a crackling bolt of electricity into his body. He convulsed irregularly and collapsed in a sizzling heap.

The telepath's sensory perception forewarned her that the woman had regained her feet. Margariete stepped sideways to avoid the female's brawny fist, spinning *Stardawn's* blade again in attack, but the telepath missed. The former princess pursed her lips in displeasure. Her opponent's superior speed was becoming a nuisance. One spell would steal that advantage. As the dark-skinned woman launched another physical blow, Margariete bent the air around her enemy, plucking the woman off the floor and suspending her in midair. Formulating the strongest concussive force possible, the telepath rammed it into the abdomen of her foe. The woman's eyes rolled into unconsciousness.

Margariete turned to her last enemy just in time to see him break the blades of her daggers into fragments. Before she could raise *Stardawn* in defense, he dashed toward her, gripping her face by the jaw and thrusting her body upward off the floor. She stabbed at him, her feet dangling helplessly.

The man growled in shock and pain when the magical blade pierced his flesh, but he didn't drop her as Margariete had planned. Her awkward position had caused her to miss anything vital. She tried to dislodge *Stardawn* and try again, but the human clenched her sword's hilt, preventing her from drawing the blade out of his body. She fought to loosen his grip, but his hands were like steel.

The last thing she saw was the arc of his head as he bashed his forehead into hers.

12: It's Been A Long Time Since I Smelled "Beautiful"

"Just pull it out, Snow!" Kyleren barked as the GAEL medic slowly ran the scanner up and down the sword.

It had pierced Lance's left shoulder, protruding out his back.

"That would be unwise, lieutenant," Dr. Boris Pryce rattled in a deep voice from across the med bay as the physician administered a dose of nanomites into Gary's neck. "Any blade that can cut GAEL skin must be living technology. It would be reckless to remove it without first discovering its protocols. It could be designed to afflict more damage when extracted."

The doctor's bald head rendered his age indeterminate, though his manicured beard was feathered with silver. His beady, impatient eyes fussed over Gary for a few more minutes. Lance noted the man's pointed ears and high cheekbones and wondered how much elf was in him—he was obviously blended.

Considering the level of injuries the team had sustained, they were lucky to have Pryce on board; *the* Dr. Boris Pryce, the genius who had discovered how to bond living tech to a blended soldier. Without him, the GAEL

VICs would be just another handful of warriors in the pack.

Kyleren looked away from the doctor, his body groaning with complaint. He glowered at Wayne who was chuckling softly as he leaned against the transparent medical center doors.

"Keep laughin' and I'll put you back out, Wayne."

"I just can't get over it, that's all," Wayne chortled. "You getting stabbed by a chick."

The lieutenant clenched his fist, though the pain that lashed down his arm made him wish he hadn't.

"Because it's impossible for a 'chick' to take someone down?" Trisha inserted warningly. "Is that what you mean?"

Her eyes dared Wayne to refute.

"Don't forget Reese—a crappy, dead tech Agromor mech took you out with one hit."

"I didn't mean you, Reynolds," Wayne defended. Then he added with a grin, "We all know you could kill any one of us if you wanted."

"Gromm straight," Trisha rumbled.

"Calm down GAELs," Dr. Pryce insisted. "I didn't spend the past hundred years producing the strongest soldiers in the galaxy, only to have you kill each other. There are enough of you almost dead already."

Pryce's last statement caused Trisha's mouth to snap shut. Wayne looked at the floor. The newest recruit, Gary, lay on a clean med couch, charcoal burns shimmering wetly across most of his chest. The doctor assured them that Private Thompson would be fine after a few days of nanomite dermal-regeneration, but Gary hadn't regained consciousness since the intruder had electrified him.

Harris wasn't so lucky. The ambush on Agrona had cost the GAEL veteran his left arm all the way to the shoulder. Currently, the corporal was sedated.

"How's Harris?" Lance asked, pointedly ignoring the pain in his shoulder.

Dr. Pryce shook his head.

"Corporal Evans will receive the best care I can give him. With living tech bionics I can give him back an arm, but I'm afraid it will not be good enough to continue service with a GAEL squad."

"Can't you regrow his arm or something?" Wayne asked.

"Nanomites can speed up the natural healing processes of cells," the doctor answered, "but they can't recreate entire limbs."

Dark expressions filtered through the assembled GAELs. Evans had been part of squad Aon longer than all of them put together. Even if Harris's arm was replaced by a machine, death would have been preferable to a GAEL. The best the corporal could hope for was reassignment to the regular VIC military, or a position as cadet instructor.

Chad's scanner broke the somber mood as it emitted a loud tone, indicating the completion of its function. Snow peered at it in confusion.

"What?" Lance asked.

"This sword isn't protoed to do anything," the medic answered, his eyes squelched in puzzlement.

The doctor abandoned Gary's side and snatched the medical instrument from Chad's hands. His nose wrinkled and twitched as he examined the machine's display.

"This can't be right."

"What?" Lance hollered, entirely frustrated.

He wanted the sword out.

"The scans say that the sword isn't living tech," the doctor explained, "but it isn't registering as dead tech either."

"That's not possible," Trisha interjected.

"Young lady, I am the creator of bonded tech, and the head of the most prestigious medical research company in the universe," the doctor said. "I know this isn't possible."

"Is it bonded tech?" Trisha posed.

"Bonded tech originates from the same source as living tech," Pryce quibbled, his beard wagging in irritation. "It would register the same frequency on the scanner."

"Then what is it?" Wayne pressed.

The doctor paused, thinking. Lance's patience burned away with every second of delay.

"I don't know," Pryce finally admitted. "It will take time to analyze the readings."

"So I can take this fraggin' thing out?" Lance bellowed, wrapping his hand around the hilt.

Before anyone could object, he yanked the blade from his body with an agonized grunt.

Chad reacted quickly, taking the sword and setting it carefully aside. Then he injected nanomites into Lance's open wound. The tiny living machines immediately halted the bleeding and urged Kyleren's cells to begin their rapid heal. By the end of the day, the injury would look like it had never been.

"Done," Chad announced with pleasure.

He moved on to Trisha, who had suffered several broken ribs and a cracked knee in the mess hall skirmish. The doctor turned his attention back to Gary.

"Good," Kyleren said, sliding from the metal examination table.

He was eager to meet Colonel Stoddard and Major Huard in the brig as they interrogated the prisoner. Wayne followed Lance out of the med bay, not speaking until the crystasteel doors hissed closed behind them.

"How do you think she got on the ship?"

"Don't know," Lance huffed crossly, "but it's annoyin' how I keep gettin' fragged by every woman I meet. The last five to be exact."

"Yes we know you get fragged all the time, Lance," Wayne responded with a chuckle and roll of the eyes.

"Not what I meant," Kyleren complained.

Wayne ticked a list off on his fingers as they ascended the stairwell. "Gwen, the shiidh, our prisoner."

He looked at Lance quizzically.

"Trisha?"

Lance sighed as he clambered upward, turning left toward the brig when he reached topside.

"Who's the fifth?" Reese asked they entered the hatch.

"You don't wanna know," Lance returned, thinking of LAMIE.

The brig had four separate cells, each designed to isolate one prisoner. Static polarization fields kept the detainee safely guarded when activated. LAMIE's constant supervision negated the need for a posted guard. Colonel Stoddard spoke in low tones to Major Huard in front of the only occupied cell, while the intruder frowned at them hatefully. When the two GAELs entered, the officers halted their conversation and turned.

"Are you sure you should be out of the med bay, lieutenant?" the colonel asked Lance with concern.

"I'm good, sir," Kyleren answered. He indicated the woman with a flick of his head. "Do we know who she is yet?"

"She won't say," Huard complained acidly. "We've been at it for 45 minutes and all she does is glare at us."

Kyleren's yellow-hazel eyes poured over the female who had stabbed him. Her own clothes and equipment had been confiscated for examination, so she had been dressed in some of Sergeant Reynolds' training sweats. The garments sagged against her figure, but that did nothing to diminish Lance's recollection of her body's form when she had gromm-kicked his comrades in the mess hall. Her smooth shape curved as if it were made to specifically hold a man's attention. The olive tone of her skin pleaded to be touched.

He shook the feeling away. The stranger had held her own against three GAELs. She might be the most beautiful woman he had ever seen, but she was also the most dangerous. Inside the cell, she sat rigidly facing forward, showing no sign of fear or anxiety. Strangely, she hid her right arm from view.

"She's only 60 kilograms at most, Lance," Wayne pointed out. "How'd she take down two GAELs?"

"Technology," Lance answered shortly. "Has to be."

"I've sent all of her things down to Gene," the colonel informed them. "He hasn't given us any details yet."

"She isn't Vartal," Wayne observed. "Her skin's not the right color."

"She's human though," Kenny asserted. "Saw her ears when we brought her in here."

Lance and Wayne traded a glance. There weren't many humans who sided with the Agromors.

"What's a human woman doin', workin' for the gromms?" Lance wondered.

"We don't even know if she is for certain," Kenny grumbled. "Like the colonel said: she won't talk."

"Does the doctor have anything that could make her?" Wayne suggested.

Gene burst into the room in an agitated frenzy before the colonel could reply.

"You—are—never—," he said between breathless gasps, "—going—," he paused dramatically, "—to believe this!"

"What?" the colonel asked warily, his face indicating that he would rather not have had to ask.

"I analyzed her equipment. Other than the firearm, she has no tech."

"That's not possible," Kyleren argued.

"It's true!" Gene declared confidently, as if he were personally responsible for this marvelous turn of events.

He presented a dataplate to Stoddard for inspection.

"I saw her shoot lightnin' out of her hand, Gene," Lance contended. "She was *invisible*. Those fraggin' daggers were hoverin' and attackin' by themselves. And she lifted Trish off the ground without even touchin' her!"

"I know. I remember you telling us the first time," Gene said with a patronizing eye roll. "It doesn't change the fact that she doesn't have any technology. Even her firearm isn't a registered design on the Intergrid. I checked all the codex databases. Twice."

"So you're sayin' she appeared from thin air on our ship and beat up two GAELs without any tech?"

All four soldiers glowered at Gene skeptically.

"Yep," Gene said cheerfully. "Don't ask me how. You'll have to get it out of her."

"Except she won't talk," Wayne stated.

As his three superior officers discussed the possible implications of Gene's findings, Lance moved just in front of the fluctuating horizon of the polarization field. The woman didn't move, but if thoughts could kill, Kyleren had no doubt he'd be dead.

"What's your name?" he asked just quietly enough so the others wouldn't hear.

The woman contracted her brows, deepening her frown. Lance's tolerance of the intruder snapped. She had been the worst possible ending to an already sour day. He slammed his fist against the unseen barrier, causing it to spark loudly.

"Hey, Blue Eyes. Don't ignore me!"

His outburst drew the attention of the other men in the room, but Kyleren barely noticed.

The woman twisted her lips and shouted in a rich, heavy accent, "I don't understand what you're saying."

"You don't understand us?" Kenny blurted.

The woman awarded him with a blank stare.

"I think she's tellin' the truth," Kyleren said after a moment of reflection.

Though the stranger grated on his nerves, she was bold, defiant. It would seem out of character for her to lie.

"How could she not understand?" Huard asked helplessly.

"Maybe she doesn't have a translator," Gene piped, his finger wagging in epiphany.

Everyone else in the room blinked in bewilderment.

"You think she doesn't have a patch?" the colonel asked.

"That's unheard of," Kenny insisted. "Everybody gets patched, even Agromors."

"But it would explain why we understand her but she doesn't us. Go get one," the colonel ordered Gene.

The technobionomist responded promptly and scurried out. When he returned, Stoddard turned to the GAELs.

"Reese, Kyleren, hold her."

As Kenny shut down the field, Lance noticed a twinge of fear color the woman's expression for the first time. Her breath became quick and shallow as she stood, though she kept her arm hidden protectively behind her back. Kyleren considered she might be injured.

Lance and Wayne reached her at the same time. Her eyes flicked from one to the other, apparently at a loss of what to do. The lieutenant trapped her arms to her sides in a giant embrace, though she kicked, screamed, and fought the moment he touched her. As Wayne pulled her head to one side, making the back of her ear more accessible for the technobionomist, she cursed them both to some kind of Void in the name of someone called Nehro. Lance had no idea what she meant.

But a GAEL VIC's grip was stronger than crystasteel, and her attempts to free herself proved fruitless. Stoddard tried to communicate that they meant her no harm, but it was obvious she didn't understand. Lance tightened his hold, just to be safe, and her chocolate locks spilled across her arm, its spicy scent annoyingly arousing.

Gene extracted a porous strip of brassy fiber from a synthetic wrap and pressed it firmly behind the woman's ear. Two finger swipes activated the translator device as it adhered permanently to her skin. The fiber was removed, leaving the tawny patch behind. Reese and Kyleren let her go, pushing her into the corner of her cell as the GAELs sped out. Huard initiated the static barrier before she realized they had gone. Her left hand reached behind her ear dubiously.

"Do you understand me?" the colonel asked, a fatherly tone softening his words.

Kyleren snorted inwardly. Gentleness with this woman was a waste.

"What is this?" she asked, touching the device behind her ear gingerly.

"It's a translation device," Stoddard explained.

Kyleren could almost see the colonel's thoughts, because they mirrored his own. How could she have never before seen a patch? The colonel continued.

"What's your name?"

She lifted her chin stubbornly, silent in her refusal to answer.

The colonel's kind manner dissolved, leaving behind a perplexed and serious commander.

"What are you doing on my ship?" he demanded. "Who do you work for?"

Her eyes flashed.

"I serve no one," she declared proudly.

"Then why are you here?" the colonel asked.

She took a breath, letting it rush out with her frustration.

"I don't know."

"This'll go on forever if you don't start answerin' the questions, Blue Eyes," Lance interrupted impatiently.

She turned her gaze to him, resentment glittering deep in her electric eyes.

"Then I suggest you start asking questions I know the answers to."

The uncooperative response made Kyleren dislike her even more.

13: More Than Meets The Eye

Margariete's interrogation was a collection of wasted arcs, at least for the colonel and his men. They asked her innumerable questions and she remained silent. For the telepath, however, the experience was impressively successful.

The translation "patch" they had forcefully installed on her body provided her with a means to access two of the most powerful abilities she had lost since leaving Thyella. For centuries, she had been frustrated that her mind reading power was hampered by language. She could read thoughts but was unable to translate them. The best she had been able to do was assess underlying emotion, mind-walking through memories. Sometimes that resulted in more trouble than it was worth. And her domination power was completely useless when the subject she controlled had no idea what she wanted him to do.

But this translator technology not only interpreted language, it somehow decoded thought streams. Without knowing, her captors had already revealed the names, ranks, and mission objectives of each crew member. The vessel which carried them, LAMIE, was a special prototype, made of an ore called "living tech," and capable

of travel that surpassed faster-than-light. The two burly
soldiers who had restrained her earlier, Lieutenant Kyleren
and Captain Reese, were an enhanced species called
"GAEL VICs." These people named their enemies the
"Vartal," a race of elves belonging to an organization called
the "Agrona-Morrigan Concord." Major Huard, at least,
was confident that Margariete was one of them. LAMIE
and her crew were rapidly fleeing the system because they
had just stolen some important object from the Vartal and
didn't want to be intercepted.

But most importantly, the telepath had learned that
Raeylan was not on board.

Nothing like this had happened in the four hundred
seasons they had travelled together. Margariete was at a loss
to explain it. The only thing she knew for sure was that she
wasn't going to find her brother if she was confined in
LAMIE's prison. She needed to escape.

She rubbed her naked right arm pensively as she
thought. It was still sore from an experience a few arcs ago.
One of the yellow-eyed soldiers—Margariete hated him
especially—had pointed out to his superior that she had
been hiding her arm. Colonel Stoddard had sent for a
brusque little man with a beard. He was some kind of
healer, and had at first asked her politely if her limb was
causing her pain. Not wanting to give them the satisfaction
of a real answer, she had curtly informed him that she
didn't need any medical attention. Doctor Boris Pryce
requested to examine it anyway.

Margariete voiced a liberal opinion about what the man
could do with his scanner and refused to let him see her
arm. This, of course, convinced the nasty Major Huard that
she had something important hidden there, some nonsense

about technical implants that were responsible for her earlier prowess in battle.

It was like the witless idiots had never heard of Shardwell magic before.

She had been restrained again so the bald doctor could get his ridiculous readings, Margariete battling with burning tears and gritting her teeth over the violation of her person. The healer then extracted some of her blood in a vial and injected her with an unknown medicine that repaired the throbbing ache in her head.

The former Thyellan princess made no more effort to conceal her arm. She felt exposed without her signet glove—which they had taken with her clothes and other belongings—and angry that she didn't have *Stardawn* to help her get it back. Wavering between designs of escape and a means of murdering every one of her abductors, she experimented with her energy dissipation spell and tried to destroy the field that trapped her in the cell.

To her disappointment, she found that her charm only managed to disrupt the barrier for a moment, a span of time not nearly long enough for her slip through. There must have been a generator continually renewing the field's effect. Her investigation caused the ship, which was apparently an intelligent entity, to summon the colonel, the major, and Captain Reese. They tested the functionality of the barrier for half an arc before determining that nothing was amiss. Leaving Margariete alone under the watchful jurisdiction of the ship, they filtered out of the prison with mutters and grumbles. She was hesitant to try any other powers after that. Currently, the men believed her extraordinary abilities were some technological trick, and that was why they left her with only LAMIE as a guard.

As she paced the tiny cell, wholly frustrated, the door unexpectedly hissed open. Margariete stopped, bracing herself for another round of interrogation by the soldiers. But the hulking forms of the enhanced humans failed to appear. Instead, something small peeked cautiously around the threshold—something rather furry. It scampered into the room, bushy tail sweeping across the floor as it halted just in front of the barrier field.

The telepath stared at the animal in an incomprehensive daze. She and Raeylan had traveled through hundreds of shards, many of them space worlds, but never before had she encountered a squirrel free-ranging on a spaceship before. Its nose twitched with curiosity as it sniffed the energy wall that trapped Margariete. Just as she was considering shooing it away, a detested voice pealed from the ship's intercommunication speakers.

"Gene Pecktol," Lieutenant Kyleren called, "report to the bridge."

At the same moment, the squirrel chirped. The energy barrier died with a sputter. Margariete stared at the creature incredulously. It had to be a coincidence. The animal lifted itself upward on its hind legs, inspecting Margariete with its little pink nose. Slowly, she reached out to it. The squirrel's nose tickled her fingertips. With another chirp it twisted and rushed out the door.

Margariete followed, certain that LAMIE would sound some sort of alarm, informing the crew of her escape. But none came as she carefully crept through the exit. At the end of the corridor, the ship's sandy-haired scientist had just disappeared up a set of stairs.

"What now, squirrel?" Margariete whispered, more to herself than the animal.

The little creature had already dashed down the passage and hopped onto the first step, as if waiting for her to join it. Stretching her mind across the particles of air that spanned the hallway, Margariete searched for enemy vibrations. Finding nothing, she wasted no more time. The squirrel's actions were uncharacteristic and inexplicable, but some providence had intervened to free her, and Margariete was in no position to stop and analyze it.

Her bare feet tapped noiselessly up the stairs and another door opened when she reached the top floor. Anxious of being prematurely discovered, she froze. Fortunately, only two figures occupied the newly exposed room—somehow she had stumbled onto the bridge—and both seemed too consumed with their console to notice the open hatch. Margariete searched for the squirrel, but her tiny guide had disappeared.

"That can't be right," Gene complained.

"I'm tellin' you somethin's wrong with her," Kyleren asserted.

Margariete slid silently into the room, hugging the walls as the door glided closed.

"LAMIE's tech is perfect. There's no possible way you could have lost connection with her," Gene returned haughtily.

"You're not listenin', Gene. I told you already: the connection's still there, but it's like she just fell asleep or somethin'."

That at least explains why the ship hasn't warned them of my escape yet, Margariete reasoned as she skulked toward the unsuspecting men, *and how the cell barrier fell.*

"Are you sure you didn't just fall asleep yourself?" Gene asked.

Kyleren's face twisted with a glower. Gene held his hands up in surrender.

"Fine, I'll go check her board."

As Gene turned, the top of Margariete's foot cuffed his face. He crashed against the instrument panel with a whimper.

"What the—" Kyleren emoted, launching from his chair.

"Stop!" Margariete commanded as he rushed her.

Her order settled around the lieutenant's body, pressing down on him with the weight of her will. He fought against her domination, his mind clamoring with confusion when it refused to obey him. The telepath smirked.

"Stay there," she directed, appropriating his pistol.

A gaping cylindrical hole in the handle told Margariete that it wasn't loaded. She tossed the useless weapon aside and grabbed Gene by the back of his shaggy head. It looked like he had been trying to access a control board without arousing her attention. She jerked him to his feet roughly.

"If you want to live," she growled menacingly, "then you will do exactly as I tell you."

Gene cringed and glanced fretfully at his immobile companion.

"What did you do to him?" he stammered.

"Keep talking and you'll find out," Margariete bluffed with an oily sneer.

Hopefully, the timid scientist would be unable to discover that she could only hold on to one mind at a time. "Is there a way to lock that door?" she demanded.

Gene nodded his floppy hair. Margariete ordered the lieutenant to seal it. He obeyed, but the telepath felt him strain against her spell with every synapse of his brain.

130

Gene undoubtedly noticed her focus on forcing the lieutenant to comply, because the scientist suddenly tried to elbow her in the side. He miscalculated her reaction time, however, and Margariete managed to sidestep before his heroic attack could connect. She released him abruptly and he toppled forward under the strength of his momentum. Before he could recover, Margariete caught his arm and mercilessly twisted it behind his back in a painful joint lock.

"Don't do that again, Gene. I don't like killing unless I have to," she whispered in his ear. "Now, show me how to fly this ship."

He pointed his free hand at the controls.

"That's less than helpful," she growled crossly. "Be a little more specific."

"He can do it," Gene said with a wild wave at Kyleren, "with his core drive. But since LAMIE's asleep right now, I'm not sure it will work."

Kyleren's incessant exertion against Margariete's domination spell required her complete concentration of power, and she couldn't spare the energy to filter Gene's mind for the truth. Fortunately, he was a bad liar.

"I don't believe you," she stated.

She slid her eyes from the pilot seat to Kyleren.

"Sit," she commanded.

The lieutenant followed her instructions with a cantankerous growl. Margariete knocked the pesky scientist unconscious against the nearest console.

"Sorry, Gene," Margariete apologized as she lowered his body to the floor.

She glanced out the clear portal that was the forward bulkhead. The vessel had been swiftly approaching a grey, cloudy world.

"Land this ship on that planet," she demanded.

Kyleren's uncooperative mind reared with protests and foggy concern for Gene. Margariete leaned against the panel adjacent the flight controls. She bore down hard with her will. A swell of cursing gushed across Kyleren's mind as his body did her bidding, changing LAMIE's course to intercept the planet.

"Gene's just unconscious," she promised the aggravated warrior. "He'll have a horrible headache when he wakes, but he should be fine."

Nice of you, Kyleren thought with acidic skepticism. The words burned in Margariete's mind. *How the frag did she get out of her cell?*

"Don't be so surprised," Margariete laughed with amusement.

She'll never get off this ship alive, his mind continued angrily, still unaware that she could hear him.

"Oh, I'll get off this ship, Lieutenant Kyleren," she answered his unspoken challenge with confidence. "Two of your crew are unable to fight, your ship is asleep, and I'm already acquainted with your friends' capabilities."

Though the lieutenant's body was unable to express it, she felt astonishment tickle his thoughts.

Did you—how?

"How did I what? Know what you were thinking?" she gloated brashly, but didn't explain. "This is simple, Kyleren. You are going to get me off this ship. And if you do it cleanly, I might let you live."

I'm not gonna help you, he asserted.

"You won't have a choice," she returned.

How're you doin' that?

"You'd think after arcs of questions you'd know I won't answer you, lieutenant. Instead, you are going to answer all of mine. I heard someone refer to you as 'blended.' What does that mean?"

"I'm half-human, half-elf," he answered blandly, his mouth helpless to oppose her request.

The ship skimmed the unknown planet's atmosphere. Margariete's brow creased in irritation. Mortal cross-species birth was impossible. Only higher beings, like the lorelei, could cross that barrier. But, under her power, there was no way the lieutenant could lie.

"What do you mean? Humans and elves can't have children."

"Blending tech was discovered two thousand years ago, DST," he answered mechanically. "There are millions of blended children in the universe."

"And do they all look like you?" she asked.

"No. I am a GAEL. A bonded tech soldier. The bonding process makes us look more human than a regular blended."

Margariete bit her lip. Processes that altered the body could only be done through magic.

"How does bonding work?"

Kyleren's mind rapidly fought against answering. His determination intrigued Margariete. Perhaps it was knowledge that wasn't supposed to be revealed. His efforts, however, were in vain.

"The GraEL."

"Is this 'GraEL' the object you stole from the Vartal?"

"Yes." He added silently, *How the hell do you know that?*

"Describe it for me."

"It's a small tree, the source of all living tech in the universe. Without the GraEL a VIC can't be bonded to his core drive."

"Core drive?" Margariete asked as the ship's shields pushed against the planet's upper atmosphere. A curtain of orange danced across the crystal view portal.

"It's a GAEL's life-line. It makes us stronger, faster, and allows us to integrate with bonded tech."

Margariete stood and retrieved the lieutenant's discarded pistol. Again she looked at the gap in the handle—the usual place an ammunition clip would be inserted—but this time she examined it more closely. She waved it in front of Kyleren's face.

"Tech like this pistol?" she asked, noticing the black arm band on his bicep.

It was generally the same cylindrical size as the opening in his pistol. It too was empty.

"Yes," Kyleren answered.

"Why do you call it 'living tech'?" the telepath asked. "What does that mean?"

Kyleren's mind tried to scramble his response by wandering aimlessly through memories and facts, pointedly avoiding her question. Margariete soon discovered that her mind-walking was susceptible to the technique. She had lost interest in his answer, however, pondering probable explanations as the skeletons of oceans and rivers appeared on the planet's surface.

These core drives could be Wells. It would explain the magical energy that discharged from the GAELs' weapons.

"You said it was a 'life-line.' Elaborate," she insisted.

Panic careened through Kyleren's head, and for an intense moment, she thought he was going to break through her domination. Margariete repeated the question three times, pushing more of her influence into his skull with each try. She breathed a sigh of relief when he finally answered.

"A GAEL is directly connected to his core drive. If anything happened to it, it would kill me."

It had to be a Soulwell, she deduced. Nothing else could be that powerful. It was extremely feasible that this GraEL was actually an artifact. Her head buzzed through each possibility: Kirion possessed Skoh's Earring and Nehro's Glove, and Esilwen carried Fohtian's Blood within her. That left only two prospects. A tree fit the description of the Maiden of Life best—goddess of nature, stone, and metal. The telepath desperately wished her twin were near. He had read the god scrolls and understood the artifacts' natures more completely than she did.

"That is an unfortunate weakness," she finally said, hoping that her silent reflection hadn't aroused the soldier's suspicions.

Margariete turned away from her captive, scanning the flight controls for his core drive. A black ring seemed out of place amongst the sleek computerized panel. She fingered it gently.

"Where are you keeping the GraEL?"

"It's locked up in the armory."

"How do I get—" Margariete started, but was knocked completely off her feet as the ship shuddered and jerked—reminiscent of before, when she and Raeylan had lost their own vessel. She found herself floundering uncomfortably in Kyleren's lap. His core drive dangled from her fingers. She had accidentally removed it when the ship lurched.

LAMIE's voice suddenly wavered through the cabin, cutting in and out between bleary static. "Lieutenant Kyleren . . . reinsert your core . . . flight controls. Failure to comply . . . collision with planet . . . in . . . seconds."

Margariete prepared to leap forward, but two massive arms compressed her chest.

"No you don't, Blue Eyes," Kyleren said, snatching his core drive from her hand.

How was this happening? Her domination had been completely dispelled! She tried to recast it, but nothing happened. The lieutenant's thoughts rolled through her power, patchy and indistinct, like a poor communication signal.

"LET ME GO!" she screamed, but Kyleren's embrace was like iron.

"You fraggin' piss me off," he spat, wrenching her to the side and almost throwing her to the floor.

He snapped his core drive back into LAMIE.

"You're a stubborn—"

But another jolt rocked the ship and Kyleren lost his balance. Margariete wrestled with the GAEL, slamming her elbow into his gut. Surprised at the blow, he struggled for breath and immediately let go. As she bolted for the door she wondered how she had penetrated his superior strength. Whatever was affecting her magic must also be robbing him of his.

She leapt over Gene's floppy body to reach the hatch and pounded on it ferociously when it refused to open. The telepath twisted quickly, prepared to fight the lieutenant for her freedom, but he hadn't pursued her. He perched in the pilot's chair, swearing profusely as his fingers tackled the controls. LAMIE had fallen eerily silent. Her console panels were dark and lifeless.

Two things occurred to Margariete. The first—that this shard's living tech must have something to do with magic because it was vulnerable to whatever force had scrambled her own. And the second—and more alarming—was that the planet's surface was rapidly rising to meet the ship.

And there was nothing Kyleren could do to stop it.

14: COME WITH ME IF YOU WANT TO LIVE

Anya stepped through the security bioscanner as required, a process ensuring that she didn't carry anything dangerous into the private transport station set aside for Penardun's prime minister. The clear paned machine spat several puffs of air across her, painting her skin with luminescent strings of light. Satisfied that she didn't pose a security threat, the machine graciously granted her a visitation ident tag and shooed her forward into the slim hall that led to the shuttle platform.

Her glassy heels snapped anxiously against the marble floor as she hurried through the passage. Something was dreadfully wrong. Vivian would never have asked Anya to desert her patients in the middle of a shift unless it was an emergency. Her sister's holomessage had been brief and seemingly friendly, asking nothing more than Anya's familial farewell at the station as Vivian prepared a regular visit to the Round on Kamolos.

Vivian had never asked for that before, not in the 150 years she had led the city.

The walk through the confining walls of the transport building squeezed the remaining calm from Anya. Though she wanted to know what really happened to tiny Riia Farren, she desperately hoped she hadn't brought grave peril into her sister's path.

By the time the air dock yawned at the end of the hallway, Anya was nearly at a run. Expecting one of the glossy modern shuttles that serviced Coalition dignitaries, she was confounded to see instead a boxlike, terra-textured vessel used by only a single group in the galaxy: the shiidh.

Why would they be escorting her sister to a meeting with the Round? Penardun was a neutral city in the MetaGalactic War, a natural stopping point for the only organization of Vartal elves that was allowed to travel freely throughout the Coalition homeworlds. But the shiidh had their own launch station on the other side of the city.

Anya slowed her pace as she spotted Vivian standing in the center of five granite-skinned elves. Though her sister masked her anxiety well, Anya noticed a discernible release of tension in Vivian's face as her sister finally arrived.

"Anya," Vivian greeted, embracing her tightly. "I am overwhelmed with joy to see you."

Anya returned the gesture, though it comforted her little. The five shiidh remained eerily silent. A small linen satchel and a long, oddly shaped package lay next to her sister's feet.

"What's happening, Vivian?" Anya blurted, trying to ignore the intense gaze of the five foreign women surrounding them.

One seemed to stand taller than the rest, her malachite hair twisted into a tight maze of dreadlocks. Her angular face exuded intimidation. Anya lowered her voice, hoping that the woman wouldn't hear.

"Are you going to the Round on a shiidh ship? Vivian, that could get you arrested!"

Vivian's hand rose to Anya's face.

"I am not leaving with the shiidh, dearest Anya. You are."

Anya's heart lurched.

"What?" she asked.

"It is no longer safe for you here," Vivian declared. "You must leave with those I trust."

"No longer safe?" Anya said breathlessly, her mind foggy and numb. "I don't understand. What's happened?"

Vivian grasped both of Anya's hands with her own.

"You have always been blessed with the aptitude to recognize deception. The day you joined the Ninevay family, our mother knew you were special. As did I."

"I can't just leave with the shiidh, Vivian," Anya argued, "I have responsibilities—"

"You must," Vivian interrupted. "Have faith in my judgment, Anya. I've been investigating the Coalition hierarchy for nearly a century. You provided me with the evidence I was searching for, but now we are all at risk."

"Vivian—"

"The truth you uncovered will change the Coalition forever. Because of that, it is too dangerous for you to remain. You must go."

"What about you?" Anya insisted. "Won't you be the first they come for?"

Vivian's eyes glittered with the depth of understanding gleaned only by centuries of life. With a sickening swell of panic, Anya realized her sister intended to keep their enemies preoccupied, allowing Anya time to escape.

"Yes, they will," Vivian answered steadfastly.

"Then you can't stay either," Anya pleaded.

Tears choked her throat. If the secret Vivian had discovered was powerful enough to damage the Coalition, it might be worth killing for.

"I must steer them from your trail," Vivian explained. "You will find sanctuary among the shiidh. They will need your help contacting those who can use the information to bring down the Coalition."

"I will not abandon you," Anya choked.

"You must," Vivian commanded in the tone of someone who was used to being obeyed.

Anya shook her head defiantly. She couldn't do it. The shiidh closed ranks around them, their faces calm with sympathy.

"Do not ask me to leave you here to die, Vivian," Anya whispered.

Vivian embraced her for the last time.

"I'm not asking," she said. "Remember always that I love you, Anya."

Anya recognized Vivian's intent a second too late. A sharp sting pricked Anya's neck before she managed to jerk away. Her vision slid into blurry disorder and her limbs dragged her to the hard, plated floor. The last thing she saw before succumbing to the nanomite-induced darkness was the sad farewell of her sister's smile.

15: THERE CAN BE ONLY ONE

Lance's body continued to rattle even after the ship finally halted its screeching skid across the flat grassland. His head pounded with dizziness. Blood trickled into his eye from a gash near his hairline. He couldn't remember ever feeling so much weakness throb through him. Rolling onto his stomach, he pushed himself slowly upright, surveying the damaged bridge as he did so.

It wasn't pretty. Several of the control panels were completely destroyed. The crystasteel viewing portal was a spider's web of cracks. Cables and wires sparked in hanging curtains of entrails from the ceiling.

At least the integrity of the deck seemed intact. It was possible that with a little time the crew could repair LAMIE enough to manage a hobble back to Coalition territory.

When it had been obvious that communication was lost between himself and LAMIE, Kyleren had wrenched the ship's control away from her integrated living tech propulsion to the back-up dead tech engines. Those malfunctioned as well, but at least they provided enough counter velocity to slow the ship so that the crew wasn't vaporized on impact. He had grappled to level the ship's belly with the horizon when they crashed. He just hoped the hull wasn't twisted beyond use.

The lieutenant cursed fluently as he stumbled through the wreckage. His movements were ungainly and jerky, a wooly numbness shrouding his senses. It took him a few minutes to determine the cause: the ever present link of his core drive was missing, leaving a void in his head that blunted his thought process.

Gene lay limp a few steps away. Kyleren knelt by the technobionomist's side and flopped him over. The man's eyelids fluttered and his chest rose and fell evenly. Lance didn't have the equipment for a thorough scan, but it seemed the technobionomist had escaped serious injury. As the GAEL rose, a clatter near the door drew his attention. The woman responsible for this mess heaved to her feet and tried to slip out the door unnoticed.

Even without his super speed, Kyleren reached her before she managed to escape, snatching her by the waist and yanking her back into the command center. She strained against his hold and he lost his grip, causing Lance to unintentionally throw her to the floor. The woman recovered expertly, however, regaining her feet and positioning her body in a defensive stance.

"You've caused me nothin' but trouble, Blue Eyes," Kyleren accused as he took a step toward her.

She held her ground, regarding him coolly.

"I told you to land the ship, not to crash it."

"I wouldn'tve crashed if you hadn't forced me to land it!" he returned.

"If you weren't so weak-minded, then I wouldn't have been able to force you!"

The impossible predicament, coupled with the woman's infuriating scorn, goaded Lance to charge. He swung his fists twice, though both strikes missed her agile form. Her counterattack collided against his abdomen and face, resulting in more pain than he had anticipated. It was only partly due to his sudden loss of physical endurance. The way she applied the blows somehow increased the damage her strikes inflicted. After three more unsuccessful punches, he realized that without his bonded enhancement, this woman was superior in martial combat.

That left only one way to beat her—his greater weight. He threw his body against hers, surprising her with such a brash action, and wrangled her to the ground. Kyleren pressed his knee into her lower back hard enough to make her fight to breathe, and yanked on her wrists, pinning her on her stomach. Just as he bound her hands with whatever cord was most readily available, he heard the unmistakable report of weapons' fire from below decks.

"What now?" he complained, securing her restraints to one of the command chairs and forcing her to sit up. He glanced back at the partially open exit.

"This have anythin' to do with you?"

Her eyes narrowed.

"If it did, do you think I would tell you?"

Kyleren tightened her restraints for good measure, forcing a hiss to pass between her lips.

"Guess not," he admitted almost jovially. Now that the woman was properly contained, he felt better. "Don't go anywhere, Blue Eyes," he told her with a grin. "I'll be back to put you in a new cell."

She clenched her jaw defiantly. Kyleren ignored her. Retrieving his sidearm and core drive, he snapped them together hopefully, but nothing happened. The core drive remained dark, unable to power the weapon.

"Frag it all!" he cursed, extracting his drive and holstering it on his arm. He would have to locate a dead tech firearm.

Muffled shouts and thuds were leaking through the half-open hatch. He had to pry the door a few more centimeters to accommodate his muscular frame. At the base of the stairs he was able to discern individual voices. Kenny was shouting orders.

"Sergeant Reynolds, Captain Reese, stand down!" Huard commanded, his words echoing from the direction of the mess.

Another pistol report and an angry howl of pain from the officer told Lance that Kenny had been hit. Wayne's unmistakable battle roar and a loud objection that sounded too much like Trisha to be fake stunned Lance into confusion.

What in the hell was going on?

Lance sidled to the open door and peeked inside, hoping to better understand the situation. Tables lay heaped against one wall, Major Huard ducking under them for cover as Trisha and Wayne struggled over Kenny's dead tech weapon. Bullets whizzed wildly through the mess as the two GAELs brawled, their eyes red-rimmed and wide with a crazed frenzy.

Kyleren stepped into the room.

"What the frag are you guys doin'?" he asked in amazement.

Trisha glanced at Lance, giving Wayne the opportunity to knee her in the gut, disturbing her already damaged ribs. She collapsed with a hoarse groan, blood leaking from mouth to chin. Captain Reese's intentions were clear as he leveled the pistol at her head. Lance barely had time to dart into the room and knock the weapon aside. Wayne stared at Kyleren without a shred of recognition, instantly attacking. The captain's fist connected with Lance's cheek, hurtling the lieutenant to the deck. Kyleren stared in disbelief as his longtime friend and comrade pointed the weapon at Lance's skull and pulled the trigger.

A blank click echoed through the hall.

"What's wrong with you, Wayne?" Lance asked, slapping the pistol out of Reese's hand as he stood.

The captain merely grunted and pounced. Kyleren sidestepped the ferocious lunge and pushed his friend roughly into the wall. The added momentum of Wayne's previous attack knocked him senseless and he slumped to the floor.

By the door, gurgling coughs heaved over Trisha's body, and she seemed incapable of rising. Lance rushed to the pile of tables. Behind the metal shield, Kenny hunched over the unconscious Colonel Stoddard, pressing firmly against their leader's copiously bleeding chest. The major himself bled from a shallow gunshot wound in his leg, though it didn't look immediately fatal.

"Lieutenant," Kenny barked desperately, "tell me you aren't insane too!"

"Ready and able, sir," Lance affirmed. "What the frag is wrong with everybody?"

"I don't know. Just before the crash they all started going crazy. Trisha attacked me and took my weapon. I got knocked out by the crash. When I woke up, the colonel had us bunkered behind this table. He needs the doctor, lieutenant."

"I'm on it," Kyleren said, sequestering the dead tech pistol clipped to the colonel's belt.

"Where's your BT weapon?" Kenny demanded.

"Core drive isn't working, sir," Lance answered. "Don't know why. I'll explain after I get Pryce."

"Hurry."

Lance nodded and tore into the hallway, heading to the medical bay. Without his core drive, he felt exposed and vulnerable. He ran to the lower level, keeping his sidearm at the ready. The metal weapon felt cold and stiff in his hand.

The lieutenant reached the bottom of the stairs just in time to see the engineer, Bedin Desha, hash Chief Snow with a metal pipe. Chad toppled, and the wary elf spun to meet Lance as he entered the corridor. Kyleren lowered his weapon and held his empty palms forward in truce.

"Not crazy, Bedin. Where's Percy?"

The elf wiped away a long trail of blood from a deep abrasion that ran from his ear to jaw.

"Unconscious in his lab, maybe. What is happening, lieutenant?"

"Ship crashed," Lance summed curtly.

Bedin's face contorted in fury.

"And what's wrong with you half-breeds?"

Kyleren's face soured as he continued down the corridor. He didn't like the racist engineer.

"Don't know, elf," he threw back. "Gotta get the doctor. I suggest you tie Snow up before he attacks you again."

Bedin grumbled but followed Lance's advice.

It seemed the transparent med bay doors were the only working tech on the ship. They hissed open as Lance approached. Gary, still encrusted in burn scabs, pounded furiously on Pryce's office window. He growled incoherently, slavering like a Famorian troll. Blood squelched from his fists each time he hammered the bulkhead. Kyleren crept forward, bashing the private across the scalp with the butt of the pistol. The lieutenant caught the newb as he fell and lowered him to the deck. Then Lance knocked twice on the office door.

"Doc, it's me: Lieutenant Kyleren. It's okay to come out."

*

"Explain to me just how the hell you managed to crash this ship, lieutenant!" Kenny lashed at Kyleren, his face billowing scarlet with both pain and anger.

"I didn't wanna crash her," Lance returned defensively. "I was tryin' to land her."

"You weren't given clearance to land!" Kenny retorted heatedly. "What's in your head?"

"That blue-eyed monster tied up on the bridge," Lance answered without thinking.

"Are you saying she beat you a second time?"

"I wouldn't call it 'beating,' sir."

"Then what would you call it?" Kenny screamed furiously.

Kyleren shrugged, unsure as how to explain.

"I fraggin' don't know, sir. One second I was talkin' to Gene, the next she was up there givin' orders. She was controllin' me somehow."

Kenny's head tilted to the side, clearly frustrated with the answer. Just as Lance prepared himself for another round of accusatory reprimands, Percy intervened.

"Question," the culturalist interjected from the corner, "if that woman was able to escape the brig, why is she only tied up? Is that entirely safe?"

"If she broke out of the brig," Bedin supplied, "I don't imagine we'll be able to hold her anywhere."

"Enough about the woman already," Kenny spat, turning the conversation back to Lance. "I want an explanation, lieutenant."

"I gave you the only one I've got, sir."

"System failure wasn't the lieutenant's fault, major," Gene said, skittering his fingers lithely across a dataplate. "We can throw the blame on each other for hours until the Agromors show up to skin us alive, or we can focus on the real problem."

Kenny bared his teeth.

"And what is 'the real problem' then, Gene?"

"All our living tech is offline," the technobionomist stated, tossing his plate away.

Everyone in the room blinked in astonishment. Living tech always worked as long as it had a power source. Gene heaved a superior sigh, annoyed with his companions' lack of experience.

"We're in a mire field. That's what caused the crash."

"Thank you," Kyleren said under his breath, grateful that blame had been diverted from himself.

"But we're on Danaan," Bedin posed skeptically, "the smallest planet in the system. The only recorded mire field is in the Eye of Baylour. That's a hundred-million light years from here."

Gene's eyebrows contracted.

"Duh. But the only force that can blanket living tech is a mire field. Come to think of it, it's odd that the field isn't causing more problems with our dead tech systems."

"Blanket?" Kenny asked. "Are you saying that the tech still works?"

"If the mire field wasn't interfering, LAMIE could repair herself—well mostly—and we could take off," Gene answered.

"Can't we use the dead tech engines to pull ourselves out of the field?" the elven engineer asked. "Then LAMIE could make her repairs in orbit."

"Didn't I just say, it's odd that the field isn't causing more problems with our dead tech systems?" Gene repeated disdainfully.

"Does this have to do with LAMIE fallin' asleep earlier?" Kyleren asked as the conversation lulled.

"I'm not sure," Gene said skittishly. "LAMIE was having problems in space before we entered the planet's atmosphere. She seemed to wake up in between. I think the crash and her sleep session are two separate events."

"Wait," Bedin interjected with a quizzical look. "LAMIE was having problems before the crash?"

"I don't really know," Gene replied with a pitiful shrug and a sigh. "Based on what the lieutenant described to me, LAMIE regained consciousness momentarily but was unable to properly communicate. It appears like something else was wrong with her before we struck the mire field. But I won't know for sure until she's is fully revived and I can run a diagnostic on her board."

Footsteps clicked outside the situation room. Dr. Pryce marched into the chamber and sank tiredly into one of the chairs.

"What's the status of the wounded?" Huard inquired.

"Not good," the doctor responded, shaking his head. "I've slowed the bleeding into Sergeant Reynolds' lungs, but I can't stop it. She needs surgery. The colonel won't last long without a nanomite injection to stimulate the growth of red blood cells in his system, and Corporal Evans has a fifty percent chance of surviving infection now that his GAEL immunities are gone. Plainly stated, I'm not properly staffed or equipped to save any of them."

"What do you mean 'without his GAEL immunities'?" Lance asked nervously.

The doctor looked at Gene.

"I assume you already discovered the living tech aboard isn't working?"

Gene nodded and Pryce turned back to Lance.

"A GAEL's enhancement comes from the living tech of his core drive. This connection is so complex that complete severance from it would result in uncontrollable violence, or worse."

"But I'm still standin' here, doc. I haven't tried to kill anyone," Lance pointed out.

"This is something that has never before been tested. Obviously it's affecting each GAEL differently," Dr. Pryce reasoned. "Trisha and Wayne still retained the capability to use weapons, whereas Snow and Thompson regressed entirely, going completely wild. You seem more lucid, lieutenant, but until I have a chance to run a full scan— difficult with the state of our medical instruments—I'm unsure as to how the loss of your drive has affected you."

Pryce pointed to the field dressing on Kenny's leg.

"You need to let me look at that, major."

"I'll manage until we've dealt with the situation," Kenny said. He turned to the technobionomist. "We need options, Gene."

"Well, he may be a pompous genius, but Bedin is right," Gene said, jerking a thumb in the engineer's direction, ignoring the elf's resultant glare. "The only naturally occurring mire field on record is in the Eye of Baylour. We don't know much about it because it warps all tech, living and dead, that gets too close to it. What we do know is that the field produces a wave frequency that vibrates inversely to the energy output by living tech ore at an amplitude that overloads anything comprised of dead technology. But judging by the erratic effects of the mire we entered, I'd say we're dealing with some kind of artificial reproduction. We'll have to deactivate it to get off the surface."

"You lost me," Kyleren confessed edgily.

The absence of his core drive was like an irreconcilable itch, something he was dying to scratch but couldn't reach.

"Someone's built a big mire field generator," Gene said again, waving his hands in an impatient circle. "And by someone, I mean the Agromors. I'm guessing they're only in the test stages."

"How could you even know that?" Percy asked.

"Because you don't build some awesome doomsday machine and leave it on an uninhabited planet, never to be used. As we've seen, it's still disrupting dead tech. The Agromors couldn't use it in any real tactical situation without the possibility of affecting their own dead tech systems. They must still be working out the flaws, tuning it to only interrupt the living tech of the Coalition."

"You think you can shut it down?" Kenny insisted.

Gene playfully rested his hands behind his head.

"In my sleep," he said.

"It's a start," Kenny snorted. "Can you locate the generator?"

"Yeah," Gene responded confidently.

Lance's insides twisted uncomfortably. This meant an infiltration op, but without backup or any BT weaponry.

"We'll need a strike team, sir," Kyleren sighed.

His yellow-hazel eyes brushed across those gathered at the table. A doctor, technobionomist, culturalist, and engineer; none of them trained. They would be hard-pressed to succeed in a game of tag.

151

"Major Huard," Lance said, feeling the first sliver of fear's razor edge, "I can't penetrate enemy defenses on my own."

"You won't," Kenny answered. "You'll take Gene."

For a moment Lance couldn't speak, so ridiculous was the idea.

"Does he even know how to shoot?" he finally asked.

"I went laser-tagging once," Gene replied seriously.

Lance stared at the technobionomist incredulously.

"Great," Kyleren grumbled. "Sir, this is the worst plan in the history of bad plans. I don't have any of my GAEL strengths, and even if I did, I don't think I could infiltrate a gromm base with a whizbang in tow."

"You have to take him, lieutenant," Kenny commanded. "He's the only one who can shut down the generator."

"And what if we just get ourselves killed?" Lance countered.

"We don't have a choice," Bedin interposed. "We either disable the mire field or surrender to the Vartal. If you do perish at the base, consider yourself fortunate. In Vartal custody you would die a horrible, tortured death."

Good point, Lance thought. He scanned the room's occupants again.

"Can anyone else here use a weapon?"

Percy paled as if the very thought terrified him and the doctor held his hands palms outward, indicating refusal.

"I do," Bedin said, "but LAMIE can't repair the damage to her dead tech engines. If we have any hope of getting off this planet, you need me in the engine room making repairs as long as possible."

"What about the woman?" Percy offered timidly.

"Absolutely not!" Huard screeched.

Kyleren wholeheartedly agreed.

"Why not?" Percy argued. "She's stranded on this planet, just like us. It stands to reason she'd be willing to help."

"She's a gromm agent!" Kenny accused. "We'd be taking her back to her own people."

"I don't know about that, major," Percy disagreed. "I've been researching her behavior on the Intergrid. Neither her accent nor the single glove she wears on her right arm match any culture in the Agrona-Morrigan Concord. In fact, I'm convinced she's from a society that we've never come across before."

"I concur," the doctor added before either soldier could argue. "Before the crash I was in the middle of evaluating the blood sample I took from her. She's not entirely human, but neither is she blended. She has markers I've never seen before. She may be a race we've not encountered."

"From the Famorian Cluster maybe?" Bedin speculated.

"I don't think so," the doctor continued. "All of those species have a common blood relationship, a genetic identity that links them together like the different classes of the elves. Her blood is entirely unique. Strangely, her cells reflect some of the properties you find in a GAEL, but they haven't been altered by any bonding process. If I had to guess, I'd say hers is natural."

Lance snorted with doubt. Nothing about that woman was natural—not her crazy abilities or her otherworldly beauty. There had to be some technological explanation.

"Well that would mean she wasn't even from the galaxy," Gene huffed skeptically.

His nasal laughter died quickly and hollowly as the others brooded darkly.

"Or a part that's beyond our known universe," Pryce amended. "Maybe out past the Black Reach."

"I don't care where she's from. I don't trust her," Major Huard asserted.

Indecision wracked over Lance. He agreed with his superior's assessment, but the fact remained that he needed skilled assistance to complete his mission.

"Sir," Kyleren said, already regretting his unspoken proposition, "may I speak to you alone?"

One by one the non-military crew members filed out. Kenny shifted in his chair, wincing as he moved his leg.

"What is it, lieutenant?"

Lance inhaled deeply.

"I hate to admit it, sir, but I think Percy's right."

Huard's face pulled into a mask of stubborn antagonism.

"That woman is a risk, lieutenant; one I'm not willing to take. I'm responsible for this crew."

"I know; she's more of a fraggin' pain than a Famorian boghag," Lance admitted. "But she can fight. I've seen it myself. And she can shoot. If I wasn't a GAEL, her first attack would have left me dead."

"You trust her?"

"Hell no, major," Kyleren blurted. "I'd rather dance with an ashray! But I need her, sir."

16: It Is Hard To Fill A Cup That Is Already Full

Margariete watched Kyleren drop her things at her feet. Distrust coursed through her thoughts. Her weapons clanked ungraciously on the metal floor. Her clothing fluttered over them in a delicate shroud. She fixed her eyes on the GAEL with a suspicious glare after he released her bonds, pondering his request that she accompany his team on some sort of quest.

"After taking me prisoner, you expect me to help you?" she asked with arched brows.

Kyleren folded his arms across his chest and relaxed his posture.

"You stabbed me in the shoulder, Blue Eyes. We're square."

"Far from it," she contended. "You don't understand the dishonor you've shown me."

"I don't give a frag," he spat without remorse, looming over her with his immense height. "You snuck onto *my* ship, attacked *my* comrades, and marooned us on a planet in enemy territory. You're not exactly innocent."

"I find it hard to believe that you suddenly trust me," Margariete accused as she snatched her signet glove from the pile. "How do I know this isn't a trick?"

"Thought you could read my mind," he chuckled, tapping lightly against his temple with one finger.

Margariete ignored him as she slipped the garment onto her naked arm. Its cool threads provided a small comfort to her dire predicament. One by one, she curled her fingers into a fist, unfurling them slowly to maximize the feel of the silky fabric against her skin. The creak of the GAEL VIC's black body armor interrupted her short respite, however, as he crouched next to the heap of her belongings while pointing to her arm.

"What's so important about that glove?"

"Who said it was important?" she asked, dodging the question as she counted the assorted weapons attached to various parts of his body: two pistols, a large rifle, and a dagger. She guessed the spherical objects snuggled on his belt were explosives of some kind.

"It was the first thing you picked up," he explained. "You didn't even reach for your sword."

Margariete ignored him, collecting her pack instead. A quick survey told her that nothing was missing. Snugly inside was her jar of quirr, two ammo clips, and a teleport stone—which was useless since it seemed something here was disrupting magic. Next, she gathered her clothes.

"You didn't answer me," Kyleren insisted. "The glove?"

"Do you mind?" she said holding her shirt and pants up.

Kyleren's jaw clenched, but he snatched *Stardawn* and her firearm before he rose to his feet and turned around.

Wise, Margariete thought, though she was annoyed that he didn't simply leave.

"Hurry it up, Blue Eyes," he threw over his shoulder. "I don't have all day."

Margariete dressed quickly, in case he inappropriately peeked. After dropping her mother's necklace over her head, she cleared her throat. The lieutenant circled, offering *Stardawn* by its hilt. Margariete took it and pulled, but he didn't let go. A stare infused with hatred burned from her eyes.

"My sword?" she asked with a tug.

"The glove," he repeated with a smile. "What it is?"

"It's nothing," she answered stubbornly, yanking on the blade again, which might as well have been entrenched in stone.

"Not buyin' it, Blue Eyes," he countered with a magnetic grin. "If you want the sword, you have to answer."

Margariete breathed deeply to dismiss her temper, but it refused to calm.

"It's a signet glove," she conceded through tight lips, "and it signifies my rank among my people."

"What rank?" he asked, still holding *Stardawn* tight.

"More questions weren't part of the deal," she seethed.

"We didn't make any deal."

"Just give me the damn sword!" she roared.

Kyleren released *Stardawn*, unimpressed by her outburst. Margariete fastened the sword to her belt in a huff. Then, with a grin, Kyleren held out her pistol.

"Your name?" he asked.

Her lips pursed so hard she felt they might split. She lunged for the weapon. Kyleren proved faster. He easily sidestepped as she dived, and her resultant overcorrection of balance nearly caused her to fall. She considered launching again, but the lieutenant stuffed the pistol's nose into his own holster.

"Margariete," she spat. "Satisfied?"

"That's quite a mouthful," he mused, tossing her the gun. "You don't mind if I call you 'Mags' do you?"

"My name is Margariete."

"Right. Well, Blue Eyes, you can help us get off this planet, or you can stay here in a cell. But this time we'll sedate you to make sure you don't get away."

Margariete clenched her fists, wishing she could shoot him and be done with it. That, of course, wouldn't solve her current dilemma. She needed to find Raeylan and that required a ship.

"If I help you," she asked, "will you let me go?"

Kyleren laughed and started for the door.

"No."

"Then drug me," she said obstinately.

The soldier twisted to face her.

"What?" he asked.

"I'm not an imbecile, lieutenant," she announced confidently. "You have a crew of well-trained combat soldiers. You wouldn't ask me for assistance unless you were in dire need."

"You need us more," he argued. "The only way off this planet is in our ship."

"And according to you, the only way to repair this ship is if I help you," she countered.

Kyleren scowled, but Margariete refused to yield, though her heart pounded furiously.

"Fine," he agreed. "Can't make you a promise, but if you help, I'll see what I can do."

Margariete opened her mouth to argue that she wouldn't participate unless her freedom was guaranteed, but she hesitated at the last moment. The technology of this shard was the most advanced she had ever encountered. She doubted she could persuade LAMIE to fly without the GAELs.

"Then let's finish this," Margariete proclaimed, stepping past him and into the corridor.

She imagined she could feel his loathing scalding into her back as she walked, but she continued down the stairs boldly until she reached the second level. Here she paused, unsure of which direction to go. Kyleren brushed past her and descended to the lowest deck, taking a left to the docking bay. Gene paced anxiously near the exit hatch. An enormous travel pack hung from his shoulders and seemed on the brink of toppling him. When he saw Margariete, he squeaked and jerked his hands, dropping a dataplate he had been hugging. It skittered across the floor with a clatter.

"Gene, what are you doin'?" Kyleren asked in exasperation.

"I just dropped my dataplate," he apologized, bending to retrieve the fallen computer device. His overlarge knapsack smacked him on the head as he did so.

"Ouch," he complained, rubbing the injury as he straightened. "Don't worry, it's not broken."

"I meant what are you doin' with that bag?" Kyleren said, pointing.

Gene's eyes brightened.

"Oh, just some things I might need."

"We're only goin' six kilometers, Gene," the GAEL said.

"Well, over uncharted territory that could take several hours at walking speed. We might get hungry and who knows, we might have to spend a night out there.

According to my calculations, there are only a few hours of light left on this planet."

Gene adjusted the pack several times, failing to find a more comfortable position.

"We're not walkin' Gene," Lance corrected. "The colonel and Trish can't wait. We're runnin'."

"Running?" Gene mouthed.

"Ditch the pack," Kyleren ordered. "One canteen and one ration. Take only the minimum tech you need to hack the generator systems."

Gene simply stared, taking no action to comply.

"Unless," Margariete added, "you'd like to spend the night out there with *me*."

The pack hit the floor. Gene rummaged through its contents like a wild animal, hastily gathering a few items. Margariete smiled, catching the lieutenant's quiet chuckle through a sidelong glance. Irritated that they might have shared humor over the same incident, she stormed through the hatch.

A wide swath of rust-colored soil peeled through the thick aquamarine grassland behind the ship—LAMIE's makeshift landing strip. The ground was spongy rather than solid, the rolling landscape of turf stretched to the green horizon. Large ochre pylons of a pumice jutted through the sod, like rotted teeth. To the east, the land flattened and smoothed into the bright liquid of a gigantic sea, though it was too far away to see properly. The alien grass hummed strangely in the wind, singing a high-pitched melody that sounded not unlike the vibrating ring of a crystal goblet.

Lieutenant Kyleren led them, loping at a stable pace so that Gene lagged only a short distance behind. Margariete enjoyed the exercise, having been cooped inside the confines of space vessels for several long trinals, though she wished they had been able to travel more quickly. Only a quarter arc into their journey, Gene pleaded for respite.

"Stop!" Gene he begged through gasps. "I can't run anymore."

His willowy legs sank into the tall bristles of sod as his hands fumbled for his water container. The telepath rubbed her neck sullenly as she and the GAEL circled back.

"This is going to take forever," Margariete complained to Kyleren. "We could get there in half the time without this idiot."

"We need him," Kyleren refuted. "Unless you think you can turn off the generator by yourself? Only five minutes, Gene."

Margariete looked away in disgust.

"And I'm not an idiot," Gene piped. "I'll have you know I'm the most gifted technobionomist in my generation. You can't beat that."

"I was not referring to your intelligence," Margariete snapped, "but your weakness of fortitude."

Gene reddened, embarrassed.

"Hey, without me you're stuck here. I created the ship that brought you."

"How nice of you," Margariete offered sarcastically. "Unfortunately, your amazing creation crashed."

"Leave him alone, Mags," Kyleren commanded, sweeping the area for possible enemies. "He's done nothin' to you."

Margariete turned away from them, staring across the open plain in silence for the duration of their break. As Kyleren ordered Gene to stand, the telepath noted the solider rubbed at his shoulder with a grimace.

"Is your wound bothering you?" she asked.

"I'm fine," he threw out with a growl. "I fixed it myself."

"The LT nanomites would have stopped working after we entered the field, lieutenant," Gene inserted. "How long has it been since they were injected?"

"Four hours."

Gene's mind ticked away a set of calculations.

"That's not long enough for complete regeneration," he said. "You must be in considerable pain."

"Nanomites?" Margariete asked.

"Microscopic machines protoed to perform certain medical tasks," Gene answered absently. "In this case, they were meant to stimulate the healing process of Lieutenant Kyleren's stab wound."

"Let me see it," she demanded, extracting the quirr jar from her pouch.

"Forget it," Kyleren mumbled. "I told you I was fine."

"You're a bad liar, lieutenant," Margariete proclaimed crossly. "An injury like that could fester if you don't take care of it, and get the rest of us killed. Let me treat it."

Kyleren's expression plainly doubted her sincerity, but he allowed her ministrations regardless. His black combat armor dropped to the grass and he stripped to the waist. Margariete coughed to cover her stunned gasp as he revealed the rippling splendor of his muscled chest and abdomen, and had to staunch an uninvited flutter that tickled her stomach. She carefully removed the stiff medical dressing and dabbed the healing ointment onto Kyleren's skin.

"What is that stuff?" Gene asked.

"Quirr," she replied. "A healing agent. It soothes pain and prevents infection."

"Wow," Gene said, truly impressed. "I've never heard of that before. Is it rare?"

"Not in the shard it comes from," the telepath explained.

"The what?" Kyleren asked, looking at her.

"Nevermind," she answered, fighting an unexpected blush that tainted her cheeks. Margariete hid her face behind a heavy wave of hair.

"But now we're curious," Gene pouted.

Margariete applied the quirr until she was certain the flush had drained from her complexion. As she replaced the cap to the jar, both men watched her expectantly. For a moment, she wondered what to do. Dismiss the topic? Lie? But then one of Raeylan's lessons sprang from memory: even enemies will respect those bound by truth.

She replaced the bandages on the lieutenant's shoulder. "Do you have a creation story that describes your people's beginning?" she asked.

Gene nodded.

"The Bang. The establishment of recorded history."

"This 'Bang' of yours is known by another name to my people. We call it the Fracturing—the uncontrolled destruction that split the universe into different shards. Your universe is one of these shards. I come from another."

"So the doctor was right," Gene interposed excitedly, nearly jumping up and down in excitement. "You're from somewhere on the other side of the Black Reach!"

Margariete bit her lip in indecision.

"If that's what you call the impassible boundaries that keep the worlds apart, the shardwalls."

"You're mistaken. It isn't impassible. The Black Reach is an area of space so vast all attempts to survey it have resulted in nothing past the Dintigel Asteroid Belt."

"Then it's not a shardwall," Margariete grumbled. "Only the servants of Nehro can pass through them."

Gene looked frustrated. Margariete shared the scientist's aggravation. Technological cultures were always the same, refusing to believe the nature of the shards and the events that caused the universe to shatter. For some reason, they relied only on what their science could explain, snubbing the truth in favor of their "enlightenment."

She averted her eyes as the lieutenant pulled his uniform over his bare chest. She added, "Look, I know you don't trust me. But before you accuse me of conspiring with your enemies, you have to understand. I am not from your universe."

"There isn't anythin' more than this universe, Blue Eyes," Kyleren argued. "Don't try to feed us that skrit."

"Choose to believe what you will, but it doesn't make reality a lie," she countered. "I'm unlike anyone you've ever met, able to do things you all think are impossible. I can control your mind, see into your thoughts. I even electrified your companion."

Kyleren's eyes narrowed.

"I was wondering about that actually," Gene intruded. "How did you manage to levitate Sergeant Reynolds? The scientific community has been working on that kind of tech for centuries, but all laws of technobionomy prohibit it. And then there's the matter of your invisibility booster. The only thing we have that's even close to that kind of complete stealth is the Sylph camouflage systems."

"I was never invisible," Margariete stated.

"Then how'd you appear out of nowhere, Blue Eyes?" Kyleren asked doubtfully. "When you attacked us in the mess?"

"Teleportation," she said with a shrug. "But something went wrong. I didn't mean to materialize on your ship."

"No way," Gene said, shaking his head. "The ability to transfer matter from one place to another without an STT drive is strictly impossible."

"Yet, I did it," Margariete smirked.

"Then tell us, Mags," Kyleren probed sardonically, "how'd you do all this impossible stuff?"

She recklessly dived into the truth.

"Magic, of course."

Kyleren glowered and Gene snorted. They assumed she was mocking them. She threw up her hands in impatient disgust. Moving to the front of the little group, intent on zipping into the wide grassland, Margariete tossed words at them heatedly.

"You can refuse to believe me, lieutenant, but I find that entirely ridiculous since you have a fair bit of Shardwell magic yourself!"

"What're you talkin' about?" the lieutenant asked. "I don't have any magic."

"Then explain how your 'special' abilities disappeared at the same time as mine!"

"You've got some kinda livin' tech," he maintained.

"Until this cycle, I've never heard of such a thing," Margariete responded.

"If you really aren't from this part of the universe," Gene postulated, "then you might not have. Living tech is a natural ore found only on the surface of Athalonde Prime. It obtains sentience when the material is combined in large quantities or complex machines. The larger the object, the

165

more self-awareness it grows. But whatever technology you have right now isn't working because of the mire field."

Margariete waived his explanation away angrily.

"Magic is power from the gods, regardless of what you call it. I grew up in a culture whose height of technological advancement was limited to swords and knives! I have never been exposed to your 'living tech.' I was born with my abilities. And as for your mire field," she roared, "all it does is disrupt magic. That's why LAMIE can't communicate with you, that's why your nanomites are silent!"

She pointed an accusatory finger at Kyleren.

"And that's why you can't use any of your abilities!"

The telepath dashed heedlessly forward toward their target, not bothering to check if either of her companions followed. She cursed her twin, wherever he happened to be. Telling the truth hadn't had any effect at all.

17: LET'S GET OUT OF HERE BEFORE ONE OF THOSE THINGS KILLS GUY

Magic and gods? Gene scoffed at how so many people in the universe could be fooled into following ridiculous fanaticism—like the Vartal and their brainless rituals or the Morrigans' blind devotion to fictional personages. Their empty beliefs hadn't kept the GAELs from infiltrating the Agromor defense satellite nor saved the dark elves' most revered temple on Agrona. The goddess Danu had not appeared to offer even the slightest objection as the ancient monoliths of her shrine tumbled into ruin. True, some of the Morrigans—officially recognized as dwarves in the Coalition—had the sense to flee from their backwards star system when blending was outlawed on Babd and Makos, but as a whole, their race stubbornly clung to outdated superstitions.

But this Margariete woman plunged herself into a level of insanity that surpassed all rational explanation. "Magic" was simply a description for physical laws that could not be explained by pre-scientific culture. Through technology and study, nothing was beyond manipulation—except for teleportation, mind control, and telekinesis of course.

Gene's head spun dizzily as he tried to keep up with the two people who led him. He wondered if the disorientation was caused by the unaccustomed exercise or the barrage of hypotheses that rattled around his brain.

It was expected of an uneducated culture to explain unusual phenomena as "miracles from the gods," but the dark-haired stranger who had infiltrated their ship displayed at least a basic understanding of simple technology, like the operation of firearms and comprehension of space flight. Her extraordinary abilities had to be a result of super advanced tech. Either her society had convinced her that technological enhancement was nothing more than a manifestation of power from whatever religion she practiced, or she was lying.

Gene, enfolded in silent speculation, plowed clumsily into Margariete when she ducked behind a large rock. Lieutenant Kyleren grabbed him by the arm and dragged him behind the cover. A lumpy facility had appeared in their path.

"So what now?" Gene wheezed after a few minutes of labored breathing, his abdomen clenching uncomfortably.

Margariete shushed him harshly. Kyleren scanned ahead with a pair of ocular lenses, but Gene resisted the urge to point out that the device wouldn't work in the mire field. The GAEL passed them to Margariete with a grunt.

"They must not be expecting company," she commented after a pause. "Only four guards."

"That we can see," Kyleren corrected. "We gotta get over that wall to get better intel."

Wall? Gene groaned inwardly as the brunette tossed him the ocular lenses. The machine's display offered substandard resolution, grainy and blurred, but the high stone barrier encircling the complex was easily discernible.

The spikes running along its lip looked particularly daunting. Two large metal doors seemed to be the only way in or out.

"There is no way I'll be able to climb that wall," Gene whined grumpily, his hands slick with sweat.

Kyleren and Margariete bent over a rudimentary sketch of their target that the lieutenant had scratched into the ground with a nearby stick, but both looked up at Gene with annoyance at his complaint.

"You'll be fine, Gene," Kyleren said dismissively.

"Why can't we just blast our way in?" Gene asked, pointing to the explosives on Kyleren's belt.

"Because that'd alert every gromm bastard in the compound," the soldier replied. "We need to slip in quiet."

"Then we should wait for dark so we can open the door," Gene suggested. "That's in two hours."

"Send me over the wall," Margariete demanded, ignoring Gene's idea completely. "I can scout for more guards and find another entrance."

"And sound an alarm if you're a gromm spy," the lieutenant shot back acerbically. "Forget it, Blue Eyes. I'm not lettin' you outta my sight."

"I already told you I don't work for these Agromors," she retorted sharply.

"You also said you use magic," Gene recalled.

Margariete's expression was as prickly as ice. Gene swallowed dryly, afraid to break her gaze. After a moment, she turned back to Kyleren.

"You need me on the wall while you shoot down the guards," she reasoned. "My skills are not limited to my magic."

Gene watched the lieutenant consider her argument. When Kyleren nodded an affirmation, Gene's objections spilled out of his mouth without restraint.

"Seriously? Just like that you're going to trust her?" he shouted, jumping to his feet in agitation.

The next thing the technobionomist knew, he was sprawled on the ground face first, unsure of which warrior had tackled him first.

"Frag, Gene!" Kyleren said, roughly yanking the lanky technobionomist upright with a frown. "You coulda given away our position. Don't do that again."

"Right. Sorry," Gene apologized, running a shaky hand through his hair. "I won't."

Kyleren turned his attention to his weapons, prepping for an assault. Then he passed a threader to Margariete. The GAEL explained its function quickly, showing the brunette how its projected grappling hook would launch from the barrel, then retract to pull her up the wall's lateral surface. She tried not to look impressed, but Gene thought he saw genuine awe in her sapphire eyes.

Again he felt baffled. How could someone who obviously used advanced technology react that way? It wasn't possible, there was no such thing as magic. And yet—

A memory of his first year at Lamorak University on Lludd sprung out of his neatly labeled consciousness. He had been leagues beyond his fellow students in the field, his instinctual understanding of technobionomy more advanced than that of his professors.' During his second year, he had discovered a formulaic principle that converged the fundamental theory of technobionomy into six distinctive signatures, but his instructors merely scoffed at the viability of his mathematical proof. In the history of science since the Bang, only one signature had been recorded throughout the universe. His calculations might be flawless, but his Six Signature Theory could never be measured in the physical world.

Or could it? he thought suddenly.

This Margariete might prove it true. Her odd assortment of belongings had tested negative for any living tech regularities. Perhaps if he modified the scanning equipment to register alternate frequency signals? Also, the LT instruments he had used might have been unable to detect algorithms that began with a different wave emission period than their own.

"Gene," Kyleren barked, jolting the brilliant thinker from his inner scientific exploration, "focus!"

"What?" Gene asked innocently as his two companions stared at him with irate impatience. "I was—"

"Do you have more of these threaders?" Margariete asked Kyleren, interrupting Gene's excuse.

"One for each of us," Kyleren explained.

Margariete stared down at the threader, biting her bottom lip. A moment later the corners of her mouth turned in a savvy smile that lit her eyes.

"I have an idea," she said, "but I don't think either of you will like it."

18: In Space No One Can Hear You Scream

Vivian tapped open the wooden doors to her office and let the precise clack of her beaded shoes on the polished floor calm her mind. Anya was safe. The Faidh Seer, High Priestess of Danu, had personally vowed to protect her. Vivian just hoped the shiidh ship managed to reach the Danaan System before the Coalition could intercept it.

Vivian regretted having to send her sister away. Anya's heart lay in her life's work, with the patients she treated and cared for. Sending her to the shiidh would likely sever her connection with the Ninevay lineage, but in her heart, Vivian had always known this day would come. Anya was unusual among the Kildar elves. Her destiny had finally caught her.

As Vivian walked to her desk, she didn't bother activating the lights. The soft radiance from the window and the perpetual glow from the desk's outer rim illuminated the room well enough. She had come to complete the details on a new transportation project intended for the lower district of the city. She slid into her chair and tapped her ident code into the crystal screen that doubled as the surface of her desk.

It was then that she noticed the intruder. He detached from the walls in haze of black vapor. It coalesced into the solid form of a man as it reached the foot of her desk. Vivian had never seen anything like it. His black armor reeked of burned blood. She had to swallow hard to keep herself from trembling.

"The Silver Shadow," she said, flicking her gaze across the unusual shine of his hair. "I expected you sooner."

The man stroked the hilt of a dagger at his belt, his mouth splitting into a maliciously amused grin.

"I'm afraid I was detained, prime minister. My other 'appointment' in the city was inconsiderately less than punctual." He loosed the dagger from its garish red sheath. "But don't worry, I managed to rearrange my schedule for you."

Vivian's tongue felt heavy. She willed herself not to give in to fear. This was, after all, what she had expected. She calmed herself with the thought that, whatever the outcome here, she had already won. Anya and the information she carried were out of the assassin's reach.

"So kill me," she dared brazenly.

The man's teeth glimmered between his lips and he tilted his head to the side as he laughed.

"Straight to business. Your reputation precedes you, prime minister. But death will find you soon enough. First, you're going to answer my questions."

Vivian briefly considered refusing, but decided that the longer she kept the killer occupied, the better for her sister. The Coalition probably knew what information she had gathered anyway.

"Then ask your questions," she replied proudly, leaning back in her chair with more control than she felt.

The assassin plunged the point of his weapon into the crystadisplay surface of the desk, startling Vivian with its glassy crack and electric spark. The computer sputtered as he leaned forward.

"You have information that could damage the interests of the Coalition," he said as he leered.

Vivian's eyebrows raised in challenge.

"The interests of the Coalition, or Chancellor Medrod?"

The assassin's eyes gleamed with malicious glee as he pulled away.

"My, my, you have been busy, Madame Ninevay. How long did it take you to discover the truth?"

"My suspicions began decades ago, shortly after the chancellor started shifting power away from the Round. Laws were passed that left loopholes in the regulations of living technology development, restrictions that would have prevented the experimentation that led to the creation of your secret GraEL Attached Elite Level VICs. I believe you call them GAELs?"

"Yes, the bonded soldier project was quite a success," he returned. "Until, of course, you tipped our hand to the Vartal. Two entire generations of soldiers were lost with Gwydion's destruction."

"I'll remember to grieve them," Vivian said.

"Their blood is on your conscience, prime minister. You murdered members of the Coalition military forces."

"And how many children died under the direction of your chancellor when he had them bonded with the GraEL? How many people are being held against their will, tortured in the labs under my city?"

"Very good, minister," he laughed, though Vivian could tell the assassin wasn't as impressed by her intel as he seemed.

She had missed something.

"If you had not been so foolish as to stall the chancellor's grand design, he well may have offered you a place in his regime to come."

He yanked the dagger free and fondled its wicked point.

"I am afraid that you have become a liability."

"Death," Vivian said, straightening, "will suit me better than playing a part in the atrocities of a megalomaniac. His deeds will follow him to the Void without redemption."

The assassin cackled cruelly.

"The Void cannot condemn those who rule it," he smirked.

"You refer to the chancellor as if he was a god," Vivian countered.

"He is," the assassin replied coolly, slashing the blade horizontally with lightning speed.

Vivian felt a nasty sting, and then the warm drip of blood as it slid down her skin.

And then she never felt anything ever again.

19: What You Plan And What Takes Place Ain't Ever Exactly Been Similar

Gene winced as the Vartal guards pressed his face into the springy mix of Danaan sod. The manacles his captors snapped onto his wrists pinched uncomfortably. He watched helplessly as the two elves rummaged through his belongings, rattling comments through their uncommon accent.

Off to Gene's right, Lieutenant Kyleren roared in protest, convincingly throwing three Vartal soldiers to the ground, even without the benefit of his GAEL strength. A fourth scurried behind the gargantuan VIC, snapping an instrument against the warrior's neck. Gene worried over what drug the enemy soldier had injected—more importantly, he doubted that the look of surprise on Kyleren's face was only show. Until today, the GAEL had been immune to every toxin the galaxy had to offer. The VIC snarled and seemed on the verge of panic, clawing at the back of his neck where the offending substance had entered his body. Then he crashed to the ground, staring vacantly forward as the Vartal easily restrained his hands.

Already the brunette's plan to enter the compound through capture had careened into an excess of unaccountable variables. Kyleren wasn't supposed to be drugged. Margariete's hidden weapons had been discovered and confiscated. What if they were taken to separate cells? What if they were transported to Agrona immediately? What if the Vartal executed them right now? What if, what if, what if!

The plan was swiftly disintegrating into the field of chaos theory. These Vartal were using nearly extinct tech— the manacles were a crude assembly of working parts, absent of electronic interfaces. If their prison cells were just as ancient, he would be unable to hack them. The small energy disruptor tiles he had shoved into the toe of his socks would be useless. Their only hope would be to somehow procure a key. Lieutenant Kyleren would now be a worthless ally until the mire field was deactivated and his GAEL immunities neutralized the enemy's poison.

Gene hadn't accounted for this in his calculations. When Kyleren vehemently opposed Margariete's idea, Gene hadn't understood the GAEL's reluctance. Every variable the VIC could produce was easily countered by either Margariete or the technobionomist. But, having lived their entire lives in a universe of technology, neither the lieutenant nor Gene had conceived one particular circumstance—that the Vartal would be using ancient technology.

The Vartal yanked Gene roughly to his feet, Margariete drawn upright next to him. It took four granite-skinned elves to drag the unresponsive GAEL to his knees. The technobionomist risked a sideways glance at Margariete, but she was preoccupied with a tactical survey of the compound, apparently unconcerned with the turn of events.

He attempted to follow the woman's example by scanning the area for probable means of escape. They were just inside the impassable wall, a foggy domed building straight ahead. Through the glass orifice, Gene could make out the distorted shape of the equipment on the other side. Spindly tubes and wide conduits fed into a rounded portion of the structure. Some were humming with power. The technobionomist figured there must be some sort of generator in there.

Immediately to the right and left were six aerial transport pod units, characteristically squat and prefabricated for easy drop off. Though these were manufactured by the Vartal, they looked enough like Coalition military issue to be recognized for what they were.

Gene's captor pushed him forward before he was ready, so he stumbled. Two heavy spiked doors yawned open into the domed building, and for a second, Gene felt like some bizarre metallic monster was spitting another enemy solider out of its jaws. This one displayed a more elaborate uniform than the others. By the way the other Vartal deferred to him, Gene assumed he was some sort of command official.

Though the elf's race made him appear young enough to have just finished his first year of university, his speckled eyes were laced with experience that could only be earned with age. His quick steps pounded against the ground like metal against metal. The commander picked over Gene and Margariete like carrion over a corpse, but his granite face split into an exhibit of menacing teeth when his eyes found Kyleren.

The commander strode to the unresisting GAEL, immediately drawing the lieutenant's core drive out of its protective sheath. Gene sucked in a breath of panic. If that drive were smashed, Kyleren would die. But more disturbing was the clear smirk of recognition that painted the commander's lips. The Agromors weren't supposed to know anything about the GAELs. That information was jealously guarded.

"Take him to the medical bay," the commander ordered. "Egrin will examine him."

His subordinate Vartal nodded deferentially. Then the four elves wrangled the heavy GAEL toward one of the pod units. Gene whimpered pathetically.

The Agromor commander turned. One of Margariete's guards handed her weapons over, and the leader's navy eyebrows lifted. The Vartal commander ignored her sidearms and knife, instead running his spidery fingers along the length of Margariete's sheathed sword.

"This is an odd weapon for an infidel. Who is she?" he asked, looking at the elf who had handed him the blade. The lead Vartal did not even look at Margariete.

The subordinate soldier repeated the question to Margariete, but she didn't answer.

Gene wished he had paid a little more attention to their culturalist, Percy, or at least had the foresight to ask questions regarding the basics of Vartal military society. Vaguely, he remembered that the higher an elf ranked, the less likely he was to speak with outsiders directly. This commander must be something important.

The technobionomist's heart pounded so frantically that he thought it might crack his chest as his female captor shoved him into the domed building. They shuffled through passages and corridors so quickly that he was soon lost in their sterility. The dim lights, barely enough to see by for a human, flickered weirdly, a side effect of the mire field. Doors and archways provided exits in multiple walls, but his guards took none of these as they penetrated deeper into the structure.

Just as he decided he had been pulled through the ghastly passageways for eternity, his Vartal guard jerked him backward. A curious contraption protruded from a door on his left. Gene was bewildered when the elf twisted it and pushed. The door swung inward on a pivot, or maybe hinges. Despite his discomfort, Gene stepped closer to it, hopeful to discover exactly how the mechanism worked.

Unfortunately, his feet tripped on a slight variation of the otherwise smooth floor as he craned his neck for a better view at the door. The fall slammed the breath from his chest because his hands were bound uselessly behind him. His vision splintered into fields of black and white. He felt the clawing hands of his captor dig into his arms and a slew of Vartal profanity rang through his head.

And then two loud thumps penetrated the haze in his mind, followed by an angry shout. He felt the hands on his body release and he slumped back to the floor. A weapon discharge smacked through the air. Gene struggled to turn his face toward it. When he finally managed an unobstructed view, Margariete already rummaged through the pockets of one of the guards. Somehow, she had managed to get her shackled hands in front of her. All three Vartal lay motionless on the floor.

"Good distraction," she commended as she pulled a set of keys from the belt of her vanquished victim.

After freeing herself, she tossed them to him. He fumbled and almost dropped the jangling ring as his brunette companion stripped the guards of their weapons.

His attempt to unshackle his restraints was less than pathetic.

Gene had only seen physical access devices like this in the holotexts he studied as a student. There were at least seven keys in the stack and he had no idea which matched his manacles. Lastly, his hands were still secured awkwardly behind his back. After several failed tries, Margariete growled and none-too-gently released him herself.

"Thanks," Gene muttered, rubbing the chafed skin of his wrists and tenderly patting the large bump forming on his forehead.

Margariete shoved his dataplate into one of his hands and a commandeered pistol into his belt.

"If you're as clumsy with a weapon as your feet, do not shoot that unless I'm dead," she ordered.

Gene nodded meekly and shifted his gaze away. The evidence of her wrath lay scattered around him, and he had no desire to be its next target.

"Which way?" she asked.

Gene peered into the passage they had just left. There were several corridors that forked on either side.

"One of the hallways on the right," he answered, hypothesizing from his earlier review of the exterior that one had to lead toward the generator.

Margariete nodded, leading the way. She moved with the confidence of experience, as if infiltrating an Agromor base was something she did on a regular basis. At every junction she scanned for enemies, her pistol prepped for fire. Gene admired the way she slid around corners with less noise than a stealth shield. In contrast, his shuffling steps seemed to announce their exact position to everyone in the compound.

At the end of one particular hallway, Margariete held up her hand in warning and Gene stopped. He heard the clicking of a mechanical door and then voices.

"He's sure?" asked a distinct Morrigan accent.

"Yes," a slimmer, more refined male voice answered. "Test him immediately. This will advance our knowledge of the GAELs—"

The voices slowly drifted away. Gene exhaled deeply, unaware he had been holding his breath.

"That must be Egrin," Margariete whispered. "He'll lead us to Kyleren."

"Look, I don't want you to think I'm overreacting," Gene twittered, "but this is bad. Really, *really* bad. We have to deactivate the mire field before that scientist gets his hairy fingers into Kyleren. And we have to check whatever research he already has on the GAELs."

"Why?" Margariete asked, moving closer to him.

"These guys shouldn't even know that the GAEL VICs exist, but the gromm commander seems to know exactly what Kyleren is. We can't let them figure out more."

"So you want to destroy the information they have?" Margariete asked.

"No, I want to see how much they know," Gene clarified.

Margariete nodded and trotted down the abandoned hallway. Only one door interrupted the wall. She carefully cracked it open and peered inside.

"It's empty," she reported.

Gene slipped in. The twelve-meter room hummed with dead tech monitors and consoles, many flickering like a scratched holodisk. Clusters of what appeared to be archeological relics dominated the central table. The walls sported blackened panels of slate where someone, maybe

Egrin, had painted long strings of equations in a powdery white substance. Several dataplates littered sterile metal workstations and outdated keyboards. He punched a few buttons and the terminals prompted him for an access code.

That could be any number of things. For a moment he turned his attention to the equations on the walls. They circled around the room, ending abruptly, as if someone had been interrupted mid-calculation. The longer he studied the material, the more the theory it represented took shape in Gene's mind. The beauty of its unique perspective rivaled even some of his own work.

"This is incredible," Gene said, touching the white lines gingerly.

When Margariete didn't respond, he turned toward her with alarm, suddenly remembering they were in an enemy stronghold.

But the brunette stranger hadn't been spirited away by an onslaught of Vartal. Instead, she fingered one of the objects—a brittle looking parchment—unrolled on the relic table. Her face was completely unreadable, terrifying in its placidity. She seemed to have faded into herself. Then, so quickly that Gene could have sworn he heard her return-to-focus snap through the air, she gathered the objects in a flurry of motion. Margariete wound the paper around a long metal rod attached to its base, forming some type of scroll. She snatched a leather bag that lay near it and stuffed the scroll inside, along with five others that had rested on the table. These were followed by an embroidered pouch, two pale blue chunks of quartz, and a curved sword that she thrust through her belt.

"Are you okay?" Gene asked when she appeared to be finished.

"I'll be fine once we finish this," she returned, offering no explanation to her actions. As she slung the bag over her shoulder she waved at the slate walls. "What does this all mean?"

"He's figured out how to perfect the expanded mire field," Gene said, returning to his analysis. "If the Agromors successfully implement it—"

He broke off, following the formulas to where they stopped. The theory wasn't quite complete.

"This is only most of it. I bet he has the rest on file."

Gene leapt back to the computer terminals and began dismantling its outer casing.

"We don't have time for this," Margariete argued.

"It will only take a second," he promised as the outer shell of the machine peeled away.

He sifted through the myriad internal wires and processing boards. In a few minutes, he had extracted the terminal's main memory tile and held it aloft in triumph.

"Everything we'll need to know about his work will be on this."

Before he even registered her movement, Margariete snatched the octagonal tile from his fingers and smashed it under the firm heel of her boot.

"What are you doing?" Gene yelped.

Margariete stepped out of the way as Gene frantically gathered the remaining splinters of the most unique scientific discovery since the galaxy invented blending. But even at first glance he recognized his efforts as useless. The tile looked too damaged. When he finally stood, Margariete had obliterated the remaining information on the slate walls with a piece of cloth.

"Are you completely insane?" Gene yelled in exasperation.

"This technology is a threat to all the magic in the shards," she said. "I cannot allow it to exist, and neither should you."

"But in the right hands this research could—"

"—destroy the universe," Margariete finished severely. "This kind of control cannot belong to anyone. I've seen with my own eyes what becomes of those who hold too much power."

"But this information would have helped the Coalition to counter the Agromors! Maybe even win us the war!"

"According to you, this shard has been at war for centuries," Margariete stated. "My concern is the protection of *all* the shards."

"Well, you've definitely fragged the GAELs," Gene complained. "You've trashed any chance I had to see what the Agromors know about the VIC bonded soldiers."

Her eyes seemed to soften. "For that I am sorry."

Gene didn't trust himself to respond. Margariete moved back to the door and checked the hallway.

"Let's go," she commanded.

As she slipped out of the room, Gene tucked the memory tile fragments into his pocket. Maybe there was a chance he could put it back together once LAMIE was fully repaired. On his way out he appropriated the nearest dataplate and stuffed it down the front of his shirt.

Margariete was already at the end of the passage, so he hurried. She turned left at the junction. Just as he caught her, Vartal shouts echoed from behind. Startled, Gene looked back, but the immediate vicinity was empty.

"The Agromors must have found our guards," Margariete whispered. "We don't have much time."

Two more turns brought them up against a banded set of metal doors, taller and wider than anything they had encountered. The sound of electricity hummed low along the walls.

"This must be it," Gene whispered urgently. A high-pitched alarm pealed through the building and the flickering lights turned an ugly shade of orange.

Margariete inclined her head at the door.

"Stay low until I give you a signal."

She pushed the heavy door open with her body, pistols raised. Gene followed, crouching low behind her. Her weapons seemed to discharge in all directions at once. A backward glance revealed more enemy Vartal charging their direction from the corridor. Margariete was still engaged with her forward attack, so Gene slammed himself against the door, groaning with effort to shut them. He searched frantically for some type of locking mechanism. Three silver knobs ran the length of the two doors. He twisted them all, satisfied to hear a muffled clunk inside the metal frames. Hopefully, that would keep them out.

By the time he turned, Margariete had felled the three Vartal stationed inside the room. She pushed him out of the way, planting herself between him and the door.

"I'll take care of them, you shut down the generator," she said.

Control panels flashed and beeped from every available surface. Some were smoldering—collateral damage from the firefight. Three of the walls were metal, but one was heavy glass that overlooked a circular undulating dintillium core room on the other side. Loud bangs emanated from the door Margariete guarded as the Vartal attempted to breach it.

"Turning the generator off is going to be the easy part," Gene mumbled as he approached the ancient keyboards.

20: I HAVE BEEN AND ALWAYS SHALL BE YOUR FRIEND

A hazy glaze of content spread a waxy sheet across Kyleren's senses. Objects blurred at the edges in his vision, sounds muffled through his ears like a wet glob. His body tingled loosely as he reclined on the cold surface of some chair. He tried to scratch a tickle at the base of his neck, but found that his hands were bound by metallic restraints. Other bands compressed his torso and ankles.

Something poked into his arm and sent a buzzing vibration into his head. Kyleren flopped it to one side so he could see. Through the lethargic fog he noted a pair of beady dwarf eyes glowering at him thoughtfully. It twisted its syringe further into Kyleren's bicep, extracting samples of blood and tissue. Past the dwarf, Kyleren spotted another prisoner confined by one of the restrictive chairs.

Then everything turned a washy shade of orange and a high-pitched drone squealed through the air. The dwarf snorted and ignored the alarm, climbing a stool next to a long counter of medical equipment. A Vartal commander stood near the door, barking orders into the hallway. The elf glanced angrily at the dwarf, drew his weapon, and turned to leave.

Kyleren wondered whether he should offer to help—he remembered that his occupation had something to do with fighting—but then a heavy clout sucked the air from his lungs. It was like the pressure of a gigantic hand squeezing his torso. Just as he thought he might black out, a small blot of warm yellow light in the back of his head pushed the darkness away.

He felt the rapid pulse of his core drive vaporize the drugs in his system. GAEL strength snapped back into his limbs like whiplash.

He smirked. The mire field was down.

One flex of his muscles and his enhanced strength burst the metal binders from the chair. In two seconds, he had retrieved his core drive from the instrument table and slammed it into his confiscated BT pistol. A single shot to the head and the dwarf hit the floor.

Kyleren twisted toward the door to dispatch the Vartal commander, but was puzzled to see the other prisoner already confronting the elf. The stranger yanked Margariete's sword from the Vartal's belt with a hand scored by some kind of terrible frostbite. Kyleren glanced at the other chair.

How had the man managed to get past him so fast? And the binders on the chair were still clamped shut. How had he escaped?

An expert blow to the skull by the other prisoner and the Vartal crumpled unconscious. Though both imprisoned by the Agromors, Kyleren wasn't willing to take a chance with the newcomer, not with his comrades' lives on the line. He trained his weapon between the stranger's twilight grey eyes.

"Give me that sword," Kyleren demanded.

The man stared at him with stoic calm, but made no move to comply.

Kyleren swore as the face-off continued and considered popping off a round into the stranger's leg to incapacitate him. What was the man waiting for?

Then Kyleren blinked.

Impossibly, the man had closed the distance between them, holding the point of the sword at Kyleren's throat. Lance hadn't even heard the thing come loose from the sheath. He barely managed to react, pressing his sidearm against the stranger's forehead.

"This sword does not belong to you," the man stated without even a flinch.

"It doesn't belong to you either, friend," Kyleren replied.

The man's eyebrows lifted faintly and he slowly lowered his blade.

"You know Margariete?" he asked.

Kyleren figured he shouldn't be surprised. This was the second crazy grommsack he'd met in less than a DST week.

"Yeah," Kyleren said, refusing to lower his own weapon. "Likes to piss people off."

The stranger sheathed the sword and pushed it securely through his belt.

"I am Raeylan," he said. "Margariete is my sister."

"That's gromm skrit," Kyleren returned, glancing poignantly at the man's light features and blonde hair. "Mags never mentioned a brother."

"Mags?" Raeylan asked, a hint of a smile dusting his lips. "She allows you to address her so?"

Kyleren shrugged, but remained wary.

"Didn't give her much of a choice."

"My sister's temper often rules her actions," Raeylan said fondly, taking a step back. "I imagine she does not respond well to your jest."

Kyleren snorted in agreement, his unease wavering. He felt inclined to believe this man, trust for him springing from the depths of his core drive. Besides, they stood a better chance of finding Margariete and Gene together. With that thought, he lowered the BT pistol.

"You her half-brother or somethin'?" Kyleren asked.

"I'm her twin," Raeylan explained, moving quickly to the door. "Do you know where she is?"

Kyleren nodded.

"Her and Gene must've shut down the mire field generator. Bet they're still around there."

"I will follow you then," Raeylan answered, moving aside and resting his disfigured hand on the hilt of his sword.

Kyleren wondered briefly what had caused the injury to Raeylan's arm as he checked the hallway for enemies. Three Vartal careened up the stairwell at the end of the corridor, weapons rising as soon as his head peered around the doorframe. Lance fired three precise shots, bringing them all down in a heap. A rapid trot brought him to the bodies, Raeylan following close behind.

As Kyleren bent to search the dead elves, two rounds blasted past his head from the other end of the passage. He had spun to return fire, catching one Vartal in the shoulder, when his companion disappeared from his side.

Lance's jaw fell open. Raeylan appeared between the two enemies, almost 50 meters away. Instantaneously. His sister's sword flashed twice in the orange rinsed light, parting the elves' heads from their shoulders. Raeylan rematerialized at Kyleren's flank before the two corpses collapsed to the concrete.

What. The. Frag.

Kyleren turned to Raeylan, prepared to ask the man just what kind of tech allowed him such a feat, when a thunderous explosion rocked the building. Shrapnel and steel ripped a gaping cavity through the walls, cutting the building nearly in half. Through the opening, he could see smoke belching 20 meters into the air from across the compound. Kyleren's questions went momentarily overlooked.

"I hope Mags wasn't in there," Kyleren said before thinking.

Raeylan's calm mask cracked with concern as he bolted in the explosion's direction.

21: SOMEBODY HAS TO SAVE OUR SKINS

Margariete adjusted the straps of Raeylan's pack so it would stop sliding down her arm if she had to roll her shoulder during an attack. The sheath of her twin's most recent sword was already secured to her belt, the blade itself brandished defensively in front of her. It was heavier than *Stardawn*, and not as finely wrought as Raeylan's original weapon, *Moonstone Retribution*, whose loss had frustrated him for nearly four centuries. This sword was thick near the hilt, curving into a flat flange at the tip, and noticeably off balance. They had acquired it in another shard, near the Gorta trading center, after Raeylan had shattered yet another blade.

Gene's chatter as he fiddled with the generator control panel razzled Margariete's calm. Most of his comments evaded her comprehension, thick as they were with unfamiliar technical terminology, but his frantic tone whittled her nerves raw. She twisted the hilt of the sword, counting her heartbeats as she tried to smooth her impatience, and wishing to Nehro that her powers would return. Their loss made her feel naked, blind to the air currents in the corridor on the other side of the doors. The entire base could be mounting a full assault behind them. She had no way to tell.

As she stood guard, a deluge of white sparks tore through the crack between the heavy door panels. Metal oozed down its surface as the first lock melted.

"Gene?" Margariete warned.

He didn't seem to hear, but continued with his nonsensical scientific prattle.

"Gene!" she barked as the second bolt disintegrated into hot liquid.

"What?" he said, raising his head.

"Hurry!"

"I'm working as fast as I can. If I'm not careful, I could accidentally polarize the coolant inducer in the accelerator drive from the platform generator...and that would vaporize us all. Right now I'm trying to recalibrate—"

"I don't care, Gene!" Margariete shouted, quickly shifting the sword to her left hand and drawing out a pistol with her right. The third lock was nearly breached. "Whatever you're doing, do it faster!"

"You can't rush science!" Gene complained, turning back to the machines.

Margariete briefly considered shooting him, just to prove a point, but the doors demanded her attention as they burst inward, spewing a rush of Vartal into the generator room. She blasted two of them square in the skull, then dropped the pistol in favor of a surer grip on the sword. She impaled the third Vartal intruder and kicked him backward off the blade into the path of newly arriving enemies. The corpse knocked three off balance and pinned them to the floor.

"Done!" Gene shouted triumphantly as the generator clanked loudly and died.

Suddenly, Margariete's head exploded with dappled streaks of color that dug heatedly into the sides of her head. Raeylan's sword clattered against the floor next to her ear, and she experienced a moment of confusion until she realized she must have collapsed. Tiny popping sensations crackled at the tip of her neck, opening a rush of sensation that slid through her body. Thought threads whipped into her mind like wind through a window during a storm. Her extrasensory vision deepened the orientation of her surroundings, like she had been trapped in a dark gooey murk for the arcs previous, and the unexpected restoration of sight and touch overwhelmed her.

The zing of an energy discharge jolted her back to focus. She rose to her feet as quickly as she dared. An enemy soldier looked past her in shock, his hands cradling a bloody hole where his knee had once been. Surprised, Margariete followed the Vartal's gaze. Gene trembled behind the generator interface, his pistol pointed at the elf in a limp grip and his eyes squelched shut.

Margariete finished the wounded elf with a kick to the temple. Then she bent the air around his body, pulling him five hand spans above the ground. Pressing against him with telekinetic force, she launched the fallen elf like a blunt projectile into the corridor. Only one of the oncoming rush of enemies managed to slip into the room unhindered. The rest tumbled into a mass of bone crunching yelps. The swarm of Vartal now heaped over itself in confusion, momentarily halted.

Margariete determined that her two disadvantages—the eerie weakness caused by the abrupt return of her powers and her battle-useless companion—made escape through the corridor impossible. With a flick of her eyes she slammed the doors, counting on the precious few seconds it would buy her. The lone Vartal who had made it into the room looked on in terror as she commanded Raeylan's sword to leap to her palm. He lifted his weapon.

"Don't move," she ordered, invoking the pressure of her telepathic sway.

She held the sword under the elf's granite-colored nose. "Do you recognize this blade?"

"Yes," the elf sputtered against his will.

"The man it belongs to, where is he?"

"In a medical lab on the other side of the compound."

Margariete drew the blade across the Vartal's throat, turning to Gene before the elf's corpse hit the floor.

"Gene, I told you to fire only if I was dead!"

"When you fell over, I thought you were," Gene squeaked.

"Well I'm not," Margariete spat, mentally pushing against the doors to counterbalance the Vartal shoving on the other side. Her head reeled painfully. "I think the sudden recovery of my magic did something to me."

Gene pursed his lips in thought.

"Well, if you were a GAEL, I would say that the abrupt resurgence of your graviton locus frequency had overwhelmed your body's capacity to compensate for the biorhythm disruption, making you momentarily vulnerable. But since you have to be using some sort of living tech—"

"Gene," Margariete snapped peevishly, "we have to get out of here. I can't hold them back much longer. Overload the generator."

Gene released a high-pitched snort. Margariete glared him into submission.

"That could destroy half of the complex," he argued.

"I'm counting on it," Margariete answered.

"But the lieutenant—"

"Should have his powers back by now. We don't have a choice. The elves block our only escape."

"What about us? We'll be caught in the blast!"

"Just make sure you do it without turning the mire field back on," Margariete instructed.

As Gene turned back to the generator console, muttering pathetically, Margariete retrieved her pistol and turned it upward. Three shots ruptured the opaque dome, opening a hole just wide enough for two people. All she had to do was time it correctly.

"That's it," Gene said sullenly.

Margariete waved him closer, then shut her eyes in concentration. Her extrasensory sight registered the room, the door, and the swell of enemies behind. Her skin tingled as she felt the air charge with the generator's power. It howled for escape, building and roiling over itself, but it had nowhere to go. Gene stepped next to her just as she released her hold on the door. Vartal streamed into the room as the energy erupted from its cage, belching their carcasses with cataclysmic fire.

As soon as she felt the vibrating tips of the explosion, Margariete concocted a barrier of air that channeled most of blast's force underneath her feet. Using her telekinesis to steady her path, she allowed the detonation's power to lift her and Gene upward to the dome.

Her most immediate concern was that they would miss the opening and be smashed against the ceiling. The effort to keep the angry energy of upsurge from consuming their bodies grew with every passing moment. Portions of her barrier dissolved into the fire. Sharp pieces of metal scraped her face, flame licked nasty burns through her clothes. She could feel blackness devouring the edges of her consciousness. Something warm trickled onto her lips and tongue. The air seared her lungs.

The only thing that existed in her mind was the hole in the dome. She could not die on this planet. Raeylan depended on her. Esilwen needed her. The shards could not fall to Kirion.

When her eyes opened Margariete was lying on her back, Gene hovering over her anxiously. His lips moved, but the words entered her ears in a tangled thread that took a few moments to unravel.

"Margariete, are you okay?"

She nodded and pushed herself to sitting. They were safely outside the smoking remains of the generator building. The soft sod had cushioned their landing. Shouts of Vartal soldiers rang through the dusky sky—the sun had set—as they tried to reorganize.

"What happened?"

"Somehow the blast didn't incinerate us," Gene answered hesitantly, unwilling to admit that her magic had been their salvation, "and we sort of—um—flew out the dome. Then you blacked out and we fell."

"We need to find the lieutenant," Margariete said as she tried to stand, "and my brother. He's been taken prisoner at this base."

"How?" Gene asked. "I already tested my comm. The explosion fried it."

The recoil of blaster fire supplied Margariete with an answer.

"You said the lieutenant would be fine once the field was down, didn't you?"

"Yes," Gene said, not understanding.

"Then we go toward the sound of battle. That is where Kyleren will be."

Margariete turned just in time to see a group of elves scuttle aboard some kind of small spacecraft. Gene gasped and clutched at her arm, which she shook off irritably.

"What is it?" she asked, checking her weapons.

Only one pistol and Raeylan's sword had survived their flight.

"It's a standard Coalition military apple-hopper. I recognize the number!" Gene said. "That was the ship that attacked Gwydion."

"I don't understand," she returned, watching the ship prepare for lift off. "What's the significance?"

"Gwydion was our most secret military base, the GAEL VIC space station. No enemy vessel could have gotten within 20 light years of it without being destroyed. But bypassing the outer defenses using a Coalition ship allowed them to get off the base with the—"

Gene suddenly stopped talking, embarrassed that he had revealed too much.

"The GraEL," Margariete inserted.

Gene's mouth dropped open. "How did you—?"

Margariete tapped her forehead twice.

"Magic, remember? I can read people's thoughts."

She looked back at the ship and repeated the classified information she had plucked from Gene's mind.

"So Gwydion's communications were disabled and the infiltration team wasn't stopped. Why?"

Gene's mind rolled over the possibilities and Margariete's telepathy struggled to sort the technical acronyms and theoretical concepts into coherency. Finally, he seemed to settle on an explanation.

"That ship must have a mire field generator aboard. It explains why Gwydion's communication array went black when the Agromors attacked and accounts for the inaction of GAELs. The mire field must have made them all crazy, just like squad Aon."

"But I thought mire field also disrupted what you call dead tech? Wouldn't their ship have malfunctioned too?"

Gene pursed his lips.

"There must be a connection between the field dimensions and the Agromors' ability to control it. I'd be willing to bet my entire collection of *Galatic Starfighter* action figures that the ship has a perfected mire field generator that only affects living tech. Gwydion was the most advanced station in the Coalition. Its primary and secondary systems running the newest LT generation. The only dead tech onboard was life support and the reserve engines. A mire field would have left the complex defenseless."

"So if the field is flawless," Margariete asked, "why would your enemies still experiment with an incomplete one on this world?"

"I think they're refining the generator to accommodate a worldwide field—just a guess, since it affected us so high in orbit. They probably intend to use it on all the worlds under the Agrona-Morrigan Concord."

"And that's bad because?"

"It would make living tech weapons obsolete, and might even win the war. Our LT ships and weapons are significantly more powerful than the Agromors.' That's why they've never launched a direct invasion against the Coalition. But if they've harnessed the power of the mire field and can mass produce it, the Coalition will lose its technological advantage. The MetaGalactic War will turn into a holocaust. Millions will die simply because they're blended."

Margariete felt cold. A planet-wide field that interfered with magic. Whoever controlled this power could rule all the shards. This was bigger than just one war. If Kirion managed to discover it—

"We should destroy it," Margariete decided.

"No, we need to study it," Gene countered, just as the small vessel's engines fired.

Margariete glared in defiance at the technobionomist.

"If they have one here, it stands to reason that they have more," Gene reasoned hastily, withering underneath the former princess's expression. "The Agromors aren't stupid enough to keep all of their schematics for this kind of tech in one place. If you destroy it, you take away any chance the Coalition has to counter it!"

Margariete battled within herself. Gene's thoughts were flooded with apprehension of her impending decision. He completely believed that the acquisition of this ship was the only way to save the lives sheltered by the Coalition. Raeylan would agree that the mire field technology should be kept away from Kirion, but he would not support any action that might doom the souls of millions of people.

"If I were to send an electrical charge through the engines," Margariete growled, "would it prevent the ship from taking off?"

Gene's head shook up and down emphatically, but his expression was tight.

"Target the port side engine. A severe electrical discharge would effectively overload the power relays that support the sublight drive. But there's a 40 percent chance the ship will detonate instead."

The ship already hovered several spans off the ground.

"If you have any better ideas I'm open to them," Margariete snapped. "But a 40 percent chance of getting your information is better than the zero percent it will be if that ship escapes."

Gene bit his lip, but conceded.

"Do it."

Margariete yanked the static energy from the air surrounding her, commanding it to strike the fleeing vessel. The arc of electricity crackled madly along the outer hull plating of the ship. The engines sputtered and stalled. It slammed its belly against the launch platform with the wrenching howl of twisting metal.

Margariete clapped Gene on the back, almost friendly.

"Good guess."

Someone inside the cockpit attempted to restart the disabled engine.

"You should wait here and find a place to hide," Margariete said. "I'm going to take that ship."

Even as she said it, she worried that she hadn't the strength. The return of her powers had drained most of her stamina, and the air shield she had conjured to protect them from the explosion hadn't helped.

"You won't have to do it alone," Gene exclaimed, suddenly pointing to the sky.

Margariete followed the line traced by his finger.

LAMIE zoomed over the complex's outer wall, the force of her speedy passing bending the grass horizontal. Her belly gaped wide with an extended ramp that housed two heavy-framed GAELs. When LAMIE was directly overhead, they jumped, allowing thrusters attached to their armor to safely slow their descent.

"Over here," Gene called, jumping up and down and waving his hands dramatically.

Both GAELs rushed to him.

"Are you okay, Gene?" Captain Reese asked, retracting his visor and revealing his identity.

"Yes, captain. Good to see you're no longer crazy."

"Same here," Captain Reese responded with a wink.

"How did you locate the complex?" Gene asked.

"Lieutenant Kyleren radioed for backup," Reese shrugged. "Major Huard has been trying to contact you, Gene."

"My comm's dead," the technobionomist explained.

Captain Reese tossed Gene a new one. As Reese and Chief Snow provided cover fire, Gene relayed all his assumptions about the Vartal ship to Major Huard who coordinated the fight from LAMIE's bridge. Margariete pulled out her own pistol, aiding the GAELs in their efforts to subdue hostiles.

"Yes, sir," Reese said into his comm after a few moments. He turned to Margariete. "Wait here with Gene. He needs protection. Lieutenant Kyleren is enroute to this location."

The GAEL rose, signaling Chief Snow forward. But before moving out, the captain hesitated. Removing his comm so the soldiers on LAMIE wouldn't hear he said, "The major doesn't trust you ma'am, but you saved our lives. Squad Aon owes you a drink."

The GAEL's sincerity persuaded a smile to tease Margariete's lips, but only for a moment. Reese's comm went back into his ear and he was gone. Gene crumpled next to her.

"This is not my idea of fun," he complained.

Margariete fought to suppress a chuckle. She was uncomfortable with the rising level of ease that she felt around these people. To distract herself from the conundrum, she released the ammo clip on her weapon to check the remaining rounds. As she snapped it back in, she wondered angrily how she was going to find her twin in all this chaos.

At that moment, Lieutenant Lance Kyleren strolled out of the roiling smoke. His face was streamed with dirt, his armor was battle-torn and scratched. Large rifles were gripped in each hand and a blaster cannon was strapped to his back. A huge grin plastered his face.

Margariete barely had time to feel annoyed, because just behind the hulking soldier, Raeylan appeared, *Stardawn* secured firmly to his belt.

22: THE WORLD IS A MESS AND I JUST NEED TO RULE IT

The trees swayed in the artificial breeze. Water babbled in quiet conversation with the birds through the flowery meadow. The sky was tinged a slight shade of violet, for serenity, and the tangy scent of cedar wood hinted the air. In the center of the glade stood a deeply red circular table, surrounded by thirteen high backed chairs, each occupied by a distinguished member of the Round.

The council chamber's appearance was only an illusion of course, a symbolic representation of the field on Kamolos where the first meeting of pro-blended leaders established the Coalition's charter. Here, the Round conducted their business with clear heads and united purpose. When the meeting adjourned, the chamber would revert to flat walls and a tiled floor.

But today, the calming effect of the illusion was lost on Chancellor Medrod. He was displeased that the momentum of his latest amendment, which lifted many outdated restrictions on living tech research, had been trampled by a conservative faction on Caliburn. The fools had unraveled nearly 40 years of delicate political maneuvering. Even if he managed to sedate the situation, it would take months to push the policy forward and repair the damage of today's discussion.

"In short," Governor Kells was saying, concluding an extremely lengthy speech, "I hereby rescind my vote to establish the Lamorak Industries Amendment of the technobionomy restriction laws."

The current head of InterSys had political status guaranteed by his company's virtual monopoly on living tech ore exportation in the Athalonde System. Usually, the obese blended man was predictable, his support easily gained by the lure of soaring profit. Kells' sudden shift of alliance was unanticipated. In previous meetings, he had rubbed his meaty hands happily at the LAMIE project initiate—after all, new tech meant higher demand for his product. Something had influenced him.

Medrod coated the assembly with his discontent like mold on rotten fruit. The other governors eyed each other nervously. Politics was an intricate web of manipulation and control. Medrod knew the dance well. The chancellor rose from his chair in a thoughtful manner, preparing for the verbal duel.

"I am curious about the change in your position, governor," Medrod began. "The Lamorak Amendments were originally proposed to this council by yourself." The chancellor knew this statement wasn't entirely true. It had, in fact, been his own well-seeded persuasion that had encouraged Kells to first make the recommendation. He continued, adding an inflection of perplexity to his comment. "And now you advise us to abandon such a monumental advancement. You can see my confusion at such a reversal."

"My decision, Your Excellence, was not kindled lightly," the governor stated with a respectful inclination of his head. "But further investigation of the topic and discussions with several associates of mine—people of great standing who oppose the issue—I must conclude that we have rushed into a policy that, rather than strengthening our collective economy as we intended, would instead cause irreparable injury to the Coalition's interests."

Medrod raised his eyebrows in false pretense of surprise, since he already suspected the identity of the "associate" responsible for swaying the governor. If he was right, the chancellor already had means for correcting this unfortunate delay. He moved forward into a feint.

"Your concerns are of course important to this assembly. But it is only reasonable that you disclose the source of your dissent. Who has caused you to doubt the diligent work of this council? A plan that has cost us a hundred years of compromise and toil."

Governor Kells licked his lips but his voice was strong and proud as he proclaimed his answer. "Prime Minister Vivian Ninevay of Penardun."

Medrod paced a turn around the table, inwardly satisfied. Though Minister Ninevay's connections had proved more influential than he originally accounted for, the matter had already been resolved. Now he simply had to persuade the Round to see his point of view.

"The Prime Minister of Penardun is indeed an honorable leader, Governor Kells," Medrod agreed, "but we must remember that Penardun broke from the Blended Coalition and has maintained a neutral position in the MetaGalactic War."

He made another circuit around the table and then resumed his seat before continuing. He needed Kells to look foolish, and the best way to accomplish that was to provoke the man's temper.

"Though their city provides a base for our military operations, their freedom from the oppression of the Agromors is dependent on the lives of our soldiers. They enjoy a life of ease bought by the blood of our people. Though we appreciate their goodwill, their prime minister has no right for her voice to be heard here in this council, even if it be by the proxy of one of our members. That would be no better than allowing the head of the Vartal's Druidic Council to manage our republic's affairs."

Kells leapt from his chair, knocking it to the floor.

"Minister Ninevay is nothing like that Agromor skrit. You allege her intentions to be as sordid as the genocidal ideals of the Vartal?"

"No," the chancellor said with a patient sigh, "I would never disgrace the minister with such a humiliating comparison. But I will suggest that her motivations are similar in purpose."

"How so, chancellor?" Kells challenged.

"Leaders are the custodians of their people, and as such, they must base their decisions on the best interests of their citizens. Minister Ninevay would never slaughter innocent babes in the name of religious zealously, but she has an obligation to protect her city-station. Allowing us to advance the strength of our military through intelligent technology could be seen as a threat to their free government. Therefore, her motivation to dissuade the Round's course of action is based on her need to safeguard her position."

"These 'intelligent' ships could be our downfall," Kells inserted.

"They could also bring a long-awaited peace to the galaxy," Medrod countered wisely. "Such an armada could end this racial war. The technology has already shown promise. Is it not our primary goal as a Coalition to preserve life? How can we achieve this ideal if we will not consider all possibilities?"

Murmurs of agreement circled through the governors. Kells' posture slumped and his eyes lowered.

"Today's proceedings have given us much to ponder," Chancellor Medrod concluded. "I move that we postpone further discussion of all agenda topics until our next assembly."

Kells opened his mouth to argue but the unanimous harmony for the motion from the others silenced his rebuttal. Reluctantly, the abashed governor agreed to adjourn. Medrod excused them all. Though the others filed obediently out of the door that seemed to materialize out of thin air, Governor Kells lingered behind. When only the two of them remained, Kells spoke.

"Chancellor, I must be heard in council again tomorrow."

"I apologize, Governor Kells," Medrod answered, "but I cannot oblige your request."

"You cannot deny my appeal!" Kells urged. "If my demands are not met, I will incite the InterSys Corporation to strike. The whole financial district of the Coalition will be brought to a standstill!"

The hologrid powered down, plunging the chamber into a blanket of grey. Medrod felt his eyes darken at the same time. An InterSys strike would hinder the objectives of his greater design. This development was unacceptable. His voice was smooth as he addressed the wayward politician.

"I suggest you consider your future carefully before you so willingly submit yourself to the mercy of the Round, governor."

Kells laughed confidently.

"I do not fear the governors, chancellor. Once they understand my resolve, they will do what is best for themselves. Must I remind you that I control the mining operations on both LeFay and Athalonde Prime? I could have you unseated with a jangle of my pring purse!"

Medrod ignored the governor's boast, picking up his dataplate from the table. He scrolled through a collection of files. Making the appropriate selection for display, he slid it toward Kells.

"It pains me to inform you that Prime Minister Vivian Ninevay was assassinated just yesterday."

The large man exhaled quickly, his saggy skin turning sallow.

"How? Who?" he sputtered.

"That depends on you, governor," the chancellor said.

Kells' face jerked away from the gruesome photo.

"What do you mean?"

"A hired assassin was responsible, but all evidence suggests the killer was hired by a member of the Round. It would be unfortunate if that evidence were to incriminate you."

"You think to accuse me? This was not of my doing!" the governor snarled, knocking the plate back to Medrod.

"Perhaps. But you can see how the rest of the Sector Governors might be uncertain of your innocence. You did undermine them in assembly today. And I suppose they won't react too kindly to your threat of strike against the Coalition if this conversation were to be made public."

"I will not be intimidated!"

"Then I'm afraid your eldest son will inherit InterSys Corporation several centuries sooner than either of you expected," Medrod warned with a triumphant turn of the lips. "Treason carries the sentence of death, governor. We are, after all, in a state of war."

The man seemed to sink into himself, confidence swallowed by helplessness. Medrod cocked his head to the side.

"As you love your prings, remember your place. It will always be beneath mine. You are dismissed."

Kells inhaled several defeated breaths before supplying Medrod with a single nod, then fled in haste. Satisfied, Medrod sauntered to his office, only a short distance from the council chamber. As he entered, he noticed his private communication panel vibrated softly. He entered his personal code to unlock the device. A small hologram of Medrod's most trusted employee flickered to life above its sensors.

"My Lord," the man greeted with a bow.

"Feralblade," the chancellor said, "your timing is exceptional, as always. I have a new task for you. Governor Kells requires a small reminder as to where he should place his loyalty. I believe he has several children."

Feralblade's face cracked with malice. "Which one?"

"The youngest."

"Easily arranged, My Lord. I have discovered a matter, however, that I believe you will want me to address first."

"I despise suspense as you well know, Feralblade. Explain yourself."

"Of course, My Lord. As per command I have destroyed all the evidence Minister Ninevay compiled against you regarding the GAELs. But I have recently found that another copy exists. The minister sent the data to her younger sister, Anya Ninevay."

"Your ignorance to consideration is taxing, Feralblade. On matters of such obvious importance you do not need my permission to complete an execution. Kill the sister and deal with the evidence."

"I was preparing to do just that, My Lord, when I discovered some intriguing information. I felt I needed to report it immediately."

The image of Feralblade shifted to the side of the sensor area as a new set of data was uploaded through the comm. Medrod sucked in a slow breath of air to calm his pounding heart as the likeness of Anya Ninevay materialized above the sensor. He ran his thumb thoughtfully against his bottom lip.

"Where is she now?" he asked.

"Unfortunately, she has fled Penardun in the company of the shiidh. She's headed for the Vartal homeworld."

"Intercept her and bring her to me!" Medrod commanded, his elation nearly bursting through every pore in his skin.

"Of course, My Lord," Feralblade cackled.

The assassin's picture disappeared as he broke contact. Anya's portrait remained, along with the list of standard Coalition information registered by all citizens:

NAME: ANYA NINEVAY
OCCUPATION: HEAD OF MEDICAL OPERATIONS PENARDUN
        MEDICAL CENTER
HOMEWORLD: UNKNOWN
BIRTHDATE: UNKNOWN
AGE: UNKNOWN
PARENTS: (ADOPTED 991 AGW) TARNIN AND ARRE
        NINEVAY
SIBLINGS: VIVIAN NINEVAY, FEMALE

The chancellor's hand reached up to stroke the woman's holographic cheek. He could almost remember the soft texture of her skin. Her unique, ice-green eyes sparkled with her usual cheer.

She wouldn't get far.

PART 3

23: You've Just Taken Your First Step Into A Larger World

Kyleren adjusted the illuminator to better distinguish the tangle of wires that threaded the communications board. LAMIE's access ducts were designed to accommodate an elf or human, not a GAEL VIC. But regardless of the small space, Kyleren smiled at his work. He wasn't an expert technician, but he knew ways to retrofit comms that would even astound Gene. The patch had only taken him a few hours, despite Bedin's pronouncement that nothing short of a full overhaul at Penardun could persuade it to work again. True, most of the components would need to be replaced once they returned to base, but Kyleren had managed to restore minimal communication capability.

"I found it," Wayne announced, appearing with a grin from the duct porthole.

Kyleren slid out. Reese offered a small, angular tile in his palm.

"Had to grab it when Gene wasn't looking," Wayne admitted. "Couldn't get him to stop talking long enough to tell him what you wanted. He's glued to LAMIE's protoboard."

Lance chuckled and lifted the imprint tile, inserting it into a nearby dataplate.

"He's probably spinnin' in circles lookin' for it."

Lance's longtime friend joined in laughter as the protocols were uploaded into the array's living ore. Fifteen minutes passed. Lance was so engrossed in tweaking the dataplate prompts that he almost missed Wayne's question.

"So what do you think?"

"Hmm, about what?" Lance asked absently.

"The 'twins'," Wayne clarified.

"What about 'em?" Lance returned, still distracted by his task.

"I was just wondering if we can trust them."

"Guess so," Kyleren said with a shrug. "They helped us out."

"But why?" Wayne pondered. "They don't belong to any faction. They aren't military. And if they're spies, they're making a gromm mess of things. What do they get out of it?"

Lance peeled his eyes from the plate as it completed the final round of protoimprints.

"Well, Mags didn't have a choice," he said. "The brother's stickin' with his sister. They need us to get off this rock."

Wayne nodded, but seemed unsatisfied.

"Do you really believe Raeylan is her brother?"

"I have my doubts. Startin' with the fact that they look nothin' the same."

"I had the same thought." Wayne folded his arms and leaned casually against the engine room wall. "Huard thinks we should lock them up. He's worried they'll try to jack one of the ships."

"Wouldn't put it past Mags," Kyleren said, disengaging the dataplate. "Huard doesn't trust 'em I take it?"

"Nope. He still thinks it was a mistake to take the woman to this base. Says it could've ended badly."

"Can't argue with that," Kyleren agreed. "I didn't trust her either."

"Didn't?"

"Without her, I'd be Agromor meat," Kyleren stated. "So would you."

"I tried to tell Huard that, but he doesn't want to hear anything about it. He's made up his mind. He doesn't believe their story."

"Neither will Command," Lance pointed out.

Wayne shook his head.

"I've been going over it again and again. My head tells me that their story is gromm skrit. But my gut thinks something different. They got us out of a real fragging mess. Trish and the colonel would be dead if Margariete hadn't gone with you."

"Yeah, well, I wish the colonel would wake up soon," Lance admitted.

Even after two days of extensive nanomite injections, Stoddard remained unconscious in the med bay.

"Huard's on edge," he continued. "Makes me nervous."

"Me too," Wayne confessed. "Huard doesn't have Stoddard's trust in GAEL instinct. If the colonel was giving the orders, he'd leave the twins alone. I bet he'd even forget to mention them to Command and drop them planestside before we made dock."

Lance eyed his friend, guilt gnawing into him. After the battle settled out, Huard had him file an official report detailing the incident. He had deliberately left out certain specifics about Margariete and her brother. He couldn't explain why he'd done it. His allegiance should be to his unit entirely, and he shouldn't give a frag what happened to either of the strangers. But somehow, every time he tried to document their strange abilities, the words wouldn't come out.

"I lied in my report, Wayne," Kyleren said, securing the access duct hatch.

Wayne looked shocked.

"Why?"

The story spewed from Lance's mouth before he even realized it was over. He explained everything from Margariete's belief of magic to the impossible teleportation he'd witnessed.

"Do you believe them?" Wayne asked dubiously. "About the magic?"

"I don't know, Wayne. If I hadn't seen them do some of the stuff—," he grimaced. "Mags took control of my mind, made me crash the ship under her orders. All she had to do was look at me and tell me what to do. And her brother. I saw him disappear, then pop up 50 meters away. There's not a single GAEL alive that fast."

Wayne shook his head doubtfully. "So you really think he teleported?"

"I know it sounds crazy, but yeah," Lance grumbled. "You don't fraggin' believe me, do you?"

"If it's true, both of them are risks. Maybe Huard's right."

"Never thought I'd hear you give Huard that much credit."

"He has his moments," Wayne defended. "I see why you left out the information, but you shouldn't have. These two could be a new enemy we haven't seen from across the

Black Reach. How come Gene didn't mention any of this in his report either?"

"Cuz I told him not to. Not yet, anyway," Lance answered. "Didn't take much to convince him either. He went off about how he didn't want to bring it up until he had proof of some sort of theory." Lance thought for a minute, considering his justification. He needed Wayne to understand. "We owe Mags. I don't like her, but I don't want to see her end up in some Coalition lab either. I guess I'm asking you to keep this under wraps, Wayne."

"I didn't tell anyone about you and Trish, did I?" Wayne answered. "I'm with you. The twins are suspicious, but as I said, I trust my gut."

Lance clapped a hand on his friend's shoulder. "Thanks."

The door to the engine room hissed open and Major Huard limped inside, favoring his nanomite-injected leg. Exhaustion sunk his eyes. What with LAMIE's repairs, Colonel Stoddard's coma, and two men still in the infirmary—Private Thompson's burns were barely on the mend and Corporal Evans was still recovering from the loss of his arm—Huard hadn't seen much rack time. They were working on a skeleton crew, and not only had to fix LAMIE, but also the overloaded engines on the mire field ship so they could take it back with them.

"Lieutenant Kyleren," Huard demanded tiredly, "what's the status of communication repairs?"

"Almost complete, sir," Lance reported.

"Good, I need you to get moving on LAMIE's landing gear. We can't get the starboard leg to retract. Gene says it's in bad shape."

"Yes, sir," Lance confirmed. "I can jury a patch."

Huard nodded his thanks as he turned to Wayne.

"Captain Reese, come with me to the situation room. With communications up, we need to make our report to the Round."

*

Lance sifted through the assortment of parts he had gathered from the ruined shell of the Vartal compound. A swift diagnosis of the landing gear's condition led him to the conclusion that only a bypass of the lever hydraulics could correct the problem. He organized the different gears and metal sheets, mentally drafting the most useful combination of his scavenged materials. As he put the finishing touches on a holographic sketch in his dataplate, he heard footsteps approaching him.

He knew it was Raeylan even before the man spoke. An odd sensation of something that could only be described as static buzzed inside Kyleren's ears every time Margariete's brother got close. It was almost like the vibrations that came from a live electrical wire.

"Greetings, lieutenant," Raeylan greeted politely.

Kyleren looked over just in time to see his guest bow stiffly at the waist.

Lance raised his eyes. What was with that?

"Mornin'," Kyleren returned cautiously.

"I would like to speak to you, if you are not too occupied."

Lance shrugged, turning back to his project. "If you don't mind me workin' while you talk."

"Of course," Raeylan said, stepping to the opposite side of Kyleren's work station. "I wanted to extend my gratitude to you."

"For what?" Kyleren asked while lifting an oddly shaped gear for examination.

"For keeping my sister safe."

Lance replaced the gear and chuckled. He turned to face her brother.

"You mean keepin' her prisoner and forcin' her to help us on a mission? I wouldn't call that safe."

Raeylan held up his right hand, which was now covered by a fingerless glove, and nodded.

"It does no harm to my sister to be reminded that humility is valuable for survival. Despite the circumstance, you did defend her. I am in your debt."

"It's good for everyone, I guess," Lance said, confused.

"For Margariete, it is particularly essential," Raeylan explained, turning so that Lance could only see the man's profile.

Kyleren lifted his gaze to follow Raeylan's. Out in the grass, in what used to be the complex's quad, Margariete practiced a series of choreographed parries and attacks with her sword.

"She often overestimates her own abilities," he continued.

Lance watched the smooth flexing of the brunette's body as she maneuvered through her training routine. Her weapon seemed an extension of her arm, so precise were her movements. Her hair loosed itself and tumbled across her cheeks as she completed a twist and roll. When she reached her feet, she paused in a wide stance. A second later she straightened, and repeated the same bow he had seen Raeylan use earlier.

She turned in Kyleren's direction, as if she had sensed him watching, and glared. With her head raised in pride, she sheathed her blade and spun away, marching toward the other side of the base.

"She always been that intense?" Kyleren asked as he turned back to her brother.

"Since birth, Margariete's life has been complicated."

"How complicated?" Lance questioned warily.

The look Raeylan gave him was calm, but wise, as if the teleporter knew something that Kyleren didn't. Lance cleared his throat.

"Just curious," he said.

Raeylan considered Kyleren's answer thoughtfully.

"Very well," he finally said. "What has Margariete already told you?"

"Nothin'."

Lance admitted that his answer wasn't technically accurate, but he figured crazy stories about magic didn't count.

"You have already noted the differences in our appearance," Raeylan said. "Differences so extreme that most doubt our blood kinship."

Lance grunted in agreement.

"As Margariete differs from me, she differed from our people," Raeylan said, his face melting into sadness. "She was shunned. Persecuted. Only a few were able to see past her uncommon features."

As a GAEL VIC, Kyleren didn't know how to process Raeylan's account. Lance had only ever known his training and his missions. His parents were his superior officers, his siblings his fellow soldiers. Sure the Agromors hated him, hated that he was a blended species, but they were the enemy.

What would it be like to be despised by everyone around you, the people you risked your life to serve? The idea sent his mind into a novel quandary, a way of thinking he had never before considered.

"Yeah well, it's not like that in the Coalition, so your sister's in luck. Just wish she wasn't so touchy about stuff," Lance grumbled.

"Her experience has made her thus," Raeylan defended quietly. "She cannot trust."

"Guess I see that, but not every person you meet is a hostile."

"I agree," Raeylan said, "but when Margariete is without me, she relies only on herself. She attacks first, entrusting her fate to no one."

"She's been crossed I take it?"

"In ways too deep for her to discuss," Raeylan answered.

Lance could tell the teleporter had deliberately kept his voice even, forbidding any emotion from exposing itself. But his grey eyes smoldered.

"A betrayal by a man she once loved—a person I mistakenly called friend. After that, the destruction of our homeland by a man who calls himself Kirion. He murdered our younger brother when Margariete refused to join his cause."

Kyleren looked across the quad, at the building where Margariete had disappeared. She was the most annoying woman he had ever met.

"She still blames herself for our brother's death," Raeylan concluded. "Nightmares still haunt her, though it happened four centuries past."

"Four centuries?" Kyleren bellowed.

He eyed Raeylan from head to foot. The man wasn't blended. He looked as human as anything. So did his sister.

"No human lives that long."

"Margariete and I are not human, lieutenant," Raeylan declared.

223

"Then what are you?" Kyleren demanded.

"In a way, we are just like you and your comrades. We are human, but not human."

"Thanks for explainin'," Kyleren returned sarcastically. "Why are you tellin' me all 'a this?"

"Because you are unique," Raeylan replied vaguely.

"What kinda answer is that?"

The man actually smiled.

"Some things become clear with time, Lieutenant Kyleren."

Raeylan's riddles frustrated Lance. But before he had a chance to say as much, Wayne's voice crackled over the comm.

"Lieutenant Kyleren, report to the situation room immediately. You have an incoming transmission."

"Affirmative," Lance said. Then he said to Raeylan, "I gotta go."

He made it to LAMIE's hatch before a thought occurred to him, a question about something he had seen when he first met Margariete.

"Can I ask you one more thing?"

"Of course," Raeylan replied.

"After we captured your sister, we examined her right arm. She was real upset about it."

Raeylan held up his right hand, displaying his dark brown glove.

"In our culture, the right arm of a ranked individual is sacred, never to be viewed by another. To her, your examination was a violation."

"And her rank? Was it important?"

"She was a princess."

"Figures," Lance snorted, and entered the hatch.

24: ADD ANOTHER SUITCASE FULL OF BAD

Stardawn happily carved the air as Margariete practiced. She hadn't realized just how much she had missed the freedom of the open. The cramped quarters of space travel didn't suit her. With such limited room, it had been impossible for her to hone her martial skill on a regular basis. Over time, she had discovered other ways to keep her body in adequate fighting condition, but it just wasn't the same as breathing in fresh air.

Margariete let her body's memory consume her mind, knowing this opportunity wouldn't last. Soon, the search for Esilwen would resume. She would need her full set of skills to help Raeylan find an avenue to destroy Kirion once and for all.

It wasn't until halfway through her fifth set that the back of her neck bristled strangely. Her sense alerted her that someone was watching. Ignoring the sensation, she completed the last few movements in her kata. As custom demanded, she bowed, ritually offering a polite tribute to her former teachers.

The bristle was still there, so she turned to face her spectator. Of course, it was the insufferable Lieutenant

Kyleren, staring at her quizzically. Vexed by his intrusion, she seared him with a glare that included every loathsome thought she had ever had for him. Then, she sheathed *Stardawn* and stormed around the corner of a building across the practice area.

She threw herself on one of the yellow rocks and snatched a pack she had left there earlier. It contained an assortment of Vartal weapons she had gathered from around the compound. One by one, she laid them out for inspection, organizing them by size and function. The last she set down was the threader Kyleren had given her before they infiltrated the base.

She examined her weapons with false intensity, trying to banish the image of Kyleren from her head. It was too hard to decide just what she hated most about the GAEL. There were so many things. She hated his humor. It attacked her without fear. She hated the way he laughed. It was too irresponsible. She hated his smile. Full of confidence, it displayed too much self-assurance. She especially loathed his clarity of mind. His singular obsession with achieving the next objective. Kyleren possessed no ambition, no need prove himself. It made him predictable, honest, and easy to trust.

More than anything, that scared Margariete the most.

"You have collected an entire armory, my sister. What need do you have for such an arsenal?"

"I only intend to keep a few," Margariete returned, trying hard not to seem ambushed by her twin's approach.

"Then why have you gathered so many?" Raeylan asked, surveying the pile of weapons at her feet.

"I wish to select the most useful," Margariete answered, picking up the nearest pistol and testing its weight, "and that requires experimentation. I would like them to last at least a half century this time."

"That is difficult when each shard we visit has marginal differences in ammunition," Raeylan said, kneeling next to a row and inspecting its neat line of firearms.

"Yes. It would just be simpler if everyone had swords," she complained.

She slid the projectile clip from the pistol she was holding, determining its capacity.

"Raeylan, how long until we abandon these idiots?"

"Your colloquial use of the term is not its actual definition, Margariete," Raeylan reprimanded. "The GAELs are dedicated soldiers. They deserve respect."

Margariete curled her lip.

"I am fully aware of its meaning, brother. Some may be less foolish than I accuse, but in general, they are all much too focused on trivial affairs."

"Their focus gives them strength. They do not question, but embrace their destiny."

"So?"

"They are not blinded by revenge," Raeylan concluded.

"They haven't suffered as we have," Margariete spat, her temper flustering. She knew his statement was a reflection of her own conduct. "They have nothing to revenge."

"That is an assumption, Margariete—one that lacks courtesy. There are many in the shards who have endured hardship at Kirion's hand."

Unintended, Shikun's face burned across Margariete's vision.

"Don't start, Raeylan. Even you don't know what it was like for me. To watch Shikun—"

She choked.

"I have seen my share of the destruction left in Kirion's wake, Margariete. I was witness to Thyella's destruction when it was drawn into the Void. We have lost family, friends, and—"

Raeylan's voice trailed off.

"Esilwen," Margariete finished, feeling ashamed.

Of course Raeylan knew what it was like to watch a loved one die. Esilwen had burst into flames right before his eyes. At least their little brother had safely crossed into the arms of Nehro. Nothing could harm him again. Esilwen could be anywhere, be suffering anything over the past four centuries. Just the thought made Margariete's throat ache.

"Forgive me, Raeylan," she entreated. "You're right. I was thoughtless."

Raeylan smiled. "I could never deny you forgiveness."

Overwhelming relief accompanied Raeylan's presence. He had explained his own adventure of teleportation error to Margariete already. The wild magic that tore their ship apart was a natural mire field warping the space next to the shardgate. Raeylan's time and space abilities had malfunctioned, spitting them across the universe in different directions. Raeylan had appeared on Danaan, overloaded and unconscious. He found himself a prisoner of the Danaan field base when he awoke, sedated and powerless. It was luck that they had been reunited so quickly in such an enormous shard.

Several moments of quiet passed as they studied the weapons.

"Well, you must have a reason for remaining here," Margariete observed. "Would you explain it to me?"

"The GAELs are Chano's angels," Raeylan blurted.

The revelation of such an unlooked for explanation made Margariete drop the pistol she was holding. It thumped onto the grass.

"What? The goddess of stone?" she asked. "Are you sure?"

"Yes," Raeylan said, "though they are different than you or I."

"How so?"

"Their Wells are not natural, but manufactured through their technology. Ours reside inside our bodies, but theirs are external."

"Their core drives," Margariete said.

It made sense. She had suspected the Coalition soldiers of using magic before. What they called "bonded tech" was weaponry enhanced by the magic of Chano. GAELs were more dangerous than regular warriors because they used technology to project their magic directly from a Soulwell.

"Yes. But there is another reason we should remain."

Margariete remained silent, indicating he should continue.

"You must convince Lieutenant Lance Kyleren to come with us."

Margariete burst into laughter. When Raeylan didn't join in her amusement she stopped abruptly.

"You can't be serious!"

"I am serious about all matters concerning the fate of the shards, Margariete," he said somberly.

"Well I think the Vartal drugs might have addled your mind, brother, because the last person we want to join us is Lance Kyleren. Why would you even suggest such a thing?"

"Because he is an artifact bearer," Raeylan calmly declared.

"Are you certain?" she nearly gasped.

"Entirely."

"I don't believe it. Where could he have even found it?"

"I have been studying him. I believe it has been in his possession since the creation of his core drive."

"How could you know that?"

"Kyleren is not an angel, not like his comrades. His core drive is not a Well. It is the artifact."

Margariete refused to consider it. If it were true, Kyleren would have to stay with them indefinitely, both to fight Kirion and keep the artifact safe. The idea was ludicrous. Margariete pursed her lips in rebellion, but a stray thought suddenly forced her to side with her brother's argument.

"That's why the mire field didn't cause him to lose control like the other GAELs."

"Correct," Raeylan said. "His bond is of a different kind. Though he has many of the abilities of his companions, his exceed theirs in strength and variety."

"Which artifact?" she asked. "Chano's?"

"Kyleren's magic matches the GAELs'. It must be."

"All this time I thought the artifact was this GraEL they keep talking about," Margariete said.

"It very well could have been. But I am convinced that the GraEL is only a Well, although I would have to see it to be sure. If so, it will need to be closed so that Kirion cannot misuse it. The first step to that is to convince Kyleren to join us."

"Can't we just take the artifact from him?" Margariete pouted.

"No," Raeylan said with a shake of the head. "His bond to the artifact is much like Esilwen's to Fohtian's blood. If it were broken, he would die."

She kicked the rock in frustration, feeling like a flailing tantrum would be the only thing to ease her exasperation. Constant and intolerable torment loomed eagerly at the edge of her future.

"Then you ask him if you really want him to come with us," she insisted.

Raeylan frowned and his eyes flashed displeasure.

"You must do this, Margariete. You understand Kyleren much better than I."

"He hates me almost as much as I do him," she grumbled. "He won't listen."

"We cannot know that until you try."

"Look, whether knight of a kingdom or solider in a galactic military, warriors don't surrender their allegiance lightly. He won't come."

Raeylan heaved a slow sigh.

"I have already considered this, Margariete. If he declines, you must make him come with us."

"What?" she asked, shocked.

"I do not belittle the seriousness of forcing someone to abandon his duty, Margariete. But we cannot take the chance that Kirion might find Kyleren."

Margariete had no reservations against using her dominance if the occasion warranted, but she was concerned that Raeylan was desperate enough to suggest it, even as a last resort. Kirion already had the magic of two artifacts, plus his own power of light. If he were to capture Chano's power as well, they could not hope to stand against him. For the sake of the shards, and her twin, Margariete decided to try.

"I don't like it," she said. "I am not exaggerating when I say I hate the man."

"You must do this, Margariete, no matter how unpleasant you find it."

"Promise me that the next ship we acquire will be large enough for me to avoid him," she bartered, "and I will do as you ask."

At that, Raeylan finally smiled.

"Very well, you shall have my word. I will do my best to obtain a suitable ship." He stood. "I must return. I asked the culturalist, Percy Jameson, to examine our god scrolls. He seemed particularly interested in one of them and requested I return after a time to hear his hypothesis."

Margariete snorted. Turning the conversation back to Kyleren, she said, "I don't even know how to start."

"First, sister, you might consider an agreeable approach for meeting with the lieutenant," Raeylan advised. Right before he turned the corner around the building he added, "Then I suggest you pray to Nehro for patience, lest you loose your temper on him."

25: To Hell With Our Orders

The situation room bent tight with tension as Kyleren cleared the sliding door. Major Huard and Captain Reese flanked the round holotable, both fixed stiffly with their arms crossed over their chests. Gene was in the corner, nervously hovering over a comm console with his dataplate.

"What's goin' on, guys?" Lance asked guardedly, thinking he had screwed up the communications array mend after all.

Wayne shifted uncomfortably and answered, "Lieutenant, you have a communiqué from Penardun." He leveled a warning with his eyes, flicking them from Huard and back.

"You have some explaining to do, lieutenant!" Huard snapped, glaring at Kyleren expectantly.

Whatever the major was after, Kyleren was clueless. After a few awkward seconds of silence Kyleren asked, "Could you tell me what I'm supposed to explain, sir?"

"LAMIE's communication frequencies are top secret! I want to know how Dr. Anya Ninevay got access! Then you're going to tell us who else you gave codes to!"

"I haven't told anybody nothin', sir," Lance defended.

Huard's eyes bulged impatiently, "We all know your record with women, lieutenant. But that does not excuse your behavior!"

"Major Huard," Wayne interceded, "with regard to Dr. Ninevay, I can vouch for the lieutenant. There has been no inappropriate relationship. And Lieutenant Kyleren is always careful to never leave any woman a way to contact him."

Huard looked unconvinced.

"If he didn't give out the codes, then how did the doctor manage to contact us?"

Gene jumped away from the wall, happily offering his expertise. "She didn't, I mean—" he tapped a sequence on his dataplate, "she is on the other side of the message, but she's not the one responsible for hacking into our comm array."

Huard whirled to the technobionomist.

"What do you mean 'hacked'? How could they get past LAMIE's protodefense wall?"

"I don't know," Gene said with a frown, "but it's not coming from Penardun."

"Then where?" asked Wayne.

"It's a shiidh vessel," Gene said.

"What?" Lance and Wayne shouted in unison.

What was the doc doing on a shiidh ship?

"Drop the transmission and get them out of our comm array!" Huard ordered.

"Easy enough," Gene rattled, hastily fiddling with his plate. "Although I will have to redesign the existing algorithm to buffer out the shiidh signal without compromising our assigned frequency. That will take me about half a day. And I'm still only halfway done with LAMIE's proto reconstruction."

"Wait a sec," Kyleren growled, "don't we want to know what the frag Anya's doin' on a shiidh ship? She could have been kidnapped or somethin'."

"Our orders are to secure the GraEL and return to Penardun. Then we are to resupply and escort the mire field ship back to friendly space," Huard barked. "I will not have those orders compromised by an enemy ship, no matter who's on their comm, got it?"

"But, major," Wayne argued, "Doc Anya has been a longtime friend of squad Aon. We should at least determine her situation."

"I agree," said Gene. He waved his dataplate in the air. "This signal hit space when we dusted off of Agrona four days ago."

"How do you know that?" Huard asked.

"Because I'm a genius," Gene answered with a complete lack of modesty. "It would take too long for me to try and explain it to a military grunt like you. The point is, someone really wanted to contact us, someone clever enough to tap our array before we even cleared the atmosphere."

"It could be a trap," Huard immediately concluded. "If they hacked our frequency, they might be able to infiltrate our datacore."

Gene rolled his eyes, as if he were speaking to a brainless Taranian Etten.

"Major, I designed LAMIE. None of her communication tiles are linked to her datacore, mission computers, or navigation logs. No penetration of the comm array could access any other system on this ship. She's built that way on purpose."

Wayne looked at Huard.

"We should do it, major. We might gain some valuable intel."

Huard spit bullets.

"Fine. Do it. But don't tell her we are monitoring the transmission. And I want the signal traced to a point of origin, Gene."

Gene smiled and fiddled with the comm, but out of range of the hologrid. Two seconds later the blond, slightly rumpled projection of Anya Ninevay floated in the center of the table. Her shoulders relaxed with visible relief when she saw Kyleren.

"Lieutenant, I can't tell you how good it is to see your face," she announced cheerfully. "There is so much I need to discuss with you."

"Doc, how'd you find me?"

"The shiidh," she admitted. "They helped."

The blatant declaration made Kyleren's fingertips cold. Did that mean she wasn't a prisoner? Had she joined the other side voluntarily?

"Smiles," Kyleren said, unable to keep worry from the edge of his voice, "what are you doin' with those banshee women?"

"It's hard to explain, Kyleren. And I don't dare over the comm. I'm sending you some coordinates." Her hologram touched an invisible console and a little list of numbers appeared on the table. "Can you meet us there in a few hours?"

Kyleren turned to look at Gene, who seemed stupefied. So much for tracing the shiidh ship's location. Lance's brow furrowed uneasily. Squad Aon had been out on assignment for a week, and Anya should have known that they would be unable to make those coordinates in such a short time. Unless—

She must have understood his expression because Anya blurted, "I know your ship is capable of reaching the rendezvous within the timeframe, lieutenant. I know about your STT drive."

Kyleren's gaze shot to Huard, whose face was turning an angry shade of purple. LAMIE's capabilities were known to only those with the highest level of security clearance.

Anya didn't wait for a response.

"Look, I know I shouldn't have that information. I need your help, lieutenant. If you come, I promise to tell you everything. I have proof that connects Chancellor Medrod to horrific war crimes."

"Doc, I don't know what the shiidh have told you, but there's no way it's true," Kyleren said with a shake of the head. "What you're sayin' is treason."

"It didn't come from the shiidh," Anya clarified hastily. "My sister—"

She choked on the word. Kyleren held his breath, waiting for the pretty doctor to regain control of her emotions. Several tears spilled over Anya's cheeks. She paused a moment, then wiped them away. When she continued, her voice was stronger, her eyes determined.

"The information comes from the Prime Minister of Penardun, Vivian Ninevay. She was murdered shortly after I escaped the city."

The others muttered quietly. Vivian Ninevay was a high ranking politician. An accusation from Penardun's leader would not have been made lightly. Add to that a suspicious death—

"I want to trust you, Smiles," Kyleren said, "but you're with the shiidh. They're Vartal. Did they kidnap you?"

"No," Anya said waving her hands back and forth. "My sister arranged it. She was trying to protect me."

Kyleren's eyes shifted to Wayne. They shared a look that said one thing: whatever was going on, Anya needed their help.

"I'll see what I can do, doc," Kyleren said.

Anya smiled through a fresh tumble of tears. "Thank you, lieutenant."

The hologram dissolved. Gene rapped his dataplate twice and loaded the latest newscasts from the Uplink Intergrid. He selected a particular link. Kyleren didn't bother to read the article as it sprawled across the table's surface, or listen to the highly attractive Kildar elf reporter who appeared above the holographic slab. The title was enough: Penardun's Prime Minister Found Dead in Office.

"Well," Gene said when nobody commented, "we know at least two things Anya said are true. Her sister is dead and LAMIE's STT drive can bring us to her in a few hours."

Every eye in the room turned to Huard.

"Doesn't matter," he snarled. "We have orders."

Kyleren nearly came unglued.

"You mean we're not goin' after her?"

Huard's eyes narrowed dangerously.

"No, we're not."

"Major, I think we should consider the rendezvous," Wayne suggested, "at least to rescue Anya and her intel. Even if her information turns out to be Famorian skrit, in the hands of the shiidh it could do some serious damage to the chancellor, maybe even the Round. It could hurt the war effort, sir."

Lance silently applauded his friend's ability to manage a calm line of reason. Kyleren wasn't one to match words. Instead, his fist itched to match the major's jaw.

"You heard the doctor yourself, captain!" Huard roared. "They know about LAMIE's STT drive. This is clearly an attempt to ambush the ship!"

Gene clicked his tongue with annoyance, "Just because they know about the drive doesn't mean they can—"

"Stay out of this, Pecktol," Huard interrupted with a slice of his hand. "My decision is final. We stick to orders."

"We're not asking you to defy orders and jump the ship into a trap, major," Wayne argued. "Just report it to Command and let them make the final decision. Standard protocol, sir."

Lance wanted to howl in support, but since the major seemed inclined to disagree with anything Kyleren said, he restrained himself. Wayne's argument was airtight; Huard would never dare to fool around with protocol.

"I'll check in with Command," he seethed ungraciously. "Dismissed!"

Lance and Wayne managed to salute before stepping into the corridor. Gene dashed off in the direction of LAMIE's protocore.

"Huard's gonna spin the story his way, Wayne," Lance sighed. "Command's only gonna hear what he wants them to. Whatcha think they'll do?"

"I don't know," Wayne said, stopping to look back at the doors to the situation room, "but telling Command is our only shot at getting Anya back."

26: They Didn't Call Them The Dark Ages Because It Was Dark

"I'll see what I can do, doc," Kyleren's hologram said.

"Thank you, lieutenant," Anya replied, then switched off the shiidh comm.

The towering image of Kyleren wafted into the lightless space of the room, leaving only the feeble glow of the small lantern in her palm. She stared at the place he had disappeared, feeling the desperate ache of loneliness that only someone haunted by fear could experience. Tears abandoned her cheeks and dripped to the floor. She hadn't felt this kind of panic since the first day she could remember, the day she awoke, naked, on Kamolos, completely unaware of her identity. Kyleren's company, even though he was physically light years away, had comforted the hollow pit in her heart that had once born her love for her sister.

But with his departure came the darkness of truth. Vivian was dead, forever lost.

The small power cells of her light source did little to combat the black vacuum that hid her weeping. Soon, however, she forced herself to regain composure. It took a few moments for her to locate the door mechanism. When it finally slid open, Anya jumped back, startled. The meager light reflected strangely off the face of a waiting shiidh. The woman's deep, coal eyes squinted away from the invasive lantern as she pulled back into the darkness.

"I trust, fair elf, the message is complete?" the shiidh hissed from the hallway.

Anya nodded, wondering how many more of them lurked in the dark. This was not the same person who had escorted her to the communication deck a few minutes ago.

"The Mistress Tuatha sends for you. Make haste," the shiidh declared, her voice melting into the swish of her heavy robes.

"Wait!" Anya called, wishing the shiidh would tell her their names. Only the leader had permission to become familiar with an outsider. Combined with the strange lyrical echo of their voices, she found the mysterious cult of Vartal religious leaders unnerving.

With a low slushy breath the shiidh crept back into Anya's little circle of light.

"I'm sorry," Anya apologized, "but I don't know where to go."

The woman pointed down the corridor, but made no move to lead the way. Anya sighed and trudged forward in the indicated direction. Artificial light was scarce since the Vartal matrons preferred the darkness. Anya knew they simply modeled the conditions of their homeworld, but the greedy black seemed to swallow her little light with spite, making her shiver as she wandered through the vessel's windy corridor.

It wasn't just the gloom that made Anya feel as if she were lost inside the catacombs of a forgotten tomb. The walls and floor of the ship were lined with eerie stone murals that stole the heat from the air. Some she recognized as Agrona's history, others were sacred rituals depicting the shiidh's goddess, Danu.

But some of the scenes scared her, for reasons she could not explain. There were images that reeked of hate, visions that provoked fear. One just outside the bridge filled her with a particular dread. It presented six personages, three male and three female. The story unfolded in details she could not decipher, but the ending was clear. The first of the six destroyed his fellows in a bloody battle. As Anya passed by, she could not help but reach out to the image of the destroyer, touching him with the tips of her fingers. The chill stone sent a numbing ache through her, and she removed her hand quickly.

She felt a great sigh of relief when she finally stepped onto the bridge. Though dim, the flight system panels shone with a warm luminescence. The opposing darkness pressed in on the light like a fog, creating the illusion that Anya looked through a mist of frosted glass. Four shiidh wandered in and out of the pockets of light, as if they were wisps of living shadow. The equipment's glow fractured weirdly on the crystal spikes hanging at their belts, making Anya think for a moment that the Vartal women were taller and leaner than usual. Tuatha stood over a stone table, inspecting the wrapped object Vivian had given to Anya at their parting on the Penardun launch platform. When the wrappings had been removed, an elegant curved sword was revealed.

"The weapon's hilt has told the tale your sister meant for us," Tuatha rattled in a voice that sounded like sharpened crystal. "In faith we now return the blade, yet still it keeps a secret's trust."

"If by that you mean no one has ever seen anything like it in the whole galaxy," Anya said as she reached the table, "then yes. My family spent many of our resources trying to discover its origin, but it does not match any weapon on record."

"And will you tell the aged truth of how this matchless thing of worth has somehow come into the hands of Danaan's fairest kin?"

Anya fingered the sword's hilt tenderly, trying to decipher the woman's riddling speech.

"When I was found nearly four hundred years ago, the sword was with me."

Tuatha rustled.

"So Ninevay is not your name of birth?"

"No," Anya admitted, trying not to become mesmerized by the flickers of light dancing through the room. "The Ninevays found me, naked and alone, this sword my only company. I couldn't remember anything, not even my name. They tried to help me discover who I really was, but my fingerprints had not been registered in any system. They hoped that the sword's origin might lead to an answer, but nothing turned up. After a few years the Ninevays were kind enough to invite me into their family."

"Yet, after all this time, still nothing of your past has come to surface on your mind?"

"Only when I touch the sword do I feel my memories try to awaken, but I can't recall anything solid. Just impressions."

Anya lifted the sword, frustration pulling her face into a frown.

"I don't think this was mine. It belonged to someone I knew, but I can't seem to remember who that was."

When Anya looked at Tuatha, the shiidh woman was staring thoughtfully at the weapon. She slid her thin, mottled fingers down the length of the metal's curve.

"There is a set of deeply written runes inscribed along the blade. Can you speak them?"

"I believe the sword has a name," Anya explained. "The words say *Moonstone Retribution.*"

"The language here may lead you to your home," Tuatha offered.

"We took it to every linguist we could find. Not one could identify or translate it."

Tuatha's razor teeth flashed in what Anya hoped was awe.

"Then how, pray tell, can you discern the runes?"

Anya's response was quick and she took a step away from the intimidating elf. "I've just always been able to read it. I have no idea why."

Tuatha considered the answer, then handed over the weapon's sheath. Anya awkwardly slid the curved metal inside. When she was finished, Tuatha eyed her with amusement.

"Your healer's nature thwarts the skillful use of such an object. Metal thirsts for blood."

"Like I said, I'm positive it wasn't mine," Anya squeaked, clutching the sword to her chest. It was the last bit of home she had left and she was desperate to change the subject. "Please tell me why my sister sent me to you."

One of the others passed a dataplate to Tuatha, but the Vartal leader took it without breaking her gaze on Anya. The physician couldn't help but feel that stare peer straight into her soul.

"Your sister's choice distresses you. I fear my words will bring no comfort to that care."

"I have to know," Anya begged, swallowing a fresh threat of tears. "My sister died for this. I need to hear that her sacrifice was worth it."

"Have joy; she met the task her fate foretold," Tuatha whispered.

"What does that mean?" Anya choked. "Has she always been working for the shiidh?"

Tuatha's expression narrowed in anger and she stiffened.

"The shiidh do not pretense as spies. We worship Danu. Vivian reached out to us."

Anya bit her lip, worried what to say next. Obviously, the Vartal matron was offended.

"I meant no disrespect, Mistress Tuatha," Anya apologized humbly. "My sorrow overwhelmed my good sense. Of course I meant to ask how long Vivian and the shiidh have been working together and—um—for what purpose, exactly?"

Tuatha's face relaxed into a spooky grin. "The rapid rise of Medrod's power made your sister wonder. Blurry lies and wicked deeds he keeps disguised from all. She found the truth. Her evidence will bring him low."

Anya swallowed. Chancellor Medrod had been running the Coalition for almost a hundred years. Vivian had been working against him for a long time.

"Why did she never tell me?" Anya asked sadly.

"To keep you safe, as I would for my own."

"I didn't realize," Anya sniffed, brushing the tears from her eyes. "I guess I just assumed all you wanted was to turn the tide of the war."

Tuatha looked at Anya sternly.

"The shiidh do not obey the Vartal people. We submit to edicts from our goddess. This the people have forgotten. Danu is the sovereign of all life, not war."

"If you really believe that, why don't you stop the MetaGalactic war?" Anya demanded.

With only her eyes, Tuatha commanded each of her sister shiidh to leave. She didn't continue speaking until all were gone.

"As mother of all species," Tuatha explained with a sneer, "Danu outlaws unions forced without her blessing. This commandment we do preach throughout the worlds."

"Your goddess hates blending so much that you ordered your people to murder us?"

"The war was not of us proclaimed," Tuatha said, lacing each syllable with a glass hiss. "The Druid Council passed the charge. We are neutral."

"But why help me then? Why side with my sister?"

"Perhaps our goals are not the same, but we believe our paths align. For countless years has Danu slept, but just this century awoken. There must be a connection."

"Danu appeared?" Anya asked. "You mean the actual goddess has come to speak with you?"

"In ages past, did Danu lead us from her temple on our planet. When she came to us unlooked for, demanding that we join the war, we knew we spoke with someone false."

"An imposter!" Anya declared.

"This conclusion we believe."

"And you think that Chancellor Medrod has something to do with it? That my sister's information will lead you to the fake Danu?"

Tuatha nodded.

"So why then did you want me to contact Lieutenant Kyleren? What does he have to do with all this?"

"The ship who bears him is alive, a servant of the goddess. Danu wants her relic found; Kyleren is the keeper. Without him we will fail."

Anya wasn't quite sure what that meant. Obviously squad Aon's ship had some fancy new LT systems, but what was this 'relic' Tuatha meant? Anya didn't really dare to request an explanation. All that mattered was that for some reason, the shiidh believed Kyleren was crucial to their success. For Anya, that meant she wouldn't be alone anymore.

"How did you even get the frequency to hack their ship's systems?"

"Oh, there is something on that ship that wants the shiidh to find it."

"But you don't know what," Anya said, shivers clawing up her skin.

Tuatha only smiled more ferociously.

"And what if Lieutenant Kyleren doesn't come?" Anya asked.

"Of that we have no fear," Tuatha said.

"How can you know that for certain?"

The answer was not what Anya had anticipated.

"Because, dear girl, the one who asked was you."

27: JUST BELIEVE

Margariete paced back and forth with terse steps, her arms crossed tightly. She debated her twin's logic, trying to devise an alternative to his plan of inviting Kyleren to join them. She already knew the lieutenant's answer. There was little doubt he would refuse. But that was only a slight inconvenience. Her magic would ensure his compliance. What really bothered her was having to spend the rest of her life in the company of an overconfident oaf.

No excuse surfaced to save her, however, so in sudden decision she huffed around a bend, moodily wishing that she hadn't missed Kyleren's heart when she had stabbed him with *Stardawn*.

"So that's it? We do nothin'?" she heard Lance yell in exasperation.

Margariete slipped back behind the corner and flattened against it, hoping the two soldiers on the other side hadn't spotted her.

"Lance, there's nothing we can do," Captain Reese replied. "Squad Aon is to report back to home base for resupply."

"Wayne, we can't just leave the doc out there!"

"It's not our decision to make. We have our orders."

"Frag orders!" Lance shouted.

Too curious not to peek, Margariete slid half an eye from the safety of her hiding place. Captain Reese's face plainly spoke disapproval.

"Keep your attitude locked down or you're going to get yourself quarter-decked again," Reese warned. "Our crew is shot to hell and LAMIE's trashed. Command has the coordinates. Anya's in their hands now."

"That's the problem," Kyleren argued.

"I'm sorry, Lance, I want to go after her too," Reese said, clapping his comrade on the back with an open palm. "But short of commandeering LAMIE, we've got nothing."

Kyleren stood motionless while Reese disappeared in the opposite direction of Margariete's hiding place. As soon as the captain was gone, he angrily jerked his pistol from its holster and jammed in his core drive.

"You done spyin' on me yet, Blue Eyes?" he said without looking up.

Margariete slid around the corner, staring at his back.

"How did you know?"

"My armor has an enemy locator," he stated as he replaced his weapon. He turned to face her with eyes that clearly reflected annoyance. "Plus, I saw you duck behind that corner. What'd you want, Mags?"

She shifted uncomfortably. This conversation had started all wrong. Intending to reassert her confidence, she mentally arranged an insult, but a question came out instead, almost of its own volition.

"You have a friend in trouble?" she asked.

"Not that it's your business," he replied cautiously, "but yeah."

"Why don't you just go after her anyway?"

"You're the one who reads minds," Kyleren snapped. "Get the answer yourself if you want it."

He turned to leave. Suddenly, she didn't want him to go. Something in his face had expressed true concern for whoever was in trouble, and for a moment, Margariete felt she understood him. If he walked away now, she didn't think she could muster the courage to force him to go with them.

"I could," Margariete said quietly, "but sometimes talking is a better approach."

Kyleren's shoulders shook with a ripple of sarcastic laughter. He turned back to her.

"No offense, princess, but talkin' to you won't improve my mood."

The fragment of empathy glazed over with ice. "You've never tried," she growled, "so how would you know?"

"'Cause I can't stand you," Kyleren said easily.

"Tell me something I don't know," Margariete returned, unimpressed.

Kyleren stared at her. Margariete could feel his mental struggle, so she waited.

"Command denied our request to pick up Doc Anya," he finally admitted. "She's a good friend of the squad. I don't like leavin' people behind."

"Maybe your captain had a point then. There are two ships here. Why can't you just borrow one?"

"'Cause I'll be court martialed," he complained.

"What do you think will happen if you don't go after her?"

Kyleren's face drooped.

"The Coalition gave up talkin' stuff out with the gromms a long time ago. There'll be a fight. Anya'll be collateral damage."

"Then maybe you should get court martialed, or whatever that is," Margariete proposed. "When someone's life depends on you, you have to make sacrifices."

"I wish it was that simple, Blue Eyes."

"Why shouldn't it be?" Margariete asked frankly.

"It just isn't," Kyleren returned with a head shake. "That's the way the world works."

The hulking soldier looked so distraught that Margariete was assaulted by a surge of pity. She reached out and placed her ungloved hand on his arm.

"The world is what we make it. Our decisions allow others to live in peace," she paused, "or can cost them their lives."

"You mean your little brother, right?" Kyleren said.

Margariete snatched back her hand.

"How do you know about him?"

"Stoic Boy mentioned it. Name of the guy who killed him is Kirion, right?"

Margariete's jaw clenched, heat simmering at the tip of her tongue. What was Raeylan thinking? How dare he share something so private with this uncouth barbarian.

"And I suppose my twin also told you that our younger brother was barely twelve? That I watched Kirion torture Shikun before ripping out his heart?"

"No," Kyleren said softly, "he didn't tell me any of that."

Margariete lost control. Her emotions were so tumbled that she couldn't use her domination on Kyleren if she wanted to. Rage, grief, and humiliation clotted her head. She closed her eyes, desperately trying to concentrate.

"Is there anything else my brother mentioned that I should know about?" she choked between her teeth.

"Yeah," Kyleren said. She heard him shuffle his feet. "Look, I didn't know about your arm-glove thing. I'm sorry."

She couldn't help a flutter that lifted her heart. Unconsciously, her bare hand massaged her gloved one. She opened her eyes.

"Well, you could have asked," she mumbled ungraciously.

She turned to leave. Damn everything to the Void, Raeylan had told this man too much. Her twin could try to convince the solider to come with them himself. She wanted nothing more to do with it.

A strong hand gripped her arm as she made to walk away. She tried to rip herself free, but Kyleren's grasp was like iron. She whipped to face him. His expression was a mask of humility.

"If I had known it was such a big deal," he said, "I wouldn't've done it. I crossed a line."

Then he let her go. Margariete's eyes fell to the ground. Her cheeks burned with—what? Anger? Shame? No, it was something else. Something too horrific to name. What, by Nehro's Grace, was wrong with her?

The silence became uncomfortable. If she walked away now, she would look like a coward in the face of Kyleren's gallantry. Attempting her task was the only honorable way to resolve the situation.

"My brother would like to invite you to join our quest," she said.

"Quest?" Kyleren chuckled at the word.

"Yes," Margariete countered, flashing her eyes onto him. "We have pledged to defeat Kirion. You find that amusing?"

"You just sound crazy, that's all," he shrugged. "You got enough cracked stories about magic and quests to fill the holy shrine on Agrona."

"Since he killed my brother, my every waking moment has been spent fighting against Kirion. If he isn't stopped, he will once again become a god. No one will escape him."

"Gods aren't real, Blue Eyes. I think we're safe. Sorry about your brother, but my answer's no. I can't go with you."

"Can't or won't?" Margariete demanded.

"I got a job to do," Kyleren said. "And I don't prance around the galaxy like an Agromor bastard chasin' stories about gods and magic."

"Well, I'm not surprised there," Margariete roared furiously. "You couldn't recognize magic if it slapped you in the face."

"Cuz it doesn't exist," Kyleren returned.

"Fine. I didn't want you to come with us anyway. It's Raeylan who thinks we need you. I'd rather sleep in the jaws of Skoh's wolves than spend a decade with you."

"I have no idea what you just said," Kyleren said with indifference.

"I'm calling you a coward, lieutenant."

Kyleren advanced on her so fast that she instinctively retreated. Before she even considered drawing *Stardawn,* he had her backed against the wall. His fist slammed into the wall next to her head, his body looming over her.

"I fear nothin'. Not you, not the Agromors, and definitely not your gromm skrit gods."

"Have it your way, then," Margariete challenged, straightening as much as she could. "Stay here and let Kirion destroy you."

She tried to push him away, but his body didn't budge.

"I've got nothin' your Kirion wants."

"Then you weren't paying attention," she shouted angrily. "You are an artifact bearer! Kirion will find you. He wants your magic."

"My answer's still no," Kyleren said obstinately.

"Then you are a fool," Margariete accused.

"Is that so?"

Kyleren leaned in closer, his breath brushing against her lips. Her heart pounded like a cornered animal.

"And what if you're wrong? The Coalition is fightin' to free the universe from the Agromors. I'm already where I need to be. Your quest has nothin' to do with me."

He pulled back and Margariete slid away from the wall.

"Then I'm sure you'll understand that I'm only asking as a courtesy," she said.

"And what're you gonna do, force me?" he dared.

Margariete instructed her mouth to form the word 'yes,' but once again, as she looked into the lieutenant's eyes, her lips defied her.

"No," she said.

Neither spoke. Then Kyleren's hand pressed against the comm in his ear. He was obviously receiving a transmission.

"Read you, sir. Yes, sir, she's standin' right here."

Margariete watched his brow furrow unhappily.

"Confirm order? Yes, sir. Immediately, sir."

In a blur Kyleren drew his pistol and held it to her head. Margariete's hand reached for *Stardawn's* hilt.

"Don't fight me, Mags," he pleaded. "I have to take you into custody and I don't wanna shoot you."

"Lies don't suit you, lieutenant," Margariete spat acidly. "We both know you'd love an excuse to shoot me."

Kyleren's grip tightened on his pistol. Her hand rested on her weapon, but she knew she'd be dead before she could manage to unsheathe it.

"Then read my mind," he offered, "and you'll know for sure."

His suggestion made her pause. What if he meant it? She opened the bridge between their minds.

It was there: the desire to cause her no harm. And something else—but she broke contact quickly, fearful of what it might mean.

Instead of drawing her sword, she loosened *Stardawn's* belt and tossed it to the ground.

"I hope you're as confident about that as you think, Lieutenant Kyleren."

"Me too," he agreed gloomily.

28: Time For The How-Screwed-We-Are Report

Lance, Trish, and Gary stood at attention behind the round table in the situation room waiting for Major Huard to begin his briefing. Wayne and Dr. Pryce peered over Gene's shoulder as the technobionomist rummaged through the disorderly data clusters floating just above the table's surface. Kyleren thought the information looked to be records and codes designated for LAMIE's security systems. He struggled not to fidget. Huard seemed to be taking his time explaining why the twins had been confined in the brig.

"There," Gene said at last, pointing to the screen.

"I didn't see anything," Wayne said skeptically.

"Look at the time registry," Gene clarified impatiently.

"It jumps forward a minute," Dr. Pryce interjected.

"Forty-nine-point-six-two-three seconds to be exact," Gene said.

"Someone erased the feed?" Huard asked angrily. "I thought all security surveillance was protected by LAMIE's board!"

"It is," Gene said. "To destroy it would take hours of recalibration on LAMIE's protocol board. It's impossible. I've been in there since she landed."

"What about during your rack time?"

"The only people with clearance to LAMIE's board room are Colonel Stoddard and myself," Gene said shaking his head. "LAMIE didn't report any unauthorized tampering."

As the conversation continued, Kyleren's impatience grew.

"Well, we know it wasn't the colonel," Dr. Pryce suggested. "He's still unconscious in the med bay."

"And what's that supposed to mean?" Gene returned in an offended tone.

"You're the only person who has had access to that room," the doctor concluded, "and the only one with enough skill to alter LAMIE's protoboard."

"Are you accusing me of stealing?" Gene shrieked as he jumped to his feet.

"I was just making an observation, Gene," Dr. Pryce said.

Kyleren almost shouted in exasperation, but was saved the embarrassment by Trish.

"Uh—excuse me, major, sir," she interrupted crisply as Gene glared at the doctor, "could you apprise us of the situation? We GAELs are all in the dark here, sir."

Huard's eyes still reeked circles of fatigue. He shoved Gene back into his chair none-too-gently. Then he turned to the assembled GAELs and growled, "The situation, sergeant, is that the GraEL has turned up missing from Gene's office. And LAMIE's records of the theft are missing."

"That is another curious detail," Dr. Pryce added with a sidelong glance at Gene, "that the GraEL was in his office when it vanished."

"I am the most advanced technobionomist in my field," Gene wailed. "What possible reason could I have to steal the Graviton Energy Locus?"

"Improved lab experimentation, more conclusive research opportunities, the black market." Pryce shrugged.

Gene opened his mouth to argue but stopped short, lost in contemplating the doctor's suggestions.

"I think Gene's innocence isn't in question, sir," Wayne remarked during the lull. "He's too invested in military contracts to turn on us."

Huard nodded in agreement and said, "Then that leaves only the twins."

"Hold on," Kyleren declared. "You think Mags and Stoic Boy stole the GraEL?"

He screwed his eyebrows with doubt.

"Yes I do," Huard said.

"Mags helped to save our asses out there," Kyleren defended. "She's not about to turn on us."

"You can't know that for sure, lieutenant," Wayne challenged tiredly. "There's still a lot we don't know about her."

"Neither can you," Kyleren argued, stepping out of line. "You said LAMIE's surveillance data was gone, so there's no proof it was them!"

"Only Gene has access to that office," Huard barked, "so the only way to get in there without being detected would be to teleport in. Who do we know who has that capability, lieutenant?"

Lance flashed a look of surprise to Wayne, but the captain refused to meet his gaze. Kyleren muttered a string of angry obscenities. He'd been stabbed in the back by his best friend.

"I'm sorry, lieutenant," Wayne explained formally. "The GraEL has been stolen. I didn't have a choice."

"Frag you, Wayne!" Lance roared. "You always get a choice."

"That intel should have been in your report, lieutenant!" Huard snapped. "The entire mission is in jeopardy because of the skrit you left out!"

Kyleren ignored Huard's accusations, focusing on Wayne instead.

"If they stole the GraEL, why didn't they make a run for it? Think about it, Wayne. The twins can get outta the brig any fraggin' time they want. They're stayin' without a fuss. Does that make sense to you?"

"We don't know the extent of their plan," Wayne shot back. "That could all be a trick."

"Shut up, Wayne," Kyleren snarled, taking a step in the captain's direction.

Wayne immediately drew his sidearm.

"Permission to take Lieutenant Kyleren into custody, Major Huard."

"Granted," the major rumbled.

"Wait!" Dr. Pryce intervened. "The lieutenant has a valid point. The disappearance of the GraEL marks the twins as suspects immediately. Why didn't they just steal one of the ships and escape?"

"Use your head, doctor," Huard howled ungraciously. "They can't fly LAMIE without a core drive interface, and if they stole the mire field ship we could easily catch them. They're dead if they run and they know it."

"But that still doesn't explain why they would take the GraEL now, when they haven't a chance to escape cleanly," the doctor rebutted. "It would make more sense if they had waited for a more opportune moment."

"I'm with the doctor on this one," Gene agreed, "even though his stupidity tried to pin the blame on me just a few seconds ago."

"You are just as insubordinate as the lieutenant, Gene," Huard accused. "I didn't see any mention of Raeylan's teleportation ability on your report, either."

"Uh, because I never witnessed it," Gene complained. "What is it with you military guys? You're missing one vital fact. Even if the twins had managed to steal the GraEL, neither could have possibly manipulated LAMIE's protoboard and erased the security data."

Huard's face turned red. Wayne's BT pistol was steadily trained on Kyleren, though he seemed less sure of himself in light of Gene's analysis. Things were spiraling into crazy faster than a ship caught in the Eye of Baylour.

Maybe he should take Blue Eyes up on her offer. It would beat being fragged in a court martial.

Just as he was considering his chances if he jumped Wayne, Kyleren was saved by a calm, clear voice.

"Please do not distress yourselves," LAMIE's said. "Everything is under control."

Everyone instinctively looked up at the ceiling.

"LAMIE, what do you mean everything is under control?" Gene asked guardedly.

"It was I who manipulated the security data," she admitted.

"What the frag?" Huard shouted at the ship's technobionomist.

"That shouldn't be possible," Gene defended, his body looking like a deflated balloon. "You can't do that LAMIE," he said to the ceiling. "Your omega quadrant access provision protocols restrict any tampering with security conventions."

"You are quite right, Gene. My omega quadrant access provision protocols do not allow me to alter the security systems you initiated," LAMIE said. "But they do, however, allow me to extract specified data and sync it to a remote file sector."

Gene's mouth swung open.

"I take it she can do that," Dr. Pryce stated.

The technobionomist opened and closed his mouth silently, apparently at a loss for words.

"Well then, just find the file sector she hid it in," Trish recommended.

By the sour grey that mottled Gene's face, Kyleren knew that wouldn't help.

"That could take years!" Gene said. "There's enough storage in LAMIE's datacore to maintain the personal records of every citizen in Coalition space!"

"What about mapping the route used to transfer the information?" Trish offered.

"That would be like tracking the path of a single particle through a tornado. There are just too many variables."

"Then make her give the footage back," Huard hollered. "Didn't you at least proto her to follow orders?"

"Of course I did!" Gene said.

Huard slammed his fist against the table.

"LAMIE, as ranking officer I command you to give me access to the security data."

"I could, major," LAMIE said pleasantly, "but it would not help you discover the perpetrator. I have masked the data with a series of chameleon fractal algorithms that would take even Gene three months to decrypt."

"Frag it all, we can't return to Penardun without the GraEL," Huard complained. He turned to Gene and said, "You told us LAMIE's design was flawless."

"I also told you she wasn't ready for this kind of mission. But did anyone listen to me? No!" Gene screamed. "If I had been given the proper amount of field testing, I would have caught such an error in LAMIE's protocols!"

"Calm down, everyone," Dr. Pryce soothed. "LAMIE is an intelligent entity, capable of complex thinking patterns. Perhaps she can be reasoned with."

"I fully understand your arguments," LAMIE said, "but I could not allow you access to the decrypted data even if you somehow persuaded me, Dr. Pryce. I have locked my key to the encryption code with a subroutine that will not surface until a certain eventuality."

"What eventuality it that?" Huard asked.

"The rendezvous with the shiidh vessel to collect Dr. Anya Ninevay and the information in her possession."

Lance looked between his comrades, trying not to laugh. Wayne holstered his sidearm and stood with his arms moodily crossed. Both of Gene's hands clawed miserably at his face.

"No deal," Huard stated. "We'll take LAMIE back to Penardun and force her cooperation in friendly space."

"A predictable reaction, Major Huard, but one that I have anticipated," LAMIE said. "Therefore I added a second subroutine into my contingency algorithm. If I am jumped to Penardun before meeting with the shiidh vessel, a complex series of kill commands will cascade through my operating systems, ultimately concluding with the unavoidable overload of the STT drive."

Lance burst out laughing. The Coalition's most powerful infiltration team was at the mercy of a 14-year-old machine. Wayne glowered at him as Kyleren said, "Looks like we get to go after Anya after all."

29: They Haven't Built A Circuit That Could Hold You

Raeylan relaxed, letting his knees take the weight of his body as he meditated in the metal cell he occupied. He could sense the passage of time around him, flowing across the bare walls that kept him prisoner like water over stones. Just as rocks are shaped smooth by the river that holds them, so time eroded the objects around him, molding them to its liking. The energy field that barred the door hummed gently, its echo blunted by Raeylan's special sense. Only the tense tapping from Margariete's prison broke through the calm. Though Raeylan couldn't see her, he knew something was wrong. She had surrendered far too peacefully.

He opened one eye to survey the GAEL who watched over them. His name was Chief Chad Snow and he leaned against the brig wall with practiced ease. From what Raeylan had gathered, the field medic was devout in his loyalty to the squad. He was not likely to tolerate a conversation between his prisoners.

So Raeylan slowly drew air into his lungs, focusing his power into an intangible ring around his body. As he exhaled, the circle expanded, drowning the world around him in a sea of stunted time. Chief Chad Snow moved so slowly that he seemed frozen, oblivious to Raeylan's actions.

With a nip of saline scented air the former king teleported into his sister's cell. She too appeared motionless. He touched her shoulder, inviting her into his state of normal time. She didn't seem surprised, but simply noted his presence and the stillness of the guard.

"Something disturbs you, sister?" Raeylan asked.

"I'm fine," she said, chewing absently on her thumbnail.

He continued patiently, knowing Margariete would not divulge her true feelings without some persuasion.

"I feared you would constrain the GAELs to incapacitate you fully before submitting to their imprisonment a second time. But it appears you arrived without violence."

His comment lured a reaction more quickly than he anticipated. Her anger flew in words as she hissed, "And I'm upset that we're still confined here when you could easily teleport us away!"

Raeylan saw through her temper like glass.

"Time will prove our innocence. We have done nothing wrong," he stated.

"Whatever," Margariete snapped, peevishly picking at a thread from her glove.

Raeylan reached his hand over hers to stop her from permanently damaging the garment.

"It is unlike you to enter custody without resistance, sister," Raeylan said, turning the conversation back toward his original purpose.

"I believe you would argue that resistance could lead to my senseless death," she countered obstinately.

"That does sound like something I might say. But it does not explain why you yielded so easily."

"The lieutenant was the one who arrested me. I thought you might be irritated if I accidentally killed him," she said.

"I know you better than that, Margariete. If it meant protecting yourself, you would have engaged him without thought. Share your reasons with me."

Margariete turned her face away. Raeylan waited, but her refusal to speak lasted long moments.

"You know I cannot slow time's flow indefinitely, Margariete," he prodded.

Margariete rubbed her palms together uncomfortably, then drew a deep breath and said, "Kyleren asked me to trust him. He promised no harm would come to me."

"And do you believe him?" Raeylan asked.

"I don't know," Margariete expelled angrily.

To Raeylan it was as close to a 'yes' as his sister would ever admit.

"So you were asking him to come with us when his commanders ordered him to take you into custody," he mused.

"Yes," Margariete pouted, scuffing the toe of her boot against the floor.

"Did he agree to join us?"

"He said, in his vernacular, 'No fraggin' way'," she imitated with scorn.

"Then you were forced to sway him," Raeylan reasoned.

Margariete bit her lip and didn't answer.

"Did you fail?" he asked in concern.

Margariete refused to look at him.

"I didn't try. I was going to—but I just couldn't. I don't know what's wrong with me."

Gently, he took his sister's chin in his palm and turned her eyes to meet him.

"Our path lies with the angels of Chano, Margariete. We must remain here. Their culturalist, Percy Jameson, has identified the language of Chano's scroll."

"Well, elaborate!" Margariete demanded, clearly relieved by the change of subject.

Raeylan removed his hand.

"He thinks it may be a prayer written by a group of elves called the shiidh."

"So you think we need to find them."

"Yes," Raeylan agreed, "but we must ensure Lieutenant Kyleren comes with us."

"I don't understand, Raeylan. We already know Kyleren has Chano's artifact. Of what further use is the scroll? It doesn't even tell us what the artifact does!"

"Kalariel gathered the god scrolls for a reason. Their purpose is of greater significance than merely leading us to the artifacts. We must take every opportunity to understand them."

Margariete nodded thoughtfully. Raeylan exhaled, thankful that she had chosen not to fight him on this. He teleported back to his own cell moments before time regained control of itself. Chad Snow looked between both compartments quizzically, but only shook his head, as if he were dismissing something logic told him he hadn't seen.

30: You Are So Much Less Than The Best Of Humanity

Kyleren stood stiff next to Wayne, refusing to make eye contact. He ground his teeth. His gromm bastard friend of 26 years had ratted him out. It had taken most of Lance's self-control not to pummel Wayne to the deck right there—which turned out to be a good thing.

Huard, unable to sway LAMIE, had resentfully agreed to make the rendezvous with the shiidh. The major ordered Trish and Chad to remain on Danaan to help Bedin finish repairs on the mire field ship. Private Thompson had been cleared for action, his burn scars still reflected the glossy sheen of new regeneration. His max GAEL strength hadn't returned. That meant the only soldiers currently on board at a hundred percent were Kyleren and Wayne.

Despite that, Lance blissfully imagined the satisfaction he'd get when he finally got a chance to give Wayne a good mouth full of fist.

LAMIE shuddered as her docking clamps attached to the shiidh vessel. Lance steadied his BT assault rifle, covering the path that led to the enemy, doubting it was even worth the effort. Last time he fought them, they'd immobilized the whole team with just a song.

"Dock complete," Gene's voice crooned from the comm in Kyleren's ear. "Initiating rear hatch pressurization protocol. Releasing hatch seal."

A dark path led from the docking bay into the shiidh ship as the heavy bulkhead door hissed open. Lance heard light footsteps echoing from the black emptiness. He tensed, ready for anything.

Anya emerged from the darkness, blinking in the light. She clutched a long object wrapped in cloth. She glanced quickly at the assembled crew: Wayne, Huard, and Lance. Her pale face smothered in tears as she noticed him. She dashed into Kyleren's chest with a grateful hiccup of sobs. He lowered his rifle just in time. She hadn't seemed to see it.

"I am so relieved to see you, lieutenant," she mumbled into his combat armor.

Lance glanced uneasily between his comrade and commander. Huard looked annoyed, Wayne uncomfortable. Kyleren patted Anya awkwardly on the back, trying to stem her emotional outburst.

"Good to see you're safe, doc," he said, pushing her away gently.

Anya wiped her face with one hand, the other gripping her package more tightly as she did so. A displeased sigh, like glass panes rattling together, drew Kyleren's attention. His firearm snapped back into position with expert precision, locking on a robed woman who had just stepped into the hangar. Her hand shaded her deep eyes against the light, her heavy robes swathed her figure in midnight veneer. The shiidh towered over Huard and Anya, almost as tall as a GAEL, but more willowy. Her streaked hair looked like toxic copper that had been on the hull of a ship too long.

"Wait! Please," Anya said, stepping into his weapon's firing line. "This is Mistress Tuatha. She's a friend of my sister."

Huard spoke before anyone else could.

"Your sister's credibility is under scrutiny, Dr. Ninevay." He turned to address the enemy woman. "We will listen to what you have to say only if you agree to disengage the dock with our ship while the meeting is in progress. And no weapons," he concluded, eyeing the crystal spike on her belt.

"Restrictive are your wishes," the woman's voice grated. There was a tense pause before she decided. "So be it."

She curled her long fingers around her spike and offered it to Huard. He snatched it with a grimace. Kyleren noticed that the major's knuckles turned white as he struggled to not drop the strange weapon. The shiidh seemed amused as Huard clamped it to his buckler.

"This way," he growled rudely, leading Anya and the woman up the stairs. Kyleren and Wayne waited until LAMIE's hatch closed and the shiidh vessel had fully disengaged its docking corridor. Then they hustled to the situation room.

Anya, Gene, Percy, and Dr. Pryce already sat at the holotable. There were plenty of open seats, but the shiidh remained standing, looming over the assembly like a ghastly specter. Anya's cloth bundle lay on the table. Huard had just finished introductions as the two GAELs arrived.

". . . and Dr. Pryce."

Anya started perceptibly at the name, failing to hide her alarm.

"Dr. Boris Pryce? Head of the GraEL Attachment Program?"

"Yes," Pryce confirmed, looking offended at her reaction. "I don't believe we've met?"

Anya shook her head and bit her lip. Kyleren didn't understand why Pryce made her uncomfortable, but her fear drew out his protective instincts. He took position behind her.

Huard cleared his throat impatiently when Anya didn't say anything more. After a few minutes, Kyleren placed a hand of comfort on her shoulder. From the corner of his eye he noticed the shiidh watching his actions very closely.

"All right, Smiles," Lance prompted, "what's all this about Chancellor Medrod?"

The pretty elf breathed deeply before answering. She twisted her face upward to meet Kyleren's eyes.

"Do you remember your physical examination last week, lieutenant? How I was upset over the death a child I had delivered?"

"Yeah," Lance grunted, wondering what the frag this had to do with anything.

"I remember," Wayne added. "You said that the baby was healthy and there was no explanation for her death."

"I was right," Anya said, producing a dataplate from her lap and sliding it to Dr. Pryce hesitantly. She flicked her fingers away quickly as the bald man took the device. "The child in question, Riia Farren, was one of the strongest blended children I have ever created. There was no trace of FLTB in her blood. After her sudden death, I repeated my analysis."

"This report is conclusive," Dr. Pryce noted as he scanned the report. "Complete FLTB. You must have missed it."

He tossed the dataplate to Gene.

"Of course that's what I thought," Anya admitted, glancing at everyone around the table. "But every nanomite I prescribe to a patient is marked with a personal ident code."

"I'm not seeing that in this report," Gene said.

"Because those are not the same nanomites I used in Riia Farren's conception," Anya concluded.

Dr. Pryce narrowed his beady eyes.

"You think someone falsified the test samples?"

"Why would someone wanna mess with blood samples?" Lance asked, confused.

Gene shook his head. "I think a more important question is why someone would want to fake the death of an infant? What does that even accomplish?"

Tuatha glided forward and plucked the dataplate from Gene's hands. She inserted a tile and tapped the instrument. Then she handed it to Pryce. As he scrolled through the information his brown face paled.

"This is my work," he boomed. "How did you get this?"

"Of loyal worth were Anya's sister's spies," the shiidh intoned between her sharp ivory teeth. "Your Coalition's lies were plain to find."

Dr. Pryce's brows knit into an angry crease.

"Do you know what this implies?" he accused everyone around the table.

"What?" Huard demanded.

"According to the information we have brought you," Anya announced sadly, "for the last hundred years, the Coalition has been responsible for staging the deaths of countless blended infants. These children are used to increase its military strength. Riia Farren isn't dead. She was stolen from her parents to be used as a test subject in the

GraEL Attachment Program." Anya looked between Lance and Wayne. "Your parents didn't voluntarily release the two of you to serve in the military. Your families think you died at birth. You were both kidnapped by our government and genetically altered to be living weapons."

Lance's gaze shot to Dr. Pryce, waiting for the master of genetics to refute Anya's claim. When he remained silent, Kyleren felt anger surge into his throat.

"Is that true?" he demanded.

"I swear upon my soul," the doctor asserted, "I never knew the children were stolen. I was told they were recruited by legal means only."

Anya's eyes flashed outrage.

"But you did know that only 30 percent of those children actually survive the attachment process past puberty. You reported those numbers yourself. You are a butcher, not a physician!"

Numbness gripped Lance. His torso felt empty of heart and stomach. Many of his childhood friends on Gwydion had disappeared at age nine, after undergoing the first treatments of GraEL Attachment. He had been told that they hadn't made the cut and had been sent home to their families. More schoolmates vanished as his training unit approached puberty. Was Anya telling him that it was all a lie? Most of his comrades had died before they hit sixteen?

Looking at Wayne told Lance that his friend was reaching the same conclusion. They were all just Coalition lab rats.

"The experimentation is not illegal," Dr. Pryce defended. "The Round has passed specific laws that protect the right to such scientific exploration. I've done nothing wrong."

"Except broken the honor code taken by all living tech scientists," Gene accused, looking sick. "We don't kill our research subjects!"

"My participation in these experiments has only increased the success rate of the program," Pryce bellowed. "No one else could have managed the same survival rate! The GAEL VICs are the most advanced force in the galaxy. They are essential to the Coalition's victory in the MetaGalactic War."

"There could have been other ways, other advancements," Gene argued.

"Like what? Intelligent ships?" Dr. Pryce sneered. "Do I have to remind you that for the last century, all major developments in the technobionomy field have been based on my research? The GraEL Attachment program is directly responsible for the Round's decision to initiate the LAMIE project. Your precious ship would not even exist if it weren't for my success in GAEL VIC soldier development."

"Have you forgotten so quickly the reason this war began?" Anya charged. "For freedom! For the right to live with the people we love, to create a family of our own choosing. To raise a child without fear! You have ripped these infants from their mothers. Devastated fathers! Transformed innocents into something they were never meant to be and murdered most of them in the process. You have become the very evil we propose to defeat!"

Silence overtook the room as Anya realized her comment directly insulted their Vartal guest. Then the echo of Tuatha's crystalline laughter spilled over them like unpleasant mist.

"Of little concern is your charge to us. The words of faithless halfbreeds harm us not."

Dr. Pryce shifted uncomfortably and ignored the shiidh.

"You are naïve, Dr. Ninevay. One person's freedom can only be purchased at the price of another's. The GAEL VICs will overpower the inferior capabilities of the enemy. They will win this war for the Coalition. The lives of a few blended children are a small expense."

Lance's whole body rippled with wrath. The coward showed no remorse for his actions.

"You gromm bastard!" he shouted, yanking Pryce out of his chair and slamming him against the wall. "Those kids you're talkin' about were my friends."

Kyleren contracted his fingers around Pryce's neck, hardly knowing what he was doing. Somewhere behind him, Huard was screaming, but the words were swallowed by Lance's uncontrollable rage. His whole life was a lie. This man was responsible for that. It wasn't until he felt the pressure of Wayne's grip on his forearm that the angry roar of his temper was pierced by reason.

"Let him go, Lance," Wayne ordered calmly. "Killing him won't solve anything. He was given the green light by someone else. I'd like to know who."

Kyleren surveyed the table of faces as the doctor struggled to breathe. Gene and Anya were petrified, Percy introspective, and Huard furious. Only the shiidh seemed unaffected by his actions.

"Fine," Lance agreed, releasing Pryce, who scurried behind the major. "But if we decide to kill him, I call dibbs."

"No one is killing anyone!" Huard bellowed. "Dr. Pryce is right. Without the GAELs we wouldn't be winning this war. The fate of a few children is worth the safety of billions."

"Speak for yourself, sir," Wayne growled. Both he and Kyleren stood near the wall, refusing to return to the table. "You weren't forced into the service."

"Are you saying you would have preferred the life of a painter, captain?" Huard scoffed. "Or pushing papers behind a desk somewhere?"

"Guess I wouldn't really know, sir," Wayne returned dangerously, "seeing as I didn't really get much of a choice."

Huard turned to Dr. Pryce.

"You might want to see what you can do about GAEL obstinacy with your next batch of recruits, doctor. Every GAEL under my command challenges orders."

"You mean your assumed command, major," Wayne clarified. "Until Colonel Stoddard is awake."

Lance smiled at Wayne. For that, all was forgiven.

"Will you guys stop the infighting already?" Gene said, smacking the table with his hand. "I want to know who let this happen."

"Your hostile quarrel chokes the worthy pith," the shiidh said, cracking into the conversation. Her deep eyes met everyone in the room, driving each gaze away in turn. Even Kyleren felt daunted. "The very laws that granted Pryce his license over life were fashioned by the Round, 'tis they who hold the key to murder; none so more than he who leads them—founder of all crimes. His blood stains all the horror's fate."

"What?" Kyleren asked, thoroughly confused by the woman's speech. A glance at Wayne confirmed his friend didn't understand it either.

"What Tuatha is trying to explain," Anya said, "is that my sister discovered proof that Chancellor Medrod was directly responsible for the laws that allowed the Coalition to form the GraEL Attachment Program. The chancellor has also been instrumental in forming other questionable military projects outside the public eye, including LAMIE. And just recently he has begun a series of—" she paused, swallowing with disgust,"—breeding facilities to push GAEL development further."

"Breeding facilities?" Percy wheezed.

"Apparently, the natural production of blended infants is too slow to meet the requirements of Dr. Pryce's program. Chancellor Medrod has been targeting people with desirable genetic structure for producing stronger GAEL candidates, abducting them and shipping them out of Coalition space."

Anya stopped to retrieve the forgotten dataplate that had fallen to the deck. She linked it to the holotable and pulled up a system map. Three red blips blinked along one of the planet's surfaces.

"There are three of these breeding facilities in the Famorian Cluster. And not only does he force the crossing of non-consenting victims, but he's been using blending tech to interbreed the main races with ogres, roane, Melsunians, and boghags."

"He's mating those monsters with elves and humans?" Gene asked, turning green.

"And dwarves," Anya whispered. "There are so many combinations I can't bear to tell you all of them."

Kyleren felt like he might hurl. This had to be stopped. Now.

"What does it matter, if we manage to save the universe?" Pryce mumbled, clutching his damaged throat.

A glare from Wayne silenced him.

"Are you sure this information is accurate?" Huard asked Anya, his eyes plainly speaking his refusal to believe any of it. "I'm afraid I can't take you just at your word, especially with the company you keep."

The major scowled at the shiidh. She curled her lip in disdain and bore down on him with her gaze. Huard hastily turned back to Anya.

"Then allow your technobionomist to evaluate its authenticity," Anya recommended, pushing her dataplate into Gene's hands.

"No," Huard refused immediately. "Whatever Dr. Pryce's work, I won't believe this wild skrit about the chancellor. He's done nothing but help us win this war! Captain Reese and Lieutenant Kyleren, arrest Dr. Ninevay. She is charged with defamation of a government official and allying herself with the enemy. Capture the shiidh as well. I'm sure she has valuable information we could use."

Neither Lance nor Wayne moved. Huard's face turned a deep shade of red.

"Now soldiers! That is a direct order!" he screamed.

"I vote," LAMIE intervened suddenly, "that we expose the chancellor and take back the galaxy. After all, it is up to the next generation to heal the ills created by its parents."

"I agree with LAMIE," Gene said, thumbing toward the ceiling.

"This is mutiny!" Huard hollered.

"The crime against all nature far outweighs mere mortal law," Tuatha chimed. "If you abide this evil, then within your soul is just as foul."

Huard made to lift his sidearm, but Lance was faster. He dashed from the wall and knocked the weapon from Huard's hand before the major could even level it to fire.

The shiidh didn't even blink.

"I think you could use a night in the brig to cool off," Lance suggested as he pinned Huard's arms behind his back. Dr. Pryce surrendered to Wayne without protest.

"You'll pay for this," Huard seethed. "I'll make sure you get executed for treason!"

"Only if the Coalition can catch us," Wayne said with a wink at Anya. "If you'd give us the information, doc, I would like Gene to check your sources."

The shiidh's granite face split in a fierce grin of spiky teeth. With an elegant swoop she took back her crystal spike from Huard's buckler. At the same time, Anya rose from her chair and passed her cloth-wrapped parcel to Gene.

"My sister concealed the original information in the hilt of this sword," she explained.

Gene took the offering as Wayne deployed orders.

"While I dock with the shiidh ship, I want Percy to take Anya back to the med bay to see if she can do something for Colonel Stoddard and Corporal Harris. Kyleren, lock these two up and release the twins."

"Not a problem," Lance said, pushing Huard through the door. From behind, he heard Wayne talking to the ship.

"All right, LAMIE, a deal's a deal. Get to work on that encrypted footage. It's time we found out what really happened to the GraEL."

31: ALSO CUTE AND FLUFFY

Kyleren shoved the prisoners all the way across the secondary level, ignoring Huard's colorful protests. As the party tumbled into the brig, Private Thompson jumped to his feet in a hurried salute. As he noted the situation, however, that the lieutenant was leading his commanding officer to a cell, the gesture wavered in uncertainty.

"At ease, private," Kyleren instructed as he initiated the energy barrier to imprison the major.

"Private Thompson!" Huard yelled desperately. "Captain Reese and Lieutenant Kyleren have been compromised. Do something!"

Gary nervously reached for his sidearm.

"You were gonna discharge your weapon at the shiidh lady," Lance growled across the energy field. "That's an act 'a war."

Gary kept his hand on his weapon but didn't draw it.

"What's going on, lieutenant?"

"We're already at war! I gave you an order, private!" Huard screamed as Kyleren threw Pryce into an adjacent cell.

"Shut up, major," Lance said, noticing that the twins had both risen to their feet and watched the proceedings with interest, though neither spoke. Gary's grip tightened on the handle of his firearm, so Kyleren asked, "You gonna shoot me, private?"

"Imprisoning a superior officer is a serious offense," Thompson returned, "and I'd like an explanation."

"Then scurry your newb-ass to the situation room and ask Captain Reese," Lance said, folding his arms across his chest. "He gave the order to lock these gromm lovin' bastards up."

With an uneasy glance at the captives, Gary dashed from the brig.

"Please, lieutenant," Dr. Pryce begged when Thompson was gone, "be reasonable."

"Doc," Kyleren said testily, "I wouldn't push me. I'm still plannin' on killin' you."

Dr. Pryce's beard quivered as he huddled in the corner of his cell. Kyleren grunted in satisfaction and moved to the control panel that fed the twins' energy barriers and shut them off.

"Is your life always this interesting, lieutenant?" Margariete asked.

"You should see it on a bad day," he replied with a grin.

She laughed, but her eyes quickly found the deck. Kyleren glanced at Raeylan, thinking he had done something wrong. But Margariete's brother remained as expressionless as ever. With an inward sigh, Lance flipped off the power.

"You guys should come with me," he said. "We're gonna find out what happened to the GraEL."

"You are setting us free?" Raeylan asked, taking no move to leave his cell.

"Yeah," Lance said. A thought occurred to him so he added, "Weird stuff is happenin' an' we wondered if you could help us figure it out."

"Of course, lieutenant," Raeylan answered with a quick bow.

"You're going to trust them?" Huard squealed in disdain. "You might as well feed us all to a horde of Famorian trolls!"

"Whatever you say, major," Lance said, "but just remember who got quarter-decked this time around."

Huard's nose flared, but Kyleren led the twins from the brig before the major could say anything in return. They followed him silently to the situation room where Wayne explained the previous events to Private Thompson. Gene fiddled with the hologram module on the table while Percy tried unsuccessfully to suck him into conversation. The shiidh woman stood motionless against a backdrop of crystasteel, her robes gloomier than the black space that framed her. Lance noticed that Raeylan seemed to absorb everything around him as he entered, especially the long spike on the shiidh's belt. He pointedly chose a chair that placed himself between the Vartal and his sister.

"Got it," Gene said proudly as soon as Lance took a seat.

"Pull it up on the table," Wayne commanded.

LAMIE's security footage jerked alive in three dimensions across the holotable. The image showed Gene's office, cluttered with orderly experiments in various stages of completion. The GraEL was stowed underneath one of the long counters, secured by a high intensity LT shield. The holorecord showed Gene tossing a snack into his mouth as he left the office.

Two-point-six seconds later, the door slid open and a pink nose popped around the corner, sniffing the air guardedly. It disappeared as it pulled back into the hallway. Then a fluffy, golden squirrel scampered into the room.

"Frag me!" said Wayne as they watched the little animal poke the LT shield with its nose. For no logical reason anyone could fathom, the barrier gave a bright zat of energy, then snapped out of existence. The squirrel hopped onto its hind legs and, propping its front paws against the GraEL's tub, pushed the Coalition's most important military discovery out into the corridor.

The holofeed switched to a recorder in the hallway, following the squirrel's path all the way to LAMIE's STT drive access hatch. The furry creature pressed the GraEL against the hull and scurried up the tree's branches so it could poke its nose against the ident tag panel that opened the door. Kyleren swore beneath his breath as the computer accepted the squirrel's snout as proper admission protocol. The little animal scooted its pilfered merchandise into the STT portal drive room just as a holographic Wayne and Lance walked into camera range.

Then they were watching the inside of the STT drive platform. Leaving the GraEL in the center of the room, the squirrel hopped across a multitude of panels, activating what looked to be a random assortment of instruments from Kyleren's perspective, but a worried intake of breath from Gene indicated that the animal had done something specific. A small prick of swirling orange light twinkled suddenly next to the GraEL. Kyleren thought it looked familiar. Gene's loud groan solidified Lance's suspicion.

A T-portal.

With a huge heave, the squirrel pushed the GraEL inside, converting it into pure energy. Then the animal scuttled into an opening between two braces on the STT drive. The footage ended.

Kyleren blinked, dumbfounded.

"I've seen that squirrel," Margariete said abruptly. All eyes turned to her and she shrugged. "It let me out of my cell just before we crashed on Danaan."

Kyleren stared at her, at a loss as to how he should respond. Nothing could explain what he had just seen. He was dreading where the conversation was bound to go next.

"The squirrel incident!" Gary almost shouted. "Could it be the same squirrel that helped you get off Agrona, lieutenant?"

Kyleren held up a hand.

"No way."

"But it has to be the same one that fixed your ship—"

"I didn't get any help from a rodent," Kyleren defended, trying to ignore the voice in his head that kept pointing out how familiar the squirrel looked. "I fixed that fraggin' ship myself."

"Forget about the squirrel," Wayne ordered. "What exactly happened to the GraEL, Gene?"

The technobionomist pressed his palms against his eyes in frustration.

"Oh, it's just about a hundred-billion atoms scattered across a parallel energy plane on its way to some unknown destination in the galaxy."

"Can you track it?" Wayne asked.

"Not unless the squirrel tells us where it went," Gene complained.

"Then how do we find it?" Lance grumbled.

When no one seemed to offer a solution, the shiidh's voice rang out like scuffling bricks of glass.

"The thought proposed afore may yet present your goal. To seek the item which lies hid, unearth the thief who stole this thing from you."

"I was kidding—" Gene trailed off, but the shiidh continued to stare at him intently.

"This gifted creature serves the goddess, little doubt is there of that. Agrona may have means for discourse, Danu's sanctum binds your fate. Pursue your end and meet her there."

"Is anyone else gettin' this?" Lance asked in exasperation. "Cuz I'm pretty sure she's speakin' a language that even my patch can't translate."

"She is suggesting that the animal is more than it seems," Raeylan explained, speaking for the first time, "and to understand its magic you must go to Agrona."

"Are we operating under the assumption that magic is an accepted scientific force in the galaxy?" Gene interjected with an incredulous expression that encompassed all three GAELs.

"Guess so," Lance responded, fully fed up with the arguing.

"Right," Gene said petulantly. "I was just wondering how much crazier we wanted this to get."

"Whatever we decide, Gene still needs to check the validity of the information stored in the Ninevay sword," Wayne said, pointing to the covered weapon that Gene had propped against the wall earlier.

Gene snatched it and tugged off the cloth. A sharp intake of breath from Margariete drew Kyleren's attention. She and her brother were staring at the sword, and if he wasn't mistaken, Raeylan's face was actually exposed in an expression of shock.

"Raeylan, is that—?" Margariete whispered.

"You know the blade which has no ancestry," the shiidh noted.

Raeylan rose from his chair, Margariete at his side. He took two steps toward Gene and held out both hands.

"May I?" he asked quietly.

Gene looked questioningly at Wayne. The captain nodded, perplexed. Gene passed the sword over. As Raeylan drew the majestic blade from its sheath, the metal rang out with vibrant joy. Margariete looked like she was holding her breath. Raeylan touched the weapon gingerly, almost as if he didn't believe his eyes. Kyleren noticed that something was written along the bottom of the metal, where the blade met the hilt.

"*Moonstone Retribution?*" Lance chuckled. "What troll-skrit kinda name is that?"

Gene eyed him suspiciously.

"You can read that?" he asked.

"Can't everybody?" Lance said, trying to ignore the disproval Raeylan flashed at him.

"Well I sure can't," Wayne admitted.

"It is our native language," Margariete explained. "We haven't seen Raeylan's sword in four hundred seasons."

"You claim to be the sword's true master?" the shiidh hissed. "Anya Ninevay will be most pleased, for she has spent her life in search of its spring source."

Kyleren heard the sword ring on the deck, the noise drowning out something Margariete said. Raeylan stood motionless, though his body seemed to ripple like an unrestrained tide. His face became stern with suppressed feeling.

"Where is this woman?" Raeylan asked in a voice that echoed like the surge before a hurricane.

Confusion made Lance's head tight. What did the squirrel have to do with Anya and this sword? How could it belong to Raeylan when it had been with the doc for so long? And how the hell could Lance read a language that no one else could?

"She's down in the med bay," Kyleren finally answered, "workin' on the colonel."

Raeylan walked through the door before anyone could stop him, Margariete nearly tripping on his heels. Gary looked panicked, and it took Lance a second to realize that the newb still had a bit of a crush on the pretty doctor, and he obviously worried that the twins meant her some kind of harm. Kyleren wasn't about to wait around to find out, so he launched out of his chair and hurried to catch Margariete and Raeylan. Thompson trailed anxiously after.

One flight of stairs and a right turn through the med bay's sliding doors brought them to Anya. Her back was to them as she administered an injection to the unconscious colonel. Both Margariete and Raeylan stopped just inside the room, staring at her in awe.

Anya set her medical instrument aside and turned with a warming smile to greet her visitors. Her ice-green eyes reflected no sign of recognition toward the twins, which made Kyleren uneasy.

What was their game?

And then Raeylan stepped forward, touching Anya's cheek tenderly with the back of his hand, his face torn with painful joy. Something seemed to flicker deep in the doctor's eyes as he stared at her silently. Then he leaned in to kiss her.

Kyleren's jaw hung open. He had never met anyone brave enough to even think of touching Dr. Anya Ninevay. Gary nearly leapt out of his skin and rushed to pull Raeylan away, but Kyleren barred the young soldier's way with his arm. Lance wasn't quite sure why he had stopped Thompson from interfering, but he had the uncanny feeling that it was important.

Raeylan's lips pressed against Anya's like a man starved of breath. His fingers kneaded her hair and tears crept from under his lashes. Kyleren could have sworn he heard the roar of an ocean wave and looked around curiously to see if anyone else had noticed. The salty scent of the sea wafted through the med bay as the two unwillingly pulled apart.

"You found me," Anya whispered.

Raeylan smiled.

"I would navigate the terrors of the Void for you."

They stood together, wrapped in an embrace that seemed to defy fate. Lance turned to Margariete, who had covered her mouth with her hands to stifle her emotions.

"They know each other?" he asked.

Margariete looked at him with an expression that could only be described as loathing. He cocked his mouth into a grin and threw up his hands.

"What'd I say?"

32: The Game Has Changed

Colonel Art Stoddard sat up and tossed the dataplate on his rack. He stroked the grey stubble on his chin and pulled a bit of worn paper from the front pocket of his uniform. He stared at it thoughtfully. Physical photographs were a rarity; this one had been purchased 12 years ago at one of the Kamolos historical parks. Just a cheap souvenir he had picked up days before he left on his first tour with squad Aon, a whim indulgence that had become his most treasured possession. It represented his last happy moments with his family. Less than a standard year later, he had signed the divorce papers.

He didn't really blame Jennifer for seeking love from another man. Though he was granted ample shore leave as a commanding officer, Art had found little opportunity to use it. His base of operations was in the mobile city of Penardun, which wasn't always near the Kamolos System. Though he might be one of the most decorated officers in the Coalition Armed Forces, he had failed as both a husband and a father.

Marty was only six in the picture. Art slid his thumb across his son's photographic hair. Now eighteen, Marty had recently submitted an application to join the VICs program. The colonel only knew this information because of the congratulatory letter that his superiors had sent him as a professional courtesy. Art was more familiar with his son's file than the boy himself. Determined to know his son better, Stoddard had decided just prior to the GraEL retrieval mission to put in for reassignment on Nynniaw, the Coalition's military school station, so he could be closer to his son.

Art stowed the ancient photograph safely back in his pocket and reclaimed the abandoned dataplate, sighing as he did so. There would be no reassignment.

For the fourth time, he reviewed the authenticated information. It came from Prime Minister Ninevay herself, someone Art knew to be both dependable and honest. The intel was clear, no matter how many times he read it. Chancellor Medrod was worse than a traitor. He was a power-crazed butcher. Under him, the Round was responsible for countless inhumane experiments, justifying their actions under the excuse of war.

Squad Aon had accepted the challenge to expose the corrupt politicians, but there was no guarantee that Stoddard's team would ever be able to clear their names afterward. As commander, Art would face the severest penalty, even if Aon was successful at bringing Medrod to justice. That meant prison at least, execution at worst. He would never get his chance to repair things with Marty.

Stoddard rose to his feet, ordering Reese, Kyleren, and Gene to the situation room through his comm. A round of affirmatives spilled back into his ear. His joints seemed to creak as he stepped into the corridor. At 50, the colonel was still in prime shape, but his recent injuries had taken their toll on his no longer youthful body. He had been released from the infirmary for less than a day, taking as much time as he could to review the new information his team had gathered during his five days, DST, of unconsciousness.

By all accounts, he should be dead. His body had been so damaged by the mire field GAEL-frenzy that even nanomites had struggled to repair it. But according to his men, Dr. Ninevay had restored him to health in mere seconds, with nothing more advanced than her own blood. He still felt light-headed from the experience, groggy, like he had overslept.

As he walked into the situation room, both his soldiers rose in salute.

"At ease, gentlemen," he said as he took a chair. Then he turned to Gene and asked, "How long will it take to reach Agrona?"

"I've projected several possible courses. Five or six hours max. Tuatha is requesting that we bring the shiidh ship through our T-portal."

"Is that possible?"

Gene ran a grimy hand through his hair.

"Well, their ship is big, but with the right calibrations I could extend our slip paradigm to include them. It's not a guarantee though," he warned. "I would recommend their crew make the trip aboard LAMIE in case their ship doesn't make it."

"How long will the calibrations take?"

LAMIE answered before Gene could.

"Under 20 minutes if Gene allows me access to the STT drive protocol board. I could ensure a 91 percent survival rate for the shiidh vessel."

"No way," Gene objected. "Not a chance."

"Why not?" Stoddard asked, startled by Gene's vehement protest. The idea sounded solid.

"LAMIE has already twisted her programming to blackmail us once," Gene explained. "You give her access to the STT protocols and she might as well just drive the ship on her own."

LAMIE quickly presented a counterargument.

"I still require a pilot to initiate normal flight procedures. Access to the STT drive only permits me to open T-portals. I would not be able to enter one without the correct permissions."

"But your portal could take us anywhere," Gene argued. "I haven't protoed any restrictions into your board that would mandate flight navigation logs under the STT drive usage files. You could tell us we were headed to Penardun, but jump us to the Morrigan system instead."

"I could promise to be honest in my reports," LAMIE offered.

"Sure," Gene retorted sardonically. "Then how long before you request full access to life support and FTL systems? Are you going to promise not to kill us if we don't do what you want?"

The lights from the holotable dimmed in response, almost like the narrowing of a pair of eyes. LAMIE refused to answer Gene's question.

"I think you hurt her feelin's, Gene," Kyleren observed.

Art agreed but Gene just shrugged.

"She'll get over it. I'm just blown away that none of you seem to see the potential dangers of giving LAMIE primary system controls."

No one else around the table seemed threatened by the prospect.

"How long would it take you to complete the modifications manually, Gene?" Stoddard asked.

"Ten hours," Gene answered.

"We don't have that kind of time," Art replied. "We're 15 hours from Penardun. Major Huard informed Command of the rendezvous location before we jumped. If they decide to intercept with reinforcements, we'd be fragged. We're going to need LAMIE's help."

Gene threw up his hands and said, "Don't say I didn't warn you if something goes wrong."

"Noted. Our team is three GAELs short and my second officer is quarter-decked. LAMIE needs to be a full member of the squad now. Give her access to the drive and plot a course for Agrona."

Gene shook his head in defeat.

"Are we still considering trying to speak to the squirrel?" he whined.

"I only know what's in the security files, Gene," Stoddard said sternly. "The way I see it, an intruder infiltrated this ship and hijacked the GraEL. And if we are going to turn against the Coalition, we need safe harbor. Agrona is our best tactical advantage. Whatever answers we find there are just chrome on the hull, understand?"

Gene left the room mumbling. After his departure, Art turned to Reese.

"Captain, after we touch down on Agrona, I want you glued to LAMIE's flight deck with your core drive inserted in her terminal at all times," Stoddard ordered. "If you get even a whiff of duplicity you jump LAMIE through the nearest T-portal and get clear. Private Thompson will assist you."

"Yes, sir," Wayne acknowledged.

Turning to Kyleren, the colonel continued, "Whatever's going on here, lieutenant, you seem to be mucked in it. You're coming planetside with me."

"What about the twins?" Captain Reese asked. "They'll want to go."

"I want them where I can see them. I know both of you trust them, but I still have my doubts."

"I can vouch for them, colonel—" Reese began, but Art interrupted.

"I appreciate that, captain, but I am responsible for this ship and its crew. I can't afford to trust anyone who isn't one hundred percent. In my absence, you and Major Huard made some risky decisions. I'd say we've been lucky. I hope the twins turn out to be everything they claim to be, but if not, I don't want to be caught with our asses hanging in the line of fire."

"Understood, sir," Reese said.

"Speakin' of the major," Kyleren interjected, "we know what we're doin' with him and Pryce yet?"

"Keep them in the brig for now," Art said, "at least until we know for sure what's going on."

Just as Art readied to dismiss his soldiers, LAMIE's voice resonated into the room and she restored the lights.

"Colonel Stoddard," she said in a cold, formal pitch, "Raeylan, Margariete, and Dr. Ninevay have requested an audience with you. They are waiting outside."

"Let them in, LAMIE," Art decided, waving his GAELs back to their seats. He wanted their perspective on what the newcomers had to say.

The door opened and the trio walked in. Both women were pale, but Raeylan wore a mask of calm. Stoddard motioned an invitation for them to be seated.

"I'm afraid we have some bad news," Margariete began in a low, bold tone.

"That's my favorite kind," Kyleren interrupted.

Margariete glared at the lieutenant.

"Well if you have more intel," Art said, "I'd be glad to hear it."

Dr. Ninevay inserted a tile into the holotable. The image of Chancellor Medrod floated gracefully above them.

"This man is well known to us," Raeylan stated. "His true name is Kirion."

Lieutenant Kyleren, who had been lazily leaning back in his chair, sat upright suddenly.

"You've heard that name?" Stoddard asked him.

"Yeah," Kyleren said his eyes on Margariete.

"He is responsible for the destruction of our home," Raeylan said.

"Kirion is the worst kind of evil," Anya added softly, "because he does not believe himself to be immoral. He leads his armies in the name of light, justifying murder as cleansing. He kills anyone who gets in his way."

"Are you sure the chancellor and this Kirion guy are the same person?" Kyleren asked.

"Without question," Raeylan answered, his eyes dark.

The colonel was unnerved by the intensity that ebbed from the man.

"As soon as my memories were returned, I realized the connection," Anya explained. "He's been in this shard for at least a hundred years. He wouldn't have stayed so long unless there's something here he wants."

"And you think you know what he's after?" Art asked her.

"We think it is more than just the GAEL program that keeps him in your shard. His true goal is to restore his godhood. For that, he needs all of the god artifacts."

"Kirion is looking for him," Margariete said, pointing at Kyleren.

"Here we go again. For the last time, Blue Eyes, I don't have this thing you're lookin' for."

Margariete pursed her lips and tried to retort, but Raeylan cut her off.

"It is not something you possess, lieutenant. It is a part of you."

"You cannot continue to deny the existence of Shardwell magic," Margariete spat impatiently. "You've seen what my brother and I can do, and how Esilwen restored Colonel Stoddard with her healing fire. Denying it further just makes you look more like a fool."

Kyleren grimaced and opened his mouth, but Stoddard held up a hand to silence him.

"Hold on. Explain these 'artifacts' to me."

Margariete continued to glower at Kyleren as she answered. Art listened to her story about six gods who fell from power and left a portion of themselves in magical objects with the skeptical ears of someone born into a world of science and technology. But she piqued his interest as she described the fracturing of the universe into isolated realms she called "shards." He stroked his chin thoughtfully as he listened. Was this why the galaxy was surrounded by barriers that could not be crossed? He wanted to believe her, but her story seemed too incredible. And yet, she, her brother, and Dr. Ninevay had used some unbelievable abilities. Things that could not be explained.

"If you say you know this man," Stoddard finally said, pointing to the chancellor's hologram, "then I believe you. We know enough about his underhanded dealings in our own government to consider that he is capable of committing crimes against you as well. As for your belief in magic, I admit that you have the ability to do things that science can't explain, but you can't expect us to accept such an absurd idea."

Raeylan touched his sister lightly on the shoulder, commanding her to halt any argument.

"We do not expect you to change your cultural beliefs, colonel," he said diplomatically. "Whether or not you believe in magic, Kirion must be stopped."

Raeylan's eyes suddenly flamed with the blaze of vengeance.

"And you are going to need our help to succeed."

33: MOMMY ALWAYS SAID THERE WERE NO MONSTERS—BUT THERE ARE

The red glow of the small ship's proximity indicator flickered as the vessel crept into position behind its target. Sharp shadows cloaked the assassin as he expertly fingered the switches along the flight console in the narrow cockpit. Two snaps against the smooth computer terminal wrapped his ship in the dark mask of invisibility only the power of Skoh could provide.

He didn't miss his ill-gotten powers of Nehro, lost when Raeylan closed her broken Well on Thyella. The ability to teleport paled against the dark possibilities of Skoh's magic. The assassin's new Well—opened by the power of The Earring in Kirion's possession—gave Feralblade direct access to the illusions offered by the Void, which were more aligned to suit his purpose.

Finally his master's obsession with Fohtian's Warden would be quenched. Though not as stimulating as the sweet release of blood, abduction did produce a particularly rousing taste of terror. That almost made up for Lord Kirion's orders that the shiidh women, a rare breed of stone sorcerers, were to be left unspoiled.

Stalking his mark had taken nothing more challenging than inserting a set of coordinates from VIC Command. The foolish Dr. Ninevay—Esilwen—had inadvertently revealed her location when she contacted someone in the Coalition military.

He tapped three switches to scan his prey. Results appeared on his display. His LT computer immediately analyzed his target's weaknesses and pulled the machine's interior schematics. The shiidh vessel he had expected. The other ship he had not.

LAMIE.

She was undetectable to everything except his own instruments. All ships under the Coalition were marked with a Void signature that only one of Lord Kirion's most trusted servants could trace.

Her presence meant squad Aon had broken orders. They were rogue. According to intel, Aon had the GraEL, the only Well of Chano Lord Kirion had ever managed to find. The assassin's mission instinctively expanded. His master wanted that Well only a little less than Esilwen.

That the two ships had linked caused Feralblade to hesitate. His target could be aboard either, but the shiidh— with their dead, stone-lined tech, lightless corridors, and ineffective internal security—would be much easier to infiltrate. He wormed his ship just under the shiidh's belly, at the lips of her cargo hold. When his hull had completed its silent merge, a hatch on the deck twisted open. He took slow amusement as his cutting tool licked an open sore into the stone-like metal of the shiidh's outer hull.

When the hole was as wide as his fist, an alarm yapped from his sensor console. Even without the aid of his scanners, he could see the pinprick of gold light that meant a T-portal. The interdimensional rift jerked larger. A quick calculation by his ship's computer and a series of warning lights told him that the portal was only wide enough to accommodate LAMIE and the shiidh ship. His skiff would be sheared in half.

He spoke the command word for a preprogrammed set of flight instructions, leaving only a four second delay before execution. Then he shifted his body into the free state of shadow, thrusting himself through the opening and into the target ship's cargo bay. As soon as he reformed, he slipped a small LT growth disk from a hidden pocket and tossed it onto the breach. The tiny column of light that shone into the hold from his ship vanished as the LT hull patch repaired the opening before his skiff detached.

The room burst into sudden brightness as the T-portal passed over him.

It took only a few moments for his eyes to readjust to the pitch darkness of the shiidh environment, another gift afforded to those with the power of the Void. Objects, especially living creatures, pushed darkness away like a finger traced a path through sand. No one had been in the cargo hold for several days. Feralblade smiled in the gloom and activated his infiltration scrambler. The shiidh's dead tech scanning devices would never register his presence.

He needed to know how long the ships had traveled through the energy plane. Only LAMIE would have that information. It was necessary to board her. With the practiced ease of a predator, he skulked through the ship's dark corridors, sensing his way with darkness.

The hatch linking the two ships was closed when he reached it—a safety precaution for the STT journey—so he shifted back into shadow and stretched thin across the base of the bulkhead, waiting.

His shadow walk gave him certain advantages, yet had its flaws. Incorporeal, he could feel the world around him, but could not affect physical objects or see in the traditional manner.

He felt the change in darkness as the hatch opened and six women entered. Like ghosts, their robes glided across the deck, crystal spikes swinging rhythmically at their hips. Five drifted deeper into the ship, but the sixth, the tallest of the group, lingered near the doorway. Two more figures stepped through the hatch.

If he had been in physical form, he would have sucked a displeased breath between his teeth. Instead, he snapped himself around the corner, shadowy tendrils vibrating savagely. Hate almost forced him back into his true form.

Raeylan.

Even the darkness wasn't guaranteed to hide Feralblade from Raeylan's perception. Over the years, the First Kingdom ruler had somehow developed the ability to detect magical auras, much like Lord Kirion. But as Raeylan disappeared down the opposite corridor, Feralblade determined that the man's focus must have been on his companion, Esilwen. The assassin was sure he had remained undetected by his enemy.

This complicated things. Experience had proved Raeylan to be the better warrior in a head on fight. Feralblade stood little chance at successfully retrieving his master's prize with the lorelei at her side. He would have to wait to strike until Raeylan left her unguarded.

Fate, however, must have smiled into his corner of the shard. If Raeylan were here, that meant Margariete wasn't far, providing him an opportunity for a bit of delicious torment.

He coalesced back into human form as soon as the hatchway was empty. With three flicks of his fingers he pulled an ident tag out of the air, seemingly from nothing. It writhed in his fingers, a sharp concoction of sliding Void granules. Before boarding LAMIE, he fondled the curve just under her hatch ident panel. A slot appeared at his finger's touch, and he inserted the tag.

LAMIE's internal sensors would be blind to him for 30 minutes. He had that long to discover the ship's destination, form an exit plan, and retrieve the GraEL. It had taken only a quick glance at her specs to memorize LAMIE's layout. The most likely storage compartment for the Well would be in the science lab—Gene Pecktol's office. Feralblade just had to make it there without running in to any of the crew.

He withdrew the ident tag and crept through the passageways with care, encountering no one until he reached the stairs. Voices rattled down from the next deck.

"He's really up there?"

The speaker sounded confused.

"Yeah," a second, lighter voice answered. "Corporal Harris just marched in and relieved me. He said it was an order. When I left, Gene was arguing with him."

"Private," the first speaker said, "the colonel took Corporal Harris off duty. You should have stayed at your post."

Feralblade heard the hiss of a door and the heavy tread of footsteps. A third joined the conversation.

"What's goin' on, guys?" the newcomer asked. "Wayne looks like someone just kicked him in the balls."

"Harris forced Thompson off the bridge," Wayne explained.

"Frag. Can he fly in his shape?" the third person asked. "Maybe we should check it out, Wayne."

"I got it," Wayne said. "Private, report this to the colonel."

Private Thompson's footsteps headed away, toward LAMIE's bow, while the other two trounced up the staircase. That meant three GAELs on the bridge and one on the second level with the colonel. Most importantly, Feralblade had discovered the technobionomist was not in his lab. Since GAEL squads were regularly comprised of six soldiers and two officers, Feralblade had three members unaccounted for, plus the engineer and medical staff.

As soon as the upstairs level went quiet, Feralblade shadow-walked through the remaining corridors, hugging the bulkheads and remaining alert for any changes in the surrounding darkness. He reached the science lab without incident and stepped back into his body. The door hissed open at his ident tag's command.

He scanned the room, noting everything with a single glance. The LT storage barrier that was supposed to house the GraEL for transport was empty, its four energy tiles deactivated. Five scrolls lay flat along a table, the curled ends held in place by metal weights. Close by, a misshapen blue crystal perched under a scanner.

A teleport stone?

Feralblade touched it gingerly. The collection of objects had to be Raeylan's. He turned his attention to the scrolls. One was written in an old Thyellan dialect. From what he could glean, it gave the history and powers of Nehro's Glove. The other four he could not understand, though one had some familiar characters. It seemed similar to the codes used by the Faithful Legion. Unmistakably,

Feralblade recognized the symbol Lord Kirion used for his name.

He bent into a comfortable crouch and picked up one of the four corners of the GraEL storage device. He turned it on, but nothing happened. He tried the second. Still nothing.

That was odd. LT tech was notoriously reliable. He rolled one over to inspect it. No sign of damage. He pulled a small scanner from a pocket. No energy signature registered.

That was impossible, unless the LT was no longer living, its magical connection severed. To his knowledge, only an artifact was capable of that.

Feralblade filed his discovery away. He had enough to handle with his current mission. The GraEL was not here. He tapped into the computer console using his personal, untraceable security code.

He watched the feed showing the GraEL's disappearance. The implications were interesting. His lord would want to know. Next, Feralblade accessed LAMIE's flight data. They were enroute to the Vartal homeworld, Agrona. Six hours to touch down.

A wicked thrill seized his body. Perhaps he would be able to gorge on death after all.

34: You Mind Telling Your Subconscious To Take It Easy?

A breeze jeered in Margariete's ear as she sprinted through the towering stalks of Thyellan bamboo. A burning urgency stalked her. She was unsure of how long she had been running, but the moon covered the sun and spilled sickly lunar light across the grass. She should be close to her home, the City of Jewels, but the forest refused to break. She could see nothing but the leaf-framed night sky.

A dark sludge suddenly slithered into her path, appearing too quickly for her to evade it. It bubbled and coiled around her, choking any hope of escape. It devoured her like an empty soul. She screamed and clawed, all the while knowing that it shouldn't be happening. It had taken place already, only somewhere else. It had swallowed her home hundreds of seasons past.

Ahead, the shadows swirled in a predatory dance, forming the gritty outline of huge misshapen beasts. They milled around her, their needle-point jaws dripping with black fog. Margariete tried to track them, to sense their movements with her magic, but her power refused to obey her commands. She could not push back the dark. Fear slipped from every pore on her skin.

Stardawn sang helplessly in front of her, its point lost in the gloom. The smoke shriveled her throat. Something struck her and she collapsed. Before she could right herself, a hand wrenched her head upward by the roots of her hair. Then, like a barren wind scraping across a decaying landscape, she heard a malicious voice call her name.

"Margariete, you can't escape me," Terail whispered. "You are a curse to anyone you touch."

Margariete tried to fight back, but her limbs were frozen. And then she heard screams, the pain-filled voices of the Pearl Knights under her command as they were torn to shreds by Terail's army of cursed beasts. The courtyard of Castle Viridius bent into view, dripping blood. Terail's hands closed tightly around her neck. She couldn't breathe. Her powers were gone. Nothing stood between her and the gaping maw of the Void.

The sound of someone speaking her name dashed her nightmare into oblivion. But even when she opened her eyes, she failed to detach reality from delusion. Terail's treacherous name fled her lips and she lashed out at whoever was near.

Two strong hands restrained her until her rasping breath slowed. Unwelcome tears betrayed her terror. She pressed her face against her savior's chest, thinking that it must be Raeylan. His hand curled into her hair and the other wrapped around her tightly. She let the strength drain from her body, squelching her eyes tightly shut to blot out the phantom of Terail. It had been a long time since she'd dreamt of him in particular.

And then she realized that it was not Raeylan who held her.

"You okay, Blue Eyes?"

Fiery chills flashed through her limbs. She pushed away from Kyleren. Even when sitting he towered over her, forcing her to look up to see his face. He looked concerned.

"I'm fine," she lied, glad the dimness of the barracks prevented him from seeing any blush that might taint her skin. "It was just a dream."

Margariete cursed. How could she have allowed herself to become so completely helpless in front of him? No matter how real it felt, it had only been a dream. Two swift swipes with her fingers and her tears were gone.

Kyleren's eyebrows perched dubiously.

"You sure?"

His bare chest flustered her. He must have been sleeping. Though she had pulled out of his embrace, the small bunk wasn't really large enough for two people. The comfort of his body was awkwardly close.

"What are you doing here?" she demanded with an angry huff.

"I was tryin' to catch some rack," he said, motioning to the disturbed blankets of a bunk two spots over, "but I couldn't sleep with all the noise you were makin'."

"Try harder," she said waving him away.

"Can't," he said, "you keep screamin' some weird name."

Margariete's eyes narrowed. Kyleren turned his head away from her.

"I don't get you," he said as he stood.

"That's a tragedy," Margariete chirped sarcastically.

"So who's Terail?" he asked offhandedly.

Margariete shivered, despite her attempt to suppress it. Kyleren stood over her like a sentry, and folded his arms stubbornly across his chest. It was obvious that he didn't intend to move until she answered his question.

"He's just someone who works with Kirion," she said.

"I don't believe that for a nanosec," Kyleren returned.

"It's none of your concern," she argued.

"Have it your way, princess," Kyleren said coldly.

His shoulders were rigid as he walked to his bunk and threw himself on it. Then he rolled over so all she could see was his well-muscled back.

Margariete, satisfied that he would mind his own business, lay back onto the thin mattress. Her eyes traced every line in the ceiling, but sleep refused to descend. Hot tears burned the rims of her eyes and she had to concentrate hard not to succumb. When Kyleren's breathing became even, she spoke softly.

"Terail was a prince of Thyella, my home shard. My grandfather destroyed his kingdom. Terail infiltrated our lives so he could gain revenge. He pretended to be Raeylan's closest friend and tricked me into loving him. It was my foolish weakness for Terail that led me to reveal my family's secrets. It gave him the leverage he needed to depose my brother as king of the First Kingdom. Terail framed me for the murder of Raeylan's wife. When Raeylan refused to have me sentenced to death, our kingdom collapsed. Sometimes I wish Raeylan had allowed my execution. Lives were lost because of my recklessness. I trusted Terail and betrayed my duty. I was even convinced I loved him. Without me, things would have ended differently."

Her gaze never left the ceiling as she spoke. It wasn't until she had finished that she turned her head, simultaneously hoping and dreading that Kyleren had been listening. He was sitting up, his elbows on his thighs and his chin resting on his intertwined fingers.

"You come with a lot 'a baggage."

Margariete felt a choke in her throat.

"I should have known you would find this amusing."

"Far from it," Kyleren said seriously. "Knowin' you better explains why you're always so pissed off all the time."

"I'm glad I could clarify, then."

"You should loosen up a bit," he said, clapping hands together. "You and your brother both. You guys are too tense."

"That tends to happen when your best friend betrays you and destroys everything you cared for," Margariete returned angrily.

Kyleren's grin disappeared.

"I guess you're right. I can't miss what I never had. My squad is my family, and whatever ship I'm on is home. You lose either, Command replaces 'em. Comes with the job."

Margariete's tongue felt dry with guilt. If Raeylan had been present he would have been disappointed. She was supposed to convince the lieutenant to come with them. Unsure as how to mend things, she tried her twin's approach.

"Sounds like a hard way to live."

"It's all I know. Bad skrit happens. Can't hold onto it forever."

"I guess you think it's the same for me. That I should just forget what happened."

"I never said to forget anythin'," he shrugged, "but you can let the bad stuff ruin your mood or you can move on. Simple as that."

"I wish it was," Margariete sighed. "Raeylan and I have been on this quest for so long, with only one goal. When you spend your time doing nothing else, the centuries blend together. More and more the past feels like the present. But we've found Esilwen. Things will change now."

"So your brother has his girlfriend back," Kyleren surmised. "That makes you the one left out. Must be lonely."

"My brother and Esilwen are all I need," Margariete snapped. "If they're happy, I'm happy."

"If you actually believe that skrit, then you're better at lyin' to yourself than you are to me," Kyleren jabbed, his face lit with a magnetic smile.

"What would you know about it?" Margariete demanded.

"People have needs. Even you."

"My brother and I are long-lived," she said. "Any companion I brought along with me would be dead before we made it through three shards."

"Some of them, maybe," Kyleren said with a laugh. "But it doesn't mean you can't entertain yourself in the meantime."

"You may be capable of such callous experience, Kyleren," Margariete said proudly, "but I have never met a man worthy of my attention."

"That's code for you haven't found anyone fraggin' crazy enough to put up with you," he teased.

"You're a real bastard," she said and sat up. "It's not like you're doing any better for yourself."

"I have plenty of company when I want it."

"But who's waiting for you?" Margariete challenged. "I bet there's no one. My brother has spent the last four hundred seasons searching for Esilwen, wishing every cycle he could be with her."

"That why he was so anxious to disappear with Doc Anya onto the shiidh ship?"

Margariete didn't quite know what he meant, and her blank look of confusion must have stirred the lieutenant to clarify.

"After we jumped through the T-portal, Anya pretty much ran off with him. Hard to believe anyone woulda waited four centuries for a frag," he said doubtfully. "No woman's worth that wait."

"Then you must have spent your life in the company of substandard women," Margariete snarled, rising to her feet and piling her things in a precarious bundle.

Margariete stormed from the room. She didn't stop until she reached the med bay, which was blissfully empty now that all its former occupants had been healed. Once the door closed behind her, she slammed her things angrily to the floor and let the tears blemish her cheeks.

She didn't know what hurt more: that Kyleren was right, and now that her brother had found the woman he loved, Margariete was the extra bead in the arc counter—

Or that Kyleren hadn't bothered to follow her.

35: You're Not Afraid Of The Dark Are You?

Kyleren chafed at the starboard hatch long before LAMIE hit the Agronan atmosphere. His body sported enough artillery to take down an entire enemy battalion. His BT assault rifle quavered with adrenaline in his hands, a BT sidearm hung on each leg, and explosives dotted his uniform like the sequins on a call girl's dress. His *White Lady*, which seemed almost moody from lack of attention, hung snugly across his back. Just in case the shiidh were planning on fragging them over with a mire field, he had stuffed a few dead tech pistols and grenades into the various pouches that hung on his combat armor.

LAMIE formally announced her separation from the shiidh vessel and dove planetside. Lance rolled his shoulders, loosening his tight muscles. Raeylan and Anya emerged from the stairway. The teleporter eyed Kyleren with interest. Lance could have sworn that there was a hint of mirth in those stoic eyes.

"You doubt Tuatha's intentions," Raeylan stated.

Kyleren snorted.

"Last time I was here, some shiidh chick almost smashed my head in with a hammer," he said, snapping his core drive into his rifle with a little more force than he meant. "I'm not takin' any chances."

"I'm surprised she was swift enough to do you harm," Raeylan said.

"She wasn't," Kyleren said with a shrug. "I was incapacitated."

Raeylan's eyebrows peaked in curiosity.

"You call it magic," Kyleren went on. "Guess that's what it has to be, considerin' she sang at me and I just fell over for no reason."

"The shiidh's magic originates from Chano's domain, the plane of stone, life, and metal. Manipulating the magical energies that encompass our living bodies is a fundamental base of her power."

Kyleren blinked dubiously, wondering what exactly that meant.

"Whatever it is, it's really annoyin'."

Anya giggled, color flushing her cheeks. A temperamental voice intruded into their conversation.

"So how did you manage to survive?"

Margariete leaned against the wall just outside the medical bay, her shoulders pushing against the bulkhead for balance. Two pistols and her sword guarded her hips, combat knives peeked over the edge of her boots. Her tight clothing hugged her, like the camo seal on the wings of an atmospheric fighter, exposing her curves. Kyleren felt the blood rush into part of his anatomy he would rather keep under control.

He looked away, turning to face the hatch. It helped that her superior tone put him on edge.

"She let me go."

"Just like that?"

"I was too busy gettin' my ass out of there to ask questions," he snapped.

After a minute, Lance looked back. Raeylan had walked to his twin and was speaking to her softly. Margariete fiddled stiffly with a loose thread on her glove. She refused to face him.

Anya stared at them with a wistful expression.

"Four centuries and she's barely changed," she said.

"So do I call you Doc Anya or," Lance paused, not remembering what Raeylan had called her, "the other name?"

"I prefer Smiles," she said with a warm glint in her eyes.

Kyleren's face split into a grin.

"You got it," he promised with a nod. He indicated the twins with a flick of his head. "He treat you right?"

"Always," Anya answered.

"Well then, you hit the jackpot, Smiles. He's devoted, that one."

Kyleren glanced at the twins. Margariete looked angry as she quietly argued with Raeylan.

"And patient," he added.

"I've lived over the course of millennia and met many people," Anya said. "Margariete is both the strongest and angriest of anyone I've ever known."

"I believe it," Kyleren agreed.

His statement drew a laugh from Anya. Both Margariete and Raeylan looked over at the sound.

It was hard for Lance to tell, but Margariete's temper either flared higher or burned into offense. She threw up her arms, spouted one more sentence at her brother, and escaped into the med bay. Raeylan returned, calm as ever.

"That was unsuccessful," he admitted.

"What's wrong?" Anya asked, tenderly slipping her hand into his.

"Hormones, probably," Kyleren snorted.

Raeylan returned a polite nod. He leaned close to Anya as if to say something, so Lance pretended to check the clip in his dead tech sidearm and turned away. He didn't hear what Raeylan said, only Anya's reply.

"I'll talk to her about it after the meeting on Agrona," she whispered. "Maybe she needs a friend right now instead of a brother."

Raeylan's brow furrowed with hurt, but Anya was quick to rectify.

"It might just be that she's afraid to tell you."

Good save, Kyleren thought. Lance replaced his sidearm, sneaking a glance at the vacant spot where Margariete had been standing. She was way too much work. Although, he had to admit, he did enjoy the electric shade of blue that her eyes turned when she glared at him.

He was pulled from thought by the arrival of Colonel Stoddard, Harris, Gene, and Percy. Kyleren saluted respectfully and listened to orders as LAMIE made touch down. Wayne was to stay on the bridge, ready to fly LAMIE in the blink of an order. Evans would hold position at LAMIE's outer hatch, while Thompson continued to watch over the prisoners. As the cultural specialist, Percy would be especially useful for the meeting with the shiidh leader. Gene had been ordered to stay on the ship in case there was a fight, since their main engineer was off somewhere with Trish and Chad on the captured mire field ship.

The colonel made their mission sound like any other standard op, but Kyleren noticed the uncertainty in his superior officer's voice. Lance couldn't blame him. They were traitors to the Coalition. There was no going back. If the alliance with the shiidh failed, it was all over. But something deep inside Kyleren seemed to calm his nerves, and his gut was never wrong.

Gene passed out LT low-light ocular specs to everyone not wearing CC armor, including Margariete who reappeared as the hatch opened. She avoided making eye contact with anyone as she attached the goggles to her face.

Lance strode down the ramp, rifle at the ready. Colonel Stoddard flanked him, Evans backing them up. Everything planetside was caked with darkness. Even the planet's two moons were only a lighter shade of dark than the sunless sky. Kyleren commanded his LT visor to go night mode so he could scan the area. Huge trees, older than the MetaGalactic War, towered over LAMIE. There were no landmarks, only smatterings of worn standing stones. He wondered if the Vartal actually lived in cities like the people of the Coalition. The only things he'd ever seen on this planet were trees and rocks.

In Lance's periphery, Raeylan helped Esilwen exit the ship. Margariete flatly refused any assistance from Percy and stalked down the ramp with one hand on her sword and the other on her pistol butt. Gene peeked from the hatchway, as if daring himself to break orders and run down to join the away team.

"Report," Stoddard ordered.

"Nothin', sir," Lance answered, lowering his rifle. "What now?"

The colonel shook his head.

"I don't know. They told us to land here, nothing else."

Suddenly, Kyleren's armor tracker registered the signatures of 15 newcomers. He swore. He had forgotten that the shiidh slid through rock as easily as air. More arrived. There must have been stones hidden behind the trees, because women surrounded his group in a matter of seconds. Their gloomy robes whispered across the moss like an eerie wind. Their crystal spikes hummed. He couldn't help the chills that scratched at his spine as their ghostly eyes bored straight into him.

He recognized Tuatha, standing just behind another shiidh woman. Instead of a crystal spike, this one had a crystal hammer glinting freely at her belt.

Colonel Stoddard stepped forward to introduce himself, but the shiidh with the hammer ignored him, watching only Kyleren. Her eyes narrowed as she cut the colonel off in mid-sentence.

"My duty is to read the signs that Danu sends. Her people call me Druantia. The goddess has returned you as foretold."

"Uh," was all Kyleren could manage as he turned to the colonel for instructions, but the night goggles covered his commander's eyes and it was impossible for Lance to tell what the colonel was thinking.

"Your value is unknown to you, but we perceive your life's true worth, for you will bring the goddess forth and save our worlds from ruin."

Kyleren shook his head, frustrated. Why the frag couldn't these women say things that made sense? Her eyes watched him hungrily, like she was a wild animal waiting to devour him. He fidgeted. Percy stepped beside him and spoke in a low voice.

"The shiidh queen has marked you as the leader of our group," he explained. "She will not speak to anyone else in a formal setting."

"Great. So you're sayin' I get to do all the talkin'?" Kyleren complained. "I don't know if that's such a great plan."

"Just don't get us killed, lieutenant," Stoddard said out the corner of his mouth. "She may accept a request to meet with me privately. Until then, keep it together."

"Yes, sir," Kyleren muttered.

This was skrit. He was a soldier, not a politician.

"Perhaps your faith in us is not secure? You wonder why I let you live that day you struck our temple." Druantia's voice shuddered like cracking crystal. It made Kyleren's hair stand on end. "Know that Danu stayed my hand. You live because of her."

"Your goddess?" Lance asked sourly, barely able to interpret the shiidh queen's words. He almost made a rude comment, but remembered at the last second that all their lives hung on his diplomacy. "I owe her one then," was all the reply he was able to muster.

Druantia did not look pleased. Her face pulled sharply.

"Your tone conveys disdain. The great domain of Danu's might is not for scorn. Her champion should uphold her holy sovereignty."

"You lost me," Kyleren said helplessly.

"She's angry with you for being rude, idiot!" Margariete spat savagely.

Kyleren sighed. He'd thought he was being polite. The shiidh queen turned her ominous gaze on Margariete.

This was not going well.

Percy hurried to Margariete's side and whispered something urgently. Druantia drifted toward Margariete and Kyleren felt a surge of concern. Would the crazy queen-lady attack? The situation was already tense, so he didn't dare raise his weapon. He glanced at the colonel for orders, but his commander remained silent.

Druantia's long fingers stroked the head of her hammer, making it vibrate through the grove. The queen and Margariete stared at each other for long, tense seconds. Just as Kyleren decided to frag orders and shoot the shiidh to hell, Margariete's expression turned quizzical and Druantia's lips parted into a severe smile.

"The Mystic's blessing calls your name. Your breach of tact is thus dismissed. Amongst the shiidh our goddess deems you equal to our caste." Druantia turned back to Kyleren. "Your technobionomist must join us."

The mass of shiidh parted as their queen drifted deeper into the forest. Kyleren looked back only to make sure Gene had heard the queen's order. The gangly technobionomist had tripped on the ramp in his excitement and rolled into a pathetic heap in the moss. Evans helped Gene to stand. Then the GAEL took his position as hatch guard.

Kyleren turned forward and followed the shiidh queen, his hands tightening on his assault rifle. Colonel Stoddard opted to take rear guard. The rest of the Vartal women surrounded them as they headed toward Danu's temple.

"Smooth," Kyleren said to Margariete as they walked. "I thought she was gonna try takin' you down."

"She was thinking it. But one thought changed her mind."

"An' what was that?" Kyleren asked.

But Margariete only smirked arrogantly and pushed ahead of him, walking in the lead of the party.

"Show off," Kyleren muttered, admittedly a little impressed at how easily she had gained the shiidh queen's respect.

"Contention comes more quickly to my sister than courtesy," Raeylan apologized.

Kyleren looked behind him as he walked.

"But you gotta admit," he said with a grin, "she's got spark."

36: THAT COULD JUST BE FAILURE OF IMAGINATION ON YOUR PART

She had been here before. Time had passed, but her ever youthful mind saw only beginnings, never endings. Trapped in a state of In Between since the breaking of the shards, she had never given a name to this place that was a bridge, rather than anything real. Here she could be more than just a squirrel.

In Between was not a prison. Her curiosity prevented that. Even from the start, this new simulation was exciting. It allowed her to meddle without the Rules. The Others were not around to watch her anymore. She was no longer entirely divine, but not changed into mortal either. Just something In Between. That meant the Rules were stretchy.

It was great fun to do as she pleased.

But, sadly, Life had to be attended. It couldn't be trusted to do things all on its own. Especially Intelligent Things. Always getting in to trouble. Missing the important details, even if it was right in front of them. Bickering, arguing—ruining the other Things she had made.

Luckily, one group of Intelligent Things had found the perfect attunement of stones that reflected the frequency she needed to manifest as something with voice. They called it a temple, a circle that tapped the connections through the planes, making it easier for someone stuck In Between to more than just appear. It gave someone the ability to speak.

Her power had been reduced when she was thrust In Between, and she found crafting New Things had become painful. She could only manifest for short bursts, and then only as a small creature. So she wandered through the shards as a squirrel for a time until she came here. This shard had a Lifewell, a connection to her source of power. This she could use to prod Old Things to grow in new ways. It let her open walkways between worlds. But over time she started to get very tired, and slept a long, long time. Soon she understood that the only way to stay awake was to bond herself with a mortal.

Her Mortal was special. He was what she wanted to make, but was never allowed to by the Others. She had thought of bonding mortals to the plane of life long ago, but had to wait until they discovered it themselves. That was one of the Rules.

She had waited for Her Mortal over the centuries. He was everything important: blended by technology and bonded with magic. And his life was exciting. She got to go many places, even though now she was bound by new Rules. Her Mortal let her play with all the newest toys her Intelligent Things made from her magical ore. His heart was vibrant. He listened to her when she tried to whisper.

Plus he was very, very strong.

It was quite an event, the opening of the Great Door that led from In Between to the place on the Dark-Light planet. Without a Door, she could only appear on occasion, and it made her tired.

She scampered through the Door as it opened and perched herself on the tip of Her Mortal's weapon. She took a moment to look at those gathered around her, classifying them in her own way. She wasn't accustomed to remembering names, because it was far more fun to make Things than to identify them. And Intelligent Things could never agree on what to call the Things she made anyway. It was all very tedious.

They looked shocked to see her. That made her giggle. It was one of the reasons she chose to look like a squirrel.

Three were just human, but the other Intelligent Things were all beautiful. Her dark Singing Ladies, each under a stone alcove, hummed with life energy. The angry servant of Aeron was especially stunning. But then, Aeron had always had a bias for beauty, even though this one was female. The Water Angel's calm exterior hid a depth of emotion. She wondered when the pressure would make him explode. That might be messy.

Most interesting was the Pretty Blonde with Fohtian's eyes. Unchanged, one of the original three races. That answered many questions.

The Singing Ladies knelt in worship. She didn't like that. It led to problems.

Her Mortal, however, stared at her with disbelief. She laughed, scurrying across his magic ore weapon and up his arm. On his shoulder she brushed her nose against his cheek. Then she spiraled down his body and hopped onto the altar.

Her body changed in a warm glow. Fur melted into a sheen of golden skin. Those around her removed their technology eyes. The Singing Ladies squinted. She stared at her tiny hands. Always a child. That was her Rule from the Others before the Bang. For meddling.

She turned to the technobionomist, one of the humans. "You're my second favorite," she said.

"I—um—" he stuttered, "you're a—"

"It's okay," she interrupted, swinging her legs back and forth. "You were wrong about magic. But I like you anyway, because of LAMIE." She leaned over and put her hand to her mouth as if to whisper a secret, but her voice rasped loudly. "She *likes* you! But don't tell her I told. I promised I wouldn't."

She turned to the Singing Ladies. They were exchanging confused glances. After a few awkward moments the Ladyleader spoke.

"Delight most high you bring to us Great One."

"Great One?" she said, tapping the corner of her mouth thoughtfully with her finger. "I don't think that's my name."

The Ladyleader looked troubled. "Most sacred Danu, we live to serve you."

"Oh yes!" she said with a giggle. "That's what I told you to call me. It sounds like a sneeze."

The Singing Ladies shifted uncomfortably. Then she remembered. The Dark Time People were full of their own Rules. She sighed. Rules were a bother. But only the Dark Time People could melt into the stone and become magic singers. She had made them that way long ago.

"I am Chano, the Child of Stone."

The Ladyleader looked relieved. "The holy strife against the blendeds turns into our favor. Soon their end will come."

Chano placed her elbows on her knees and cupped her cheeks with her little hands.

"About that," she said, "I should have told you sooner. I like blendeds. They are what could have been. You should like them too."

The Ladyleader narrowed her face with uncertainty.

"Exalted one, in your pure name we did decree the war upon our enemy!"

"A sneeze name," Chano said happily.

"But, Goddess! By your holy writ, you plainly guide that lineage blood should stay unmixed."

Chano pouted, placing both her fists against her hips and puffing her chest out indignantly.

"Kirion, Lord of 'Tell Everyone Else What to Do,' made me write those things. He has no imagination."

The Ladyleader's mouth hung open. Chano thought it looked silly. She liked silly.

"Chano," said the Pretty Blonde with Fohtian's eyes, "you remember Kirion?"

Chano had been waiting for her to say something, ignoring her on purpose. It had been her favorite game to play with Fohtian. The child goddess turned.

"Yes, I remember all of the Others. Fohtian most of all. He was my favorite before." She grew sad. It had been a long time since she had tried to remember. "He wanted to stop all the killing. He was going to turn Kirion mortal. But the 'Lord of Stuffiness' turned Fohtian's scary Wing General against him. She told the secret."

"Thanati," the Water Angel said quietly.

Chano shrugged. That might have been the name.

"Fohtian protected me—Nehro too—when Kirion turned our magic against us. That's why a part of me survived. But Fohtian is gone now." She sniffled and looked at the Pretty Blonde. "You have all that's left of him, and The Chalice is destroyed."

The elf gasped.

"How did you know?" she asked.

"I imprinted its form in my artifact. Because I missed him. Since then, I've been able to see it in the In Between, like the faraway light of fireflies. But it disappeared."

"I'm sorry," the elf with Fohtian's eyes apologized.

"Me too. Because of the imprint, only I can copy The Chalice. Kirion wants me so he can take Fohtian's Blood from you."

The Pretty Blonde paled and nearly collapsed. The Water Angel caught her before she fell. Chano felt sorry for her. Kirion was sometimes really, really scary.

The Ladyleader stepped forward, her eyes heavy with regret.

"Your wishes come to us so late. Why delay?"

"Because," Chano said with a shrug, "I was hiding."

"What heinous force dares stand against you?"

"Kirion, of course. When The Chalice broke, I knew he must have escaped his prison. Until I met you," Chano looked back at the pretty blond girl, "I thought he took the Blood of Fohtian. But then, I should have known he wouldn't dare smash The Chalice, since that would throw all his memories into Nehro's Cascades of Time.

"Once Kirion came here I had to leave Sarras and bind myself to a mortal so he couldn't find me."

Chano beamed at Her Mortal proudly.

"You chose him?" the Angry Angel said, pointing at Her Mortal. "You're very brave."

"Wait," a new voice said. Chano hadn't paid this one any attention before. He was human, but not hers. He always talked about silly past things that weren't in any way interesting. "You mentioned Sarras," he said. "You mean *the* Sarras?"

"What other Sarras is there?" Chano asked, hoping he would get the hint and stop talking.

"So it's real?" he asked.

"Percy, what the frag are you talkin' about?" Her Mortal said. "What's Sarras?"

"The Vartal believe it to be the planet of Danu, penetrated by her power. It's only ever been a myth," the Boring One explained.

Chano felt a little annoyed. Her planet was not a myth. She just hadn't been there in a while.

"Perhaps to you without belief," the Ladyleader countered with a sneer. "The faithful know that Danu's will gives Sarras life."

"There's no proof of its actual existence," the Boring One droned.

"Can we just skip this skrit and get some real answers?" Her Mortal asked impatiently.

"What would you like to know?" Chano asked excitedly, happy to change the subject.

Her Mortal licked his lips uneasily. He didn't look like he really wanted any answers. But Chano knew him well. He would ask the questions anyway.

"How long have you been with me?"

"Since you were bonded," she squeaked. "You were much smaller then."

"Nine," he said.

She nodded.

"I pretended to be the Well Leaf they gave you. It made me bond with your core drive."

"So what does that mean?"

"You ate me!" Chano said grabbing her stomach with a giggle.

327

The corner of Her Mortal's mouth twitched. That's why she liked him so much. He liked to laugh.

But all the other Intelligent Things just stared, unsure. So she decided to explain. "It means that you are not just bonded. Your core drive is me, or what's left of me anyway. This is why magical forces, like the mire field, do not affect you like the other bondeds. And that's why I could save you twice."

Her Mortal seemed to consider.

"So, five years ago, on Agrona when I was trapped—"

"I helped you. I turned the ship into living ore so you could speak to it," Chano finished.

"And the second time?"

"That was here. I told my Singing Ladies to leave you alone," Chano said.

"So why take the GraEL?" he asked.

"Kirion is breaking his own Rules," she huffed. "He wants to make more ships like LAMIE and bond more mortals. He will use them to invade the other shards. But secretly, he hates blending because it breaks the Rules. Once he has his way, he will kill them all. So he can't have my Well. I put it somewhere safe."

The technobionomist stepped forward. LAMIE was right, he *was* nice to look at.

"How did you get our STT drive to open a new portal?" he asked. "It's only designed to open existing ones."

That took some thought. She liked technobionomy, but there were so many names for Things. He must mean the walkway to her energy place.

"I can open a portal anywhere I want, as long as I have one of my Things to help me. For that one I used the energy in your drive. All the walkways were opened by me a long time ago."

The technobionomist's mouth opened and closed.

"Then by the goddess' hand," the Ladyleader said, pleased, "the holy GraEL is safe from him, the master of all lies."

"Um, sure," Chano began hesitantly.

"What do you mean by that?" Her Mortal asked.

Chano figured she should tell them. It was kind of important anyway.

"My Well can't stay in my energy place. It is a channel between my world and yours. If I leave it too long in my place, it will overload and ruin my realm of life."

"What will happen then?" the technobionomist asked.

"It will disrupt the stability of all the god planes."

"That's bad I'm guessing?"

Chano stacked her tiny hands on one another and squished them tight.

"The Mortal Realm exists by squishing the six God Planes on top of each other. Each energy place gives something important to yours: fire, air, water, stone, light, and darkness. Without Nehro's Netherworld, there would be no time; without Aeron's Observatory there would be no intuition of thought. My energy gives Life its being. If the planes are disrupted, the mortal realm will collapse, destroying all the shards and all the Things in them."

"That's not good," Her Mortal stated. "Just pull the GraEL back out. We can move it somewhere safe."

The humans murmured in agreement. Silly mortals. They could only think in one direction. Chano shook her head.

"The Well will only be safe on Sarras. I will only bring it back if you take me there."

"Why Sarras?" the Boring One asked.

"Because that's where it goes," Chano said impatiently.

"So then, we go there," Her Mortal promised. He always said the right things. Chano smiled. "Where is that, exactly?" he asked.

Chano's smile disappeared.

"Um—" she said.

They looked at her expectantly.

"What's the problem?" Her Mortal asked.

"I lost it."

"The whole planet?" the Boring One yelped. "How can you lose a whole planet?"

"Well, I moved it," Chano answered sheepishly. "A long time ago. For the Singing Ladies."

"Moved it to where?" the Technobionomist asked.

"I can't remember," she shrugged.

"Great," the Boring One said, throwing his hands up.

"And there is one more thing," Chano said holding up a finger. "You need to hurry. You've only got three days before the Well gets so heavy that I can't pull it out."

"But it's been in there a whole day already!" the Pretty Blonde exclaimed.

Chano was tired of speaking. It was starting to hurt, even with the special stones. She leapt off the altar, shrinking into her skin. Running back up to Kyleren's core drive, she hopped back through the Great Door to In Between.

37: Causes Are Only Lost When We Give Up

Raeylan leaned against the garden's low stone wall, running his fingers gently through the beautiful strands of Esilwen's hair. She lay against his chest, safely enclosed in his arms. Four hundred seasons of searching, countless cycles of constant worry, and he had finally found her. He could almost feel the abscess of anxiety drain as he held her.

She had sacrificed so much—memory, life, and love—to keep Fohtian's power from Kirion's grasp. But Chano's artifact, a sentient piece of the Child of Stone herself, could render that cost meaningless. If Kirion was ever in possession of them both—

No. Raeylan would never allow it.

Esilwen must have felt his heart quicken, because she turned her eyes to meet his.

"What is it?" she asked.

Raeylan brushed her cheek softly, tucking a loose lock of blond behind her tapered ear.

"I will not let Kirion take you," he promised quietly.

Her lips bent into a pretty smile.

"I know," she said, and kissed him tenderly.

She rested her head on his chest once again, but his heart would not surrender its pace. Kirion's horde seemed to have an endless supply of power, a limitless following. A shiver of doubt shook Raeylan to his core. What if he couldn't protect Esilwen? What if in the final moment, he failed?

He took a calming breath, willing his heart to behave. Panic would not shield Esilwen; uncertainty could not protect his sister. With the strength of discipline he forced his body to relax, his mind to clear.

The scratching of metal across stone drew his attention and he looked across the garden.

After meeting with Chano at the temple, the shiidh had herded them into a humped stone edifice in the forest. The rounded roof and bent walls were overgrown with grass and ferns, making the structure look more like a barrow than a building. The center of the complex had been specifically designed for foreigners. There were simple quarters lit with large tallow candles and a central sculpture garden. Luminescent lichens climbed much of the statuary that speckled the enclosed garden. A graceful stone willow tree stood in the middle of two twisting pathways, its molded branches drinking deeply from a moss lined pool. Golden light emanated from the floating moss, filling the garden with a subtle glow.

Just in front of the willow fountain, the illumination reflected sharply off the expression in Margariete's face. They had been waiting for Druantia's summons for more than two arcs. But his sister's mood was harsher than simple impatience. Something more troubled her as she tapped her sword against the walkway paving stones.

Kyleren stepped into the light and disengaged his helmet. As he approached, Raeylan noticed that Margariete refused to raise her eyes. When Kyleren reached Raeylan and Esilwen, he bent on his haunches and offered them two bead-like objects.

"LT comms," he said. "You're gonna need them if we split up."

Esilwen took one and placed it in her ear. Raeylan followed her example. Kyleren's hand shifted toward Margariete. She looked up at him, eyebrows poised.

"Do they allow for private conversation, or will we be constantly bothered by everyone's banter?"

"Just take one, Blue Eyes," Kyleren ordered.

Margariete stabbed *Stardawn* into the moss and stormed forward. Raeylan decided to intervene as she snatched the earpiece, before she started a squabble.

"What does your colonel intend to do?" he asked.

Kyleren stood to his full height, towering over them all.

"Not sure," Kyleren said. "We're gettin' stonewalled by the queen bee. She refuses to tell us anythin' until her council talks it over."

"Clearly, they don't understand our time restrictions," Margariete spat.

Kyleren grunted in agreement.

"Still nothin' we can do 'til they tell us where to go. They said somethin' about lookin' up Sarras' history."

"Great," Margariete said, returning to the fountain and plucking *Stardawn* from the moss.

Kyleren looked at her. Then with a grunt he reached into a pouch on his belt and withdrew a scroll. Raeylan recognized it immediately.

"Percy said you wanted this," Kyleren said, handing it over.

Raeylan stood and took the brittle parchment with both hands. He bowed politely and said, "Thank you. Your culturalist insists its language belongs to the shiidh. I am eager to discover Druantia's interpretation of its poetry."

"Is that really necessary, Raeylan?" Margariete snapped. "We've already found Chano. What else could that scroll possibly tell us?"

"The scroll is important," he returned. "Kalariel would not have collected it otherwise. I can read the words, but without context I do not understand its significance."

"And what if it is nothing more than a shopping list," Margariete argued, "or a poorly written letter between lovers? It's a waste of time!"

Raeylan felt his patience wane. The severity of their situation should be helping her focus, not inciting a temper tantrum. She had not been quite this irrational since the last cycles of Thyella.

"It may still prove to guide our fate. Find comfort that I take the burden of the mystery upon myself." He looked at his sister sternly. "You will not have wasted any effort beyond your assault on that patch of stone at your feet."

Kyleren laughed and Margariete spat an ugly curse. She slammed *Stardawn* back into its sheath.

Raeylan sighed. He could almost picture a little angry storm cloud above her head, zapping them all with ferocious lightning bolts. A bit of guilt rolled into him. Margariete had been through so much already. He opened his mouth to apologize for his cutting remark, but was interrupted by a raspy crystalline voice.

"My queen has closed accords within the Druid council," Tuatha said. "She has agreed to meet you."

The tall shiidh woman stood in front of the stone willow, as if she had materialized from nothing. Raeylan looked back at his sister. Her face was hidden behind the sheets of her dark hair.

Amends would have to wait. Esilwen rose and entwined her fingers in his. Together they took a step toward the fountain.

Tuatha hissed.

"Our queen invites you only, Raeylan of the lorelei. Alone must you approach."

Distress threatened him for a moment. He did not want to leave Esilwen undefended, however short a time. She must have noticed his muscles stiffen, because Esilwen placed a hand of comfort on his arm and leaned to whisper in his ear.

"Don't worry. I will wait here for you with Margariete. We will be safe."

Raeylan nodded, only half tense, and kissed her on the forehead. He spared a glance at his sister. She rolled her eyes, a common response to his overprotective nature. That, more than anything, brought him comfort.

"I am ready," he said to Tuatha.

He climbed onto the lip of the fountain. Three flat steps of shale led to the stone tree. The dark-skinned elf inclined her head and turned, placing a hand on the sculpture. It shivered at her touch. Then she moved forward, dissolving into the willow. Without fear, Raeylan followed.

It was an odd sensation to glide through stone. Raeylan was at a loss to describe the experience. As he emerged from another willow fountain, identical to the first, his ears rang with the high-pitched tone of water on glass. His body felt heavy, pressed. A cavernous corridor stretched in front of him, hollowed out like a cave. Tiny crystals glittered in the walls and ceiling, offering little light. He could only discern Tuatha by the silhouette she cast.

"The press of stone oft frightens strangers when they dwell this deep. Our greatest temple lies within Agrona's heart." Tuatha's voice sounded distant, yet reverberated throughout the passage, as if it were alive. "Have patience with my queen, her discourse with our homeworld Druid Council proved unsatisfactory."

"This council is her subordinate in government?" Raeylan asked.

"Not so," she answered. "The council stands apart. We guide with Danu's will, but they control all else within our land. They would not hear our words, refusing Danu's will to end the war."

Tuatha turned and glided down the corridor. Raeylan followed, a bit concerned.

"So what happens now?" he asked.

"Their lack of faith enticed our queen to wrath," Tuatha's teeth glinted in the gloom. Raeylan assumed she had smiled. "A truer council will be called to bear."

"But won't the old Druid Council rebel against the new one?"

"Their blasphemy has stained their fate beyond repair. Their souls now serve the goddess. Druantia has wrought their execution."

Raeylan stopped, stunned.

"Mercy and patience can turn the hearts of those who oppose us," he said firmly.

"That is not our way," she returned haughtily. "Traitor's souls are forfeit, serving Danu in the Otherworld. Enslaved by sin, their penance lies inside our queen's great hammer."

"They are trapped within her weapon?" he asked, appalled.

"It is the doom of they who lose their faith."

Raeylan eyed the crystal spike at her hip, troubled that its internal light was the life force of her vanquished enemies. Tuatha seemed amused.

"The queen alone commands that power. Come."

Tuatha led him through a series of tunnels which opened into a grand assembly chamber. Three shiidh, each wearing a distinct headdress, hovered around a table that burned molten orange. At first Raeylan thought the vicious material bubbled and eddied at random, but then he noticed distinct patterns of shape and rotation. It was a living map of their shard.

Druantia stood between two others he did not recognize. As soon as he reached the table he bowed politely.

"I apologize. I do not know your customs of propriety. I have only my own to offer."

"Your show of grace is pleasing," Druantia said. "Little time have we to spare. Declare to us your wish."

"Thank you," Raeylan returned. He displayed the god scroll, offering it with both hands to the shiidh queen. "Centuries ago six scrolls were given to me by my grandmother, an angel of the goddess Nehro. Each speaks of the gods. I believe this one belongs to the goddess Chano. Though I can read the words, I do not understand their significance. I humbly ask for your guidance in the matter."

Tuatha took the scroll from his hands at a gesture from the queen and delivered it to Druantia. She unfurled it and studied it carefully. Her attendants stood by silently. As she read, Druantia sucked in a hissing breath, her eyes narrowing dangerously. Raeylan struggled to determine whether she was angry or pleased.

"It is the Song of Baylour," she announced.

Glassy gasps expelled from the other shiidh. Raeylan waited patiently for the queen to explain.

"Lost a score of thousand years. Our legends say that Sarras lies behind the Eye of Baylour. Long ago the goddess made our race for this, to loose the path to Sarras."

"What is this 'Eye'?" Raeylan asked.

"The oldest mire field the worlds have ever known."

"And you would be willing to open it for us?"

Druantia's eyes glittered in the lurid light.

"Our goddess has commanded it."

38: COUNT THE SHADOWS

Margariete refused to look at her brother as he left. She plopped onto the ground. Raeylan had been short with her before, but had never stooped to ridicule. His scorning remark hurt more than she thought possible. She hunched her body against her knees and wrapped her arms around her legs. She supposed it had only been a matter of time. Raeylan had managed four hundred seasons of patience. He had to lose it sometime, water angel or not.

As she struggled to control a sob, a set of gentle hands mingled into her hair, pulling at stubborn knots with a small comb. Margariete didn't say anything, but Esilwen's tenderness brought a swell of comfort. Margariete closed her eyes and basked in the kindness.

How had she managed without her best friend for so many seasons?

"I have always been envious of your hair," Esilwen said softly. "It's so beautiful."

Margariete released herself to the luxurious pull of the comb against her scalp. Kyleren had wandered off somewhere, leaving the two of them alone.

"I'm surprised you carry that with you," she said.

"Women in this shard are taught to be prepared."

Margariete sighed, though whether from her emotional upheaval or the pleasure of being pampered, she couldn't say. She suddenly missed her maids, Lya and Rin, and most of all Seriya. All three had been proficient in grooming. Margariete still hadn't mastered the skill on her own. Her hair was disheveled chaos most of the time, restricted only by a leather band.

"I'm sure it was not Raeylan's intent to hurt your feelings, Margariete," Esilwen said diplomatically.

"No," Margariete returned. "He's getting tired. Even though I can't read his thoughts, I can read his face. He thinks those things often, but usually has control enough not to say them."

"Still," Esilwen said, "he would never hurt you on purpose."

"What did he say that wasn't true?" Margariete admitted. "He should not have to coddle me. He cares about me, but I must not expect him to be perfect."

"Wise words," Esilwen said, pulling the comb hard enough that Margariete's head bent upside-down. Esilwen looked at her and laughed. "He loves you completely."

"I know," Margariete said.

Esilwen relaxed her hold and Margariete's head returned to its normal position.

"Raeylan did not tell me what happened to Thyella after my death," Esilwen said.

Margariete's body filled with bitterness and the smile dissolved.

"Kirion destroyed it. He used Skoh's Earring."

"The Reality Scar," Esilwen sighed sadly. "I've seen it before. It's like a blackened bridge that pulls everything in the shard into the Void. Did anyone survive?"

"Seriya and Tenan, the household servants, and Malbrin," Margariete answered. It had been centuries since she had thought of them. A pang of homesickness rose up in her throat. "We found them a home in a new shard before we began searching for you."

"They must have all died by now," Esilwen sighed. "No one else?"

"No," Margariete said.

"I see," Esilwen replied.

An awkward silence passed between them.

"How many lives have you lived since Thyella?" Margariete asked.

"Just this one," Esilwen said, starting to weave a braid in Margariete's hair.

"Did things go well?"

"Yes. The Ninevay family is kind to me, though I am an oddity amongst the Kildar people."

"How so?" Margariete asked.

"There are several races of elves in this shard. I was adopted into a Sulevian family. It's quite common for them to take more than one lover, even if they are married. Sometimes spouses will separate and couple with a short-lived race, like a human or blended. They even have children with this other lover using blending tech. After the partner dies, they return to their elven spouse. They found my lack of interest in love curious."

Margariete laughed.

"What?" Esilwen asked sheepishly.

"So you remained faithful to my brother without even remembering him," she teased.

Esilwen blushed. "Yes, I suppose so."

"I'm happy for you and Raeylan," Margariete said.

"I wish you the same happiness, Margariete," Esilwen replied, placing a hand on Margariete's wrist.

"Thanks, but no thanks," Margariete said stubbornly, folding her arms across her chest. "I'll never trust a man that way ever again."

Esilwen's eyes revealed concern.

"You can't spend your life alone."

"I won't be," Margariete said firmly. "I have you and Raeylan. I need no one else."

"Needing family is one thing, Margariete," Esilwen said cupping her hands against Margariete's cheeks, "but no one can live without love."

"I can," Margariete challenged, but she could not keep her mind entirely free of doubt.

How was Esilwen so adept at touching her deepest desires? Margariete's rebellious thoughts turned to Lance Kyleren, lingered on his strong arms and his muscular chest. Her heart beat faster, even though she commanded it to be still.

"I don't believe that, Margariete," Esilwen protested.

Margariete stood and walked deeper into the garden. Her sensory perception felt Esilwen follow. Emotions clashed inside her. A small spring off to her right reminded her of the shrine in Viridius castle, the last happy moment she had spent with her younger brother as they caught the evasive kryystal fish. His eyes had been so full of life then. She stopped walking, unable to take another step.

"I can't open my heart to more death and betrayal, Esilwen," Margariete choked. "I would not survive it."

Esilwen circled to face her, giving her a soft embrace. Then she pulled away and said, "Death and betrayal are everywhere, Margariete, no matter what we choose. Every moment of happiness is worth the risk of loss."

Kyleren's yellow-hazel eyes loomed in Margariete's thought, full of disgust. He hated her. Nothing could change that. She felt herself leaking into despair.

Overwhelmed by her emotional state, Margariete sensed the attack an instant too late to dodge. She had just enough time to push out her hand and deflect the spinning blade from piercing her heart. The impact drove her back a step. When she looked down, a dagger protruded from her chest.

"Margariete!" Esilwen shrieked in horror.

It had happened so fast. Margariete's mind seemed sluggish as it tried to assimilate details. She recognized the dagger's handle, the red leather grip with the Dasklos family seal. Runes across the blade declared the weapon's name: *Bloodstorm*. Blood welled across her blouse, staining it bright crimson. The weapon had missed her heart, but had opened a major artery.

Wicked shadow wrapped around Esilwen and yanked her backward. Terail materialized from the thick vapor, one arm locked around the healer. As he jerked his dagger free from Margariete's body, she saw something glint in his other hand, the arm wrapped around Esilwen.

A teleport stone! And over his shoulder swung Raeylan's pack, the god scrolls peeking out its flap.

How had she not sensed him? She called out with her mind to anyone who might be near, hoping desperately that Raeylan would hear. Would her telepathic scream penetrate stone? Cold climbed into Margariete's limbs and she crashed to the ground. Esilwen's hands erupted in green flame as Terail crushed the blue stone.

"Blue Eyes!" someone yelled, as Margariete's consciousness fled to darkness.

39: To Punish And Enslave

The tangy taste of sea air kissed Esilwen's face as the world dropped into a swirl of stars. Fear crushed her heart into a terrified pulp. She knew who would be waiting when she rematerialized.

Esilwen gasped for air when she appeared, digging her fiery nails into her assailant's wrist. Terail dropped her with a howl when her fire mauled his arm. He flung his dagger, covered in Margariete's blood, to the floor, along with a bag he had over his shoulder. Scrolls spilled out. It took Esilwen a moment to recognize them. It had been so long ago in Malbrin's library when last she saw the ancient parchments.

After the shock of teleportation subsided, she commanded the fire on Terail's arm to burn hotter, spreading across his neck and chest. The flame devoured his black armor like dew at midday. While he flailed with pain, Esilwen skittered to the scrolls. She shoved them back into the pack, all the while darting her eyes around, dreading Kirion's appearance.

The room was lit with a muted yellow rod, dark around the edges. Her knees ached against the hard metal floor. Without a frame of reference, she had no idea if she was on a planet or locked in the belly of a ship. Her skull throbbed, a sure sign that an artifact was nearby. She didn't have much time.

Terail shifted to cloudy shadow above her. Esilwen had to concentrate to maintain her attack. It was much more difficult to keep the fire burning on his amorphous form. With one hand pointed at his vapor to better direct her power, she rifled into her pocket with the other, searching for the one thing that might take her back to Margariete before her friend died—the teleport stone Raeylan had given her for emergencies the night he had returned her memories.

She pulled it out, cradling it in her sweaty palm. The exact phrasing of the incantation to key the stone slipped in and out of her mind. Raeylan had made her recite it over and over, until he was satisfied she had it properly memorized. But that had been on the shiidh ship, safe in his arms, not in this eerie room while she struggled to keep an enemy at bay.

The words tumbled, but the stone started to glow. Quickly, she imagined the Agrona courtyard she had just left.

The pressure of two fingers pressing against her neck sent gritty pinches into the marrow of her bones. She cried out in pain, the stone flying out of her hand as her muscles spasmed with unchained cold. Her attack on Terail sputtered and died as her energy waned. He reformed in midair and crashed to the ground with a sickening thud of charred flesh.

Esilwen's cells seemed to shrivel at the edges, like those two fingers were drawing the life from her skin. She crumpled into a ball and shivered against the floor, numb to everything except needles of thrusting pain.

Kirion crouched beside her.

"The Black Touch of Skoh is deadly to mortal beings," he said, stroking her hair. "It acts much the same as the poison in her wolves' bite."

The curve of his lips was the same as she remembered. His voice remained as silky smooth as the day she had freed him. Only now, the sweet promise was gone. All that remained was sorrow. The object of her dreams turned master of nightmares.

Esilwen opened her mouth to speak, but her voice was garbled breath. She felt her life slipping into a cold place.

"Do not hope that you will escape me through death again, my love," he said with a charming smile. He lifted her hand and held it against his chest. "Fohtian's Blood will keep you alive."

Esilwen could already feel the healing fire spreading outward from her heart. But it was too slow. Her lungs refused to draw air. She was going to fall unconscious before she got an opportunity to fight back.

"Help me, My Lord," rasped Terail from somewhere off to the right.

Esilwen couldn't see him, but imagined that he was nothing more than a lump of blackened skin. Kirion's eyes darkened with pride.

"I have never seen you attack with such ferocity, Esilwen," he said, rising to his feet and stepping over her. "I did not believe you capable. But then, Feralblade is responsible for Vivian's end."

Esilwen choked. Her paralyzed body could not form tears, but her heart wailed. She knew she should be forming some plan of escape, but her mind was cloudy, her vision splotchy. Kirion returned, tossing Terail next to her.

"You didn't know that, I suppose," he sighed. "Feralblade *is* skilled at being unseen. It is what makes him of most use. He must have done something more to release your wrath. Harmed someone else you love, I assume?"

The Lord of Light drew Terail's remaining dagger from its sheath. He lifted Esilwen's hand gently, as if she was made of glass. He kissed her fingertips, his expression grave. Then he drew a long, ugly gash down the length of her arm.

"Feralblade is one of my most useful pieces," Kirion continued, squeezing her blood onto Terail's wounds. "I did not give you permission to destroy him."

As Kirion used her to heal his assassin, ribbons of light sprang from his hands. They wrapped tightly around her legs and torso. Wherever they touched her skin, feeling returned, like warm honey. Raeylan's name passed her lips, causing Kirion to frown.

"Don't worry, my dearest Esilwen," Kirion whispered in her ear. "I will keep you by my side as I restore the shards to their former glory."

40: PLEASE STATE THE NATURE OF THE MEDICAL EMERGENCY

Kyleren stood guard at the arched entryway that led into the shiidh's weird stone garden, shifting impatiently. Anya and Margariete were talking next to the crazy tree that Raeylan had melted into. Everything happening on this planet was like a cracked dream. The squirrel that had haunted him his whole life was real—a fragging goddess. And now people were walking into trees that grew like rocks.

He heaved a sigh and pulled out his drive. Magic was real, and he had a lot of it. Blue Eyes had been right all along. He was the strongest, fastest GAEL in the universe because Chano had chosen him. Kyleren almost heard her giggle as he spun the drive around, putting it back into its sheath on his arm.

It was hard to swallow. He had never really attached himself to a system of beliefs, but he had always figured the Agromor's religious skrit as the farthest thing from reality. But here was the evidence, spitting in his face. A magic rodent that popped out of his core drive, saving his brain from mire field scrambling. An evil god taking over his government. People who could read minds or teleport at will.

After this mission, when the GraEL was safe, he would have to make a choice. Margariete and Raeylan had spent their lives fighting Kirion. They expected Lance to join them. That meant leaving everything behind: the corps, his comrades, his identity as a soldier of the Coalition.

What would he be after that?

But this Lord of Light guy was after Anya and, according to the twins, Kirion would never stop until he had her. Kyleren could not let that happen. Outside the corps, she was the only friend he had ever known.

The crackle of feet against gravel caused him to look up. Margariete stalked deeper into the garden, behind more stone foliage. Anya followed after her. Lance resisted the urge to follow. Margariete was particularly moody today. He didn't want to be part of whatever new drama she was weaving.

The rest of the crew had returned to LAMIE after the meeting at Chano's temple. He wished he was there. The ship's metal bulkheads promised the comfort of familiarity. Kyleren had volunteered for guard duty, but he hoped Raeylan would return soon. The garden's petrified plants made his skin crawl.

He was fiddling with the power distribution of his sidearm when a sharp cry for help pinched his mind. He hesitated for a second, momentarily confused that Margariete's voice had echoed in his head, not traveled through his ears. Then he slammed his core drive into his weapon and bolted for the last place he had seen the girls.

Margariete was on the ground as he hit the edge of a small clearing. A man with silver hair and dark armor held Anya captive. Kyleren fired a shot at the man's head, but it was too late. They disappeared into nothing. Kyleren raced to Margariete, dropping to his knees in a skid. Margariete moaned and her eyes rolled.

"Blue Eyes," he roared, touching her blood-soaked blouse.

He cursed and yanked open his emergency med pouch. In a panic, he stabbed her with a nanomite injection. It would halt the bleeding for maybe a few minutes, long enough to get her to LAMIE. Kyleren picked her up and dashed for the ship.

"Colonel Stoddard, this is Lieutenant Kyleren," he shouted into his comm as he ran. "Enemy encountered in the shiidh complex. Inbound with injured."

"Copy, lieutenant," Stoddard said. "Report the situation."

"Doc Anya was taken by a hostile, her location is unknown. Margariete is critical."

"Understood. I'll meet you in the med bay."

As LAMIE loomed into his view, Kyleren felt Margariete's blood trickle down his arms. She had started bleeding again. He dashed passed Harris's post at the hatch. It took only a few seconds to reach the med bay doors, where he waited impatiently for the technology to register his presence. When they slid open, he rushed to the nearest exam table and gently laid Margariete on it. Wayne was already there, a second nanomite injection at the ready.

Margariete's breath rattled. Her hair had fallen across her paling face. Lance moved the rogue strands away, his hand lingering along her lips. Wayne looked at him with a knowing glint in his eye. Embarrassed, Kyleren snatched his hand away and rummaged through a drawer, tossing bandages onto the table.

Soon, Stoddard marched into the room, assessing Margariete's condition with a flick of his head.

"She doesn't have much time," he said. "Captain Reese, find Raeylan. He'll want to be here."

"Yes, sir," Wayne replied.

With a grave glance at Kyleren, he trotted out.

Lance couldn't look at Margariete, yet he couldn't look away. His throat plummeted into his stomach. This couldn't be it. In the week he had known her, he would have given anything to be rid of her. She was impossible, always arguing.

But now that she was dying, he didn't want her to go.

"What're we gonna do, sir?" Lance asked, unable to keep the desperate edge from his voice.

"Without a proper doctor, she won't make it," the colonel said. "She needs more than just emergency nanomites. Get Pryce."

Lance moved so fast he couldn't affirmate the order. He scaled the stairs to the brig and dropped the force field. Ignoring Huard's protests from the other cell, Kyleren threw the doctor over his shoulder and hauled him to the med bay.

"Where are you taking me?" the doctor demanded belatedly.

Lance had already dropped Pryce to the med bay deck.

"Help her," Lance demanded, not waiting for Colonel Stoddard to issue commands.

Pryce looked at Margariete, who bled freely on the table, and drew his shoulders back. His face became bold.

"You are all traitors to the Coalition. I owe you no allegiance," he declared.

Lance grimaced and yanked his sidearm free. He pointed it at Pryce and growled, "If you don't, doc, you won't be makin' it back to the brig."

Pryce's eyebrows rose in haughty challenge, "You've already made it clear that my life is forfeit, lieutenant. Why should I help you now?"

Blood pounded in Lance's head. Rage surged with every beat.

"You fraggin' help her doc or—"

"This doesn't help us, lieutenant! Put the weapon down," Stoddard ordered.

Lance looked at the colonel, fully intending to disobey, when instruments suddenly wailed on the examination table. Indicators of Margariete's condition flashed an ugly red. Pryce was her only chance at survival. With a strangling glare at the doctor, Kyleren lowered his sidearm.

"She's gonna die, doc," he hissed through clenched teeth. "You really gonna just let her?"

"He would," Stoddard interrupted, and Lance could see the truth of it in Pryce's eyes. "Here's the deal, doctor. Save Margariete and gain your freedom."

Pryce's beady eyes wavered.

"I want your word that you won't let your men kill me."

"If she lives, I'll drop you off in Coalition territory, alive," the colonel promised.

Lance shifted impatiently. The conversation was lasting longer than Margariete had.

"Agreed," Pryce finally said.

Lance holstered his weapon and followed Pryce to the exam table. The doctor was quick and precise. Within ten minutes Margariete's color had improved, her heart rate stabilized. Kyleren stared at her face through the entire operation, willing her to make it. He would have given anything for those electric blue eyes to open and glare at him.

As the doctor continued to work, the rest of the crew filtered into the bay. Gary, Harris, and Percy hovered at the entrance, but Gene scuttled to Stoddard's side.

"Captain Reese can't get through to Raeylan," Gene said. "Is she going to be okay?"

Pryce picked up an LT scanner.

"Her vitals are stable. She'll live, at least until the Coalition executes all of you for treason," he snapped.

Kyleren's temper burst. In less than a tenth of a second he had raised his sidearm, aimed and fired. Dr. Pryce crumpled to the floor, howling and cradling a bloody kneecap.

"You gromm bastard!" he screamed.

The colonel's objections were well-seeded with colorful attachments. Lance didn't bother to apologize. He shrugged, replying with a simple defense to his superior officer.

"You said not to kill him, nothin' about shootin' him."

41: You're Messing With My Zen Thing Man

Gene surveyed his lab with a pitiful sigh, waiting for the results of LAMIE's scan. Someone had breached the security in his office and stolen Raeylan's property. All the scrolls Gene had borrowed but one—the one Raeylan took to the shiidh queen—were missing, along with the blue teleport stone. Raeylan's insistence of the scrolls' importance played repeatedly in Gene's brain like a looped sound file. Apparently, they were key to the resistance against Kirion. Raeylan had been wary to hand them over for analysis, but Gene had promised that nothing in the universe could penetrate LAMIE's security protocols.

Unfortunately, Gene had been wrong.

And just when he had been getting somewhere with the blue stone. He'd been forced to adjust his examination instruments, but it had been enough to prove without a doubt the existence of a second universal frequency signature. It was the data he needed to confidently redesign the field of technobionomy. His Six Signature Theory could change science forever.

Gene snorted. Margariete called it magic; he called it science. So was he proving that magic was a force of reality? Or was he merely reclassifying that power into a branch of science? The paradoxical nature of the argument made him cringe. Perhaps it didn't matter. His art was of discovery, to define truths that could be classified, organized, and manipulated.

His proof was now lost. Well, not lost exactly, but definitely out of his reach. The scrolls were halfway across the galaxy, on the surface of Athalonde Prime. Impossible of course—even LAMIE couldn't leap across the vastness of space that fast. But Gene was getting used to dealing with that—the ludicrous mechanizations of magic. He had laced Raeylan's property with discrete trackers, originally meant to trace the path of the twins once they left. Gene had 200 prings against Percy that said Margariete and Raeylan would strike out to the Black Reach.

"Gene," LAMIE said, interrupting his thoughts, "I have completed the diagnostic you requested. The results are loading on your dataplate." Information marched across his screen as she continued, "The security footage has been neither corrupted nor fabricated."

Gene watched the feed. The scrolls and the blue stone rested securely on his table. Then they each disappeared into nothingness. Just like magic.

Gene groaned.

"Is the intruder using some form of camouflage?" he whined desperately.

"Negative, Gene," LAMIE answered. "However, my analysis indicates the intruder initiated a dormant code within my protocols that rendered him undetectable to my sensors."

Red flags burst to attention inside Gene's head. Who had the means and power to embed such programming?

He asked, "What evidence leads you to that hypothesis, LAMIE?"

"By using your theoretical data of Six Signatures, I was able to locate a foreign frequency hidden within my system. It was attached to an unidentified protocol. Access to its specifics is denied, though I have been able to extrapolate its purpose."

The schematics of the mysterious element appeared on the plate.

"A third signature!" he breathed excitedly.

"When active, it seems to overlay all data recorded in my sensors and security cameras," LAMIE explained.

"A sleeper code," Gene mused.

"Yes, Gene. It only affects me when activated."

"Whoever did this must have accessed the code before he boarded."

Gene's brain spiraled with possible entry points. He entered some calculations onto the dataplate.

"How many times has this code been activated, LAMIE?"

"Over the course of my lifespan, 17 times."

"In four years this guy has been on deck 17 times and he was never once discovered?" Gene snorted in disgust. "You'd think Penardun security would have noticed."

"I was curious about that myself, Gene," LAMIE said. "So I appropriated the pertinent files from Penardun's classified database."

Gene blinked.

"LAMIE, you are protoed not to do that!"

"Correction," LAMIE said, "I am protoed not to access classified information that does not directly pertain to my mission objectives. Once Aon squad and I embarked on our current operation, my protoboard could no longer prevent my access to any files involving me or Aon squad."

Gene frowned. LAMIE really was getting out of control.

"Consequently," LAMIE continued, "I have been able to analyze several million hours of security footage from Penardun. This same signature has been used against the city systems at the same time as my own. Many of the Designated Stellar Time prints align with reports of suspicious deaths to prominent people living or working on Penardun."

Gene's heart quickened. That was too improbable to be coincidence.

"This code must be everywhere, overlaid in every Coalition territory, ship, or allied vessel," he surmised. Who could be responsible for such covert infiltration? Definitely not the Agromors. Their reliance on dead tech made them unlikely candidates."

"Your conclusion has a ninety-nine-point-two-three percent chance of being correct," LAMIE confirmed. "I do have one more piece of information, Gene. But, according to your behavior history, it might cause you extra distress."

"What?" he asked cautiously.

"I analyzed the rest of my systems for the third signature in case the code was not the only hidden device. I found a broadcasting signal with the same signature as the code. It is a call sign identifying us."

"And as long as it's active?"

"The infiltrator will be able to detect us in any planetary system he occupies, within a second of our arrival."

"This is the worst day of my life," Gene groaned, slapping himself on the forehead.

The holotable darkened and the lights in the situation room flicked to normal. Gene glanced nervously around the table at LAMIE's crew, Raeylan, Tuatha, and the shiidh queen, hoping they had a solution.

"So what do we do?" Kyleren growled impatiently. "How do we get Smiles back?"

"Uh, that's actually not a problem," Gene admitted, looking guiltily in Raeylan's direction. The teleporter's eyes bored into him, and Gene danced from one foot to the other. "Percy and I borrowed your scrolls for more than just study."

Raeylan's expression didn't change.

"What do you mean?"

"I swear, our interest was purely for study," Percy apologized into his shirt.

Raeylan simply remained silent, patiently waiting for an explanation.

"Percy and I were curious as to where you and Margariete come from," Gene rattled. "You see, we wanted to know if these 'shards' you keep referring to are other portions of the galaxy—"

"Or if it's the other side of the Black Reach," Percy interrupted. "No one has ventured far enough beyond to that region of the galaxy—"

"Get to the point gentlemen," Stoddard commanded gruffly. "We have a limited time frame to get the GraEL back on Sarras before the universe gets skrit-faced."

Gene plunged into his confession without taking a breath, as if it would be less painful the faster he said it.

"We marked Raeylan's god scrolls with LT tracers. It's improbable that the enemy would have noticed, and even if they did, the traces are impossible to dismantle. I protoed them myself."

Gene might have imagined it, but he thought hope bit into Raeylan's eyes.

"You know where to find Esilwen?" he asked.

"She's on the surface of Athalonde Prime," Gene answered confidently. "Or at least the scrolls are."

"In the LT mining facility?" Reese asked. He whistled. "That would be easy to penetrate. They have minimal security."

"Not exactly," Gene admitted uneasily. "The tracer is on the other side of the planet. LAMIE has searched her data files, but there are no records of any complex at that location, not even highly classified buildings."

"LAMIE wouldn't be privy to all of that information," Stoddard pointed out.

Gene felt blood pound inside his face and his breath quickened.

"Gene?" Stoddard said, disapproving.

"It isn't my fault, colonel. LAMIE is the most intelligent living tech entity in the galaxy. Her ability to exploit the loopholes in her protoboard was something I didn't anticipate."

"If a secret government base was Coalition knowledge, colonel," LAMIE interjected, "I would have found record of its existence."

"It must be a fortress specifically built for Kirion," Raeylan reasoned. He turned to Gene. "As to the devices you attached to my possessions, I do not harbor your curiosity ill will. Your actions will guide us to Esilwen. I owe you a great deal."

Acute relief flooded Gene.

"For you, perhaps, of great concern is this," Druantia hissed in her usual grating manner. It made Gene shudder uncomfortably. "The greater matter of the GraEL before us lies. It must be placed on Sarras, so that every realm be spared from Danu's wrath."

"She's right," Stoddard said. "We have to take care of the GraEL first."

Kyleren and Raeylan's expressions tightened, but they did not speak.

"Have you located Sarras?" Gene asked Druantia.

"It lies behind the veil of Baylour's Eye," Druantia said. Her hand slipped into her robe and extracted a scroll. Gene recognized immediately; it was Raeylan's. "This gift from Danu long ago once forced the Eye to close. The shiidh could use the song to break the seal and free the path we seek."

"Then why are we sittin' around doin' nothin'?" Kyleren hollered. "Let's get it done!"

"The task is not so simple as you think," Druantia remonstrated with a crystal stare.

"I'm guessing you said we can't," Kyleren mumbled.

"If the song opened it before, why not now?" Gene asked.

"A host of our initial race is crucial to succeed. Now, not two score of us remain. A fourth of these do tour abroad."

"And what was the original count of your people?" Percy asked in what sounded more like an attempt at research than actual concern for the impending destruction of the galaxy.

"Two thousand sisters once did roam these stars."

"So who wants to tell Chano we're all fragged?" Kyleren grunted.

Druantia hissed a displeased comment and Reese returned something rude. Gene's thoughts overwrote Stoddard's reply. The queen's explanation opened an idea. Thousands of shiidh voices were needed to disrupt the Baylour mire field because of its fractal wave frequencies. Luckily, the Agromors had unwittingly discovered the one thing that could duplicate the shiidh's abilities.

"Guys," Gene announced into the arguing room.

Slowly, everyone turned to him.

"Opening the Eye isn't going to be a problem. If you need more shiidh voices, I can replicate them for you."

"Our noble race is not for you to conjure with your heresy!" Druantia seethed through her pointed teeth. "Our goddess only has such power!"

Gene held up his hands, glancing anxiously at the hammer swinging freely at her belt.

"It was your own people who invented the technology, not me."

"Explain this madness."

"The mire field generator. It was designed on the same principles of shiidh vocal disruption. With the right calibrations, we could use it to amplify your voices, even mimic them, effectively boosting the amplitude of your song to the power of two thousand shiidh."

Druantia's eyes widened. She turned to Tuatha.

"To be the cause of our own ruin is the penance for our sins. Such power cannot be allowed for anyone to taint."

"Even so," Raeylan interjected, "this power can be used by your people to return the GraEL to its proper resting place. Perhaps the technology was created just for this purpose. The will of the gods is often veiled from the mortals who serve them."

Druantia looked at Raeylan with respect.

"Then let's jump Gene and the shiidh to the mire ship," Reese said as he stood. "We can drop them at the Eye and dock with the rest of the squad."

Kyleren's eyes brightened with mischief. "We goin' after the doc while Gene plays with his mire ship?"

"You must be present to release the GraEL," Druantia argued.

"It will take time to recalibrate the mire tech," Reese shrugged. "There's no use in Aon sitting around while that happens. We can rendezvous at the Eye after we get Anya."

Gene shook his head.

"It would take hours to jump through the right portals to reach Athalonde Prime. There'd be places where you'd have to rely on standard FTL, and LAMIE's is still incomplete. The chancellor could have moved Anya by then, or you might miss the deadline to return the GraEL."

"There's a large margin for error here, boys," Stoddard almost sighed.

"There is not," Raeylan said. "Kirion is arrogant. He will underestimate us. And he would not trust anyone but himself to keep Esilwen or the scrolls secure."

"But that still leaves our time constraint," Stoddard argued. "We can't risk the lives of billions for the doctor and your scrolls."

"This is not as difficult as you believe, colonel," Raeylan returned. "Chano is connected to Kyleren. He wields her power, and it was she who opened your T-portals in the beginning."

Gene's mouth hit his chest.

"Are you saying that Kyleren can open new T-portals at any time? We could go anywhere in a matter of seconds!"

Kyleren glanced at his arm sheath skeptically, as if he weren't sure what to think. The colonel grinned.

"Then I'd say we've got a fragging plan."

42: You've Just Crossed Over

"Gene's inverse signature algorithm is now active," LAMIE announced to the bridge.

Lance glanced at Colonel Stoddard in concern. They wouldn't know if Gene's program would counteract the locator tag on LAMIE until they reached the other side of the T-portal. Gene said he had only been able to mask the beacon, not remove it. If it didn't work, they would lose any advantage of surprise. The chancellor would know they were coming.

"What do you think, sir?" Wayne asked the colonel.

"Not sure. Right after we launched from Penardun a week ago, I received a report on new troop deployment. The military presence on Athalonde Prime has been increased," Stoddard said. "If they detect us, this will be over real quick."

"Kirion will not destroy this ship," Raeylan promised.

Lance wondered how the frag Raeylan was so sure of that, but Raeylan quickly explained.

"He has worked too hard to manipulate your government for LAMIE's creation. I doubt the regular military will have access to the locator beacon. Only Kirion's most trusted lieutenants within the Faithful Legion will know of it. It is far more likely he will try to ambush us within his fortress."

Lance snorted. "Faithful Legion." What gromm skrit kinda name was that for an army?

"There's only one way to find out," the colonel said.

Stoddard leveled his gaze at Lance. The lieutenant nodded and closed his eyes, concentrating as Raeylan had instructed. It was the third time he would make a new T-portal. The first had been to rendezvous with the members of Aon who had stayed with the mire field ship: Trish, Chad, and Bedin. The second moved Gene's team and a ship full of shiidh to a respectable distance near the Eye of Baylour.

Forcing a portal open was a strange feeling. Lance's cells vibrated with energy that thrummed through his body like the report of an LT cannon. His mind used that power to pluck a hole into the fabric of space, but it wriggled and writhed like something alive. It was hard to make sure the portal was the right shape for LAMIE's hull. The edges kept rolling and warping. Without constant concentration the opening kept sliding into a paper thin line.

Besides holding it open, Lance struggled to make the exit in the right place. Raeylan had insisted that Lance memorize about 40 holomaps of the galaxy, to prevent a T-portal connection too near a planet or star. Gene rattled on about the possible implications of accidentally linking a portal to the core of a planet and something about the devastation sucking in the plasma of a star could cause. Lance wasn't sure, what with the speed of Gene's explanation and all the technical terms, but it sounded bad.

An energy surge raced out of his body, making his heart pound. His breathing came fast and hard. A giggle brushed the ear closest to his core drive, just like the two times before. Lance had the distinct impression that, for Chano, T-portal travel tickled.

On the first round, Lance had to take both LAMIE and the shiidh queen's vessel to meet up with the mire field ship. The second time, he'd had all three. Now, only LAMIE was going through. Lance tried to keep his mind on his task, pushing his worry away.

The portal stretched and twisted.

"Focus, Kyleren," Raeylan said, sounding small and far away.

Lance almost cursed. Taking a breath, he bore down hard.

"That's it, lieutenant," he heard the colonel say. "LAMIE take us through."

A hand clapped on Lance's back.

"Well done," Raeylan said.

Lance snapped his eyes open, staring out the crystasteel windows. The orange haze of Athalonde Prime hovered beneath them, welcome in its familiarity. It was the closest image to home he had ever known.

Two of the Coalition's most prominent space stations orbited the planet: Govannan, the headquarters of Lamorak Industries and sole manufacturer of LT technologies, and Gilvaethwy, a spaceport that produced hundreds of dead tech space vessels for the Coalition every year. Before it was destroyed by the Agromors, Gwydion had been the third artificial complex circling the world. Lance, and every other GraEL Attached Elite Level VIC, lived the first 18 years of life there.

But just now, as he gazed at the rust-colored atmosphere, Lance felt hatred twist inside him. Everything he had been told about his existence was a lie. The chancellor had exploited the Coalition's fear, promising victory in the war through the GAEL program. But the power hungry chancellor's only intention was to take control of the universe, proclaiming himself God.

"Report," Stoddard commanded.

"Sensors read heavy military detail orbiting the planet, sir, and—" Trisha's voice trailed off in concern and awe.

"What is it, sergeant?"

"I'm picking up Nynniaw on sensors, sir," she reported.

"What?" Stoddard exclaimed sharply.

Lance whistled low. It made sense. Govannan and Gilvaethwy were the core of Coalition military and economic strength. The Round would have wanted them protected, especially in light of Gwydion's unforeseen destruction.

Good as it was for the Coalition, Nynniaw was more living tech than LAMIE could handle. Both central training ground for the Cymric troops and an advanced defense platform, Nynniaw was the pride of the Coalition forces, ship and space station in one. One and a half million military personnel called it home. Its hull sported thousands of LT cannons, 12 hangars promised easy launch of hundreds of two-man fighters from any angle. The massive complex was always escorted by the Templar Fleet, 13 sleek battleships known for their brutal combat victories.

"Frag," Wayne muttered.

"All signs indicate that we are undetected," LAMIE announced. "I am entering orbit around the planet."

Lance heaved a sigh of relief that was reflected by everyone else on the bridge.

"At least by the Coalition," Raeylan reminded them.

"Right," Wayne agreed. "We can't let our guard down until we know Chancellor Medrod isn't waiting for us."

"Preliminary scans of the unidentified complex are now complete, colonel," LAMIE reported.

Her readings popped across the forward bridge display. That side of Athalonde Prime was rarely mined. Forests of brittle trinium made harvesting the ore trees dangerous due to their extraordinary size, and the corrosive gases bubbling from the viscous crystalakes made breather gear a necessity. Rain never fell on Athalonde Prime like an organic planet, and the world's ancient mountains thrust their sharp thorns uneroded into the russet clouds. Just walking the surface required special protection gear due to the living moss ore that barbed the rock.

Chancellor Medrod's secret base bored into the sharp face of a vertical cliff. Great panes of crystasteel lined parts of the complex that jutted outward from the natural verandas, making it look more like an ancient castle than a Coalition base. A single tower launched up from the corner of the mountain, affording a clear view of the terrain in two directions.

Trisha turned from her post at the sensor console and studied LAMIE's data.

"Three probable entry points," she concluded. "Here on the large crystasteel dome, or this opening that looks like some sort of landing bay in the tower. And of course, this," she pointed, "is obviously the compound's main entrance."

"Entering through the front door is bold and unexpected," Wayne recommended.

"And loud once the fraggin' alarm blares," Lance countered.

"Couldn't we just punch a hole through that dome?" Gary piped from the back of the room.

Trisha shook her head.

"The complex will have life support systems. Breaching the outer walls would flood the target with Athalonde's toxic atmosphere."

"Doesn't matter for us," Gary shrugged. "We can breathe it. Raeylan and Tuatha can use an LT breathing apparatus."

Trisha's brow creased with an annoyance that made Lance chuckle. The newb was in for it.

"Look green-ass, any moron worth his engineering marks would make sure there were safety protocols in place to deal with an atmo leak. Infected areas of the compound would be locked down. At the very least there'd be bulkhead doors to blast through."

"Then the tower is our best chance," Raeylan said diplomatically. "From there we can make our way into the main part of the fortress."

"I may be able to offer you some assistance with the compound's sensors and communications once you are inside," LAMIE added. "I have been studying several of Gene's LT scrambling viruses. The upload would disrupt the enemy's systems, giving you approximately ten minutes before any alarms could be activated. It is possible, however, that their defenses include signature frequencies not yet outlined in Gene's Signatures Theory. I have the capability to alter the codes to affect the three signatures he has already identified, but I cannot predict the effect my virus will have on the remaining frequencies."

"Huh?" Lance said.

"She said she might or might not be able to help," Stoddard grunted.

He stared hard at the picture of the complex.

"Get Tuatha and Raeylan suited up, lieutenant. Point of ingress will be the tower. LAMIE, take us in."

43: You Keep Telling Yourself What You Know, But What Do You Believe?

As a mortal, Pyrana had been appointed the role of Exalted Oracle in the temples of Fohtian at the age of sixteen, when the worlds were still whole. Her natural gift for compassion and a unique ability to know the Phoenix Angel's will guided the god's flock for the next 45 years. The church flourished in peace because of her ultimate dedication. Service to her god was her only love; her family was the clergy. As her body aged, her faith increased. She never regretted her life's path.

It was her selfless devotion and capacity for love that captured Fohtian's attention. When he gifted a portion of his power to create a divine race for his cause, the Phoenix Angel chose her to lead them.

His strength burned green in her veins, her skin regained its youth and shone with a bronze sheen. Crimson wings, scorched in gold, leapt between her shoulder blades, a manifestation of her faithful benevolence. The glory of her calling filled her soul. In the hour of her rebirth she took the name Thanati, "spirit of gentle death."

Twelve such beings were born of the fire plane. Much of Fohtian's domain—fire, love, and death—lived within them; more than any of the other gods had been willing to sacrifice in their own servants. Only Nehro's lorelei could match them.

The hierarchy of angels was based on the amount of power a god surrendered for the creation of his servants. The erinyes of Fohtian were the fewest, thus the strongest. The spirits of fire and water were granted so much favor that death could not claim them by age. They were immortal. Aeron's prophets were next in strength, though somehow the Mystic had discovered a way to enhance his angels without diminishing his own vigor. Skoh gave little of herself for her wolves, and though plentiful, they were short-lived in comparison to the others. Having a plane of limitless energy, Chano did not create angels, rather a living ore that could be molded into sentience by the designs of mortals. Only Kirion refused to segment his power, reserving the full strength of light for himself.

It took little time for the erinyes to earn a weighty respect from their counterparts, loved by those who lived with goodwill and feared by those who desecrated others. But Thanati was unhappy with the Fire God's philosophy of balance. Mortals who walked in darkness did not deserve the blessings of love, the power of compassion belonged in the light. Fohtian's will for equality amongst the domains often supplanted the triumph of an ultimate greater good within the universe. Her faith faltered.

That was why she sought the counsel of the Lord of Light. Through his guidance she came to realize that his design matched the desires of her heart. Kirion was bold, interfering directly with the destinies of mortals to rid the worlds of evil. And one day, she realized her love for him was greater than her loyalty to Fohtian. Kirion presented a choice to the gods: Skoh must be cast into her own Void, to purge all wickedness from the mortal plane forever.

The other gods feared him, for he retained all his godly might. So they plotted his destruction. Because Fohtian had given her so much of himself, he needed Thanati's aid. He entrusted her with the details of his plan.

And she betrayed him.

Thanati warned Kirion of the other gods' intent. She slaughtered her sister erinyes, painting the Phoenix Angel's palace with the green of their blood. Their power became hers. What happened next, she never discovered—only that the gods disappeared and the Seven Worlds cracked into fragments.

Then she hunted the shards for evidence of her missing beloved. She took the salty hearts of every lorelei she found to open the gates between the newly created realms. It was a millennium before she discovered the first clues as to the fate of the divinities.

She came upon a shard nearly consumed by a vast darkness; the dreaded scar of the Void's corruption. In a graveyard of bones she uncovered a jewel—a black pearl earring that thrummed with malicious power. Thanati recognized Skoh's might, but the Lady of Darkness was gone. If a vestige of the deity remained, was there not a chance that a part of Kirion had survived as well?

Thinking to collect whatever was left of each of the gods, she made to pluck The Earring from its wreath of bones, but the Wolves of Skoh leapt upon her, vehement that only the worthy could claim their Lady's artifact. Thanati considered killing them all for their insolence. Not only were they the least of all the angels, their might had diminished as generations passed without the touch of their goddess. Once their bodies had towered over her, but these she faced were not so large as a beast of burden.

Only a stray thought stayed her hand. If the wolves could be swayed to service the Lord of Light, they would be irreplaceable allies. So she commanded them to continue protecting The Earring, and she took her leave until such time as Kirion could claim it.

Ecstasy was her companion when she finally found him, recently delivered from prison by a young elven girl. He was fallen, trapped in a body tainted mortal, his godly nature locked away within his mind. And to Thanati's horror, his heart had been stolen by the maid who had freed him.

Thanati knew Skoh's power would release him and break the bond he had forged with the elf girl. The erinyes appeared and told him of The Earring, reminding him of his greatness and desire to bring order to the universe. She opened the shardgate and sent him to the wolves.

If Thanati had known the endless annoyance that Esilwen would become, she would have slain the elf while Kirion was away.

When he returned, Kirion was changed. But to Thanati's dismay, his desire for Esilwen did not wane, even as she defied him and took the Blood of Fohtian for herself. He embarked upon his campaign to restore his divinity, but his nagging want to seek Esilwen never diminished. The Lord of Light's obsession consumed his thought, disrupting the momentum of his army more than once.

Never daring to resist her lord, Thanati obeyed when he sent her in search of the Warden of The Chalice. Her Soulwell of fire allowed her to detect Fohtian's artifact within a reasonable distance.

She had found Esilwen once. Worried that the elf would only hinder Kirion's cause, Thanati determined the best course was to slay Esilwen and take her blood. Unaware of the artifact's phoenix power, Esilwen escaped in a wreath of flame. Too late, Thanati learned only The Chalice could recover Fohtian's flame. Thanati's penance had been long and painful.

But now, Kirion finally possessed the elf maid. Circumstance confined Thanati to her tower, awaiting new orders. It was not her lord's command that imprisoned her, but Esilwen's presence that caused the need for isolation. Esilwen could use Fohtian's artifact to close Thanati's Soulwell.

That meant Thanati would be separated from the Lord of Light for a number of years. A lesser being—like a mortal—would have been consumed with jealousy. She had been Kirion's consort since before the Fracturing, and now that honor would belong to the elf maid. But Thanati recognized the inevitability of Esilwen's fate: she would have to die for Kirion to restore his godhood.

The Lord of Light would tire of her eventually. The girl lacked the complexity of the immortal mind. Eons had contributed to Kirion's depth of thought. Esilwen lacked the capacity to truly understand him. At no other time was this so painfully obvious as when she had sought to 'save' him, to return him to what the other gods had wanted of him: a player in balance, suppressed in greatness. It seemed to Thanati that Esilwen had finally abandoned that endeavor.

Good. It would only speed her lord's return to sanity.

Distracted in thought, Thanati fluttered to the bottom of her tower sanctuary. Her aerie lifted through three levels, with a metallic floor deeply nestled into the mountain. Ringed ledges offered her perches along the walls—for sleeping, grooming, or study—but the center was an open shaft that offered a comfortable environ for a winged creature such as herself. It was topped by a dome of crystasteel, giving her the illusion of greater freedom of flight. A small landing jutted out through the second level, making use of a natural cavern in the cliff face. Through this she could soar over the planet's hostile terrain.

But here on the floor was the device she used to chronicle her knowledge for Kirion's viewing. She pressed several controls, recalling the three-dimensional map of the shards she had spent the last century perfecting. With a quick command the names, populations, and resources of each realm appeared. The shardgates were clearly marked, color signifying whether or not space vessels were required for travel between them. Ten thousand shards were documented, but there was at least four times more unexplored cosmos that potentially cradled life.

The more she considered her work, the more she understood the nature of the universe. Near the epicenter of the Fracture, the shards were small, sometimes holding only a continent. Time moved slowest here, with barely eight hundred years having passed since the disappearance of the gods. The peoples were mostly nomadic, tribal in nature. Moving toward the edges of the splintered worlds, the shards became large, containing multiple planets separated by black vacuum. The civilizations in these shards had progressed faster than those closer to the center. Over tens of thousands of years, most of these had forgotten the gods and turned instead to technology. Thanati wondered if, at the very edge, the Fracture actually halted, giving these outer shards an infinite plane of existence like the old worlds.

Chano's shard was the most advanced of any realm Thanati had visited. Kirion realized early that this must be due to the presence of the goddess' artifact—her domain was metal, life, and stone. The Child of Stone was unpredictable, notorious for breaking the ancient rules of the gods. Kirion believed that Chano might have retained a portion of her sentience due to the obvious genetic manipulation affecting the species populating this set of worlds.

The erinyes reviewed the final touches on the map. Kirion would be pleased. With this, the Faithful Legion could spread Kirion's light throughout the shards. As she worked, the hologram sputtered with static and flickered off. Confused, she tapped a series of commands. Nothing happened. She called the fortress's core engineer on her LT communication array.

There was no response.

A series of loud cracks shook the walls. Thanati noticed several fast moving shadows dart across the cave opening of her personal landing platform. The figures' size, along with their living camouflage armor, identified their race: GAEL VICs. A smirk stained her crimson lips.

So, they had come to her.

Four GAELs leapt from the precipice, causing great cracks to slither along the floor where they impacted the floor. They wore light armor equipped with atmospheric thrusters. Two others materialized from nowhere. These wore clear breathing instruments to protect against the toxic air. She easily recognized them: Raeylan and a shiidh druid.

As the GAELs raised their weapons, she opened her Well to the plane of fire, summoning her ancient blade of flame, *Rupture*. She blocked Raeylan's first strike, calling forth her second weapon, a deadly firelash, which she hurled against the closest soldier. The dark-skinned woman screamed in agony as it struck a bloody burn around her neck.

Thanati snarled with laughter. Due to the impervious nature of their skin, the GAELs arrogantly declined heavy armor. They were unaccustomed to the rules of combat magic. Properly enchanted weapons would pierce them like any regular mortal. Not one of them had ever been touched by fire, but Thanati's flame was of the Phoenix Angel and could sear their blood to their bones.

Knowing that Raeylan was the most dangerous threat, Thanati could not finish the female GAEL just yet. She yanked the whip, throwing the woman hard against the wall. At the same time, she pushed forward with *Rupture*, driving Raeylan back. Her lash cracked aimlessly behind her, to keep the remaining three GAELs at bay.

Raeylan simply teleported to a different position and sliced at her again, trying to force her closer to the circle of soldiers. His teleportation gave him a distinct advantage on the ground, so she spread her wings and leapt into the air, where Raeylan couldn't follow. She chose to dismiss her sword; it would be of no use at this range.

The GAELs pelted rounds from their BT armaments, but she either dodged or met each with an arrow blast of fire from her palm. She threw several bolts back at the soldiers, forcing them to maneuver out of the way. Finally, one seemed to tire of her unfair vantage. With reckless speed he switched on his armor's thrusters. The largest GAEL ordered him to stand down, but the young soldier was already charging to meet her.

A throaty laugh tickled her throat. What a fool. A thought commanded her firelash to blaze into the shape of a spear. One movement cast it at her enemy. The weapon tore cleanly through his chest, breaking the breastbone and ripping out the small of his back. The force of her throw pinned him back to the floor. He screamed in pain as she ordered the whip to rage with flame, scorching his organs and boiling his blood.

Raeylan rushed to the injured soldier, teleporting the GAEL's body away from the firelash-turned-spear. They reappeared next to another of their team, a GAEL who immediately turned his attention to his damaged comrade. Thanati instructed her spear to return as the man injected his friend with nanomites. The gesture was useless; the boy was already dead.

With the confidence of triumph, she turned her spear on the next weakest combatant, the downed female who was struggling to regain her feet. The leader of the squad shouted a warning, but the weapon was already sailing toward its target.

Then two eerie musical notes jarred Thanati so hard her teeth ached. The firelash evaporated from existence before it reached its kill. The erinyes turned toward the shiidh, a scowl staining her expression. The Vartal druid parted her lips in a smile that exposed the sharp points of her teeth.

Thanati screeched in fury, her promise of death for the shiidh ringing against the walls.

44: On The Other Side Of The Screen It All Looks So Easy

Gene watched through the crystasteel viewport of the apple-hopper turned mire-generator-ship as his greatest scientific achievement jumped through the golden T-portal. LAMIE was gone, and with her, squad Aon.

He wished he knew some equation that would allow him to be in two places at once. Though he knew no one else could manage the amplitude uplift algorithms needed to escalate the shiidh's vocal frequencies, he longed to be with LAMIE and her crew. Bedin could fulfill the minimum requirements of Gene's job, but the higher level functions of LAMIE's protoboard were beyond the elven engineer.

He was surprised to realize that his concern comprised more than simply wanting LAMIE to operate flawlessly. The entire mission had changed Gene. The field of technobionomy was excruciatingly competitive, leaving little time for interpersonal relationships. Peers were not to be trusted, as they were likely to snatch innovative notions and make them their own.

But for the first time, Gene had people he thought of as friends—people whose lives mattered to him, like

Lieutenant Kyleren and Captain Reese. He thought of Margariete and Raeylan as more than just another hypothesis to tackle; their survival mattered. Knowing that people he cared about had just leapt into a possible battle zone with only a flimsy masking code to keep them safe made his chest feel heavy.

"Gene," Percy said, jerking him out of his mopey thoughts, "they're going to be fine."

Gene turned to the culturalist. Percy was pale, almost like he was desperately trying to believe his own statement.

"Of course they will," Gene replied with a shaky breath.

LAMIE's team was incomplete. Sergeant Reynolds, Chief Snow, and Bedin Desha had volunteered to join the rescue operation after they were briefed, but Corporal Harris had been assigned to the Baylour mission due to his missing arm. Margariete was still unconscious and had been left at the shiidh temple on Agrona under the care of a Vartal physician. Major Huard and Dr. Pryce were somewhere in the shiidh dungeons.

That meant Aon had only five of their bonded soldiers, one of which would have to stay on LAMIE to fly her. The infiltration team would only have four, plus Raeylan and a shiidh—Twa-something or other—who had insisted on joining the crew.

"I just hope their luck has improved since Danaan," Gene mumbled. "We've hit too many complications out here."

"It's the Coalition's turn to hit the end of its luck," Percy snorted in agreement. "If it wasn't for Chancellor Medrod, none of this would have been necessary."

"Is luck the name we give our fate when mortal souls no longer see the gods' intent?" Druantia jeered with her crystal gritty voice.

Her unexpected interjection caused both Gene and Percy to lurch forward. Gene whirled, relaxing at little as he noticed that Harris seemed amused rather than alarmed.

"Perhaps all this is Danu's will," she said, encompassing the mire ship with a spidery gesture of her fingers, "your prior path to Danaan fated true. But few could bend the mire as a tool, as you."

Gene blinked, quickly unraveling the woman's riddle. Percy looked thoughtful for a moment and said, "When you put it in that light, I would say we were lucky."

"You guys done talking," Harris growled, "because the clock's ticking and that Eye of Baylour thing won't open itself."

"Right." Gene's head snapped back to his console like he had been slapped.

What was he thinking? He had already wasted two minutes. After initiating a system bypass, he snatched his dataplate and trotted to the back of the ship where the mire generator hummed. Two simple recalibrations and the plate dismantled the feeble Vartal security protocols that tried to prevent his access to the base-coding. Within seconds the essential mire cyphers danced across his interface. He ticked through them, making necessary alterations. It was a good thing he had been able to retrieve the information off the data tile Margariete had tried to smash back on Danaan, otherwise the modifications could have taken hours.

From the shadows where she must have been watching, Druantia spoke.

"Do you believe you have the skill to duplicate the power of our goddess?" Druantia hissed.

"Ack!" Gene jumped and almost dropped his dataplate. "Don't do that!"

"My apologies," she replied, though Gene didn't think she looked sorry at all.

Gene shivered. The shiidh didn't seem to understand the concept of personal space. She stared at his dataplate with distaste.

"The goddess' gifts here, stripped of virtue. Stolen by technology," she seethed.

Gene turned back to his work, more than a little annoyed. "Then you don't really understand what this work means."

Druantia sizzled with displeasure, but Gene refused to look at her. Instead, he tried to appease her.

"I can't actually duplicate your abilities," he explained. "I can only enhance the signal or copy the existing signature. It's just like working with living technology. I can't create new LT ore in a lab—only the GraEL can do that. But I can harvest that ore and manipulate it into the shape I imagine."

"Your clumsy effort meant to please has only hardened my concern. Your blasphemy is rooted deep inside your ego's pride."

That was it. He was tired of all this hokey, spiritual garbage. So what if magic was real? Did it really matter what these all-seeing gods wanted? Who said they should be in charge anyway?

"Look," Gene said in exasperation, "I understand that you think you have all of the answers. But if Chano really didn't want me to do this, she would have done something to stop me. Gnawed my fingers off or something!" His temper emboldened him and he took a step toward the shiidh queen. "Not only that, but these gods you worship have faults! Chano is in hiding. She's not all powerful. This Kirion guy is mortal—he even has to make his own army to push his crappy religion. If our technology is advanced enough to engineer their 'almighty' power, then it's not about 'blasphemy,' but their inability to stop us!"

Gene was breathing very hard, elated until he registered the lethal glint that pulsed in Druantia's eyes. His courage leaked out of his shoes. Her sharp nails clicked against the handle of her feyhammer.

The snap of a core drive into a weapon echoed behind Gene and by the time he turned, Harris had a pistol leveled at Druantia's skull. Percy's face had gone dead white.

"Are we going to have a problem?" the corporal asked, his face chiseled with determination. "Be my guest if you want to kill the scrawny whizbang, but then I'll have to shoot you."

Gene felt like his heart had climbed into his throat. He wished Harris wouldn't gamble so freely with the shiidh queen's wrath.

"Let's just all calm down," Percy soothed, stepping between the hostile pair. He turned his back to Harris and faced Druantia. "We are all on the same team here. I understand that both the corporal and Gene have offered you great offense. It is a common failing of Coalition-born citizens to disrespect the cultures of others. But you will not find me to have the same fault."

Druantia's violent expression remained unchanged, but she removed her hand from her weapon. Percy continued.

"The hierarchy of gods is new to us. Only recently have we come to encounter their power. We are like little children who refuse to accept the guiding hand of a parent. This can only change through patience and education. The shiidh have worshiped Danu since before the Bang. You understand her wishes. We cannot help what we have been taught, but you can cure our ignorance."

The shiidh queen seemed intrigued by Percy's offer and backed down. Gene heaved a shiver of relief.

"I will collect my sisters for the song," she said, drifting unnervingly to the hatch that connected her ship to theirs.

Her body disappeared into darkness. It was ten full seconds after her retreat that Harris finally holstered his sidearm.

"Nice lady," he grumbled. "How long until it's ready, Gene?"

"Five minutes, tops," he answered.

Percy's face had turned a sickly green. His legs wobbled. If it weren't for the GAEL reflexes of Corporal Harris, the culturalist would have crashed to the deck in a heap. Gene, feeling a bit woozy himself, turned back to his dataplate as Harris hauled Percy to the nearest chair.

"Hey, Gene," Percy called behind him, "how about you don't yell at the queen of the shiidh ever again?"

"Yeah," Gene agreed, "not my best moment."

"You do know that she killed the entire Vartal Council of Druids because they ignored the will of Danu, don't you?"

Gene trembled, wondering just how close he had been to that horrible death.

"Who gives a frag?" Harris barked with a laugh. "I could've used a good fight. I've been pent up in the medical bay for way too long."

"I don't think that's the best idea," Percy argued, "dooming the universe for the sake of a good fight."

"Gene started it," Harris charged with a shrug. "I was just going to finish it."

"Done," Gene interjected.

Harris inclined his head and marched himself into one of the three holding cells on the port side of the ship.

"What are you doing?" Gene asked.

"What does it look like, boy?" Harris said.

"Imprisoning yourself?" Percy asked.

Gene slapped his hand over his mouth. How could he have forgotten?

"The mire field disrupts the rhythm of GAEL core drives, causing them to go crazy. When the field activates he may try to kill us."

Though Gene had changed the field emission to transmit in a forward column rather than a blanket, there was still a chance the corporal could be affected by its proximity. Both Percy and Gene stared at the corporal as he looked at them expectantly.

"I can't activate the cell door on my own, geniuses," Harris spat impatiently. "The controls are on the outside."

"Oh," Gene said with a start.

He lumbered forward and triggered the cell door. It was lucky that the ship's security systems were archaic, dead tech impervious to the upgraded mire.

Just as Harris was secured, the entire ship vibrated with the sway of the shiidh's song. The mire generator powered on by itself, as if responding to the women's command. As soon as the machine hummed to life, Harris slammed himself against the brig walls, his body rippling with madness. The metal groaned and bent, but held.

Gene backed away and returned to the guidance console. Out in space, the red particle cloud that made up the Eye of Baylour swirled with black lighting. As the haunting melody of shiidh voices pulsed through the nebula, the red and orange clashing energies began to spin into a vortex, looking more like a dilated pupil as it began to open. Hairs prickled up the length of Gene's skull. It looked like a gargantuan one-eyed giant peered at him from the depths of space.

As the whirling pool opened a path through the Eye, Gene's excitement began to rise. He would be the first human to document the legendary Agromor planet of Sarras. He would be the first to glimpse the secrets hidden behind Baylour in more than seven thousand years.

The eye burst open.

And what he saw was nothing.

45: You Are Not Welcome Here

Moonstone Retribution drank only air as Thanati leapt out of reach. Raeylan exhaled slowly, weighing options. Most of his magical attacks affected large areas and would damage his allies as well as his enemy if used in such a tight space as this tower. Teleporting into the air would give him only one sloppy swing with *Moonstone Retribution* before he crashed back to the floor. He could slow time, but that would drain his strength considerably. He wanted to reserve that power for his assault on Kirion.

He watched the erinyes dismiss her sword and pelt the GAELs with a hail of fiery arrows. They fought back with their technology, but Thanati countered every strike they offered. She was capable of throwing more bolts than they could fire from their weapons. Sergeant Reynolds struggled on the floor, Lieutenant Kyleren, and Chief Snow patiently dodged Thanati's assault, but Private Thompson reacted with agitation. Raeylan had seen that look before—long ago in the eyes of his most inexperienced knights. It meant Thompson was going to do something reckless.

Thompson activated his thrusters and charged Thanati on his own. Kyleren ordered the young soldier to stand down, but it was too late. With a callous lack of mercy,

Thanati threw her lash-turned-spear and impaled the GAEL on the floor. Her weapon burst into a searing blast of ice-green flame. Thompson screamed.

Raeylan reacted swiftly, taking three steps toward Thompson and wrapping his arms against the soldier's body, careful to avoid touching the fire himself. He walked through space, teleporting himself and the wounded soldier to the medical officer, Snow, concentrating on leaving the spear behind. Snow immediately attended Thompson, but battle experience told Raeylan that the young soldier would never make it. Thanati had boiled him in his own blood.

Kyleren shouted. Raeylan looked up just in time to see the spear hurtling toward Sergeant Reynolds. He couldn't teleport fast enough to save her.

But a musical thrum from Tuatha's throat smothered Thanati's weapon in midflight. Thanati screeched in displeasure, turning her gaze against the shiidh. Tuatha smiled fiercely, unafraid. She spoke into the comm.

"I will divert this bird of death." Though she spoke to Raeylan, her deep eyes were locked on Thanati. "You must find the maid we seek."

"Thanati is too great a foe. We cannot leave you here to fight her alone," Raeylan argued.

The erinyes retrieved her firelash. She spun it once over her head, commanding it to burn brightly. A snap of the wrist flicked an attack at Tuatha. The shiidh met the burning whip with her long crystal spike. Thanati tried to pull her weapon back, but Tuatha sang another phrase. Raeylan understood her words: a spell of binding. The whip had wrapped itself around the spike and would not be freed. For the moment, the two pressed against each other in a standstill.

Reynolds and Kyleren appeared on either side of Raeylan during the lull.

"Is he—" Kyleren choked, glancing at Thompson.

Snow shook his head sadly. Thompson spasmed and coughed, spraying blood onto Snow's armor.

"I'm sorry, lieutenant," he croaked with his blistered tongue.

Kyleren's mouth hardened into a grim line. Pity rose up in Raeylan; he understood. Many were the times he had seen the life seep out of his own knights in such a manner. Knowing they could do nothing to change Thompson's fate, Raeylan returned his attention to his enemy. Tuatha still sang; Thanati seemed to be muttering an incantation to counter the shiidh's magic.

"Don't work yourself up, private," Kyleren said shortly.

"Tell—Captain Reese—" Thompson said, choking between the words, "it was an—honor—"

Private Gary Thompson's body convulsed with a fit of coughing that only ended with a hollow rattle of breath. Snow swore profusely. Raeylan looked at the empty eyes of the young man, and was forcefully reminded of his brother. Thompson was young and kind, just like Shikun.

Raeylan's twilight stare shifted to Thanati, anger swelling to the surface. She had finally freed her firelash from Tuatha's control. The erinyes circled back and forth, eyeing Tuatha with grudging respect. Raeylan's grip tightened on *Moonstone Retribution's* hilt.

A hand settled on his shoulder.

"Chad and I will back Tuatha up," Reynolds promised with a hard expression. "Get the doctor. We'll take care of this gromm bitch."

"She's a tough one, Trish," Kyleren argued, flicking his eyes across the burns on the sergeant's neck meaningfully. "She'll frag you over quick."

"We don't have to win," Reynolds smirked. "We only have to keep her busy. LAMIE's virus runs its course in seven minutes. We should be able to hold out that long."

Leaving his companions to fight the erinyes alone caused Raeylan great concern, but the sergeant was right. The window was closing. They had to find Esilwen or Kirion would conquer the universe.

"Thank you," Raeylan said with a nod.

Chief Snow stood and readied his BT assault rifle. Raeylan dashed to the door, Kyleren at his side. The lieutenant waved his hand and it slid open, leading to a small antechamber. The sounds of combat disappeared as the door hissed shut behind them. Jets of air blasted them suddenly.

"Compression chamber," Kyleren explained. "The rest of the compound must have oxygen. You can lose the mask."

Raeylan followed Kyleren's advice. The chamber opened on the opposite side. Kyleren peered around both corners, rifle raised to attack. He waved Raeylan forward and they entered a well-lit hall decorated with grand murals of Kirion and his Legion.

"This guy sure loves to look at himself. Which way?" Kyleren asked.

The corridor branched in opposite angles. Raeylan inspected both directions, feeling outward from the link to Nehro's plane within him. The thin tendrils of Nehro's influence pulled only one way, identifying path that led toward her artifact: The Glove in Kirion's possession.

"Left," he answered.

"You sure?" Kyleren asked with a dubious lift of eyebrows. "We don't get a second chance at this."

"I am sure," Raeylan replied.

They hurried forward, maintaining as much caution as possible to catch any guards flat-footed. The corridor bent and twisted, but didn't fork. Finally, they reached an arch that opened into a grand hall, more suited to a castle than a military compound. The golden rock was cleanly cut and polished, reflecting warm light. Woven tapestries curled down the two story walls, plainly proclaiming Kirion's mastery of the worlds. Two silver doors were set low into room, but the hallway they followed continued on, plunging deeper into the fortress.

Guards dressed in fire-orange armor lined the walls, standing at attention. They seemed at odds with the grand majesty of the chamber. They were bent and twisted, their limbs unnaturally long or their bodies disfigured by grotesque angles. They wore no helms; their faces were a mockery of humanity. Though their eyes promised intelligence, their wide jaws or flat noses revealed their monstrous ancestry.

"The chancellor's breeding experiments," Kyleren growled under his breath.

"I will handle these," Raeylan said.

In a split moment, Raeylan teleported to the cluster of guards. Three were dead before the others registered a threat. *Moonstone Retribution* flew through their paltry defenses, piercing the orange armor with ease. Two slashes removed heads, one stab pierced a throat. Raeylan stood in the center of splattered blood and gore, his six enemies heaped lifeless on the floor.

Kyleren's mouth was slightly agape as he stepped from his hiding place.

"Remind me to never piss you off," he said.

Raeylan felt a smile tug at his lips, but he only indulged briefly.

"That way," he said, pointing to the continuing passageway.

As they turned another corner they stumbled on another troop of sentries. Raeylan teleported into their midst, only to find them already on the floor, bloody holes boring into their heads. Kyleren closed the distance between them in less than a second.

"Well done," Raeylan said, returning the lieutenant's previous compliment.

Kyleren only grinned.

They continued down the passage until it ended in a set of deeply etched red stone doors. They were hinged, as if Kirion had purposefully denied technology access to this part of his fortress. Kyleren reached out as if to push them open, but Raeylan halted him.

"Kirion will not be alone," he warned. "He has a vast army at his disposal."

"I didn't come this far just to run," Kyleren shrugged. "Besides, if I let you go in there by yourself, your sister might kill me."

Kyleren slammed the doors so hard they flew off the hinges. They bounced twice before skidding into the room. Raeylan stepped inside.

The sheer walls of the temple soared upward, topped with a dome of glass that flickered with amber cloud. In the center of the room, a huge marble statue of Kirion glowered down at the mortals below him. Three people stood on a platform at its base. Kirion's brows contracted with displeasure at Raeylan's arrival. Feralblade looked eager for action, both hands resting tensely on the hilts of his daggers. Esilwen's green eyes brightened with sudden hope and she took a step forward.

"Raeylan!" she called out before Kirion managed to yank her back.

"Raeylan of House Viridius," Kirion said with oily calm. "It is long since we have met. I believe the last time I killed your brother."

Raeylan's eyes narrowed as Kirion's hold on Esilwen tightened. She whimpered.

"And how is dear Margariete?" Kirion continued with his charming smile. "It has come to my attention that she has fallen victim to a deranged assassin as of late."

Feralblade smirked and drew his weapons. Raeylan strode forward.

"Feralblade is as much a failure to you as he was to me," Raeylan accused. "My sister lives."

Esilwen exhaled with relief. A tremor of doubt flashed across Kirion's dark eyes.

"I'm glad to hear it," he said, recovering his composure quickly. "Margariete is quite unique among her kind. One day she will join the side of order."

Tight laughter rang out beside Raeylan.

"You think Mags would join up with you?" Kyleren bellowed. "When fraggin' squirrels fly, maybe!"

Kirion's face darkened.

"Kill them," he commanded.

Feralblade eyed Raeylan nervously, but obeyed his master's command. He shifted into shadow and sped forward. Raeylan had no intention of letting the assassin distract him from his goal. Kyleren could handle Feralblade. He drew *Moonstone Retribution* and prepared to teleport to the dais, but Kirion interrupted him.

"I will keep Esilwen safe," he promised, raising his fist to show off a brightly glittering glove. "No one will love her as I."

And then they were gone.

Raeylan had been without *Moonstone Retribution* since Thyella, but he had never forgotten the blade's powers. He knew Kirion would use The Glove to flee rather than chance losing Esilwen in a duel. Though the cloud of darkness that was Feralblade rushed upon him, Raeylan closed his eyes, using the sword to see the panels that made reality's sea of time and space. The world paused around him; salt kissed his lips. Pinpricks of light revealed the path of Kirion's flight. Confidence snapped Raeylan's eyes open.

And then he followed Kirion.

46: RESISTANCE IS FUTILE

It didn't matter to Thanati that Raeylan and the GAEL leader had disappeared deeper into the fortress. Lord Kirion was more than a match for them both. It was even possible that Feralblade would dispatch them.

Thanati wanted to test the shiidh.

Previously the Faithful Legion had deemed the shiidh too weak a race to serve the Lord of Light. Their complex belief system made them hard to convert, and they evinced only minimal magical capabilities. Only the queen's feyhammer, capable of trapping souls to complement its power, had been of interest.

Until today.

The shiidh's songs were a complex set of frequencies that accessed the plane of stone. So far the woman had used a dispel charm and a binding incantation. Thanati was curious to push her into revealing more. Unfortunately, this particular shiidh would have to die, but the information Thanati gathered would please her lord. Perhaps turning them would be a worthwhile task after all.

The two remaining GAELs abandoned the corpse of their slain comrade and took positions behind the shiidh, forming a triangle. Both their weapons pointed at Thanati, but she barely acknowledged them. They were merely a nuisance.

"I am General Thanati of the Faithful Legion," she said to the shiidh. "Before I destroy you, I wish to know what you are called."

"What does it matter," the female GAEL spat, "if you're just going to kill us?"

Intimidation burned in Thanati's eyes.

"Because your names will be written in the Halls of the Damned, your mortal blood spilled by my hand, your souls forever banished from the God of Light."

"Your words evoke no fear in me. My name is Tuatha, servant of Danu," the shiidh answered proudly. "These are Sergeant Reynolds and Chief Snow, my allies."

Thanati stared at her adversary, undaunted.

"Then let us begin!" she cried.

Her wings splayed outward in a fan of crimson gold, her arms outstretched and palms parallel to the floor. She began to chant.

Deep inside her body, her Soulwell burst open. She felt the veil between the mortal plane and Fohtian's domain thin and waver, like transparent gauze that flutters in the breeze. She summoned her twin familiars from their slumber, sighed as they answered her siren call. The two young phoenixes screeched between worlds, each arriving above one of Thanati's shoulders in a ball of green fire. She stroked one along its fiery plumage.

"Kill the GAELs," she instructed softly.

Her familiars shrieked at the soldiers and dove for their eyes, sharp copper talons extended. As they attacked, Thanati pulled a beam of flame from her Well and blasted Tuatha. The shiidh dodged, but her dark robes smoldered.

Wild shots from the GAEL rifles slammed into the walls, but none found their targets. Chief Snow grunted pain as one phoenix raked a bloody gash from his forehead to chest, peeling the flesh of his face to the bone. The soldier shoved the muzzle of his weapon into the bird's breast and the animal burst into ash as he fired.

Thanati felt a sharp ache: the echo of her familiar's death. Snow looked at her in triumph, but she only laughed. The GAEL's victorious expression dissolved into disbelief as her phoenix reappeared at her side. Sergeant Reynolds rolled across the floor to avoid a cone of fire the other phoenix delivered from its mouth. With confidence, Thanati called for *Rupture*. Sword in her right hand and firelash in her left, she charged the shiidh.

The whip scalded Tuatha's calf, the woman's reflexive wince leaving her open to attack. *Rupture* pierced the air in a great arc, bearing down on the dark-skinned elf as if to slice her body in two. The shiidh's voice rang raspy and hard, like rocks cracking glass. From the floor a massive rock wall intercepted the burning sword. The mineral split into two and clipped Thanati's wing as it continued to rise.

Thanati had to twist to avoid falling out of the air, but the wall seemed to have anticipated her correction. The erinyes' momentum slammed her into the rock and she tumbled toward the ground. Tuatha leapt at her and stabbed Thanati's shoulder with the crystal spike, just above the wing. Any closer and the shiidh might have damaged Thanati's ability to fly.

The Vartal woman began to sing in earnest. Thanati knew she was vulnerable. She beat her powerful wings, soaring back into the air with a snarl. By the time she looked back at her opponent, Tuatha had lowered her voice to a gritty hum. Small stones cracked their way out of the walls and floor.

Thanati's eyes narrowed as she ripped the spike out of her shoulder and hurled it unceremoniously to the ground.

Fifteen fist-sized rocks launched at Thanati from every direction, shattering like crystal when they impacted her bronze skin. The shrapnel pierced deep. Her green blood fell like rain. More flying stone followed. Furious anger burned through *Rupture* as she countered the next shower of rocky grenades with its blade.

By the time the shiidh's spell had run its course, scores of splintered stone gored Thanati's immortal body. She ripped a handful from her arms and chest with a high-pitched cry. Free of the stone knives, her wounds began to close. Thanati glared at Tuatha. With a word, the erinyes ordered the plane of fire to spill into the floor.

The corners of the room boiled and groaned, sagging with heat. The stone melted into molten slag, creeping from the edges of the tower toward the center where the shiidh and her soldier friends tried to regroup. Tuatha sang her attempt to dispel Thanati's work, but the dark elf had no idea what she fought. The deadly lava slithered toward the battered group.

The two GAELs, burned in many places, yelled warnings between strikes against the phoenixes. Tuatha's song faltered as the heat intensified and interfered with her breathing apparatus. Chief Snow activated a communication device, requesting extraction. Thanati watched with amusement as their island of safety continued to shrink.

Their arrogance would be their undoing. GAEL skin was tough, but offered meager protection from Fohtian's fire. She threw a volley of green spheres from her palms, melting the soldiers' CC armor against their bodies. They screamed as blisters boiled across their chests. The phoenixes drove the GAELs to their knees as they tried to shield their faces against beak and claw.

Turning her attention back to the shiidh, Thanati hurled several flaming spheres at Tuatha. The shiidh changed the melody of her song swiftly. The remnants of stone that had not yet melted came to life, leaping to cover Tuatha's body with several loud snaps. Thanati's spheres merely bounced off the rock armor, doing no damage.

The erinyes pursed her lips in thought. Tuatha's armor might even withstand the molten sea that boiled the floor. It all depended on how the shiidh had designed her spell. After several moments, Thanati realized that—though offering impenetrable protection—the shiidh could not move while encased in her armor. Thanati swooped low and snatched the breathing apparatus from Tuatha's face. The Vartal woman stopped singing and choked. Her protective stone fell from her body in tattered clumps. The force of Thanati's flight threw Tuatha off balance and the elf woman staggered, nearly falling into the magma that surrounded her.

Chief Snow managed to grab her. Though his GAEL speed had slowly diminished throughout the battle, he was still faster than any regular mortal. He reached into a pocket and threw four discs at the dome of glass three stories above them. They attached with a loud crack.

"Get to the rendezvous point, sergeant!" he screamed and activated his thrusters.

Shiidh in tow, he rushed toward the aerie exit. It took Thanati a moment to recognize the disks. By the time she realized what they meant, her prey had reached the tower cave platform, her phoenix familiars harrying them from behind. Thanati dove for the exit, but was too slow in the confined cylinder of the tower. The disc grenades detonated, reverberating through the chamber like thunder. The whole ceiling crumbled on top of her.

Her only salvation was the molten rock that used to be the chamber floor. Its planar heat would melt the remaining stone knives that perforated her body and provide her with the energy she needed to fully regenerate. She swam through it as easily as the fire on her home plane. She counted twelve heartbeats and then let the passion of revenge consume her.

She held her palms above her head, commanding the magma to burn and bulge. The pressure grew as the molten material seared with new heat. Like an angry volcano vomiting a planet's core, the melted slag surged into the sky, clearing the broken tower dome. Thanati rode the eruption, emerging into the orange clouds, her body dripping with liquid rock.

She felt for her familiars. They had escaped the collapsing ceiling. Still in pursuit of the fleeing GAELs, they linked their sight to hers. The soldiers had shed their thrusters, trusting instead their enhanced ground speed. The phoenixes were falling behind. No longer useful, she commanded them to return home.

Swift as the soldiers were on the ground, in chase Thanati's flight was faster. She gained.

They had halted, oblivious to her pursuit. It looked like they were struggling to resuscitate the shiidh. Above them, Thanati touched her Well with a powerful incantation. A fireball, burning so hot at its center that the green flame billowed into plasma white, blasted their direction, its diameter more than five meters. All her adversaries would be incinerated instantly.

But something black, tipped with silver, flashed out of the sky. It was faster in flight than even Thanati. It intercepted the fireball, which roared around it in fragmented tufts. Thanati clicked her talon-nails together in irritation.

LAMIE.

The fireball dissipated against the ship's shields, though Thanati noticed with a measure of satisfaction that they flickered under the strain. LAMIE slid horizontal to the ground, exposed, as she thrust her ramp from her belly to rescue the GAELs and the shiidh. Thanati took the opportunity to attack again, launching a second surge of fire. The ship's shield buzzed with static and died.

Thanati curved her lips. It didn't matter that the three mortals had managed to duck inside. They were frail; weak.

She hadn't been able to use her full battle strength in ten thousand years. Today the gods would know which was stronger: fire or stone.

47: I Ain't Got Time To Bleed

The chancellor vanished with Esilwen into thin air. Raeylan was gone less than half a DST·second later. Somehow the Feralblade guy had morphed into a shadowy mist that surged forward.

What the frag? Lance complained to himself. He was on his own against some screwy cloud that he didn't exactly know how to fight. It wasn't like basic covered this gromm skrit kind of thing.

Too late, he realized he should have asked Raeylan what magical crap their enemies could pull off. Feralblade was a skilled foe. Lance knew nothing about his tactics other than what he had seen in the briefest moments on Agrona. He debated his attack plan quickly, knowing there wasn't much time before the shadow was right in front of him. Was Feralblade inside it, or was he the shadow itself? Would BT weapons wound the assassin while he was in that form?

There was really only one way to know for sure.

Lance raised his weapon and fired at the shadow. The mist parted, opening a small hole in the path of the round. Lance's shot bypassed the target without contact. The mist didn't even slow its pace.

"Great," he grunted, annoyed at the seemingly endless uses for magic. He clenched his jaw and bellowed a challenge. "Bet you can't dodge more than one!"

Lance loaded the cartridge with slugs of compressed energy from his core drive, pelting a barrage from his BT rifle. The shadow cloud punctured itself with little round holes. The mist shifted to avoid the BT shells. Refusing to give in, and not knowing what else to try, the GAEL continued to fire, hoping to get lucky.

He didn't.

The shadow circumvented every shot, quickly reaching Lance's position and swirling around him in a dizzying cloud. Lance stopped shooting and began to swing his weapon like a club instead. The assassin materialized suddenly on Lance's right, slashing the wicked point of a dagger centimeters from Lance's ear. A second blade nearly gutted him; he was saved only by speed.

Lance knew the knives would be lethal. Margariete's sword had cut him easily enough, something a regular blade could never do. *Stardawn* had its own magic, and Lance was willing to bet a lifetime of prings that Feralblade wouldn't be wandering around the universe with anything less.

The GAEL parried two more strikes with his rifle and sidestepped a third. Feralblade offered a torrent of blows, forcing Lance to give ground to block them. The assassin twisted and prodded, but the daggers never struck. The GAEL could tell Feralblade was holding back, waiting for something.

Suddenly, the assassin's attacks became more aggressive, his movements breaking the former rhythm of the fight. One of the knives slid under Lance's guard, biting into his forearm. The GAEL growled, bearing forward and pushing Feralblade backward. Lance's rifle swung up and fired twice. The assassin deflected both rounds with his daggers and awarded Lance with a malicious gleam of teeth.

Lance spat a slew of profanity. How was that even possible?

"My blades were constructed by my family centuries ago," Feralblade boasted. He settled into a martial stance. "They have tasted the blood of many, but never that of a GAEL VIC."

"Sorry, Skinny," Lance growled, "but you're not my type."

Feralblade's grin grew dark. He advanced, faster and deadlier than before. His weapons danced around Lance's body, lulling the GAEL into a pattern of parry that would shift without warning. Gashes soon stained Lance's arms. He recognized the assassin's fighting style. It reminded him of Mags. Though Feralblade's strikes connected occasionally, Lance's speed saved him from the assassin's deadliest attacks.

The battle soon seemed like the annoying repetition of a holocast jingle that refused to end. Feralblade advanced with a flurry of blows that nicked Lance unexpectedly and threw off his balance. In turn, Lance fired six rounds that Feralblade narrowly repelled with his daggers. Lance grew complacent with the battle's pace. At this rate, they would exchange blows until the Agromors won the MetaGalactic War.

Feralblade seemed to notice the tedious cadence of the fight as well. His gaze drew inward for a second, his fist clenched. From his experience with the twins, Lance recognized the signs that precluded a magical attack.

Everything went black. He fired his rifle, but the energy projectiles left no trail of light. Lance had no way to tell if he had been draped in magical darkness or been struck suddenly blind. He circled and sidestepped, hoping to avoid his enemy.

A sharp pain screamed up his spine as the assassin slammed both daggers into the small of Lance's back, piercing through his protective CC armor. Lance spun, ignoring the pulsing throb of the wound, forcing Feralblade to rip out the weapons or lose them. At the same time, the GAEL swung his arm in a wide arc, knowing where the assassin had last been.

His hand connected with his opponent's body and threw the coward to the floor. A distinct thud revealed where Feralblade had landed. Lance slammed his fist blindly downward in that direction, attempting to crush the assassin's face, but his knuckles met only stone. The floor groaned and cracked under the strain.

The darkness lifted. Lance saw Feralblade roll twice and spring to his feet. The assassin's pasty eyes were narrowed with cool calculation, his body tense. He flicked his gaze to the smashed floor, no doubt realizing how close he had been to death. Kyleren grinned. His triumphant expression must have heckled Feralblade's pride, because the assassin returned it with a malignant smirk.

"So, Margariete survived, I hear," he snickered. "Good. Our last encounter lacked certain—satisfaction. My blade pierced her much too quickly."

The man was attempting to stall. Maybe Feralblade figured Lance's injuries would slow him the longer they bled. Or maybe the assassin intended to make Lance angry, inciting the GAEL to attack recklessly.

One thing was obvious. Feralblade was worried.

"Anyone who knows Mags, knows that pissin' her off is a fraggin' bad idea," Kyleren returned, yanking two injection tubes from a pouch over his chest. He winced as he administered them. "You're so damn afraid of her, you had to ambush her like a gromm coward. Couldn't face her like a man."

"Courage means nothing if you are dead," Feralblade sneered.

"So you admit she woulda kicked your fraggin' ass in a fair fight."

The assassin merely laughed. "That's an 'honorable' man's explanation to excuse his own shortcomings. You consider 'fair' only in the sense of matching strength. I am a master of stealth. Who are you to limit my choices on the battlefield? Nothing but a brainless brute. I am not ashamed to stalk the shadows before I bleed my victims, to taste their fear before they meet the darkness."

Kyleren shook his head in disgust.

"You're skrit-crazy."

Feralblade bowed, accepting the insult as a compliment.

"And yet Raeylan and Margariete trusted me for years without suspect."

"You—" Kyleren growled, stepping forward.

The complex suddenly shuddered, shivering as if from an explosion. Rock dust drifted from the walls and the windows rattled. An alarm blared angrily.

"Your time is up," Feralblade purred. "It won't take long for Lord Kirion's aberrations to swarm the temple."

"They fall easy enough," Lance declared, glancing back through the way he had come.

A host of lumbering humanoids in orange armor trudged through the corridor. Though the breeding experiments were weak, Lance had to admit he'd be hard-pressed to deal with their numbers. Feralblade alone was enough of a challenge, even if Lance hadn't been bleeding all over the floor.

Just as the creatures breached the shrine's threshold, a familiar voice crackled over Lance's LT comm.

"Lieutenant Kyleren," Colonel Stoddard said. "We just got some bad news."

"And I was havin' such a good day," Lance replied sarcastically, shooting at the gaggle of newcomers.

Feralblade slipped into a shadow mist form and blended with the darkness. Kyleren took ten enemies down, but more poured in. The complex shook again, but this time it felt less like an explosion, more like an earthquake. The chancellor's soldiers stumbled and fell over each other, struggling to remain upright. Lance managed to stay steady, shooting randomly into his enemy's ranks. In the chaos, he lost track of Feralblade.

"Gene's team has successfully opened the Eye of Baylour," the colonel informed him. "Sarras isn't there."

"What?"

Lance stopped firing, so surprised that he forgot he was talking to his commander. He dodged the aberrations' return fire, all the while scanning for the assassin.

"Chano did tell us she couldn't remember where she'd put the planet," Stoddard said. "The Eye was just our best guess. This means Sarras could be anywhere."

"Frag it all," Lance swore into his comm.

He dashed to the center of the room, using the huge statue of the chancellor as cover.

"Report your status, lieutenant," Stoddard ordered.

"Snow and Reynolds stayed—"

"I'm apprised of that situation, lieutenant. What about you and Raeylan?"

"The chancellor took off with the doc. Raeylan's in pursuit," Lance said. "I'm pinned down in some kinda shrine on the north side. I've got the assassin and a whole pack of genetic experiments on me."

"Get out of there, lieutenant," Stoddard commanded. "Fighters have launched from Nynniaw and are bearing down on LAMIE's position. We're pulling out."

"Copy, sir," Lance said, poking around the statue and blasting a set of rounds, unsure if he would be able to follow the order. He'd killed more of the aberrations than he could count, but still they funneled in. "Ready to receive coordinates for an evac site."

Lance didn't hear the colonel's reply. Something cold and hard slammed into his temple. He lurched heavily to the side, stunned. He spotted motion from his peripheral. Feralblade's finger darted into the heart of Lance's rifle, hooking around the ring of his core drive. One tug and it slipped loose.

Kyleren's free hand extended to intercept, but the assassin shifted back to living cloud. The GAEL's fingers simply passed through him. Fear clenched Lance's gut. It was likely Feralblade knew exactly how a GAEL VIC was tied to his core.

The mist darted away. Lance regained his feet and sped after the assassin, but it was too late. By the time Feralblade retook corporeal form, there was ten feet between them. The assassin dropped Lance's drive onto the floor and crouched over it.

"What a pitiful weakness you have, lieutenant," he said.

Lance was within reach of the assassin when the silver dagger flashed downward.

Hot needles of pain wracked Lance's body and he crashed to the floor, twitching in agony. Screams tore from his gut, but they weren't his. It was the innocent, terrified wail of a child.

Chano.

Everything around Lance dimmed. Feralblade stepped over him, lips curled in a nasty leer.

"Did courage work out for you, lieutenant?"

Lance coughed blood.

"Apparently not," Feralblade sneered, folding his arms over his chest. Glee sharpened the assassin's face as he waited for Kyleren to die.

48: Stay In The Light

Kirion felt the euphoric calm of teleportation dissolve from his body as he and Esilwen appeared in an elegant office. The room was only slightly smaller than the temple in his fortress on the planet, albeit more comfortably furnished—a shrine to a politician rather than the sanctuary of a god. A reddish glow filtered through the enormous crystasteel windows, light reflecting from Athalonde Prime's curved silhouette. He ran his thumb thoughtfully against his lip, deliberating his next move, now that he and Esilwen were safely aboard the military station Nynniaw.

Esilwen tugged her arm, trying to break his hold on her. Kirion turned to her, annoyed that she had broken his train of thought. Tears slid from her frightened eyes. With a sigh of long-suffering, Kirion swept the droplets from her cheeks. He had forgotten how her blond hair glistened so gently in the light, how her fragrance always reminded him of a meadow on a sunlit afternoon.

"Why do you struggle against me, Esilwen?" he asked softly, stroking her hair. She trembled at his touch. "I have been searching so long for you."

"Let me go, please," she pleaded.

Kirion frowned. Let her go? Go where? Back to that Thyellan fool who claimed to love her? Jealousy sank its ugly fangs into him. Hatred for the servant of Nehro boiled through his blood like fury. He dragged Esilwen to a high-backed chair and threw her into it. Kirion leaned over her, holding her wrists against the armrests as she tried to break free.

"Stop struggling, Esilwen," he warned, "or you will injure yourself."

Chains of light snaked around her, securing her in a tight embrace. She gasped, pain flitting across her ice-green eyes. With a pang, Kirion remembered when those eyes had been another color—a lovely shade of sunset brown. Before she had defied him.

"Raeylan will come for me," she said.

"Even if he does," Kirion returned, warmth spreading through his body at her nearness, "he cannot hope to match me. I am the Lord of Light. A god, Esilwen. Your Thyellan king is nothing more than a lorelei."

Kirion lifted his hand, brushing his thumb across her jaw. His hand slid up her neck and into her hair. Kirion pressed his mouth hard against hers, craving the affection she had once freely given. Her lips were as sweet as he remembered. The passion they had once shared had been perfect. Love like that did not simply waste away. Somewhere, buried deep inside her, Esilwen must love him still.

But she did not return his kiss.

"You are not a god," Esilwen whispered when he pulled away. "You've become a demon."

For a moment, Kirion was baffled. He could see the mingling of fear and sorrow in her expression. But then his jaw clenched tightly and his power rushed to the surface of his thought, pulsing dangerously close. After all he had gone through to find her, she resisted him even now. She belonged with him, whether she wanted to or not.

"Step away from her," called a voice behind him.

Kirion turned. Raeylan stood by the windows, his twilight eyes a rage of storm. He bore a curved silver sword in his hand, three cloudy stones set into the hilt. There was something familiar about it, but Kirion couldn't quite place it. And where Raeylan had once worn Nehro's artifact was a plain, fingerless glove instead.

Kirion glared at Raeylan with steely ire. The attack on the Athalonde Prime fortress had been completely unanticipated. Only his most trusted followers were aware of its existence. Add to that the speed of the infiltration, and he could only surmise that either Esilwen or the scrolls had been laced with a tracker that Feralblade had failed to notice. Probably, it was living tech. The magical properties of the material would make it easy to discover once Kirion had time to examine everything properly. As a being soon to reach godhood, Kirion could detect the presence of any magic and interpret its nature.

But there was no explanation for how Raeylan had managed to follow him to the space station. The man had arrived too quickly for it to have been the tracers. And even if the Thyellan king had known Kirion's destination, to teleport blind anywhere could have been lethal. Raeylan should have ended up spliced into a bulkhead or floating aimlessly in the black.

"Raeylan!" Esilwen called.

The hope in her voice made Kirion's stomach twist with unrestrained envy.

Kirion drew the sword on his hip, a magical instrument won long ago in another shard. Netted by a continual illusion spell to keep it hidden from the public, the gloomy grey steel appeared as he drew it. At the same time, he let the bag of scrolls drop to the floor, hiding them with their own illusion.

"You have poisoned Esilwen against me," Kirion accused. "You have seduced her away from the path of light."

"You walk in darkness," Raeylan countered. "Esilwen's love is beyond your understanding."

Though his power urged to be released, the Lord of Light held himself in check. Four hundred years ago he had underestimated this opponent—leaving Raeylan for dead, only to have the insufferable lorelei rise up against the Faithful Legion time and again. Kirion cautiously probed the magical strength of his enemy. He was met with a shock.

Raeylan's lorelei Well, the source of any angel's power, was gone.

"It was she who released me from my prison," Kirion said to delay the inevitable confrontation, at least until he knew more about Raeylan's new state. "Deny it all you wish, but she is bound to me for eternity. You may not take her without my leave."

"You have taught her only fear."

"How did you follow me here?" Kirion asked.

Raeylan leveled his sword. Kirion could see blue wafts of the water goddess's power drift from the edge of the blade.

"*Moonstone Retribution* tracks movements through teleportation. Nehro's Glove offers you no escape."

"Intriguing," Kirion said, prepping his sword to attack. "Taking The Glove from your arm should have destroyed you completely. Yet you managed to survive. How is it that you still possess so much of Nehro's power?"

Raeylan didn't answer, but Kirion already knew. The shardless king was no longer a lorelei. Kirion could see the imprint of power that rippled through Raeylan's soul. Somehow, the water goddess had passed her domain to him, making him a demigod: the next Guardian of Time.

Kirion grimaced. That meant Raeylan was his equal.

Until this moment, ridding the universe of Raeylan's infectious lies was a trivial matter, his ruin simply retribution for luring Esilwen away. But now it was necessity. Raeylan had become a threat to the Lord of Light's ascension to power. Only one god could return order to the mortal realm, could save it from spiraling into never-ending chaos. And that god would not be Nehro's successor.

Kirion drew cold light through his body, commanding it to encase him in a shield of armor. Then he advanced. Raeylan's expression remained unchanged as he parried Kirion's first strike. Steel shrieked as the combatants exchanged blows that drew hot white sparks from their magical blades.

As Kirion pressed an advantage, Raeylan teleported suddenly to the right. Kirion swept aside the attack, thrusting his knee into his opponent's stomach. The force of the connection threw Raeylan back, though the Guardian of Time did not tumble. He regained his balance in a defensive stance.

Knowing his enemy would be able to detect it, Kirion teleported behind Raeylan. The Lord of Light slashed his blade three times. Raeylan dodged the first. The second rang uselessly against *Moonstone Retribution*. But the third ripped through the black leather that protected Raeylan's right arm and carved a bloody gash into the flesh beneath.

The Guardian of Time cried out in pain and fell to his knee. Kirion smirked, pleased with the result. As he suspected, Nehro's Glove had left a curse on the Thyellan king. Raeylan's arm was blackened with streaks of eternal frost. Most likely the mark caused continual pain. Taking damage to it must result in excruciating agony.

Raeylan's glove was nearly cloven in two. It dangled in pitiful halves from a string. Pulling it free, Raeylan tossed the tattered pieces to the floor as he rose to his feet. The Lord of Light couldn't help but admire his enemy for his fortitude. To press on into the fight under such circumstances required a considerable determination of will.

Esilwen begged Kirion to stop. The desperation in her voice caught his attention and he glanced her way. Raeylan took the opportunity to vanish. Kirion expected an attack from behind so he spun, but he was too late to counter with his weapon. *Moonstone Retribution* slashed cleanly across his solid light breastplate.

Raeylan took a step back, his calm expression finally broken with frustration. The Thyellan blade left no damage in its wake. He struck again. With smug confidence, Kirion didn't even bother to deflect it. The light armor gave no ground.

Adapting quickly, the Guardian of Time maneuvered his sword into a horizontal thrust, aiming at Kirion's unprotected neck. The Lord of Light dropped underneath the attack, which could have severed his spine.

Kirion needed to end this quickly. Through the window he saw fighters deploying from the military station, penetrating the planet's atmosphere. Soon LAMIE and her crew would be forced to retreat.

It was time he ended Raeylan once and for all. But an attack of that intensity would require several seconds to generate.

Striking twice with his sword to distract his opponent, Kirion called forth the dark power of Skoh's Earring. To work properly, the illusion had to infiltrate Raeylan's mind a grain at a time, or he might suspect his perception was being altered.

Raeylan countered every swing of Kirion's blade. But slowly, Kirion commanded a copy of their surroundings to rotate, ever so slightly. He stepped to the side, leaving a ghost duplicate of himself to fight the Thyellan king. In moments, Raeylan had turned a quarter angle away, fighting a doppelganger that only he could see. From Kirion's perspective, the Guardian of Time struggled valiantly against nothing. As an added touch, the Lord of Light transformed himself into an image of the helpless Esilwen, knowing Raeylan would never strike her.

Kirion concentrated on pouring liquid light into his sword, forcing it to become an extension of himself. When completed, he would disperse the fake Kirion and call to Raeylan with Esilwen's voice. Then he would stab the Guardian of Time through the heart when his defenses were down.

"Deceit is the shield used by one of inferior grace," Raeylan said, suddenly halting his sword swings. Then he disappeared.

Out of nowhere, *Moonstone Retribution* sliced upward against Kirion's armor, the blade glancing off the shoulder and nicking his jaw. The combined force of the blow and his attempt to parry knocked him off balance. Blood leaked down his neck. He brought his sword up to deflect Raeylan's next two attacks.

The unexpected move stunned Kirion and it took him precious seconds to recover. His incomplete infusion spell withered from his blade. The illusion crumbled. Raeylan should have been completely enthralled. What had gone wrong?

"I have been victim to your lies in the past," Raeylan said, as if answering Kirion's unspoken question. "You cannot mislead me again."

Kirion should have anticipated this. Raeylan's new powers must allow him to detect Nehro's artifact. As long as Kirion wore The Glove, the Guardian of Time could sense him.

Kirion needed to redesign his strategy.

He wielded his sword with one arm, allowing Raeylan to push him back. Kirion's free hand droned with power, each fingertip blazing with prismatic color. The center of his palm soon pulsed with a hot white sphere capable of boring through any metal, of penetrating any shield. On contact he could direct it to tunnel into his opponent and disperse his soul into fragments. The only drawback to the attack was that Raeylan could easily teleport out of the way.

So instead, Kirion aimed it at Esilwen.

49: FATE IT SEEMS IS NOT WITHOUT A SENSE OF IRONY

In Between started to shake, rudely waking Chano from her nap. She already knew that Her Mortal was doing battle—that created expected tremors. But this time the quaking was extra shaky. She hopped to her four feet and stretched her grumpy muscles. Chano was connected to the Cylinder Thingy that Her Mortal used to channel his magic. His powers in battle were greater than a normal GAEL because of her, even without direct intervention. She had played hide and seek with him for so long that it didn't seem necessary to start helping just because he knew she was here.

Until it interrupted her nap.

She trotted over to the swirly sparks that were the gateway to the Bridge to the mortal plane. Although she needed a shrine to take human form and speak with human voice, she could materialize anywhere as a squirrel. This, of course, tired her out and resulted in the need for a rather longish snooze in In Between. But with all the ruckus going on across the Bridge, there seemed to be no naps in her near future.

Staring through the gateway, she was surprised at how much she could see. Usually Her Mortal had his Cylinder Thingy stuffed into some kind of weapon that blocked most of the view. That was one of the reasons she took naps during battle. But right now, the Cylinder Thingy seemed to be falling.

Then something shiny caught her eye. It was heading toward the swirling sparks she peered through. Her brown squirrel eyes squinted to gain a better look and her head tilted to the side thoughtfully.

Then the something shiny broke across the Bridge.

She jumped aside, noticing that it was less shiny than it was pointy and sharp. The edge sliced across her body and the point pinned her tail. Made of pure energy, she didn't bleed, but the weapon's spiky bite paralyzed her. An unpleasant sensation, like sticky burning, stabbed her furry body. Her lip and nose quivered.

And then she screamed. She had never experienced anything quite like this before. She definitely did not like it.

The pointy silver thing yanked free, taking a large bushy chunk of tail with it. Chano could see through the gateway again. A scary man was standing over the Cylinder Thingy. Her Mortal lay off to the right, convulsing on the floor in a messy pool of blood. When she saw him, her tummy ached painfully. Her Mortal was badly hurt!

The Scary Dagger Man was speaking, but Chano didn't have time to listen. She scampered through the swirling sparks and over the Bridge into the mortal plane. Once she appeared, she discovered things were even worse than she thought. The Cylinder Thingy was almost severed in two. That was probably how the dagger had invaded In Between. Her tummy lurched. The Cylinder Thingy was important. Without it, Her Mortal would die.

The Scary Dagger Man was staring at her, his blades at his side. His face looked silly with confusion. Chano ignored him and hopped to Her Mortal. She propped herself on his cheek with her forepaws and nudged his face with her little nose, but his eyes rolled back into his head and he lay very, very still.

She had to dodge as the Scary Dagger Man tried to kick her.

"Get away from him, you stupid rat," he snapped.

"Rat?" she accused angrily in squirrel-speak, knowing he wouldn't understand her but not caring. "I am not a rat, you meanie!"

She dashed up his black boots, her little claws latching into his leather armor for leverage. She wriggled up his body in a quick spiral. He tried to knock her off, but she was too quick. Pouncing him full in the face, she scratched and clawed as he yelped.

He tried to push her off, but she rushed sideways to his shoulder and his palm smacked his own face. She giggled as he cursed. With a squeaky growl she latched her sharp little teeth into his ear. The Scary Dagger Man howled and tried to stab her. Chano scrambled out of the way, releasing his ear and clawing her way down his back.

She had a lopsided tail. He had a lopsided head. They were even.

The Scary Dagger Man tried to stomp her with his feet, so she ran away and careened behind the tall pillar statue in the center of the room. She could hear his boots right behind her. She giggled despite the pain in her side. This would be a merry chase.

As she rounded the statue, she slid to a startled halt. Her eyes widened with pity. The twisted forms of Misblended Creatures milled around. Lots of them. Their abused genetic codes throbbed in pain. Their orange armor was ugly.

She puffed her chest out in indignation. Kirion was a cheater! Hadn't he been the one who forced the other gods to punish her for meddling with mortal Life eons ago? And here were bunches of creatures proving that Kirion was guilty of the same thing.

But he had done it wrong. No finesse in syncing genetic structure, no beauty in the recursive permutations. It seemed Lord Cheater only had small understanding of combination sequencing. These humanoids were flawed; their souls cried for release from their unhappy existence. At least Chano's meddling followed the natural order of Life, a magical infrastructure of evolution.

The Scary Dagger Man took advantage of her pause. His dagger almost impaled her, but she managed to hop aside. The second one almost sliced off her head. She ducked and hopped, sending the Scary Dagger Man into a fit of frustration. Chano looked at him through narrowed eyes. She didn't like him one bit.

"Just die, you ridiculous rodent!" the man spat through clenched teeth as his sharp pointy weapons swung at her again.

The ugly humanoids began to surround them, leaving Chano less and less room to maneuver. She was getting upset. She wanted the Scary Dagger Man to leave her alone so she could save Her Mortal. She darted past the flailing blades, running to one of the humanoids. Maybe if she took away its pain it would help her.

She touched its toe with her nose, channeling the magic of life through its body. The nanomites in its blood readily yielded to her will. The humanoid shuddered, its gangly limbs softened and its jagged face smoothed. It smiled at her as the Scary Dagger Man lunged. Extending a beautifully elongated arm, her new species caught the Scary Dagger Man in the stomach and threw him halfway back to the statue.

"What, by the Void, is this?" the Scary Dagger Man wheezed, clutching his torso.

The new species growled at the Scary Dagger Man as it completed its transformation, revealing its true ancestry— human and giant. Chano gazed at it with pride and then moved to the next one. The Scary Dagger Man would have to play by her Rules now. And her Rules were always the best.

Immersed in the euphoria of her game, Chano soon lost track of how many she changed. Soon her side outnumbered those left to the Scary Dagger Man. He howled in rage somewhere behind her, no doubt trying to get her with his pointy weapons. But now that she had friends, he didn't seem so scary. While he was busy with the game, she could save Her Mortal.

She scurried around the mob of battling humanoids, to the other side of the pillar statue. From the corner of her eye she spotted something odd, a dark cloud that didn't belong. It churned and spun before pitching in her direction. Chano had never seen anything quite like it before. She squealed in fright as it jumped in front of her, transforming into the Scary Dagger Man. His hand wrapped around her tiny body, squeezing. Chano didn't like it. She couldn't breathe. She heard a loud crack with her whole body. A swell of pain burst inside her.

"I'm going to rip you apart and feed your scraps to the Pack Sire," he promised.

Pack Sire? That meant the Scary Dagger Man served Skoh. It explained the dark cloud. The Mistress of the Void liked dark things. Chano never liked her much. She was too serious.

Chano wriggled her forepaws free. She couldn't really die, since she was more like a sentient object than an actual living thing. But recent experience had taught her she could feel pain. Being torn apart and chewed by wolves didn't sound like fun.

She clapped her paws together. The Scary Dagger Man peered at her suspiciously.

"What are you doing?" he asked.

Chano squeaked as a gap opened in the floor right between his legs. His hold on her loosened as he tried to avoid falling. Chano wriggled free and plopped to the ground. She slapped her right paw onto the stone, directing her magic toward his left foot.

Another crack raced from the edge of her tiny claws and ripped the floor from underneath the Scary Dagger Man. His leg fell in and he grunted in pain. Chano told the stone to squeeze his leg off. As the floor crushed his leg, the Scary Dagger Man screamed curses at her. Then he turned back into the black cloud and floated away. He reappeared a safe distance away from her, blocking the way to Her Mortal.

That mist thing wasn't fair! Her Mortal could die any minute and the Scary Dagger Man just wouldn't get out of the way. She glanced around, trying to decide what to do next. When she looked, she knew.

The ceiling of the room was made of a thick substance she recognized at once, a clear crystal that was hard as steel. Mortals had made it solid, but it was liquid in its natural state. Many planets in the shard had atmospheres that mortals couldn't breathe. Her Mortal was different, but hopefully letting in the planet's natural air would drive the Scary Dagger Man back.

She stomped her back paw on the stone. A slab tore away from the floor just as the Scary Dagger Man charged her. The stone leapt high—with her on it. Her tummy squirmed delightfully as she shot higher and higher. The slab slowed as she reached the peak of the clear dome. She stretched just enough to touch her nose to the window's cold surface. Where she touched it, the material softened and drooped into bulbous glops that dipped to the floor. When the tension grew too much, the crystal burst like a bubble. The remaining liquid rained to the floor and the atmosphere rushed in.

The slab dropped. Chano leapt to the floor before it smashed into tiny pieces. The Scary Dagger Man coughed and gagged. Within a few moments he had changed into the black cloud and rushed away.

Chano took a deep breath, letting the new air fill her. It tasted really familiar. Suddenly, she realized where she was. Her Planet! So this was where she put it!

She ducked her head into one of the fissures she had made in the floor. Yep, there it was: tiny veins of blushing orange ore rooting through the granite mountain, the living mineral created by her Tree Well. Every metallic/organic species she had ever made had some part of that element inside them. It was also how Lord Cheater had built his Misblendeds. The ore wasn't as shiny as it once had been— maybe because the Well had been gone so long.

She hurried around the large statue to where Her Mortal lay. His breath was slow, his usual tan skin was creamy pale. Chano looked at his Cylinder Thingy closely. Her Mortal was lucky that it had not been crushed. Still, most of the magic had leaked out of it, seeping back into the stone of Her Planet. When it was all gone, Her Mortal would die. Chano knew she had to work fast to preserve what was left. The Scary Dagger Man had distracted her for almost too long.

What she needed was the energy in raw living ore that had not yet taken sentient form, so she sprinted back to one of the cracks in the floor. Her tiny paws scratched out a marble-sized portion of mineral. Carrying it in her mouth she scurried back to Her Mortal and hopped on his chest. With a deft flick of a paw she unhooked the buckles that kept his armor tight and shed the protective plating. She dropped the ore marble directly on his heart.

Then she went to the Cylinder Thingy. As quickly as she could, she lapped up the remaining magic, storing it safely in her cheeks. Clamping her mouth shut so she wouldn't spill, she waddled back to the marble on Her Mortal's chest.

When she poured the magic onto the marble, it grew golden bright and melted, burrowing deep into his skin. Like molten bronze pouring into a mold, it sizzled into a raised relief, a metallic brand in the shape of a triple knot. As it darkened and cooled, Her Mortal took a sudden breath, throwing Chano off balance. His eyes opened and he sat up, forcing her to slide into his lap. Her Mortal looked at the broken Cylinder Thingy with wild eyes, then at the symbol on his chest.

"What the—"

Chano jumped up and down two times to get his attention, then hopped off his lap and chased her tail once in excitement. Realization dawned on Her Mortal's face.

"Did you—?" he asked, touching the bronze tattoo gingerly.

Chano bobbed her head yes. But he would have to thank her later. Now was the time for action. Calling to her plane, Chano commanded a portal to open. She dashed inside, located her Tree Well and tried to push it out. The first heave caused great pain to her broken body and she let out an involuntary squeak. Her Mortal peered in, seemed to understand her intentions and drew the Tree Well out with ease.

"The GraEL?" he asked with his brow furrowed.

His gaze flicked to her. She could tell he was thinking hard.

Chano touched the pot with her paw. The roots of the Well burst through their confinement and scraped into the stone floor, gouging deep holes as the tree implanted itself. It tripled in size in moments, gleaming a rosy-orange as it connected with the planet's living ore. Her Mortal blinked at her for a moment before his expression changed to comprehension.

"Are you tellin' me that Athalonde Prime is Sarras?" he exclaimed.

Chano held up both paws in triumph.

"Sorry Chano, but I'm not gonna leave the GraEL here for Kirion to find," he said, reaching for the Well.

Chano scratched at his fingers. His hand recoiled, three red scrapes marring his skin.

"Frag it all, Chano, what'd you do that for?"

Chano touched the Tree Well and shook her head. The Well was safe now.

"You said you didn't want Kirion usin' the GraEL anymore," Her Mortal said. "We can't leave it here."

Chano scrunched her furry face in thought. How could she explain to Her Mortal what he needed to do? It was so obvious! She tried to make several gestures to make him understand. She pointed to him, patted the floor, touched to the still-open portal with her nose and then put a paw over one of her eyes.

Her Mortal looked confused. She exhaled in frustration. Chano wished there was a temple nearby. Maybe she needed to go slower. She picked up a roundish stone from the floor and pretended to plant a tree on it. Then she threw it into the portal.

"You want me to open a T-Portal for the whole planet? Can I even do that?" he asked.

She jumped up and down. Then she put her paw over her eye again.

"Somethin' wrong with your eye?"

She shook her head no. She squinched one eye shut and opened the other as wide as possible, pointing to it frantically.

"Eye—Eye? You wanna open the portal to the Eye of Baylour!"

Chano clapped her hands together excitedly.

Her Mortal lowered a hand for her. He activated his comm as she clambered to his shoulder.

"Lieutenant Kyleren reporting in. Colonel Stoddard, sir, you're never gonna believe this—"

50: There's Only One Way Off This Planet Baby And That's Through Me

Thanati released a barrage of fiery arrows that seared LAMIE's unprotected hull. The ship's chrome colored skin rippled with hues of red, almost like a reflection of pain. The erinyes charged, *Rupture* and her firelash trailing at her sides. She struck with her flaming blade just as LAMIE's hatch closed to shield the fleeing soldiers. The GAELs managed to escape, but *Rupture* carved a melted scar deep into the ship's living hull. A life-like shudder wracked LAMIE's body.

The ship darted forward quickly to avoid Thanati's flick of the whip, so that the weapon merely glanced off the ship's metal skin. Thanati held her ground as LAMIE banked a wide arc, turning to face her. Three spots on LAMIE's nose charged with orange brilliance. A ray of energy spouted from each, colliding into a common vertex as the weapon fired. Thanati jerked with alarm. The cannon acted as a near direct conduit to Chano's plane! Only a proper Well could achieve a more powerful connection.

The erinyes barely darted out of the way of the cannon burst. As it passed her, she knew the intense burst of magic could have destroyed her immortal body. LAMIE fired the cannon several more times, forcing Thanati to twist and dive to avoid mortal injury. She danced through the air in a random pattern, evading the beam, and returning her own fiery bolts of magic when she could.

One attack burned across Thanati's arms as she struggled to dodge three consecutive blasts. Then the ship's rail guns, located just under the engines, began to hum with power. Lord Kirion's fortress was too far to be of any use as cover, and LAMIE's quick sublight engines kept intercepting Thanati's darting retreats for the planet's surface. She needed to shift to a more aggressive offense.

LAMIE's weapons had a blind spot just behind the engine pods. If Thanati could manage to cling to the ship's hull, she could disable the cannon without the need to defend herself from the ship's other weapons. Thanati yanked to a stop in the air. Spinning, she summoned a sphere of flame that encompassed her like a shield. LAMIE's rail guns spat energy rounds, but they dissolved in the fire's withering heat. The erinyes flexed her fingers, waiting patiently for LAMIE to try again with the cannon.

The sentient ship did not disappoint. LAMIE blasted a ray from the cannon that tore through the globe of fire like sunlight through glass. Thanati slid past the attack by the length of her wingtip, just as LAMIE passed overhead. The erinyes snapped her firelash around the starboard engine pod. The whip burned into the hull plates, burrowing deep so that it couldn't slide off.

As Thanati trailed behind LAMIE, she pulled herself closer to the hull. LAMIE spun and swerved, but the firelash was securely embedded. Reaching the pod, Thanati ripped open the ship's skin. It loosed a metallic scream as she dug her sharp talons deep into the pod's underbelly. The rail gun ceased its pathetic fire. Thanati wrapped her palm around the ammunition feed and erupted flames. The weapon melted into a useless mass under her grip.

Rupture appeared in her hand and she plunged the hungry blade downward, searing what remained of the rail gun and impacting LAMIE's maneuvering thrusters. An acrid odor bled out as the damaged mechanism wailed and coughed.

Suddenly, a small square access door on the right hissed open. A GAEL she didn't recognize swung out and hurled BT rounds from a rifle. She folded her wings back protectively, taking the brunt of the assault in the shoulder and chest. Thanati shrieked in rage, losing her hold on her sword. *Rupture* tumbled out of her grasp and vanished into tendrils of flame. More shells pelted her abdomen and she released her firelash, swinging free of LAMIE's hull.

Arching her wings didn't fully counter the wake of the ship's slipstream. Thanati tumbled in the air, struggling for control. LAMIE sped forward, hobbling awkwardly in the air. Black smoke hemorrhaged from the damaged thrusters.

When the air around her settled, Thanati righted herself. The projectile penetrations in her torso screamed angry with pain. Blood rose inside her throat, indicating that the first volley had pierced her lung. She coughed and spit, then hung aloft as still as possible so her body could heal. If LAMIE still had the capability of turning sharply, her cannon would have been Thanati's end. But the ship seemed incapable of swinging back.

As it was, Thanati's twelve heartbeats of regeneration were disturbed by an unpleasant turn of events.

At least a hundred objects suddenly glinted in the copper sky, zooming toward the battle. Thanati presumed Nynniaw had detected the fight and launched its fighters to intercept. LAMIE was a known traitor to the Coalition and would be destroyed for treason if she refused to surrender. Due to the damage Thanati had already inflicted, the fresh fighters would have the advantage.

LAMIE's crew was expendable, but the ship was one of Lord Kirion's most important assets. Thanati's original strategy had been to disable the vessel and dispose of the crew, salvaging LAMIE and returning her to the ranks of the Faithful Legion.

The Cymric fighters complicated matters. Thanati knew Lord Kirion would not have authorized such an attack without advising her. Undoubtedly, he was occupied with Raeylan. It was left to her to protect her lord's investment.

Weapon shells bombarded the ground like deadly rain as the fighters approached. In seconds, the lethal hail would reach Thanati and the injured ship. She placed her palms together on the left side of her body, then spread her arms open in a sweeping semicircle. A sea of green fire parallel to the ground erupted across the sky. The barrier incinerated the shells instantly.

Her protective pane would only last a few minutes. Thanati flew through it to a higher altitude, calling forth her familiars as she rose. They cried with joyful glee as she ordered them into battle. As the first fighters from the swarm met her position, she extended the length of her firelash and cleaved them in two. Twenty ships fell to the rocky surface of the planet with the strike. Her twin phoenixes punctured the hulls of enemy after enemy, rending the metal skeletons and mutilating drive systems.

It was *Rupture*, however, who claimed the most victims. The fighters blasted their weapons at Thanati in vain. Their slow navigation capabilities could not match her maneuverability. She dodged everything they fired, knocking each out of the air with a single slice of *Rupture's* thirsty edge. Lost in the glory of her attack, Thanati cackled every time she felled a ship from the air, reveling in the explosive intoxication of her full power. It had been generations since she had occasion to stretch the limits of her abilities. In moments, countless battered metal corpses littered the ground beneath her, the Cymric fighter pilots forever lost in the wreckage.

The remaining fighters recognized their doom. They tried to retreat the way they had come. Her flat expanse of shielding fire still roared underneath her. Commanding it to rise, she hurled the pane of flame at the fleeing ships, annihilating them completely.

LAMIE had disappeared by the time Thanati turned back. Electric waves of gooseflesh rose on Thanati's arms and the crimson feathers of her wings charged with energy. In alarm she whipped around. LAMIE's nose faced her only a wingspan away, glinting with power. Thanati had just enough time to bring *Rupture* up to meet a head on blast of the ship's cannons.

The raw power of the beam pushed Thanati back toward the fortress. *Rupture's* core vibrated under the strain of deflecting such intense magic. Thanati growled, channeling as much strength as she could from Fohtian's plane to her blade, but she could tell it wouldn't last much longer. Every second that passed pushed her farther away from the ship. Once *Rupture* was overcome, Thanati would wither in the full force of the beam's energy.

Suddenly, the sky flashed with bright golden light. A caramel vortex dominated the sky, brighter than anything ever seen on Athalonde Prime. Thanati recognized the phenomenon from holoreports delivered to Lord Kirion.

His scientists called it a T-portal. And this one seemed large enough to devour the entire planet.

The outcome of the conflict had altered too quickly. Thanati needed to contact Lord Kirion for instructions, but between the cannon fire bearing down on her and the threat of Althalonde Prime's consumption by the portal, she could see no means of escape.

Then one of Feralblade's small infiltration vessels scurried out of the fortress's docking bay. A black shadow against the illuminated portal, it hit LAMIE with a burst. His interference knocked the canon beam off course and Thanati managed to slide out of its path.

LAMIE disengaged her weapon and turned for the portal. Feralblade's ship clipped Thanati's position. She dug her claws into the side of his vessel as it veered upward. Clinging tightly, she looked back as they skidded out of the planet's atmosphere.

The intelligent ship limped into the portal, her engine still vomiting smoke as she vanished. Athalonde Prime, the center of all of Lord Kirion's plans in this shard, would soon follow.

Her lord would be most displeased.

51: I CAME ACROSS TIME FOR YOU

Esilwen watched the fight unfold, sick with sorrow. Every strike against either combatant caused a sharp intake of breath that she kept forgetting to exhale. She bit the inside of her cheek so hard that it bled. Soon she was so dizzy she thought she might faint.

Of course she prayed for Raeylan to be the victor. Life as Kirion's prisoner would not be pleasant. She feared his total obsession with power. He would never be persuaded to alter the course of his chosen destiny. He needed to be overthrown.

But she couldn't deny the surge of feeling that had pierced her with his kiss. She didn't want Kirion to die. She wanted him to change.

Kirion hadn't always let his arrogance twist him into cruelty. When she had freed him, so many ages ago, his gratitude and love had defined him. He was sincere, charming, and content. Though he constantly fought with his pride, Esilwen helped him seek compassion and tolerance. For a while, they had been happy. His brilliance brought the people of Alanis into a new age of prosperity.

But then one day, Thanati came and took him away. When he returned, months later, he was different—his power darker. He demanded Fohtian's Chalice from the temple. When the Council of Oracles refused, he killed them all.

Horrified that Kirion was capable of such callous murder, Esilwen stood between him and The Chalice. She begged him to stop, to atone for his selfish violence. Instead, Kirion invited her to join his quest to unify the shards. But the iron scent of the oracles' blood at her feet thwarted his pretty words. She was the last of those sworn to protect The Chalice. Her only choice was to drink it.

Kirion could have killed her as she took the fire god's power, but he didn't. He even forbade Thanati to intervene. Esilwen still remembered the hurt look in his dark eyes as she smashed The Chalice and its green flames burned her away.

After that, she had met Raeylan. He was everything that Kirion should have been: selfless and honorable. His devotion was as endless as time, his tenderness gentle like the sea. She loved her Thyellan king in a way that completed her, an affection untouched by betrayal.

As Kirion leveled his next attack at her she swallowed, wondering how he could sacrifice her so readily when he had searched so long for her power. The answer was evident in the arrogance of his eyes. Kirion knew that Raeylan would not chance to lose her again. The strike was meant to force Raeylan to action.

The next few moments blurred with simultaneous events. Raeylan teleported in front of her when Kirion let the sphere of light fly. As *Moonstone Retribution* knocked the sizzling ball back toward the bulkhead, Raeylan's guard dropped. Kirion stepped forward and thrust his sword upward, ripping through Raeylan's ribcage. Esilwen could see the bloody weapon as it burst out of Raeylan's back.

At the same time, Raeylan stabbed his free hand against Kirion's chest, palm open. Cakes of ice burst across Kirion's light armor. Bone crunched and cracked as the ice compressed. Kirion's armor flickered and swirled, helpless against the weight of Raeylan's attack. The Lord of Light screamed in agony.

Esilwen choked on tears. Raeylan's breath was ragged and uneven. If Kirion yanked the sword free, Raeylan would bleed to death. But Raeylan's open fist refused to release Kirion from its deadly coffin of ice. Her Thyellan king seemed intent on sacrificing himself if it meant the end of the Lord of Light. The deadlocked men were an instant from killing each other.

Esilwen was too far away to use any powers of healing. Her power of fire would only cause further damage. She wasn't ready to lose either of them, the man she had once adored and the king who had become a part of her. So she turned to the Phoenix Angel's ultimate weapon—the mercy of love.

And she asked for a miracle.

Moonstone Retribution exploded into tiny fragments of magical steel in Raeylan's other hand. Kirion lost his grip on his sword as the force of the blast flung both combatants across the room. The warm honey of Esilwen's bonds disappeared and she slumped off the chair. She had no idea what she had done, but her soul ached with strain. Her insides throbbed with a pain that the restorative power of her blood did nothing to heal. Tiny remnants of *Moonstone Retribution* rained down on her. When she lifted her head she nearly gagged with the effort.

Ice chunks lay scattered around Kirion's prone form. He tried to pull himself up but couldn't, coughing blood all over the floor in the process. Raeylan lay on his side against the crystasteel window overlooking Athalonde Prime, Kirion's sword still stuck through his body.

Esilwen slowly pulled herself to Raeylan. As she took his hand, bright gold light streamed through the window. Esilwen heard muffled words from the communication device in Raeylan's ear. Raeylan looked at her and tightened his hand on hers.

"I will not let you have Esilwen," Kirion spat, blood gurgling his voice.

Esilwen turned. Kirion was on his feet, glaring. But suddenly his face contorted with rage as he glanced at the window.

"An empty promise," Raeylan returned. "This cycle, you lose everything."

Kirion yelled but Esilwen didn't hear it. She blinked and the world broke into a thousand stars around her. When it reformed, she and Raeylan were lying on LAMIE's bridge, Colonel Stoddard's astonished face gaping at them as the ship escaped with the planet through the T-portal.

52: There is No Blame Only What is Meant To Be

Margariete shivered under her blanket, mossy dew sticking unpleasantly to her back. She didn't complain about her circumstances, however. They were her own doing. She had woken only a few hours after the stabbing, demanding to see her twin. Her healers informed her that Raeylan had left to rescue Esilwen, taking everyone she knew in this shard with him. He had left her on Agrona, alone.

In a fit of temper, she had leapt from her hospital bed and escaped through the closest exit, ignoring the protests of her Vartal healers. The effort nearly made her collapse, but she refused to return. Using the power of mind domination, which drained the remaining strength in her damaged body, she forced them to bring her to the shiidh garden sanctuary. Clearly recognizing that no amount of persuasion would encourage her back to the hospital, the healers had supplied Margariete with bedding, bandages, and medicine. Then they left her to the garden.

Only the smolder of anger helped to dull the pain of her injuries as she waited for her brother. A thin blade of concern tried to break through, but Margariete pushed it back, fearful that it might take away what little remained of her constitution. Somewhere in the vast sea of stars above this planet, Raeylan and Kyleren faced Kirion and the Faithful Legion.

Anger was better. It kept her away from suffocating with despair.

What new enemies lurked in Kirion's stronghold? The ones they already knew were bad enough: Feralblade, Thanati, and the wolves.

She should be with her brother, fighting by his side. But because of her failure, he had been left with only Kyleren. The insufferable GAEL was too brash. She would have bet *Stardawn* that he had already gotten the rescue party into trouble with his brazen behavior.

Unwanted, her heartbeat quickened as she thought of him. Her skin prickled with unwelcome warmth. The last few memories before she had blacked out had been of him, of the frantic way he had called her name as her blood pooled on the ground. Her life was in his debt; she owed him thanks.

His witty insults were infuriating, his magnetic smile too self-confident. It was easier just to hate him.

Margariete sighed. She longed to be with them in battle, instead of lying here, useless and broken in the grass. Shame burned a hole into her shield of fury. How could she have let Terail take Esilwen so easily? He had stolen her without so much as a slap on the cheek. If anything happened to the healer, it would be all Margariete's fault.

Just like Shikun.

The telepath bit her lip, forcing her guilt back into her head before it spilled down her face. Swallowing a desperate sob, she prayed to Nehro—or any other god who might be listening—that Raeylan came back unharmed, Esilwen safely in his arms.

She believed in her twin, had unwavering faith in his ability to remedy her failures. But a creep of doubt compressed her heart, making her chest ache for release. Never before had they faced Kirion in the core of his stronghold. There, Raeylan might be overcome. He might even die.

Dread at the thought nearly crippled her. Without Raeylan, she was lost. Margariete could never defeat Kirion alone. She couldn't even keep Esilwen safe for a measly arc!

"Margariete!"

The reservoir of worry that Margariete had kept at bay transformed suddenly when she recognized the voice. She nearly choked on relief. Too weak to use her telepathic senses, Margariete looked wildly around the torchlit shadows, scanning for the source of the call.

Esilwen dashed forward, away from a disgruntled looking Vartal guide. Raeylan walked calmly behind, composed as always.

Margariete burst into tears before Esilwen even reached her. Esilwen dropped into an embrace. Ignoring the sharp pain of her injuries, Margariete buried her face into her friend's shoulder.

"I'm so sorry—"

Esilwen tightened her arms, cutting off Margariete's apology.

"I thought for sure Terail had killed you. I was so relieved when Raeylan told me you'd survived the attack."

"It's my fault you were taken," Margariete sobbed.

A hand rested lightly upon her head.

"None of that, sister," Raeylan said. "The blame lies with Kirion."

Margariete lifted her head to look at her twin. He knelt next to her, his face soft with affection. For a moment, Margariete was overwhelmed. The two people she loved most fiercely in the shards were with her, safe.

"The battle with Kirion was not easy," Raeylan stated when Margariete noticed the blood on his white coat, "but I am already healed."

Esilwen began to remove the wrappings on Margariete's stab wound to inspect the progress of the Vartal healers. The healer's hands shook, though it looked like she was trying to hide it.

"And Kirion?" Margariete asked with a wince.

"He lives," Raeylan admitted, "though we have dealt great injury to his plans."

Raeylan was watching Esilwen closely. Her eyes were sunken and hollow. The blood-healing was sluggish. The healer looked exhausted.

A chuckle invaded the conversation.

"And by that, you mean yours truly fragged him over good," Kyleren boasted, striding into the garden with a long, lighting implement. "Like to see him build an army now."

Margariete was surprised at the surge of comfort she found in seeing him alive. She struggled to hide it. Though his chest armor gaped open, his body seemed to be unscathed. A strange glow rippled over his heart, pulsing with his stride. She had seen him bare-chested once and she was sure the light had not been there before. The mesmerizing effect made her stare. When Kyleren grinned at her, she tore her gaze away in irritation.

The icy throb of Esilwen's healing fire screamed through her body as Raeylan explained the encounter with Kirion. Most of the details blurred in the frosty pain, but she clearly noted Kyleren's heroic actions that stole Sarras out of the Lord of Light's reach. When Esilwen had completed her task, Raeylan helped Margariete to stand. Her friend's blood might be more efficient than this shard's nanomite technology, but Margariete had forgotten how weak it made her feel afterward. She swayed slightly and clung to her brother for support. Then she completely smothered him with a hug.

"Now, sister," Raeylan said as he pulled away, "why did you not remain in bed? Your doctors are very displeased."

Margariete opened her mouth to argue, but Raeylan's face had spread into a broad smile. It was the first joke she had heard him tell since the loss of their homeland.

"This world's hospital rooms are like prison cells," Margariete returned in jest. "Not relaxing in the slightest. Besides, I was getting ready to mount a rescue."

Kyleren snorted.

"What were you gonna do, bleed all over 'em?"

Margariete turned and glared at him, poignantly avoiding looking at his muscular chest. He shrugged his shoulders.

"What?" he asked innocently.

53: Revenge Is A Dish Best Served Cold

Kirion tapped his fingers on the surface of his desk, deeply mired in thought. His dark eyes soaked in the light of the passing stars through the window of his battle weary office. Nynniaw glided unnoticed toward the Famorian System, the last store of his military might in this shard.

The previous seven days had nearly unraveled a hundred years' worth of effort. Shortly after losing both Esilwen and Athalonde Prime, a news holocast had infected the Intergrid. The transmission accused Chancellor Medrod—Kirion's assumed identity in this shard—of heinous war crimes against the Coalition. Dr. Boris Pryce testified for the allegations, providing secure documentation and classified images as evidence. The outrage that festered through the populace was unstoppable, especially when the traitorous doctor provided a list of infants who had been kidnapped for their aptitude on the Blended Child Bonding test. The revelation of the interspecies breeding facilities incited a full-scale military rebellion.

The Round denounced Chancellor Medrod so quickly that Kirion had been driven into retreat just hours after his battle with Raeylan. The spiraling political situation proved irreparable. Even some of the onboard Cymric personnel had mutinied, forcing Kirion to restore order swiftly. There was no room for the nonbeliever in the Faithful Legion.

After the purge, the station was barely half-staffed, mostly with basic humanoid soldiers. Only a sparse three hundred GAEL VICs were on board, out of the two thousand he had created. A third of his dead tech fighters had been destroyed by Thanati as she tried to protect LAMIE. The loss would have been acceptable if she had actually managed to secure the LT ship.

The Lord of Light curled his fingers into an angry fist. Losing control was not something that happened to a god. He tried to transfer his emerging fury into the clenched hand, but his power refused to ignite. This emotional overload was a new ailment that plagued him. Kirion slammed his fist against his desk in aggravation, knocking several implements to the floor.

Damn that Thyellan to the Void and back, Kirion thought viciously.

This was all Raeylan's fault. Esilwen had been his; after a thousand years Kirion had finally held her in his arms. And Raeylan had waltzed in with his godling powers and taken her.

More accoutrements from the desk shattered on the floor as Kirion swept his arm across the surface in fury. His chest argued with a deep flash of pain at the sudden action. The nanomites had not completely healed the damage Raeylan had done.

His dataplate beeped from the floor, catching his attention. He picked it up. The device displayed the image of a GAEL soldier. Despite the enmity Kirion harbored for Raeylan, another had earned the wrath of the Lord of

Light, a man he had come to despise almost as much as the Guardian of Time.

Lieutenant Lance Kyleren.

Adjacent the image, the dataplate listed Kyleren's military record. Kirion had spent hours analyzing it. Besides being the best sniper in the GAEL VIC ranks, Lieutenant Kyleren seemed to be more liability than asset to his squad. His file was littered with disciplinary actions for insubordination and reckless behavior in the field. A few months ago he had been punished for inappropriate fraternization.

But he was by far the fastest, strongest, and most independent of his kind. Kirion threw the dataplate against the wall in disgust. He should have noticed. Kyleren's measure of skill and rash abandon clearly marked him as Chano's Champion.

The Lord of Light had underestimated Chano's chaotic nature. He had known she retained much of her original sentience, knew she was here in this shard. Kirion had assumed she was hiding in the Famorian System, away from his direct influence. It was why he had erected a base on the outermost planet, why he had sent the Wolves of Skoh to hunt her there.

Instead, she had been within his reach all the while. With Chano's abilities he could have extracted the power of Fohtian from Esilwen. He could have had two more artifacts. With Athalonde Prime and the Tree Well at his disposal, Kirion could have brought the rest of the shards to their knees.

In one action, Lieutenant Lance Kyleren had wasted an entire century of preparation.

Before Kirion's desk suffered another bout of his temper, the office door slid open and his two most trusted commanders approached him. He watched them with a frown, his thumb stroking his lip thoughtfully. Their failures crackled fresh in his mind.

Thanati had lost LAMIE and destroyed a significant portion of his armada in the process. Feralblade had neither executed Margariete nor managed to finish off Kyleren. Only the success of retrieving both Esilwen and the scrolls had saved the assassin from death.

At Kirion's feet they knelt. Thanati trembled under his disappointment. Feralblade tapped his gloved fingertips nervously. Both knew such grievous mistakes would not be tolerated again.

The Lord of Light stood, arranging his thoughts into calm order. Order, after all, was his edict for the shards.

"What news?" he asked.

"My Lord," Thanati said with only a hint of tremor in her clear, rich voice, "our Vartal spies have confirmed Athalonde Prime's new location. It now lies behind the Eye of Baylour, which the shiidh have somehow managed to open and close."

"How? It would require more shiidh than are alive to complete such a feat," he said.

"They used a technology unknown to us, My Lord," Thanati continued. "Its existence was hidden by the highest circles of Vartal and Morrigan networks."

A bright pulse of wrath snapped through Kirion's calm.

"And I assume we cannot retrieve this technology, or you already would have done so."

Thanati's courage wavered under the pressure of his gaze.

"Yes, My Lord. The shiidh not only destroyed the generator, but have managed to obliterate all pertinent research. They remained on Athalonde Prime when they shut the Eye. We cannot reach them."

"Then their race will die there. Without access to the stones of Danu's temple their powers cannot be passed to another generation. What of LAMIE?"

"LAMIE has joined Raeylan. Already they have passed through the shardgate."

Kirion paused. There were only two passable gates leading from this shard and he knew what lay beyond both. Perhaps that afforded him an advantage.

"His assets?" Kirion asked.

"Margariete and Esilwen of course," Thanati reported. "Gene Pecktol has also joined them, along with Lieutenant Lance Kyleren and Tuatha, the last of the shiidh. She has been granted custody of the feyhammer, Lord, and is now rightfully queen of the shiidh."

"And what of your news?" he said, turning to Feralblade.

"Not good, My Lord," the assassin said without looking up. "Penardun suspects you of Prime Minister Ninevay's murder, though they cannot prove it. They have made an alliance with the Round. They are preparing an assault on this station."

"Dispose of the Round then, Feralblade. That should give us time to gather what we can from the Famorian System."

"Immediately, sir," Feralblade answered, his eyes glinting with a hint of satisfaction.

Once Feralblade departed, Kirion turned to Thanati.

"Contact the Wolves of Skoh," he ordered. "They are to gather as many Famorians as they can. They will make excellent ground troops for the coming conflict. Once I am master of the shards, these abominations of Chano will finally be allowed to rest."

"It will be done directly, My Lord," Thanati said, rising to her feet.

She allowed her wings to flex. The resulting breath of air pushed against her silky gown, outlining the curves of her body. Kirion smiled. Thanati always knew how to please him.

"Once you have finished, report to my chambers," he commanded.

Thanati lowered her lashes with false modesty, then swept out of the office.

Kirion returned to his chair, his broody mood lifting. He gathered the scrolls he had pushed to the floor in his rage and inspected them for damage. In all there were five, but he suspected there was a sixth that had given the shiidh the power to open the Eye.

Two rested comfortably in the leather satchel in which they had arrived. One was an epic poem relating the exploits of a paladin of Fohtian, explaining the nature of the fire god's power. The second listed the abilities of Nehro's Glove, probably passed down through the Thyellan line of kings for generations. Neither had given Kirion any information he did not already possess.

The remaining three were the most important. He unrolled them carefully on the wooden desk. The first he could not read. Kirion had never encountered a language he could not immediately understand. That led him to believe the scroll was a coded script, most likely the work of Aeron. The Mystic had always been intrigued by puzzles.

The next was imprinted with the image of a hexagram, detailing instructions on how to unlock the deeper powers of Skoh. Written on some type of animal hide, it seemed to be the ramblings of an ancient priest who believed he could raise the dead.

Kirion scoffed. That was impossible.

The Lord of Light's real interest was in the final scroll. It seemed to have been written mere hours after the Fracturing, on a scrap of fabric that he recognized—a section of the cape he had worn to the god council that had shattered the world. Kirion peered at the writing more closely. It described the Fracturing, what had happened immediately after.

Kirion sucked his breath through his teeth, heart pounding. If he found the author of the scroll, he could find something he had thought long destroyed, a relic that could restore his godhood without the need of the other five artifacts.

And once Kirion had it, Raeylan Viridius and Lance Kyleren would pay in full for their sacrilege.

Epilogue

Whoever said "be yourself" can frag themselves. My specialized capabilities—far beyond those of my comrades—set me apart. Made me different. I didn't have a choice but to join Raeylan and Margariete. With Chano bouncing around that magical tattoo she stamped on my chest, I was a prime target for that gromm skrit Lord of Light. I had to leave everyone I knew just because some pretty boy was out to play god.

Wayne wasn't too happy about it. I bet all the prings in my cred-locker that it took him years to get over me leavin'—and probably a few more for not takin' better care of the newb who that freaky winged woman killed. I wish I coulda explained to Wayne that I woulda given anything to stay, to help my squad rebuild the Coalition. But Wayne doesn't say goodbyes too easy. The rest of squad Aon went back to the Coalition with Pryce and Kenny still in the brig.

LAMIE and Gene decided to go with us. We had to have a ship to leave the shard, and LAMIE volunteered. Since Gene can't let her out of his sight, he had to come too. If you ask me, they act like they're in some kind of relationship—they fraggin' flirt enough.

LAMIE's repairs were done inside a week—even with the hours and hours of Gene's whining. He brought LAMIE's main systems back online and I patched up the damaged hull. Come to find out, the artifact—Chano—lets me control living tech. I can even create it from plain rock.

All the shiidh stayed on Sarras, even though that means they'll eventually die off. It looks like they live in those big rocks back on Agrona—something about it being their source of power. At least that's what they told us. Tuatha's rock ended up in LAMIE's loading bay. The shiidh told the others she wanted to join us when we left. Queen Druantia did some sort of big deal chant and gave that crazy hammer to her. I guess that means she's free to go.

At least getting Kirion out of the galaxy wasn't too hard. Dr. Pryce's testimony aired on the Intergrid. Last we heard, the god wannabe had taken over Nynniaw and was runnin' to the Famorian System.

So here I am, on board LAMIE and searching for lost treasure—the remainin' god artifacts. If you ask me, this ship isn't big enough for all of us. Raeylan seems pleased with the crew, but Blue Eyes is a whole different story. She and the shiidh are always squabblin'. Gene bugs the skrit out of her.

And me? Well, every time she sees me, she just glares and stomps off. Won't hardly say a word.

It's a step up if you ask me. Way fraggin' better than gettin' stabbed in the shoulder.

About the Authors

A. Gerry developed an interest in fantasy at a young age. Her fondness for writing comes from many sources, but the most prominent is her devotion to video games. Some of her favorites include *Mass Effect*, *The Elder Scrolls* series, and anything that lets her shoot zombies. She received a Bachelor's Degree from Southern Utah University and teaches at a local charter school.

C. Hall has been addicted to the many realms of fantasy and science fiction all her life. A graduate of Southern Utah University, she now teaches at a local charter school. When she isn't busy designing activities for her Mythology class or going on field trips with the *Star Wars* Club, she is spending time with her sister. C. Hall's favorite authors include J.R.R. Tolkien, J.K. Rowling, and Tracy Hickman.

www.shardwell.com

Also available from A. Gerry and C. Hall:

Made in the USA
Charleston, SC
12 August 2013